HOT MAMA

Hot
MAMA

Jennifer Estep

BERKLEY BOOKS, NEW YORK

THE BERKLEY PUBLISHING GROUP
Published by the Penguin Group
Penguin Group (USA) Inc.
375 Hudson Street, New York, New York 10014, USA
Penguin Group (Canada), 90 Eglinton Avenue East, Suite 700, Toronto, Ontario M4P 2Y3, Canada
(a division of Pearson Penguin Canada Inc.)
Penguin Books Ltd., 80 Strand, London WC2R 0RL, England
Penguin Group Ireland, 25 St. Stephen's Green, Dublin 2, Ireland (a division of Penguin Books Ltd.)
Penguin Group (Australia), 250 Camberwell Road, Camberwell, Victoria 3124, Australia
(a division of Pearson Australia Group Pty. Ltd.)
Penguin Books India Pvt. Ltd., 11 Community Centre, Panchsheel Park, New Delhi—110 017, India
Penguin Group (NZ), 67 Apollo Drive, Rosedale, North Shore 0632, New Zealand
(a division of Pearson New Zealand Ltd.)
Penguin Books (South Africa) (Pty.) Ltd., 24 Sturdee Avenue, Rosebank, Johannesburg 2196,
South Africa

Penguin Books Ltd., Registered Offices: 80 Strand, London WC2R 0RL, England

This is an original publication of The Berkley Publishing Group.

First edition: November 2007

Library of Congress Cataloging-in-Publication Data

Estep, Jennifer.
Hot mama / Jennifer Estep.—1st ed.
p. cm.
ISBN 978-0-425-21734-4
1. Heroines—Fiction.   2. New York (N.Y.)—Fiction.   I. Title.
PS3605.S687H68   2007
813'.6—dc22

2007025825

PRINTED IN THE UNITED STATES OF AMERICA

10 9 8 7 6 5 4 3 2 1

To my mom, the best person I know.

And to Andre, who coined the phrase "So, are you going to eat that?"

ACKNOWLEDGMENTS

Once again, this book would not have been possible without the help of many people.

Thanks again to my super agent, Kelly Harms, and fantastic editor, Cindy Hwang. You both help me make my books the very best they can be, for which I am always grateful.

To artist Stanley Chow. Thanks for another great Bigtime cover. They just keep getting better.

To all the readers out there who wrote, e-mailed, and talked to me about *Karma Girl*. Thank you for your kind words. Your enjoyment and enthusiasm mean more to me than you know.

Happy reading!

PART ONE

Wedding Bells

★ 1 ★

My wedding day.

It was supposed to be the happiest day of my life. A time of joy and celebration and new beginnings. The day every girl dreams of from the time she's old enough to play dress-up in her mother's clothes.

It was exactly that sort of day.

Joy. Hope. New beginnings.

But it wasn't *mine*.

Carmen Cole twirled in front of the full-length mirror. Her white satin wedding dress swung out in an arc then gathered back in on itself. Thousands of Swarovski crystals dotted the fitted bodice and full skirt, giving the dress a shimmering, ethereal air. A matching crystal necklace sparkled like a ring of stars around her neck.

"How do I look, Fiona?" Carmen turned her blue eyes to mine.

I hated to admit it, but Carmen looked fantastic. Absolutely fantastic. A rosy flush tinted her cheeks. Excitement brightened her eyes. Even her auburn hair glistened underneath her simple lace veil.

"You look fabulous. After all, you're wearing a Fiona Fine original."

Carmen frowned at her reflection. "I know it's one of your more subdued designs, but I still think it's a little much."

I crossed my arms over my chest. An errant spark flew from my thumb and landed on the beige carpet. I squashed it with my stiletto. A little much? Please. If Carmen had gotten her way, she would have worn holey jeans, worn-out sneakers, and a ratty T-shirt with some cutesy saying on it to the wedding.

Luckily, hotter heads had prevailed. Mine. Then again, it was easy to get your way when you had the ability to shoot fire out of your fingertips. Getting my way was one of the prime benefits of being a superhero. My favorite benefit.

Just because I moonlight as a superhero doesn't mean I can't be a little selfish—or enjoy the perks of having superpowers. Usually, I'm perfectly happy just being Fiera, one of many superheroes in Bigtime, New York, fighting evil, cracking skulls, and making life miserable for all those pesky ubervillains who want to take over the city, then the world. But every once in a while, I enjoy showing off my fiery skills, especially when it's for the greater good, such as making sure Carmen didn't look like a bag lady at her own wedding.

A knock sounded on the door, the knob turned, and Lulu Lo zipped her motorized wheelchair into the room. A royal blue dress covered the Asian woman's slender form, bringing out the smoothness of her porcelain skin and the cobalt streaks in her spiky black hair. Since we were both bridesmaids, I wore a matching gown, but with a few modifications—a lower bodice, a tighter fit, and a higher slit up the side.

"Nice dress, Sister Carmen." Lulu whistled. "That'll make Sam sit up and take notice."

Carmen grinned. Another spark shot out from my thumb. Sam had already taken plenty of *notice* of Carmen, despite my efforts to the contrary. The two of them were always sneaking off to have wild sex in some corner of the manor house.

"Of course Sam will notice," I snapped. "I designed the dress. Ours too, if you'll remember. They're all fabulous."

"Well, you do look very *hot*, Fiona." Lulu laughed.

I glowered at Lulu. Just because I was a member of the Fearless Five, one of the most esteemed superhero teams in the world, didn't mean that I didn't get snarly from time to time—or that civilians like Lulu had the right to poke fun at me.

Of course, none of this would be happening if Carmen, aka Karma Girl, hadn't insisted we tell Lulu our secret, superhero identities. Carmen had argued that Lulu deserved to know the truth, since she'd helped save us from the Terrible Triad, a group of ubervillains. Lulu was also the main squeeze of Henry Harris, aka Hermit of the Fearless Five, and he'd wanted to tell her the truth as well. The other two members of the Fearless Five, Sam "Striker" Sloane and Sean "Mr. Sage" Newman, had agreed with Carmen.

So the four of them told Lulu everything, despite my protests. Once the shock wore off, Lulu ingratiated herself with the rest of the Fearless Five. Now, everybody else treated her like one of the gang. She even had her own room in the top-secret, underground compound with the rest of us.

I ignored Lulu whenever possible. It was bad enough she knew our real identities. I didn't want to invite her any more into our lives. Lulu was a computer hacker. She did all sorts of highly illegal things, like breaking into the FBI mainframe and swapping corporate secrets, but nobody cared except me. Not even my father, the esteemed police chief of Bigtime as well as a member of the Fearless Five.

In return for my blatant hostility, Lulu zinged me with heat-related puns whenever we crossed paths. *Fiona's hot. Fiona's smokin'. Fiona's on fire.* Like I hadn't heard them all a hundred thousand times before. Ha, ha, ha, ha. Lulu could have at least come up with something original, if she was going to mock me on a daily basis.

My eyes fixed on Lulu's hair. I could turn those blue streaks red in a heartbeat. Heat pulsed through my body. My fingers twitched. Just one little spark . . .

"Fiona," Carmen warned. "There will be no flare-ups today. You promised Sam."

I had promised Sam. And my father. And Henry. And even Carmen. Three times each. I let go of the fire coursing through my veins and banked it deep inside me. It didn't matter anyway. Carmen would have just done her empathy thing and used the ambient energy in the room to buffer Lulu and herself from my heat. Carmen had the ability to tap into other people and use their own energy against them. I hated her power, mainly because I hadn't figured out a way to counteract it yet. Most of the time, I either punched or flambéed my way through danger. But I couldn't do that with Carmen, because she gave just as good as she got.

Lulu smirked at me and motored away. She'd probably max out my credit cards or do some other devious, identity-theft thing as soon as the wedding ended. I didn't know what Henry saw in her. Maybe he was just glad that he'd finally found someone who understood all the techno-babble he spouted on a daily basis.

Lulu left the door open, and classical music drifted in,

along with the murmur of distant conversations. I eyed the clock on the wall. Five minutes to go. Good. The sooner this spectacle was over with, the better. I wasn't in the mood for a wedding today. Not any day. Not anymore.

Carmen picked up on my dark thoughts and stared at me in the mirror. "I know this has been hard for you, Fiona. The engagement, the wedding, everything. I'm sorry. I wish things were different. I wish Tornado was still here . . ."

Her soft Southern twang trailed off under my hot gaze. Hard for me? She had no idea.

It'd been over a year since my fiancé, Tornado, had been murdered. Carmen had exposed the superhero's secret identity as Travis Teague to the world, including our arch-enemies, the Terrible Triad. The ubervillains had killed Travis and used Carmen to get to the rest of us. We'd been captured, stuffed in glass tubes, and almost sucked dry of our superpowers, before Carmen had saved us by getting dumped into a vat of radioactive goo and developing superpowers herself.

Sometimes, I couldn't believe the irony of it. Carmen exposing superheroes, becoming one herself, and now marrying one. Things never seemed to turn out the way you thought they would, especially in Bigtime.

Mostly, though, I still couldn't believe Travis was gone. Forever. My heart twisted, and the burning fire inside me flickered and dimmed. My eyes dropped to the square, diamond engagement ring on my finger. Travis had given it to me a week before he'd died. I hadn't taken it off since.

"Fiona? Are you okay?" Carmen asked.

I wasn't. Not even close. But this was Carmen's big day, and I didn't want to ruin it for her.

"I'm fine," I lied. "In fact, I was thinking that it's time for me to get out and start dating again. I've done the men of Bigtime a cruel, heartless injustice, depriving them of my fabulous company all this time." I tossed my long blond hair over my shoulder for effect.

Carmen's face lit up like I'd just hit her with a fireball between the eyes. "That's wonderful, Fiona! Just wonderful!"

Her blue eyes grew cloudy and distant, the way they always did when she was listening to the strange whispers in her head. Carmen called them her inner voice, her instincts. I thought she had more than a few loose rocks rattling around in all that empty space.

"Maybe you'll meet somebody at the reception," she murmured.

I huffed. Please. I'd been active on the social scene ever since I'd moved to Bigtime some fifteen years ago, and I knew everybody invited to the wedding. There wasn't a man among them that I'd date, let alone sleep with.

I twisted the ring on my finger. The silver solidium band heated up on my hot hand, and the diamond glowed like a tiny moon. Still, I would like to find somebody. It'd be nice to be part of a couple again. To laugh and talk and have dinner with someone who wasn't a relative or an employee or a fellow superhero. To find somebody who looked at me the way that Sam looked at Carmen.

Plus, I liked sex. A lot. It sucked to go without.

My hand stilled. Maybe that's what I should do. Get drunk at the reception, have a one-night stand with some anonymous guy to take the edge off, and then start looking for someone suitable. Someone more long-term. The only problem with my plan was that it would take an ocean of champagne to get me drunk, given my fast-burning metabolism. Well, it was a good thing Sam was richer than almost everyone else on the planet put together. He could afford a couple hundred thousand dollars' worth of bubbly if it meant me getting lucky.

The music quickened and swelled, and the conversations faded away. The air hummed with energy and anticipation.

"Time to go." Carmen smoothed down her billowing skirt. Her hand trembled just a bit.

I picked up her long train, careful not to singe the fabric with my fingers. I'd spent too much time sewing the damn thing to ruin it now. Carmen turned and grabbed my arm.

"Do you think this is the right thing to do? Do you think we should go through with it? Do you think we're ready? You know how badly my last wedding turned out." Panic filled her blue eyes.

Badly was the understatement of the century. Right before the wedding, Carmen had found her fiancé boinking her best friend and discovered that the two were her town's resident superhero and ubervillain. That, of course, had set Carmen off on her little mission to expose the identity of every superhero and ubervillain who crossed her path. Which, of course, is how Carmen had met Sam and the rest of us. Karma, she called it. Destiny, kismet, fate. I just thought of it as bad luck on our part.

But I bit back the sarcastic retort I'd been ready to let loose. The nosy reporter had grown on me, despite my best efforts. And she had saved my life and everyone else's. I owed her for that. Plus, it was my solemn duty as a bridesmaid to support the bride—even if Carmen occasionally made me want to put my fist through a wall.

"Do you love Sam?"

Carmen nodded. Some of the tension left her body. "With all my heart."

"Then, it'll be fine," I said. "Sam loves you, and you love him. You're going to have a fabulous wedding, a fantastic honeymoon, and a wonderful life together. Plus, you're wearing a Fiona Fine original couture gown. And what could possibly be better than that?"

After Carmen calmed down, we made our way through Sublime, Sam's mansion on the outskirts of Bigtime. Roughly the size of a small country, the manor house contained just about every antique and art object known to man and super-hero. Polished suits of armor, colorful paintings, detailed sculptures, exquisite tapestries. Even though I'd been prowling the halls for years now, the rich furnishings still impressed me. And it took a lot to impress me.

Carmen tiptoed her way through the manor, struggling to stay upright in her towering heels. I stalked along behind, holding up the train so it wouldn't get snagged on a piece of furniture, and wishing the bride-to-be would move a little faster. I could always zing Carmen with a hot flash. That would get her moving. But I couldn't risk ruining the gown. Not now. I'd already had to redo it twice because of some temperamental flare-ups on my part.

Carmen stumbled on the edge of an Oriental rug and almost fell on her face.

"Stupid shoes," she muttered, glaring at me.

Her three-inch strappy sandals had been another hotly contested point between us. Carmen had wanted to wear these ugly, flat, ballet slippers that had gone out of style twenty years ago. I'd told her point-blank that she wasn't wearing those monstrosities with a Fiona Fine wedding gown. She wasn't ruining my hard work with her fashion faux pas. Of course, I had to roast most of Carmen's wornout tennis shoes before she agreed to wear the sandals, but the important thing was that I, and designer fashion, had triumphed yet again.

"I don't see how you walk in these things," Carmen said, tugging on one of the white straps wrapped around her ankle.

"It's easy," I snapped. "Millions of women do it every day. Now quit whining and walk. You've got a superhero to marry."

Carmen gave me another annoyed glance, but she shuffled forward. Despite Carmen's time covering the Bigtime society beat, fashion wasn't her forte. That was my domain. And I knew, like all good designers know, that no outfit is complete without a pair of killer shoes, preferably stilettos. The higher, the better.

After a couple more stumbles and a string of curses, we stopped in front of a pair of doors that led outside. Lulu sat there waiting, along with Chief Sean Newman. Sunlight streamed in through the glass, warming the alcove where we stood. The ceremony was taking place in the luscious gardens that surrounded the enormous estate, as befit a traditional May wedding.

I peeked through the doors. Henry Harris, the best man, and Sam Sloane, the anxious groom, had already taken their places in front of the minister at the far end of the long aisle.

"Carmen, Fiona," Chief Newman rumbled in his deep Irish brogue. "You both look beautiful."

"Chief." I kissed my father on the cheek.

I'd always called my father *Chief*, ever since I was a little girl and had first seen him in his police uniform. It was a habit I continued out of necessity. Nobody knew about our family connection, except the other members of the Fearless Five and now Lulu. It was safer that way. Since people, and more importantly ubervillains, didn't know about our relationship, they couldn't kidnap and use us against each other, either in our real lives or as our superhero alter egos, Fiera and Mr. Sage.

The first notes of the classic wedding march sounded, and the hundreds of guests outside rose to their feet.

"Here we go," Carmen whispered, her face pale and slightly sweaty.

"Heaven help us all," I muttered.

Two ushers stepped forward, and the double doors creaked open. The chief took Carmen's arm, while Lulu motored out. I waited for her to get halfway to the end before stepping outside and strolling along the rose-covered aisle.

A thick white carpet stretched three hundred feet toward a raised dais, which stood beneath an enormous trellis strung with silver roses and purple pansies. Oak and elm trees hovered in the background, providing splashes of green to the scene. Men and women dressed in dark tuxedos, sparkling gowns, and flashing jewels stood on either side of the aisle, adding even more color to the gardens. The sweet, thick scent of the flowers mixed with the men and women's spicy colognes and heady perfumes. A full orchestra sat on one side of the dais, but their instruments couldn't quite drown out the low, steady drone of bumblebees in the distance. The sun hung like a ball of orange sherbet in the evening sky, and a faint breeze ruffled my long hair. Late spring was a perfect time for a wedding.

My blue eyes traced over the area, drinking in the sights

and sounds. Everything that I'd wanted for my own wedding was right here. Everything except Travis. I clutched my bouquet of roses and turned my engagement ring around.

I took my place next to Lulu and winked at Sam, trying not to look as sad as I felt. I was happy for him and Carmen, truly I was. But I couldn't stop the pang of longing and jealousy that stabbed my heart with every beat of the soaring music.

The businessman-superhero gave me a nervous grin and tugged on his sleeves. With his dark hair and light, grayish eyes, Sam looked like he'd just stepped out of a men's magazine.

So did Henry, for once. The black man's glasses gleamed in the late-afternoon sunlight. He flashed me a shy smile and yanked on his tie. Like Carmen, Henry would have worn his usual attire to the wedding—a rumpled sweater vest, plaid pants, and a polka-dot bow tie—if I hadn't intervened. I'd had to melt a couple of the wires attached to his precious computers, but Henry had eventually seen things my way. Most people did, sooner or later. Especially when I turned up the heat.

The music swelled to a thundering crescendo, and Carmen stepped into view. Sam's face grew soft and dreamy and dopey at the sight of her. I smiled. Too much? Please. Score another one for Fiona Fine Fashions.

My father escorted Carmen down the aisle. She beamed like a neon light. If she got any happier, she'd blow a bulb. A few people tried to catch her gaze, but the only one Carmen acknowledged was her friend Jasper, Bigtime's resident mad bomber. Then, Carmen turned her attention to Sam, and the rest of the world fell away. She only had eyes for him, and he for her. The two of them couldn't stop staring at each other. Cold envy frosted over my aching heart.

The music faded away, and the minister stepped forward. "Dearly beloved, we are gathered here today . . ."

Thirty minutes later, Carmen and Sam professed their true and undying love for each other. They kissed, everyone cheered, and the wedding ended. I half expected to see white doves and fluffy bunnies stampede down the long aisle, but thankfully, people just blew soap bubbles at the happy couple.

The blushing bride, handsome groom, and other members of the wedding party stayed in the garden to pose for the all-important, postceremony pictures. Meanwhile, the rich, distinguished guests drifted out onto the mile-wide lawn where hundreds of tables, gallons of champagne, and thousands of pounds of chicken cordon bleu and other choice foodstuffs waited. Waiters and caterers zipped through the crowd, dishing up food and drinks as fast as they could.

I spotted Kyle Quicke among the caterers. I'd gone to Bigtime University with Kyle, and his family owned Quicke's, one of my favorite restaurants in Bigtime. I watched Kyle cut a slice of chocolate cake and hand it to a waiting guest. My stomach rumbled. I could use some food. A lot of food.

"Come on, Fiona. It's time for the pictures," the chief murmured in my ear, dashing my hopes of a stealthy getaway.

I rolled my eyes and turned back toward the dais.

Forty-five minutes later, I tapped my fingers on my arm. "How many pictures are you going to take?" I snapped at the photographer. Patience was not one of my virtues. In fact, I didn't think it was any sort of virtue at all.

The short, fat man wilted under my hot gaze. Most everybody did. My eyes went to his digital camera. One little flare-up, and it would look like something that came out of a kiln. There'd definitely be no more pictures then . . .

"Fiona." The chief's blue eyes narrowed in warning.

I shot him a sour look and dampened my temper. That was the problem with your father being a psychic superhero. You could never get away with anything.

"Actually, I'm done with the wedding party. I just want to get a few more shots of the bride and groom," the photographer said.

"It's about bloody time," I muttered.

I stomped out of the garden and onto the lawn. My stilettos sank into the damp earth, but I yanked up my feet and kept going. Another benefit of having superstrength. Henry, Lulu, and my father followed at a more sedate pace.

Most of the male guests had settled down at the tables and were busy stuffing themselves with chicken, spring vegetables, and sourdough rolls baked in the shape of curling vines and flowers. Not so for the women. Every woman under sixty gathered around the wide, long bar, downing glass after glass of champagne. Some stared at nothing in particular. A few snuffled into their crystal flutes, while others dabbed at their runny mascara. They weren't tears of joy. Quite the contrary. Three hundred women's dreams of becoming Mrs. Sam Sloane had just been dashed by a lowly society reporter. It was more than enough to make the stoutest society matron weepy, depressed, and drunk as a skunk.

I shoved my way through the crowd, zapped a few people with hot flashes to make them move, and grabbed the biggest champagne glass I could find. Bubbles fizzed up in the golden liquid. I drained the glass and twitched my nose to ease the sudden tickling sensation. I didn't need to sneeze flames in front of hundreds of people.

"Fiona! Fiona Fine!"

I turned at the sound of my name and spotted Joanne James fluttering her hand at me. Joanne was a tall, skinny woman with a rather large chest and too-smooth features. Hair blacker than shoe polish brushed her slender shoulders, contrasting with the ropes of pearls that encircled her gaunt neck.

Oh boy. I was going to need something a lot stronger than champagne. I ordered a gin and tonic from one of the bartenders and downed two doubles before Joanne sashayed her way through the crowd to my side.

"Fiona, darling!"

"Joanne, darling!"

We airkissed the way society women are supposed to. My eyes raked over Joanne's outfit, a gunmetal gray halter dress with a slinky, sequined skirt. Not bad, but it wasn't one of mine. Joanne also sized me up, her gaze critiquing everything from my shoes to my chandelier earrings. Standard operating procedure among the women in Bigtime. Once that was out of the way, we made polite chitchat about how fabulous and thin we both looked before Joanne got down to business.

"I'm getting married again next month. I was wondering if I could come in and talk to you about another gown."

I almost choked on my drink. "What will this one be? Number five?"

Joanne James went through husbands like they were tissues—she used one up and then tossed him aside for another.

"Six actually."

"Who's the lucky fellow?" My lips only twitched a little. It was amazing the things you could say with a straight face.

"Berkley Brighton, the whiskey billionaire."

"Of course."

Joanne James didn't waste her energy on small-time fish. She only went after the big, big catches. She was Bigtime's resident black widow, but she didn't kill her husbands. Instead, Joanne bled her hubbies dry, added their money to her own considerable fortune, and somehow managed to wiggle out of paying for anything—even her own divorce attorneys. In a way, it was her own personal superpower. Joanne was a legend in Bigtime, and more than a few society mamas urged their daughters to emulate her marriage merry-go-round.

"I thought you would have asked Bella Bulluci to design your gown. She did your last two, didn't she?" I couldn't resist the dig. Joanne had gone to Bella after complaining that my services were too expensive. As if. Fashion genius like mine was priceless.

Joanne swallowed some champagne. "To be honest, I did ask Bella first, but she turned me down."

"Really? Why?"

Joanne waved her hand, and I squinted at the sudden glare. The diamond boulder on her finger could easily feed the people of a third world country for years. "Oh, she said she was taking some time off to concentrate on family affairs because of her father's death. I think she just didn't want to bother with it."

Bella Bulluci was one of Bigtime's most popular designers, next to me, of course. Bella had plenty of talent, but I'd always thought her creations were a bit conservative, tame even. Bella was very fond of solid colors and subtle pinstripes. I was more of a polka-dot, plaid, and leopard-print girl. All rolled into one. With neon sequins and a feather boa to match.

I signaled the bartender and ordered another drink. I didn't like being anyone's second choice, but my eyes strayed back to Joanne's ring. That thing had to be at least ten flaw-less carats.

Being a superhero had plenty of perks, but there was one major drawback—it was a pricey occupation. We all had to pitch in to keep the Fearless Five out and about fighting crime. Carmen and Henry didn't contribute much to our annual budget. They couldn't with the pitiful paychecks they earned as newspaper reporters at the *Exposé*. My father wasn't much better off. Even though he was the chief of police, his salary wasn't what it should be, mainly because most of the city's budget went to repairing the municipal buildings, bridges, and overpasses that we superheroes and ubervillains obliterated during our epic battles.

That left Sam and I to shoulder the monetary load. With his various business interests and billion-dollar bank balance, Sam gave the most for the greater good. But I chipped in at least five million every year. Sometimes more. Outfitting Joanne James with wedding gown number six would keep us all in black leather and orange red spandex for the foreseeable future.

"Have your assistant call the store, and we'll set something up for later this week," I promised and downed my third gin and tonic.

Joanne smiled, her lips lavender against her pale face. "Fiona, darling, it's always a pleasure doing business with you."

We airkissed again and exchanged more meaningless pleasantries. Then, Joanne strutted back through the crowd to Berkley Brighton, a short, square man who'd made his fortune selling Brighton's Best whiskey. Joanne latched on to his arm, and the pretty young things who'd been clustered around the boisterous billionaire scattered like minnows fleeing a hungry barracuda. Joanne wasn't someone you wanted to mess with—especially when she was husband hunting. Berkley actually beamed at Joanne, happy to see his honey.

I snorted. Poor guy. He might as well just sign over his family's secret whiskey recipe to Joanne right now. It would save him a lot of trouble and hefty lawyers' fees down the road.

While I'd been talking to Joanne, Carmen and Sam had joined the festivities. They walked from table to table, greeting the wedding guests and basking in the afterglow of the ceremony. After paying their respects to the bride and groom, people finished their dinners and drifted out onto the tile dance floor that had been planted on the lawn for the grand occasion. A twelve-piece band to one side of the floor played a loud, brassy version of "The Right Thing to Do" by Carly Simon, Carmen's favorite singer.

My eyes scanned the glittering crowd. Joanne and Berkley. Carmen and Sam. Henry and Lulu. Even my father was dancing with one of Bigtime's rich, lonely widows. Couples, couples, everywhere. But no Travis.

No Travis.

The happy society scene and all the couples burned me out. I needed some peace and quiet. Now.

I shoved through the crowd, wrenched open a side door, and stomped inside the manor. The usual rich, shiny trappings greeted me, but for once, I didn't pay attention to them. Sam wouldn't like it if I accidentally melted some ancient knight's suit of armor or fried another one of his Monets. The mood I was in, they'd go up like dry newspaper.

The music and laughter and happy sounds faded away, replaced by the *thwack* of my heels on the hardwood floors. I walked into one of the many game rooms that populated the manor and sank down onto the smooth leather couch. A big-screen TV took up one wall, while a pool table crouched in the middle of the floor. Dart boards and various other sportslike contraptions filled the rest of the area, but I didn't really see them. I didn't see any of it.

I twisted the ring on my finger. It wasn't nearly as big as Joanne James's was, but it meant the world to me, even now. Travis. My heart squeezed like a dishrag being wrung out.

"A beautiful bridesmaid alone by herself. What a sad, sad cliché," a low, cultured voice called out.

I looked up. A man stood in the doorway. He topped out at just over six feet, with a mane of tawny blond hair that curled around the collar of his impeccable tuxedo. Flashing green eyes contrasted with his golden skin, making him look like a sleek lion in the gathering shadows. He strode into the room, his black suit flowing with easy grace around his perfect figure. It fit him well. Then again, just about anything would have looked good on him.

My eyes widened. If Sam resembled a male model, then this guy was the Goliath of male models. Yummy.

The man stared at me, and his eyes crinkled in amusement. The merriment dancing in his sharp gaze made him look that much better, even if he seemed to be making fun of me. I didn't like people making fun of me, and I especially didn't like being looked down on. I got to my feet and tossed my long hair back. With my stilettos, he only had half an inch on me.

"I'm not a cliché," I snapped.

"Really? You were one of the bridesmaids, right?"

"Yes."

"And you're sitting here all alone."

"Yes."

"And you certainly are beautiful."

"Oh, yes."

Modesty is another one of my nonexistent virtues. On a scale of one to ten, I'm a solid eight and a half. With my blond hair, blue eyes, and up-to-there legs, I've got the Barbie look men love down pat. The only problem is they think I'm as dumb as one of the plastic dolls. The same thing goes for my alter ego, Fiera. But more than one ubervillain had gotten badly burned by underestimating me.

Still, the compliment pleased me. Every woman likes to be told she's beautiful, but coming from Mr. Model, it sounded . . . better. Truer. Sexier.

"If all that's not a cliché, then I don't know what is." His voice was deep with a hint of an accent I couldn't quite place. White teeth gleamed in his tan face, adding to his already staggering sex appeal.

I crossed my arms over my chest and flipped through my mental Rolodex of Bigtime society players. No match. He must be new in town. I certainly would have remembered him. My eyes drifted over his suit, which draped perfectly over his broad shoulders and chest. Oh yeah. I would have remembered him.

I suddenly realized that I was twisting the ring on my finger. Bloody hell. I'd gone from pining over Travis to ogling a complete stranger in the space of a minute. I really did need to get lucky before my hormones made me have a total meltdown. Literally.

The man continued. "You certainly looked sad and lonely sitting there, staring into space."

"I was doing nothing of the sort."

I couldn't tell him that I'd been looking at the ring my murdered fiancé had given me before he'd died. My pain was my own. I didn't go blabbing about it to strangers. Besides, no one except the Fearless Five had even known Travis and I were engaged. It was another secret we'd decided to keep to ourselves.

"I was just taking a break from the festivities," I replied in my best, cool, bored society voice. "All that happiness can be a bit grating after a while."

"Really? You know we could create our own festivities, you and me."

I stifled a laugh. That was one of the lamest lines I'd ever heard. "Really? And how could we do that?"

"Let me show you."

He flashed me a devilish grin, pulled me into his arms, and planted his lips on mine.

★ 3 ★

For a moment, I couldn't believe it. Who the bloody hell did this jerk think he was, kissing me? I was Fiera, for crying out loud. Superhero du jour. Protector of the innocent. Defender of democracy. I could snap his neck like a pretzel stick. I could light his ass up like a firecracker with a mere thought.

I thought of doing both—at the same time. Then, something strange happened.

I realized that I liked kissing him.

A lot.

A whole lot.

He had fantastic lips. Soft, firm, smooth. He tasted like fizzy champagne and smelled of some subtle, spicy soap. The combination made my head spin more than the three drinks I'd just had.

At five-foot-nine, I'm no small, petite thing, but I felt dwarfed by him. His sculpted chest felt like sun-warmed stone under my hands, and his heart thumped under my clenched fingers. His arms held me securely in place. I opened my mouth to tell him something, I wasn't quite sure what, and he dipped his tongue in. The taste of him, the feel of his mouth, his tongue on mine overwhelmed my senses. I felt like I'd been zapped with a couple dozen stun guns—all weak and twitchy.

He plundered my mouth like a pirate seeking buried treasure. Nibbling my lips. Skimming my teeth. Probing with his tongue. I couldn't resist him, and I didn't really want to. I'd been thinking about having a one-night stand. Let's see how Mr. Model measured up.

So I opened my mouth wider, and my tongue met his. Then, I went on the offensive. Nibbling on *his* lips. Skimming *his* teeth. Probing with *my* tongue. He pulled me closer until I thought we would melt into each other. I certainly felt like I was on fire in more ways than one.

His fingers skimmed my neck and traced down to the tops of my breasts. He slid his hand inside the scooped neckline and stroked my chest. My nipples sprang to attention. His other hand went through the slit in the side of my dress and moved up my leg with quick, sure purpose. Damn, he didn't waste any time. Smooth, sexy, and bold. I loved it. Absolutely loved it.

A warm, pleasant tingling started between my thighs and spread throughout my body. My stomach quivered the tiniest bit, and my breath came in soft gasps. My hormones had already kicked into overdrive. If he kept this up much longer, I'd have to throw him onto the couch instead of through the wall. Or on the floor. Or maybe on the pool table. It looked sturdy enough—

"Ahem."

A cool, feminine voice dampened the liquid fire burning inside me.

"*Ahem.*"

The man sighed in disappointment against my mouth. He pressed his lips to mine once more, withdrew his hands, and stepped back. I tried not to stagger. I felt like I was drunk. And I never got drunk.

"Hello, Bella," the man said. Regret tinged his deep voice, and his hot, green gaze burned into me.

The intensity of his stare made me shiver, a rare thing for me.

I turned my head. Bella Bulluci hovered just inside the door. A forest green dress of her own design clung to her curvy body, while a simple silver necklace accentuated her graceful neck. A small pair of angel wings dangled from the end of the chain. Bella's foot tapped out a rapid pattern, smacking onto the wooden floor.

"Fiona."

"Bella."

I not-so-discreetly yanked the bodice of my dress back into its proper place. It didn't have far to go, really.

Bella's hazel eyes flicked to the man beside me. "Well, I see you've met Johnny."

"Johnny?" So that's what his name was.

"Johnny Bulluci. My older brother."

"Your brother?"

"Guilty as charged, I'm afraid." Johnny strolled over to his sister and planted a chaste kiss on her cheek.

My eyes zipped back and forth between them. Side by side, the resemblance was obvious. Same tawny hair, same golden skin, same killer cheekbones. The only difference was their eyes. Bella's were a soft hazel while Johnny's were as green as polished jade. Johnny also had almost a foot on his sister. Bella was a bit on the short side.

Bella looked at me, then her brother. She shook her head and looped an arm around his waist. "Seducing another unsuspecting bridesmaid, brother dear?" she asked in a teasing tone.

"Make a habit of it, do you, Johnny?" I asked, smoothing down my skirt.

"Only with the exceptionally beautiful ones." He winked.

I crossed my arms over my still-tingling chest. His sister had just caught us making out like a couple of sex-starved teenagers, and the man still had the nerve to wink at me. Johnny Bulluci had no shame. I rather liked that about him.

"Johnny's moved back home from Greece," Bella explained. "He's been looking after our business interests overseas."

So that's why I hadn't seen him around Bigtime before. It explained the accent too.

"He arrived in town several weeks ago, and I thought the wedding would be a perfect opportunity for him to meet and mingle. I didn't know he was going to disappear. I should warn you, Fiona, my brother is a notorious playboy. Always has been." Bella's voice was light, but there was a hint of disapproval to it. Her foot kept up its annoyed, tapping pattern.

"No harm done," I said in a cool voice and flipped my hair over my shoulder. "Johnny and I were just getting better acquainted."

"Indeed," Johnny said, his eyes catching mine again. "Indeed."

Suddenly, frantic screams slashed through the air. A bright, white light flashed outside, followed by a crack of thunder. The ground trembled as though it was going to split open beneath our feet.

We stood there, stunned.

"Grandfather!" Bella shouted.

She ran out the door. Johnny gave me another quick, regretful look and rushed after her.

I stuck my head out into the hall to make sure they weren't going to double back and drag me with them, but the pair had already disappeared from sight. Damn, Bella could scoot in those heels. Carmen could definitely learn a thing or two from her.

I locked the door to the game room, ran to the pool table, and twisted a knob hidden underneath one of the corners. The green felt top slid back with a whisper, revealing a row of neatly folded costumes, masks, and shoes. The pool table was one of many objects throughout the manor that held more than just a good time.

It took me about thirty seconds to ditch the bridesmaid dress, stilettos, and earrings, and shimmy into my costume. The orange red spandex molded to my body like plastic wrap, familiar and comfortable as always. I shoved my feet into my chunky, steel-toed, kick-ass boots and slapped on my flame-shaped mask. Then, I stuffed my dress and heels into the pool table and twisted the knob. The hidden compartment disappeared from sight.

The screams had quieted down, but cracks of thunder ripped through the air like gunfire. My hands curled into fists. Sparks flared to life in my hair. Flames licked at my fingers.

Unless I missed my guess, it was time for Fiera to go kick some ubervillain ass.

Goody.

I ran through the halls until I reached the doors that led outside, zoomed down the white carpet that had served as the aisle, and sprinted to the edge of the garden. A row of thick holly bushes separated the lush, flowering plants from the smooth lawn. I slid to a halt and peeked through one of the small gaps in the glossy greenery.

Bigtime's finest stood on the lawn, blank looks on their faces. They seemed not to notice the overturned tables, broken dishes, spilled food, and general chaos that surrounded them. Acrid smoke snaked up from an oak tree that had been split in two. Smoldering, snapped branches and shredded leaves littered the singed grass.

A woman dressed in a neon blue suit stood in the middle of the dance floor. Siren. She had a tangle of black curls and an hourglass figure that would make even a blind monk look twice at her. The silver zipper on her suit was open almost to her navel, showing off enough buoyant cleavage to raise the *Titanic*. A mask in the shape of a zigzagged lightning bolt covered her bright blue eyes.

But she wasn't alone. A woman in a shiny silver suit hovered next to Siren in a floating chair. Intelligal. Thick, black goggles highlighted her dark eyes, making them seem as big and round as quarters. A silver cowl clung to her egg-shaped head, hiding her hair from sight, and her suit was zipped up to her neck. It was a good thing too. Intelligal didn't have the body to pull off the evil sexpot look. She had about as many curves as a board.

So, our new neighborhood ubervillains have decided to crash the wedding. I wasn't terribly surprised. Siren and Intelligal had come to town about six months ago, right after the members of the Terrible Triad had disappeared. The two had been raising hell ever since. Breaking into computer companies, stealing electronic and media equipment, robbing anyone and everyone they could get their hands on.

But even worse than the general mayhem the pair caused were their powers. It was bad enough Siren could create powerful lightning bolts and energy balls with her bare hands. But her real weapon was her voice. One throaty whisper from Siren was all it took to turn most people into mindless, willing slaves. Her power especially seemed to work on men. Naturally. Of course, her looks didn't hurt either when it came to turning men into helpless puppets.

Intelligal didn't seem to have any superpowers of her own, but she really didn't need them. Her Intellichair did the work for her. The device was a flying, open-topped tank that wrapped around the ubervillain's legs and torso. Equipped with heat-seeking missiles, machine-gun turrets, and a force field, the chair was like something out of a James Bond movie. Only better. The Intellichair was also scratch-proof, fireproof, and virtually indestructible. Most things made out of solidium were. I knew. I'd been trying to melt and smash the chair to pieces for months with no success. I hadn't even been able to put so much as a dent in the dull gray metal.

"Ladies and gentlemen, I'm terribly sorry if I frightened you, but I'm afraid my invitation to the wedding got lost in the mail," Siren cooed into the microphone she'd taken from the band leader. "And I just couldn't miss *the* social event of the season."

Her voice was low and husky and throaty. To the men, it whispered of sexual fantasies come to life. To the women, it was the conspiratorial tone of a trusted friend and confidant. Just about everyone in the crowd nodded their heads, accepting Siren's explanation for her lightning storm.

Siren's dulcet tones curled through the air, seeking out everyone within hearing distance. I felt the humming melody in her voice coiling around me like a boa constrictor, trying to squeeze my will into hers. Trying to make me one of her mindless lackeys. But I was too strong willed and too temperamental to be manipulated by the likes of Siren. I grabbed on to the roaring fire inside me and concentrated on the heat. The coils burned away, and my head cleared.

So was Carmen. The blushing bride eyed the busty ubervillain with open hatred. Soot streaked her white dress, and her auburn hair had tumbled out of its elegant updo. Carmen's fingers twitched, and I knew she wanted to tap into Siren's powers and give the ubervillain a taste of her own medicine. But she couldn't. Not without blowing her cover as Karma Girl and ruining what was left of her wedding.

I looked for the other members of the Fearless Five. Sam and Henry both wore slightly vacant, dazed expressions. Sam's tie had come undone, and Henry's glasses dangled on the end of his nose. They'd been getting better at resisting Siren's call, but her hypnotic voice still affected them. I snorted. Men. Please. They really were the weaker sex, in every sense of the word. The first time we'd gone up against her, Siren had convinced Sam aka Striker to attack me. It had taken one of my fireballs to the chest to bring him back to his senses. But since Striker regenerated, the only thing my fireball had really hurt was his pride.

My father looked bemused and a bit pained by the whole thing. Siren purred into the microphone again, and the chief massaged his temples. With his psychic powers, he was well beyond Siren's call, although her voice always left him with one hell of a headache.

Lulu sat next to the chief and gazed at Intelligal's chair. A calculating expression filled her smooth face, and her fingers tapped against the arm of her wheelchair like it was a keyboard. The computer hacker was probably wondering how she could get Henry aka Hermit to make her a similar contraption. I didn't blame her. Although I had little use for gadgets, given my natural superpowers, even I had to admit the Intellichair was a cool, deadly gizmo. Especially since it had been kicking our asses for the last six months.

"I do hope you all will forgive my rude outburst," Siren continued. "I really want to make a good impression on everyone, being so new in town. I've heard such lovely, lovely things about Bigtime and all of you. I just want to fit in."

I rolled my eyes. Good grief, she was simpering now. Did the woman have no pride? She was giving ubervillains

everywhere a bad name. As much as I hated evildoers like
Malefica, Captain Sushi, and Noxious, at least I had some
respect for them. They would never have lowered themselves to play to a crowd of civilians.

"Oh, get on with it, Siren. Quit showing off," Intelligal
snapped and crossed her arms over her flat chest. The geeky
ubervillain had little use for her partner's sexy antics. That
was two of us.

"You always spoil my fun." Siren stuck her lip out and
pouted.

"I'll kill her for you, Siren!" one of the wealthy businessmen volunteered.

"Me too!"

"And me!"

"No, let me do it!"

Siren smiled, and several of the older men in the crowd
clutched their chests, ready to have coronary episodes if she
so much as crooked her pinky. "Thank you, darlings, but
that won't be necessary."

I thought she muttered the word *yet*, but I couldn't be
sure. The two ubervillains might work together, but they
definitely were not the best of friends. Too bad they wouldn't
take each other out and save me the trouble.

"Intelligal is going to come over to you now. If you'll be
so kind as to put your necklaces, watches, rings, and other
valuables into her bag, we would greatly appreciate it."

Siren's husky voice wrapped around me again, and I
burned away the tight, grasping tendrils. Intelligal zoomed
into the glassy-eyed crowd. She hit a button, and the side of
her chair opened up. A mechanical arm holding a soft, cloth
bag stretched out.

The ubervillain floated through the crowd, robbing Bigtime's richest, while Siren cooed into the microphone and
kept them in line. Although I wanted to lob a fireball or

three her way, I couldn't risk it. There were too many people around. Frying civilians was not good for my image. Or for sales of my action figures, calendars, and other officially licensed merchandise.

Intelligal motored round and round, collecting millions in jewels, watches, and other baubles. Of course, there were a few willful holdouts who weren't under Siren's spell and didn't want to give up their precious shinies. Joanne James was among them. Intelligal had to threaten to shoot Berkley with the machine guns mounted on her chair before Joanne parted with her pearls and enormous engagement ring. Even then, it took her a while to decide between imminent, bloody death and going without her status symbols.

To my surprise, Johnny Bulluci was also among the people who resisted Siren's throaty call. Unlike the others, he didn't have a blank look on his face. He and Bella hovered protectively over an old man in a navy tuxedo. That must be the grandfather they'd rushed out to save. What was his name? Something with an R. Reed, Reynolds, Richards, Roger, Rob, Roberto! That was it. Roberto Bulluci. Bobby for short.

Intelligal drifted their way, and Johnny's eyes narrowed to slits. He shifted his stance, and his jacket opened up, exposing his white shirt. I remembered the solid feel of his chest next to mine. His lips on mine. His hands on my body. I could still smell his spicy scent. My temperature roared up a few hundred degrees. The man was sexy, there was no doubt about that. None whatsoever. Even now, I was thinking about how we could pick up where we'd left off earlier. But I pushed that thought aside. My duty as a superhero came first—pummeling ubervillains whenever possible.

Intelligal stopped in front of the Bullucis. Johnny stepped forward to shield his family from the ubervillain. His hands clenched and unclenched into fists, and Johnny looked like he wanted to leap onto Intelligal's chair and punch her over and over again. The old man put a wrinkled, restraining hand on Johnny's arm and shook his head. Johnny shot his grandfather an annoyed look, but he relaxed just a bit. To my surprise, Bella's lips tightened into a thin line, and her hazel eyes glittered with rage. Bella? Angry? The mild-mannered designer never got angry, not even when she lost out on the Bigtime Fashion Designer of the Year Award to me. Despite his age, Bobby was just as worked up as his grandchildren. Even he shot the ubervillain a look of disgust and loathing.

Johnny handed over a thick watch and his engraved cuff links. Bella took off her silver chain and charm and threw them into the bag, while Bobby passed over a diamond pinky ring. Intelligal moved on to her next victims, but all three of the Bullucis kept their eyes on her, wishing that looks could kill.

After about twenty minutes, Intelligal finished her mission. The mechanical arm clamped down on the bag, securing it and the goodies inside. She floated back to the dance floor, where Siren waited.

"Well, ladies and gentlemen, it's been a real pleasure. But I'm afraid it's time for us to leave."

"Siren, don't go!"

"Please stay!"

"We'll do anything you want!"

Men and a few women called out to the ubervillain, pleading with her to stay.

Siren smiled. "I know you will, darlings, but I really must go before the Fearless Five show up. Now, why don't you all do me a favor and talk quietly among yourselves for, say, ten minutes? That would make me *so* happy. And you want to make me happy, don't you?"

Just about everyone in the crowd immediately turned to each other and began chatting about the weather, the wedding, and how fabulous Siren looked. Siren tossed the microphone back to the befuddled band leader and hopped onto the arm of Intelligal's chair. The two of them zoomed up off the dance floor.

Ah, my cue at last.

I grabbed the fire pulsing through me, and my body exploded into flames.

★ 4 ★

I plowed through the prickly holly bushes and pointed my finger. Flames arced outward, and a line of fire roared up between the ubervillains and the crowd. A few people snapped out of their trances, but most just stared at the flames. I pointed my other finger. Another line of fire sprang up, cutting off the ubervillains' escape route. I sprinted forward through the flames toward the evildoers.

Siren and Intelligal froze. The chair hovered in midair, and their heads snapped around to me.

"You!" Siren screamed.

Her voice morphed from sultry and simpering to sharp and jagged in an instant. It felt like cold razors slicing into my brain. I clapped my hands to my head, trying to block out the horrible sound.

A bluish energy ball popped into her hand, and Siren reared back to throw it at me. But a streak of lightning cut through the air and slammed into Siren's back. Shocked, the ubervillain flew off the arm of Intelligal's chair and hit the ground. Behind her, Carmen waved at me and smiled.

"Get her, Intelligal!" Siren shrieked through a mouthful of dirt. The harsh tone in her voice cut through me again.

Intelligal zoomed up over the dancing flames and punched some buttons on her floating chair. Two flaps opened on the front of the metal contraption, and missiles rocketed out—straight at me. I waited until they were in range, lobbed two fireballs at them, and rolled out of the way. My fireballs slammed into the missiles, and they exploded in midair. The thunderous roar and resulting shockwave jolted the rest of the crowd out of its sheeplike state. People screamed and stampeded and sprinted down the lawn toward the metal gates a mile away. Smoke, soot, and ash darkened the spring sky.

Siren scrambled to her feet and sent a lightning bolt my way. I ducked it and retaliated with a fireball. Intelligal zipped back and forth over us, trying to get a clear shot at me with some more of her pesky missiles.

Out of the corner of my eye, I spotted Johnny Bulluci. He ran through the wall of flames and launched himself onto Intelligal's chair like it was something he did every day. What the hell did he think he was doing? I was the hero here, not him. The fool was going to get himself killed, and me along with him.

But I was too busy trying to dodge Siren's energy balls and fry her alive to pay much attention to Johnny. I tried to get close enough to touch Siren, but she kept flinging lightning bolts at me. She was too smart to let me get within arm's reach. Siren knew I could crush her to goo with my bare hands. I would, given half a chance. I'd wrap my hands around her neck and squeeze her like an orange.

After a few minutes of back-and-forth action, I started

to wear Siren down. Her lightning bolts grew weaker, shorter, and slower, and she started backing away from me. I crouched down, ready to pounce on her, when something smacked into me.

"Oof!" I hit the ground so hard my flame-shaped mask left an impression in the smoldering grass.

It took me a second to realize Johnny Bulluci had fallen on top of me. Intelligal must have shaken him off her chair. Johnny didn't look like it, but the guy weighed a ton. I knew. That's what I bench-pressed.

"Move, move, move!" I roared.

Johnny rolled off me, onto his feet, and pulled me up in one smooth motion. I shoved him aside and raced toward the ubervillains. Too little, too late.

Siren hopped back onto Intelligal's chair. A helicopter rotor sprang up from somewhere inside the device and started to whine and whir. Good grief, how many gadgets did the woman have on that thing? The two of them motored up, up, and away. I tossed a couple of fireballs in the air, but Intelligal easily steered clear of them. Seconds later, the ubervillains disappeared from sight.

Damn. Just when I was getting warmed up.

"Fiera! Fiera!" someone shouted.

I turned. Chief Newman pointed at the lines of fire still burning on the lawn and threatening to scorch the gardens. I concentrated, pulling the heat back into my own body, and the flames snuffed out. The chief and the others started forward to see if I was injured. I waved them off and marched over to Johnny, who was staring into the sky as if he could see where the ubervillains had gone. Bella and Bobby Bulluci stood next to him, alternating their gazes between Johnny and the wild blue yonder.

"What the hell did you think you were doing? You almost got yourself killed," I snapped.

"I was trying to take back what was mine and everybody else's," Johnny growled, not the least bit intimidated by the orange red flames surrounding my body.

I leaned forward and focused my anger—and heat—on him. "That's not your job, your responsibility. That's what I'm here for. And I didn't just go a couple of rounds with some ubervillains so you could try to play hero and die a horrible, static-charged death."

"As you can see, I'm fine." His green eyes narrowed. "And if I want to 'play hero,' as you put it, it's no business of yours. Just because you're a superhero doesn't mean you can tell the rest of us what to do."

That's exactly what it meant, at least to me. Putting life and limb on the line for the fine citizens of Bigtime entitled me to a few perks. Bossing people around was one of them.

Johnny continued to glare at me. My hair sparked and cracked with fire. Arrogant man. First, he tried to seduce me, and now he thought he knew how to do my job better than I did. Johnny Bulluci didn't know how close he was to getting strangled. I also had the oddest desire to singe his clothes off, yank him toward me, and kiss him until his eyeballs melted. Well, I'd stop before the eyeball-melting part. That could get a little icky.

I opened my mouth to berate Johnny some more when a white blur zipped by.

Swifte stopped in the middle of the lawn and struck a heroic pose. Hands on his hips, chest out, chin up. He was a tall, thin man who reminded me of a string bean. As his name suggested, Swifte was built for speed, not strength. The afternoon sun hit his back, and all the colors of the rainbow shimmered in the superhero's opalescent spandex suit. Silver sparkles glittered on the edges of the wing-shaped mask that covered his face. I eyed him with distaste. Swifte's getup was rather over the top, even for me. Superheroes, especially men, should not wear head-to-toe white. Ever. He so needed a makeover.

The superhero was so quick that he didn't even stir up any of the sooty dust or hot embers that coated the grass. A black bag dangled from his gloved hand.

"You're a little late, aren't you, Swifte?" I sniped. "The party's over."

The superhero relaxed his media pose. He shrugged. "I was around. I heard the commotion and thought you might need a hand, especially since none of your friends showed up to help. Where's the rest of the F5 gang?"

"Oh, they're around somewhere," I replied in a vague voice.

"Of course they are," Swifte murmured, looking at Carmen.

I thought Carmen blushed. But it was probably just the heat lingering in the air that painted her cheeks a bright pink.

Swifte gazed out at the smoke and debris. "Well, you acquitted yourself nicely, Fiera. Even without your friends' help."

I flipped my hair over my shoulder. "I always do."

"Well, I'll just drop these off and be on my way." Swifte shoved the bag at me and tipped his head to Carmen and Sam. "My congrats to the happy bride and groom."

The superhero put his hands back on his hips and struck another pose. Then, he disappeared. One second he was here, the next he was halfway to Metropolis.

I hefted the bag. The telltale clink and rattle of jewels and chains sounded.

"Is that what I think it is?" Henry asked, pushing his soot-streaked glasses up his nose.

I opened the bag and peered inside at the gleaming gems. "Yep. Somehow, Swifte lifted the stolen jewels off Intelligal's chair."

"That's pretty impressive," Lulu chimed in. "I didn't even see him."

"Swifte is quick, I'll give him that," I said.

He was also rather annoying, popping up when you least expected him to, sort of like a zit. And he always zoomed off before you had a chance to talk to him. The only people who ever got to say more than twenty words to Swifte were the reporters from the Superhero News Network and other media outlets. He always had plenty of time to stop and talk to them. Showboat.

"Well, now that everything's settled, can I have my watch back?" Johnny said.

I couldn't believe his nerve. He'd gotten in my way, let the ubervillains escape, and now he wanted his shinies back? How shallow. Even for a rich, spoiled playboy.

"I don't think so," I snapped. "Not after the way you behaved. You can wait. The Fearless Five will get your items back to you in a few days."

It was standard operating procedure in cases like this. We'd sort through the items, determine what belonged to whom, and mail them back to the rightful owners. It kept people like Joanne James from claiming that certain pieces of jewelry belonged to them when they really didn't.

Johnny's face hardened, his lips forming a tight line. I tore my gaze away from them and tried not to think about just how firm and warm they'd been earlier.

"Let's go, Johnny. Now." Bella's voice was sharp as a stiletto and twice as pointed.

"Yes, come along, Johnny," Bobby Bulluci added. "I hardly think Fiera's going to keep anything for herself. We can get the watch back later."

I eyed the grandfather. Even though he was over seventy, Bobby Bulluci was still a handsome man. He stood straight and tall, with a trim body. His hair was a burnished silver, but his eyes were the same remarkable green that Johnny's were. If Bobby was what Johnny would look like in another forty years, then the younger Bulluci was one lucky devil.

Johnny stared at his sister and grandfather. He turned back to me and took a deep breath. "The watch was my father's. I'd like it back. Please. It has a lot of sentimental value to me, to my whole family."

I started to say no, but something in his eyes stopped me. A bright flash of pain I knew all too well. The pain of losing someone you loved. I remembered what Joanne had told me about Bella's father dying.

I held out the bag. "Take it."

Johnny reached for the bag. Our fingers brushed, and I felt the need to blow off some steam. A few sparks flew out of my fingertips and landed on Johnny's torn, dirty tux. He paused and patted them out.

"Sorry about that," I said. "Job hazard."

"No problem."

Johnny dug through the fancy baubles until he found what he was looking for—a simple silver watch. All that decorated the timepiece's black face were a pair of wings, inlaid in mother-of-pearl. No diamonds, no jewels, nothing fancy. It wasn't even a Rolex. Odd. Given how much he wanted it back, you'd think the watch would have been made out of solid platinum.

Johnny fastened the timepiece around his left wrist. "Thank you."

"No problem."

Johnny took his grandfather's arm, and the Bullucis headed toward the gates, where the rest of the wedding guests milled about, waiting for their stretch limos to come take them home. That left just the six of us.

The chief put a concerned hand on my shoulder. "Are you all right, Fiona? That was a pretty nasty fight."

I stretched my arms over my head and did a mental inventory of my body. I felt a little sore in places, but that was it. With my superstrength, it took a lot to hurt me.

"Oh, I'm fine. It's nothing a little liquor won't cure. I need a drink. Fighting ubervillains is thirsty work."

I strolled over to the bar, which had somehow survived the fires and explosions and lightning bolts, and grabbed a bottle of champagne. I yanked the cork out, took a long swig of the warm, bubbly liquid, and raised the bottle to the others. "Cheers."

★ 5 ★

"Are you sure we don't need to stay here?" Carmen asked.

I rolled my eyes. "If you ask me that again, I'm going to burn your tongue."

The five of us, plus Lulu, were down in the secret library underneath Sublime. Superhero Central, Carmen called it. To me, it was our War Room, despite the books and magazines and encyclopedias clustered on the floor-to-ceiling shelves.

After calming down the frantic wedding guests and escorting them off the grounds, the Fearless Five had gone into full-fledged superhero mode. We'd spent the last couple hours in the library trying to track down Siren and Intelligal. With no luck.

"Intelligal must have some sort of cloaking device on that chair," Henry muttered.

He was using his power, mind-melding with his super-computer, to try and locate the ubervillains. A soft, bluish white glow connected his fingers to the keyboard. The monitor reflected numbers and letters onto his round glasses, making them gleam. The symbols flashed by too fast for me to follow, but Henry had no trouble deciphering them with his photographic memory.

"There's no trace of them. Not even a heat signature on the radar."

"I'm sure you'll find her, babe," Lulu said, pounding away on her own computer nearby. "You always do."

"Maybe we should stay here," Carmen repeated.

"And abandon your honeymoon plans?" Chief Newman said. "There's no need for that."

Carmen paced around the room. She picked up one of her Rubik's Cubes and turned it round and round in her hands as she slid the plastic rows of colors back and forth. "I feel like Siren and Intelligal are up to something. Something big."

"Aren't they always? It's sort of what ubervillains do." I leaned back in my chair and put my feet up on the round table that dominated the middle of the room. My black stilettos rested on top of the giant *F5* insignia carved into the heavy wood.

Carmen shook her head. "This feels bigger than that. Like world-domination big."

"Chief?" I asked my father.

He laced his fingers together. "I think Carmen's right. They're definitely up to something. They took a big risk crashing the wedding, and I've got the headache to prove it."

"See? We should stay. Besides, those bitches ruined my wedding. They should pay."

Carmen's eyes flashed neon blue with rage. They only did that when she was very, very angry. Even I didn't like to go up against Carmen when she was angry.

Sam put an arm around her shoulder and hugged her to

him. Carmen's eyes brightened, taking on a different sort of glow.

"Don't worry, they will," Sam said. "The chief and the others will take care of them. You don't want to cancel our trip, do you?"

An extravagant, no-holds-barred, month-long honeymoon around the world was Sam's wedding present to Carmen. She'd be a fool to cancel on him just to track down a couple of measly ubervillains. But if she did, I'd be happy to take her place, and eat and shop my way around the globe. I could use a vacation, especially after today. As much as I loved being a superhero, there were times when the epic battles got a bit old. Unfortunately, ubervillains were a dime a dozen in this town, and somebody was always up to something. Which meant that we superheroes always had to be on the lookout for trouble with a capital T.

"No, of course not," Carmen said, leaning into Sam that much more. "But you know how I worry."

"There's nothing to worry about, Sister Carmen," Lulu said. "Henry will track them down, and then Fiona will fry their asses."

"Sounds like a plan to me," I said. "I'm always up for a good barbecue."

In the end, Carmen gave in. She and Sam got into a limo and headed for the Bigtime Airport, where Sam's private jet was waiting to take them to London. They didn't even make it out of the driveway before they tinted the windows and started canoodling in the backseat.

After seeing them off, in more ways than one, the rest of us talked for a few more minutes about the ubervillains and what they might be up to. But nobody had any bright, earth-shattering ideas, so we sorted through the stolen jewelry and packed it up to mail back to its rightful owners. Then, we closed down shop for the night. Too tired to make the drive back to my apartment in the city, I went to my suite down the hall.

Our underground lair beneath Sublime took up almost as much space as the manor house did aboveground. Wing after wing contained training rooms, gyms, kitchens, sick bays, and everything else a superhero could ever want or need. My suite was an enormous area, bigger than most apartments, and featured a bedroom, bathroom, living room, and kitchen all rolled into one, along with a pitifully small closet. The others' suites all had a similar setup except for one thing—mine boasted three oversized refrigerators.

I rustled around in one of the metal behemoths and came up with a platter of cold cuts, three kinds of cheese, and a loaf of crusty French bread. I made myself seven sandwiches and downed them with a six-pack of lemon-lime soda and a box of chocolate snack cakes. Due to my fiery metabolism, I could eat whatever I wanted to, whenever I wanted to, and never gain an ounce. A whole pizza for breakfast, ten burgers and a bucket of fries for lunch, a couple of steaks and a pound of pasta for dinner. The only downside was that I constantly had to eat to keep up my strength. It got a little tiring sometimes. Not to mention grossed people out. My father and Travis were the only ones who didn't seem disturbed by my never-ending hunger and enormous appetite.

Travis. An icy hand squeezed my heart. I plopped down on the king-sized bed and picked up the picture of him on my nightstand. Blond hair, brown eyes, terrific smile. Travis Teague beamed at me. I'd missed him today. A lot. Carmen and Sam's wedding had only reminded me of what I'd lost when Travis had been killed over a year ago. Of what I should have right now. I turned my ring around on my finger.

But as I looked at Travis's picture, my thoughts drifted

back to Johnny Bulluci and our encounter in the game room. The man could kiss, that was for sure. A couple of sparks flew from my fingertips and landed on the tile floor. If Johnny could work with his hands as well as he did with his lips and tongue, well, he could seduce me anytime.

Johnny Bulluci could be my rebound guy, I decided. Someone to have a little fun and a lot of steamy sex with before I started looking for the next Mr. Right. Travis had been my Mr. Right, but he was gone now. I would always miss him, but he wouldn't want me to be a nun the rest of my life. Travis had been generous to a fault. He would understand me moving on. He'd encourage me to. I put Travis's picture on the nightstand and carefully positioned it so he was smiling at me.

Yes, it was time to get out and live a little.

It was time for Fiona Fine to get back into the dating game.

The next morning, I drove my convertible into the city. I put the top down, stepped on the gas, and let the warm wind whip my blond locks into a tangled mess. The sporty car had been my present to myself for my thirtieth birthday a couple of months ago. I loved the sleek design, the smooth ride, the fire engine red color. The four hundred horses under the hood weren't too shabby either.

Before work, I swung by my apartment, located in the penthouse in Tip-Top Tower, one of the most expensive and exclusive buildings in Bigtime. I opened the door, flicked on the lights, and tossed my keys onto a table. My apartment featured ivory-colored granite floors and walls, fireproof up to three thousand degrees. No thick shag carpet for me. I'd ruined too much of it in my life to risk having it in my home. No chintzy curtains either. Instead, metal screens covered the tall windows like blinds, giving me privacy from prying eyes, without being a fire hazard.

I walked into the living room. A long sofa the color of Bing cherries sat against one wall, flanked by four black armchairs. The rest of the furniture was done in various shades of red, black, and white. Sometimes all three. Paintings behind shatterproof and fire-resistant glass added even more color to the pale walls.

I took a quick shower, dried off in about two seconds, and moved to my favorite part of my apartment—my closet. I flicked on the lights in the walk-in closet, which took up more than two thousand square feet. Rack after rack of shirts, skirts, slacks, shoes, and more, along with drawers full of jewelry and handbags, crouched inside the massive space. The bright fabrics, outrageous patterns, and bold colors always brought a smile to my face. Life was too short for drab beiges and tame taupes and basic blacks. Give me electric blue and lime green and shocking purple any day.

Now, on to the most important question of the day. What to wear? So many color combinations, so little time. I flipped through the racks of clothes, choosing a short, hot pink skirt and a sleeveless black V-necked top with huge pink polka dots. A pair of matching kitten heels, a heart-shaped bag, and plastic hoop earrings finished off the look.

I left the convertible in the building's parking garage and walked the few blocks to my store. It was just after nine, and most folks were grabbing a last cup of coffee and a doughnut before heading off to work. I stopped in front of Bryn's Bakery, eyeing the delectable-looking bear claws through the windows. The bag of blueberry bagels, tub of cream cheese, and quart of apple juice I'd had for breakfast were already long gone.

A siren screamed out, and a brigade of fire trucks roared by. I squinted into the morning sun. Black smoke boiled up from a building a couple of blocks away. I stood on the sidewalk, torn between the bear claws and whipping my spare Fiera costume and boots out of the special, air-compressed compartment in my purse.

"Out of my way! Move it! Now!"

A black woman dressed in a formfitting ebony jumpsuit strutted by me. Green and gold snakes curled around her arms like bracelets, hissing and snapping at people to get them to move out of the way. More snakes writhed on top of her sky-high headdress. Ah, Black Samba was coming to the rescue today.

Black Samba marched into the street and held out her hand. She chanted in an odd, sibilant language. Five seconds later, a city bus rounded a corner and stopped in front of her. Along with the snakes, Black Samba had some sort of magic voodoo powers I didn't really understand. I preferred a simpler style, punching and smashing and frying to get things done. But the mumbo jumbo worked for her.

Black Samba leapt up onto the hood, told the driver to head toward the fire, then scampered up onto the roof. Bus tops were her preferred mode of transportation around the city. For some reason, her snakes didn't like the subway. At least, that's what I'd heard through the superhero grapevine.

"Wait for me!" an older, feminine voice called out.

A diamond-topped walking stick snapped against the sidewalk, and the crowd parted to let Granny Cane through. She looked like your average grandmother, except for the flowered purple mask that covered her face and the capelike flow to her matching angora sweater. Granny Cane prowled the streets of Bigtime, getting thieves to try to mug her before wailing on them with her enormous handbag and walking stick and dragging them to the police station. Granny was a lot stronger and sturdier than she looked.

"Hurry up, old woman!" Black Samba snapped, stalking up and down the top of the bus. Her snakes hissed in time to her footsteps.

"Don't make me wash your mouth out with soap, missy." Granny pointed her cane at the other superhero. "There's no need to be disrespectful to your elders."

Granny hopped onto the bus, and it pulled away into traffic. Well, with Black Samba and Granny Cane on the way, there was no need for me to get involved. They could handle a simple fire-and-rescue operation. Besides, too many superheroes on the scene wasn't really a good thing. Everybody always wanted to get in on the drama. When there wasn't enough danger to go around, the stronger superheroes tended to assert themselves, which often led to ego-bruising and spats. We all wanted to be the best—and most popular. It was sort of like being back in high school. With superpowers, a good image, and action-figure sales to maintain—instead of a cool quotient, high grades, and clear skin.

I did, however, still need to get to work. So, I forced myself away from the bakery and walked on.

Fiona Fine Fashions sat in the middle of Retail Row in the heart of Bigtime's downtown shopping district. The front of the multistory building housed the runway and store, while workers sewed garments and more in the back. A huge, marble F towered three stories above the sidewalk and announced the store's presence to shoppers.

I breezed through the front door. A bell chimed, letting

everyone know that I had arrived. The inside of the store was rather like my apartment, in that it featured white marble walls and floors. Everything was simple and clean and colorless, the better to focus attention on my bright, bold, daring clothes. Racks of the Fiona Fine originals sat throughout the store, while a long runway cut through the middle of the open space. Models in various shapes and sizes trotted up and down the catwalk, showing off the latest, greatest designs to customers, who sat on plush leather chairs enjoying champagne and chocolates. Techno music pulsed out a snappy, happy beat through the sound system. Clerks bustled back and forth, fetching food and taking orders. I waved to them and to the society women I recognized. They fluttered their hands at me and kept on eating and drinking. I'd learned a long time ago that society ladies felt they deserved to be pampered, so I catered to their whims.

My eyes traced over the store with pride. The gleaming marble and pricey clothes were a long way from the simple home where I'd grown up in Ireland. Like so many others, my father had moved the family here in search of the American dream. I was one of the lucky ones who'd gotten mine. I sewed until my fingers bled to get to the top of the fashion world, and I did everything I could to stay there.

I strolled through the store, punched in the security code on the back door, and headed for the factory floor. The whine and whir of sewing machines, ringing phones, and other equipment replaced the pulsing music. Men and women sat in colorful ergonomically designed cubicles and sewed dresses, tops, skirts, and more. Some placed dainty crystals on supple leather handbags, while a few worked with sapphires, rubies, and emeralds. The gems glistened and sparkled under the white lights. My jewelry line was launching this fall, and it was going to be just as fabulous as everything else I designed.

More than a few folks called out and waved to me, and I answered them in kind. My workers earned top dollar and excellent benefits for their time, diligence, and quality craftsmanship. I could afford to be generous. Most of my creations retailed for at least five thousand dollars, and everything was back-ordered for six weeks. The only other designer who commanded similar prices was Bella Bulluci.

Johnny Bulluci's handsome face flashed through my mind. I'd have to ask around and get some more dirt on him. I remembered the suave way he'd kissed me at the wedding. A spark sizzled on the tip of my thumb. Oh, yes. I definitely wanted my rebound relationship to ramp up as soon as possible.

I put that thought away and stepped into Piper Perez's office, which was next to mine. Piper typed away on a keyboard and murmured into a headset. She was an average-sized woman with black hair, tan skin, and warm brown eyes.

Piper also was my chief financial officer and anal to a fault. Everything on her desk was arranged from tallest (her computer monitor) to shortest (a pink sticky pad) and sorted by color, shape, *and* times used during the day. Piper was insanely proud of her straitlaced, obsessive tendencies. She should be. Her organizational and accounting skills earned her more than most CEOs.

"Morning, Piper."

Piper said her goodbyes to her caller, punched a button on her headset, and ended the conversation. "Morning, Fiona."

She stopped typing and handed me a stack of papers. "The front desk gave me your latest messages by mistake. I went ahead and placed the oldest ones on top so you can return those calls first. I also put the cost-comparison reports about the fabric and gemstone suppliers on your desk. And Joanne James called me personally, demanding to know when you would be available. Her highness wants to come in for a fitting."

I groaned, tempted to burn the message and drop the charred remains in Piper's spotless steel trashcan. Then, I thought about that flashing rock on Joanne's finger. I really could use a couple of new Fiera suits, and the flame-proof fabric I had to make them out of wasn't cheap. I might be rich, but I wasn't going to turn down a hefty payday, even if I had to deal with the black widow of Bigtime. "All right. Have somebody set it up. But be sure we have plenty of champagne on hand that day."

"For Joanne?"

"No, for me. I'm going to need it."

"If you think you're going to need it then, just wait a minute," Piper said.

"What? What did you say?"

"Oh nothing," Piper chirped in a cheery voice that didn't fool me for a minute.

My eyes narrowed. "What are you up to?"

Piper blinked. "Nothing. Nothing at all, Fiona."

At times like this, the chief's mind-reading powers would so come in handy. I thought about sweating the truth out of Piper but decided against it. She'd just spend the rest of the morning in the bathroom touching up her makeup until it was perfect again. Piper was as obsessive about her appearance as she was about her desk. I gave her a last suspicious look, opened the door to my office, and stepped inside.

Words escaped me.

Flowers, flowers, and more flowers covered every inch of my desk, surrounding shelves and windowsills. Roses, tulips, orchids, and more painted the room in a wild, vivid rainbow

of color. My nose twitched at the heady, rich scents all min-
gled and mashed together.

Piper leaned against the door frame. "They've been arriv-
ing every half hour since eight this morning."

"Where and who did all these come from?" I fingered the
petals on a blue orchid. I loved flowers, especially orchids,
but I never bought them for myself. Unfortunately, they had
a tendency to go up like smoke around me.

Piper pulled out a card embossed with silver filigree.
*Fiona. So sorry we got interrupted yesterday at the wedding. Din-
ner tonight? I'll pick you up at seven at your apartment. Johnny
Bulluci.*

I managed not to squeal. Instead, I took the card from
her and read it myself. Three times.

"Who's the guy?" Piper asked. "I haven't heard you mention him before. Then again, I haven't heard you mention
anyone in a long time."

"Bella's brother, he's new in town," I said in an absent
tone, my eyes still fixed on the card, which was made out of
thick, creamy paper. I traced over the silver letters with my
finger, careful not to scorch the stationary.

"Bella? As in Bella Bulluci? Our archrival in the design
world?"

"The one and the same."

I read the card again. Tingles spread through my heated
body. Johnny Bulluci liked me. Enough to want to see me
again. Either that or he just thought I was extremely easy. I
remembered his spicy smell, his firm hands on my feverish
body, the way I'd offered no resistance to his skillful advances. Yeah, he probably thought I was easy. Didn't bother
me any.

"You know, I don't remember seeing you with this guy at
the wedding. So what exactly were the two of you doing
yesterday? And where?" Piper's dark eyes sparkled. "Or

should I even ask? It must have been something to get this kind of enthusiastic response."

I flipped my long, blond hair over my shoulder. "Why, Piper, don't you know? It's always something with me."

Piper just snickered.

★ 6 ★

I spent the rest of the day working on my new fall lines.
Fiona Fine Fashions was an empire unto itself, and I had my
fingers in everything from evening wear for society matrons
to couture wedding gowns to sportswear to baby clothes.
Yes, baby clothes. It was never too early to start teaching
kids about fabulous fashion.

Today, though, my main focus was on Fine Finds by
Fiona, an affordable businesswear collection for professional
women debuting in stores across America later this year. I
was taking the basic black work suit and dressing it up with
stripes, plaids, paisleys, and most importantly, color. Your
job might be boring, but your clothes should never be.

At least, I tried to work. I kept staring at the flowers clustered around me. It was like sitting in my own personal jungle. My eyes traced over the kaleidoscope sprays with their
soft, velvety petals. Inspired, I fished a large pad out of my
messy desk and started sketching. Two hours later, I had over
a dozen drawings, each one bigger and bolder and better

than the last. I'd been looking for a theme for next year's spring line. *Flower power* would be perfect. After all, flowers featured everything that I loved—wild patterns, brilliant colors, sleek designs.

A knock on the door interrupted the flow of my creative juices.

Piper held up three white paper bags that looked like they were ready to pop. "I went to Quicke's for a meeting and thought you might be hungry. I got you a couple of grilled chicken sandwiches, a Caesar salad, large fries, a dozen cookies, and the biggest raspberry tea I could find."

I glanced at the clock. Three in the afternoon already. My stomach rumbled. "Thanks, Piper. You're a lifesaver."

Piper deposited the bags on my crowded desk. She'd long ago grown used to my enormous appetite, although she thought I had some sort of eating disorder, like binging and purging. Every so often, I'd come into the office to find pamphlets on anorexia and other eating-disorder clinics and programs on my desk, courtesy of Piper. I reduced them to ash, ignored Piper's prying looks, and continued to eat like there was no tomorrow. I couldn't exactly tell her the truth—that I was a superhero with a superhigh metabolism. Piper was my friend, but I had a secret identity to protect. The Terrible Triad had taught me the importance of anonymity.

I polished off the food in about fifteen minutes under Piper's watchful eyes. She stuck her head into my office several times that afternoon, probably hoping to catch me hurling into one of the empty paper bags, but I disappointed her by slaving away at my desk.

In addition to my work as head of Fiona Fine Fashions, I also had to attend to my duties and business as Fiera. Being a superhero was just as much about public relations as it was about saving kittens from trees and babies from burning buildings. Most of us had our own Web sites, merchandise, fan clubs, and more so we could control who did what with our image. The same went for the ubervillains. Unfortunately, evil appealed to just as many folks as good did.

Some superheroes, namely Swifte, really hammed it up. They blogged and did Web casts and wrote tell-all biographies, regaling the masses with their latest daring adventures and narrow escapes. I, and the other members of the Fearless Five, were much more restrained. We had a simple Web page where folks could e-mail us and sign up for our newsletter, as well as buy our merchandise, namely copies of my annual calendar and latest action figures.

But I didn't keep any money I made as Fiera. Neither did the rest of the Fearless Five. Not a penny. We split the profits evenly and donated them all to worthy causes. My cut went to a charity that helped burn victims get reconstructive surgery and to the Bigtime Municipal Building Restoration Fund. After all, if you tear it down, you really should help rebuild it. And I'd destroyed more than one building in Bigtime over the years.

Of course, some folks like Gentleman George and the Baseballer spurned the spotlight, preferring to keep to themselves and avoid the hoopla. Sometimes, I thought about going that route. Taking down the Web site, discontinuing my annual calendar, canceling my few public appearances. But part of me liked the attention. Modesty wasn't one of my virtues, and I enjoyed being recognized for saving the city every couple of weeks. My father had taught me long ago that I had special gifts that I must use to help others. He called it my duty, my purpose in life. I just thought it was fun. At least, it was most of the time.

I logged into my Fiera accounts and checked on sales of the calendar and a few other things that needed my attention. All of the money flowed from the Web site through untraceable numbered overseas accounts to our favorite charities. Sam was a real whiz at setting up things like that. Plus, Henry had put tons of security gizmos on my computer, ensuring that only I could access the Fiera files hidden on my hard drive.

Once that was done, I switched over to my e-mails. I got dozens of e-mails and instant messages every day, most of them from fanboys who wanted me to autograph their inflatable Fiera dolls or their tighty-whities—sometimes both. I usually ignored those. I also got a lot of letters from kids asking me to find their lost puppies or to please, please, *please* bring their pet hamster back to life. Those I answered as best I could. Despite my superpowers, I couldn't help everybody, couldn't save everybody. I did what I could, when I could. That was another thing my father had taught me. You could be a hero, do your duty, and still have a life outside the masks and capes and spandex costumes. If you didn't, you'd drive yourself crazy.

By the time I finished my sketches, returned messages, and caught up on my paperwork, superhero-related and otherwise, it was after five. Time to go home and get ready for my night out on the town with the delectable Johnny Bulluci.

Goody.

I walked home in record time. Thankfully, there were no more fires or other emergencies to distract me. After grabbing a couple of apples from the fruit bowl on the kitchen counter, I strolled into the bathroom, peeled off my clothes, and ran some water into the claw-foot tub. While I chomped on the tart fruit, I fluttered my fingers, heating the water until it was nice and toasty. Then, I did the whole *I-have-a-hot-date-and-might-even-have-sex-tonight* routine. Lathered up with some vanilla-scented soap. Washed my hair. Shaved everything.

I dried off in about three seconds, went into the bedroom, and flicked on the light in my closet to begin my search for the perfect first-date outfit. I wanted something cool, something sophisticated, something that said, *We'll probably have sex if you behave yourself and buy me a nice, big dinner first.* After flipping through three racks, I picked a tight scarlet dress covered in matching sequins that set off my blond hair and rosy skin. Heavy black eye shadow, red lipstick, a ruby solitaire pendant, and red stilettos polished off the outfit. The dress didn't have too many buttons down the back, and the short skirt would provide easy access, if desired. I closed my eyes and thought of Johnny's lips on mine. There would probably be some desire tonight. Maybe even some satisfaction, if Johnny was a very good boy. Or a very bad one, depending on your point of view.

I twirled around in front of the mirrors that lined one wall of the bedroom. I looked hot. Smokin' even, as Lulu would say. I put my hands on my hips, admiring my reflection. My engagement ring caught the light and flashed it back to me. I twisted it around on my finger. My good mood vanished.

Should I really be doing this? Going out with somebody else? Thinking about sleeping with someone else? Travis was gone, but I still loved him. I always would. I didn't know if there was room in my heart for someone else. If I could even love somebody again. If I really even wanted to.

If you loved someone, you gave him power over you. Power to hurt you, whether he did it on purpose or not. I didn't ever want to feel the way I had when Travis died. Alone. Grief-stricken. Helpless. Numb. Maybe I should wait awhile longer to get back into the social scene. Maybe I should cancel—

The phone rang, interrupting my troubled thoughts.

"Fiona Fine."

"It's me," the chief's voice rumbled through the receiver. "I just wanted to check in with you. I'm on call tonight."

Each member of the Fearless Five took turns sitting in the underground library and monitoring SNN and the local police scanners in case an ubervillain decided to wreak havoc or some natural disaster tore through Bigtime. The rest of us were equipped with cell phones, ready to respond in case bad stuff went down. With Carmen and Sam gone on their honeymoon, the chief, Henry, and I would be pulling double duty for the next month.

"How are things at the manor? Any sign of Siren and Intelligal yet?"

"Not a trace of them so far. Everything's quiet. Henry and Lulu are working on tracking them down. Carmen and Sam called earlier. They're having a wonderful time in London, although Carmen's still worried about the ubervillains."

I was surprised the happy couple had found time to call or to actually see any of London. You'd think they would have spent all day in bed, given their propensity for doing so at Sublime. Their happiness was so annoying sometimes.

My father paused. "Have fun on your date tonight. Make sure he treats you right."

I rolled my eyes. "How many times have I asked you not to peer into my mind?"

"I'm your father, Fiona. I'll be doing it until the end of time."

"Just because you're psychic doesn't give you the right to use your powers on others whenever you want. Remember that lecture? You used to give it to me whenever I'd singe one of the bullies in my class with a fireball or pick them up and spin them around until they screamed for me to stop." I'd gotten more than a few of those talks.

The chief chuckled. "I remember you spent more time in the principal's office than a classroom full of kids." His voice grew serious. "You should go out, Fiona. Travis would want you to get on with your life."

I looked at the ring on my finger. "I know he would. But it's easier said than done."

"Get out. Have fun. Be your usual charming self."

I sniffed. "I'm always that."

"I know. Now, I need to go. Henry wanted me to look over some new computer program he's invented to track Siren and Intelligal's crimes."

Henry and his computer programs. Sometimes, I wondered if the man was even human or just a robot in disguise. If he was a robot, though, you'd think his designer would have given him some fashion sense. Polka-dot bow ties and sweater vests were not the stuff women's dreams were made of. Except maybe Lulu's.

"Well, you two be careful tonight. Call me if you need me. I love you." I always ended our conversations like this now. I'd learned the hard way that just because we were superheroes didn't mean we were invincible. Quite the opposite, unfortunately.

"I love you too," the chief rumbled.

I hung up. For a moment, I stared at my engagement ring. Then, my eyes went to the mirror. I smoothed my dress down and turned sideways. I did look good tonight. Damn good. Self-esteem was another area where I didn't have a lot of problems.

I let out a long hot breath. I might as well go out. The chief was right. It was time for me to move on, whether I thought I was ready to or not.

Besides, it'd be a shame to get all dressed up for nothing.

The doorbell rang at exactly seven o'clock, just as I was powdering my nose. My date had arrived right on time. I loved punctual men.

I opened the door to find another bouquet of orchids

outside. These were picture-perfect and more beautiful than all the rest combined. They made the ones in my office look like cheap plastic imitations. I could just make out Johnny's green eyes through the exquisite purple and white petals.

"Do you know where I might find a beautiful bridesmaid?"

His voice was just as rich and cultured as I remembered. His faint accent sounded sophisticated, sultry, and utterly sexy. I'd always been a sucker for accents.

"I'm not a bridesmaid anymore," I said, stepping back to let him inside.

"But you're still beautiful."

"Aren't you the charmer?"

He winked. "Always, Fiona. Always." Johnny tossed the flowers onto a nearby table and swept me into his arms. The man didn't waste any time, that was for sure.

His lips covered mine, and all thought vanished. I wrapped my arms around his neck and pulled him closer. He opened his mouth, and I slid my tongue inside the hot depths. He tasted like mouthwash, tart and tangy. His spicy soap wafted up my nose, and I breathed in, enjoying the aroma. Whatever that scent was, it complemented him perfectly. Johnny's hands traced circles up and down my back as I explored his mouth with my tongue. It was a long, slow, lingering kiss. The sort that whispered of even better, slower, longer, harder things to come.

After a good two minutes, we came up for air.

"You know, we could just order in," Johnny murmured, pressing a kiss to the hollow of my throat. My pulse roared under his lips.

"Dinner first," I said, stepping back.

I had an image to maintain, and I didn't want him to think I was too eager. Or know that single kiss had me ready to toss him over my shoulder, carry him back to the bedroom, and ravish him from head to toe. Three times over.

The truth was the intense attraction unnerved me. One
look, one kiss, one minute alone with him, and I was all hot
and bothered. At least, more so than usual. I'd never be-
lieved in love at first sight, but lust was another matter. Or
was it? Did Johnny Bulluci really have that much of an effect on me? Or were my hormones just hot to trot because of
the long drought?

I didn't know the answers to my questions, so I concentrated on him. His tawny mane of hair glistened under the
dim lights, and his eyes were as green as polished turquoise.
Johnny wore a navy blue suit with a faint pinstripe. It looked
fantastic on him. Or he looked fantastic wearing it. I couldn't
decide which one it really was. Maybe I should get him to
model some designs for me, provided I could lure him away
from Bella. With him in the store, sales would go through the
roof. If I could stop the society types from tearing off his
clothes, something I was dangerously close to doing myself.

"Well, I suppose you're right," Johnny said. "We really
should eat dinner first before getting to dessert."

Johnny smiled. A sly, impish, wicked sort of grin spread
across his face, while his eyes devoured me from head to toe.
I had no doubt what he meant by *dessert*. I shivered, something I never did, not even when Frost hit me with his freez-
oray gun.

Johnny offered me his arm, and away we went. A limo
waiting downstairs took us to Quicke's, a restaurant famous
for its speedy service, reasonable prices, terrific food, and
most importantly, generous portions. A blue neon light
flashed on and off above the revolving door, announcing the
restaurant's name. Quicke's was located downtown, a couple
of blocks from my store, and it was one of my favorite places
to get a fast burger or ten for lunch. I practically kept the
place in business with my massive orders.

Johnny opened the door for me, and when I stepped

through, he put his hand on the small of my back to guide me inside. Some women would have been insulted by this, but not me. Maybe it's because I moonlight as a superhero, but I like strong, take-charge men. They're the only ones who can keep up with me.

Kyle Quicke was working as the host tonight, the latest in a long line of Quickes to run the restaurant. With his chestnut hair, light eyes, and thin physique, Kyle was cute in a harried sort of way. We'd gone to college together, back when we'd both been penniless nobodies. I, of course, had made my fortune in fashion, while Kyle had gotten his business degree and taken over the family restaurant. During his tenure, Quicke's had increased its already healthy profits so much that the restaurant had opened a number of smaller cafés and eateries throughout Bigtime.

"Hello, Kyle."

"Fiona Fine. Always a pleasure."

I threw my long hair over my shoulder. "Of course it is. And you as well. Loved the food you did for the wedding." What little of it I'd gotten to eat had been delicious as always.

"Thanks. I aim to please." Kyle's eyes flicked over us. "Table for two?"

"Obviously."

"This way."

Kyle grabbed a couple of leather-bound menus and zipped through the crowded restaurant, darting around tables and bustling waiters with a grace I didn't know he possessed. I followed, and Johnny put his hand on my back again. Another shiver swept through me. A girl could get used to that strong, firm touch. In all sorts of places.

The inside of Quicke's looked like your typical bar and grill, only a bit nicer. Round tables covered with white linen tablecloths took up most of the first floor and part of the second. Roses perched in tall vases on every table, along with skinny votive candles. A bar with a gleaming brass rail and mirror behind it ran the whole length of the building. Shouts and curses drifted out from behind the swinging doors that led to the kitchen, along with the sizzle of frying meat and the yeasty aroma of baking bread. My stomach quivered in anticipation at the mouthwatering scents.

The restaurant's patrons wore everything from torn jeans and sneakers to designer ball gowns and tuxedos. Quicke's catered to all segments of Bigtime's population, including superheroes and ubervillains. Framed posters, newspaper clippings, and autographed pictures of heroes and villains covered the rust-colored brick walls. Action figures crouched in mock-fighting positions on the shelves behind the bar, along with car replicas and plush toys. I was pleased to note there were more than a few Fiera figures among the mix, including one scene where a six-inch-tall version of me pummeled Scorpion. I smiled.

I scanned the tables, but I didn't see any neon-colored costumes among the crowd. Quicke's was one of the few places considered to be neutral territory in Bigtime. Both superheroes and ubervillains could eat here without worrying about being hit with heat rays or thrown through the plate glass windows. In fact, with its fast turnaround time, more than one superhero and ubervillain grabbed a sandwich or salad at Quicke's before heading out to do battle for the night. Sometimes, right in the middle of a fight. Debonair, a sometimes hero, sometimes thief with teleportation powers, was particularly fond of doing that.

Kyle seated us at a cozy table in back next to one of the windows that fronted part of Paradise Park. The colorful lights of the carousel spun round and round in the distance like a never-ending comet. Shrieks and shouts of glee penetrated the window, along with the jingle and jangle of the various other rides and attractions at the park.

Kyle gave us our menus and went back to his post at the front of the restaurant. A fat waiter named Ray came over to fill our water glasses and take our orders. Johnny decided on a black pepper–seasoned steak with the usual trimmings, and the waiter turned to me.

"Your usual, Miss Fine?" Ray asked. Most of the staff at the restaurant knew me by name.

I started to say *you betcha*, but caught myself just in time. My *usual* consisted of a half dozen various sandwiches, five jumbo orders of fries, onion rings, hot-'n'-spicy buffalo wings, two bowls of soup, a couple of liters of soda, and the cake of the day. Three of them.

"I'll have the grilled chicken special." It came with only a couple of measly sides. It wasn't going to be enough food. I tried not to cringe.

The waiter looked at me, waiting for the rest of my order.

"That's all."

"That's all? Are you sure, Miss Fine?"

"Positive." I snapped the menu shut and gave it to him.

The waiter gave me an odd look, but he bowed and walked away.

Johnny grinned. "They seem to know you pretty well here, Fiona."

I shrugged. "My store's a couple of blocks over. I eat here a lot. I was rather surprised you decided to bring me here for dinner. I expected Chezanne's or one of the other fancy French places."

"Why's that?"

I stared at his expensive attire, then at the rough brick walls and simple bar that made up the restaurant. "This place seems a little tame for you."

It was his turn to shrug. "I like good food. And Quicke's has the best in town from what I remember."

"From what you remember?"

Johnny nodded. "I've spent the past few years mostly overseas looking after our European interests, but I grew up in Bigtime and went to college here."

From what I'd read and heard on the society circuit, Bulluci Industries was a massive corporation. The Bullucis had immigrated from the Mediterranean region a couple of generations ago, and they'd achieved the American dream of owning their own business and becoming fabulously wealthy. Besides Bella's fashion empire, the Bullucis had several oil wells, mining interests, olive oil plants, and even a couple of automotive and motorcycle factories.

"You went to Bigtime U? I don't remember you." And I certainly would have. My eyes traced over his firm body. Oh yeah. I would have remembered. And done everything in my power to make sure he remembered me too.

"I think it was a little before your time. I'm seven years older than Bella. You were probably still in high school when I was at Bigtime U."

Actually, I was probably still in Ireland at the time. We hadn't come to America until my mother died after a long battle with breast cancer. Seven years older than Bella? Let's see. That would make him about thirty-six, thirty-seven. Not too old. That was another mark in his favor, along with his surprisingly good choice of restaurant.

I opened my mouth to ask Johnny another question, when a soft, breathy voice cut in.

"Well, if it isn't Fiona Fine, designer to the rich and famous."

My eyes narrowed. I knew that voice, and I didn't like the person it belonged to one bit. I looked up to find Erica Songe hovering over us. Erica was a news reporter for SNN, the Superhero News Network. She was one of SNN's rising stars, having gone from being the substitute late-night weather girl on the weekends to an evening news on-air personality in a matter of months.

Now, I don't like reporters in general. They're always getting in the way when I'm trying to roast some uber-villains, shoving a camera in my face afterward, or attempting to uncover my real identity, just like Carmen had done. Why did they have to be so nosy and demanding all the time? I couldn't understand why reporters just didn't stay away and let me do my kick-ass thing. It would work out better for everyone. At least the photographers and videographers knew enough to steer clear of me. Or at least stay a couple hundred feet away. Ruin a few five-thousand-dollar cameras and people aren't so eager to take your picture anymore.

But Erica Songe was the worst of the worst. Just because she was on television, she thought that made her special. Erica had come into my store when she'd first gotten into town and ordered several pricey suits for her on-air appearances. The clothes she wanted were on back order, along with everything else. The reporter had hit the roof when I told her that she'd have to wait just like everyone else. She thought she deserved special treatment just because she was a member of the media. Please.

Erica Songe had acted more spoiled than Joanne James ever dreamed of being. Screaming. Yelling. Threatening the staff. Demanding that we treat her like the princess she was. Or else. It had taken every bit of patience I had not to drop-kick Erica out onto the sidewalk. I'd settled for ripping up her orders and barring her from the store. For life. She tried to act cool about it, always coming up and speaking to me and being as sweet as honey whenever we crossed paths. But I knew she hated me. The feeling was mutual.

"Nice to see you too, Erica."

"Who's your *handsome friend?*" she asked, her eyes zeroing in on Johnny.

Erica had long black hair, blue eyes, and lips that had so much collagen in them they looked like they were about to explode. Her size-two figure was poured into a black dress that showed off as much tanned flesh as it concealed. Erica had a sultry sex-kitten vibe to her that turned more than one head in the room, not all of them male.

"*My handsome date* is Johnny Bulluci." I reached over and put my hand on top of Johnny's, staking my claim for the evening.

His warm thumb drew lazy circles on the back of my hand. I looked up. Johnny's eyes were on me, not Erica. Score another one for Johnny Bulluci. I loved attentive men.

"Care if I join you?" Erica asked.

"Actually, we were right in the middle of a very intense, very private discussion. We don't really feel like company tonight. Sorry, Erica. I'm sure you understand."

A tight, annoyed smile curved Erica's oversized lips, and I knew she wanted to wrap her purse strap around my throat and strangle me with it. But her face smoothed over after only a few seconds. Nothing rattled her for long.

"Of course, Fiona." Erica drew a small piece of paper out of her handbag. "Just let me leave my card with Johnny. In case he ever gets tired of . . . well, whatever." She licked her lips and gave him her best *I'm-so-slutty-I'll-do-you-under-the-table* stare.

I snatched Erica's card out of her hands before Johnny could even reach for it and tore it into pieces. "So sorry, Erica. The only number Johnny needs to remember tonight and for the foreseeable future is mine."

Erica's mouth opened and closed. She seemed shocked that someone would spoil her fun when she was trying to be cute and coy and seductive. Erica turned on her heel and stalked off. I watched her sashay over to the bar, where Kelly Caleb, another SNN reporter, perched on a round stool.

The two of them couldn't have been more different. While Erica's barely there clothes screamed *trashy whore*, Kelly wore a navy dress with a modest neckline that brushed the tops of her ankles. Kelly's blond hair was pulled back into a ponytail, and her face was free of the heavy makeup she wore on television. Erica had enough lipstick and eyeliner on to paint a clown's face.

Erica snapped her fingers, and the bartender rushed to get her a drink. Erica turned to Kelly, gesturing wildly and no doubt saying all sorts of horrid things about me. Kelly's gaze met mine, and her eye twitched, almost in a wink. The blond woman's wide lips quivered, as though she was trying not to laugh at Erica's tirade.

I didn't particularly care for Kelly either. She was, after all, a reporter and thus the enemy, but I waved at her and smiled. Erica might think that she was the baddest bitch in the room, but she had nothing on me. I was Fiona Fine, for crying out loud. I'd been playing the society game in Bigtime before she'd even thought about having fat stuffed in her lips or silicone in her breasts.

"Well, that was interesting." Johnny leaned back in his chair and crossed his arms over his chest. "I take it she's not a friend of yours."

"I can't stand that woman. Something about her just rubs me the wrong way." Actually, it was everything about her.

"Well, I'm glad you got rid of her. You're the one I asked to dinner, not her."

Johnny's eyes met mine. My heart fluttered.

Our food arrived, and we spent the next half hour eating, talking, and laughing. Johnny Bulluci had a teasing, devilish sense of humor I found refreshing after all the posing, pretentious playboys that populated the Bigtime society scene. He was frank, honest, and not above telling humiliating stories about himself. I particularly enjoyed the one about him stealing his father's car when he was thirteen and taking Bella to ride on the carousel in Paradise Park. And he had the most fantastic laugh, warm and throaty and deep. It made me smile, something I hadn't done much of in a very long time.

The only problem was that I polished off my grilled chicken, vegetables, a side salad, and half a bottle of wine before Johnny was even halfway done with his steak, baked potato, and cheddar cheese soup. And he didn't seem too interested in his food. He'd put his fork down ten minutes ago and was listening intently to everything I said. Now, I didn't really mind that, as it was always nice to be the center of attention, especially when that attention was coming from a handsome man. But ignoring a black pepper–seasoned steak from Quicke's? That was just criminal.

"So, are you going to eat that?" I asked, eyeing his half-finished steak.

Johnny stared at the meat, then at me. My stomach chose that moment to let out an ominous rumble. Mount St. Helens needed some fuel. I cringed. My enormous appetite and related bodily functions were the only things that ever really embarrassed me.

"Sorry," I said. "I didn't have any lunch today." Lame, but it was the only excuse I could think of.

Johnny laughed and pushed his plate over to me. "I don't mind. I like a woman with a healthy appetite."

Healthy appetite? Please. If he only knew.

I polished off Johnny's steak, a basket of sourdough rolls, and an enormous chocolate soufflé.

"Didn't have lunch, eh?" Johnny asked, amused by the stacks of plates, glasses, and silverware littering the table.

"Or breakfast either," I lied.

We finished with our meal. Johnny insisted on paying, which I found to be very old-fashioned and charming. I might be a modern liberated woman, but it was nice to be treated to an evening out every now and again, especially since my big hunger pangs led to so many big bills. It was another point in his favor.

Once the check was squared away, we went out through the restaurant's side exit. We stood there in the warm twilight, listening to the cheery carousel music from the park. Now came the tricky part of the evening. Did I really want to invite Johnny back to my apartment? Sure, we'd made out at the wedding and shared a steamy kiss earlier this evening, but did I want to go the rest of the way? Was I ready to do that? Especially with someone I'd known only two days? It had seemed like a terrific idea at the wedding, but now, I wasn't so sure.

Oh, I liked sex, and I wasn't ashamed of it. I'd had my share of ill-advised, torrid affairs in college, including a couple of one-night stands. But with Travis, sex had come to mean something else entirely. It had been making love, sharing my body with someone who cared about me as much as I cared about him. Not to mention the fact that we'd been together five years. I wasn't sure I knew how to be with anybody else. My hand crept to my engagement ring. Or if I even wanted to, sex or no sex. There was always self-fulfillment, so to speak.

"How about a stroll through the park?" Johnny suggested.

"That'd be nice," I said, relieved I wouldn't have to make a decision just yet.

We crossed the street and entered Paradise Park, one of Bigtime's biggest tourist attractions. The park featured just about every carnival ride and game in the known universe.

A carousel, Ferris wheel, ring tosses, water guns, strength tests. Even now, after nine in the evening, thousands of people crowded into the park to eat funnel cakes, get dizzy and sick on the spinning rides, and try to win overpriced stuffed animals for their honeys.

The air smelled of popcorn and grease. Still hungry, I got the biggest cone of cherry-flavored cotton candy the vendor had. The pure, spun sugar melted on my tongue and quieted my stomach. There was nothing better than sugar for a quick boost of energy. That was why I kept an emergency stash of PEZ in my desk at work.

Johnny and I wandered arm-in-arm through the park, just another couple taking in the sights and sounds. To my surprise, he seemed content to stroll along the gum-littered pavement alongside the harried parents, shrieking children, and bawdy vendors. All the other men on the society circuit would have blown up like a balloon if they so much as scuffed their polished wingtips. They would have sneered in disdain at the noisy families and demanded that the park be closed down just for their visit. Not Johnny.

"You know, this doesn't exactly strike me as your kind of scene," I said.

"Why not?"

"From all appearances, you seem to be just another rich, spoiled playboy." Subtlety was another area where I was lacking. "Yet here you are walking through a park instead of some posh art gallery."

"Oh, I'm all of those things," Johnny said. "Rich, spoiled, a playboy. But I happen to like parks. Posh art galleries are so boring. Besides, you're one to talk."

"Oh?"

"You seem . . . different from the other women I've met in Bigtime," he said.

"Different? Different how?"

He shrugged. "Like you've got more on your mind than what you're going to wear to the latest society bash. Sometimes, you look almost . . . sad."

Sad? My cool, haughty mask must be slipping. "Sad?" I forced myself to laugh. "I'm a fabulously wealthy woman who designs fabulous clothes. What do I have to be sad about?" Just because my fiancé had been murdered by ubervillains was no reason to feel blue. Yeah right.

Johnny stared at me with his gorgeous green eyes. "I don't know. But I can see it."

I didn't respond.

Johnny bought two tickets for the Ferris wheel. We climbed on board and sailed up into the night sky. We went round and round and up and down. Finally, the ride stopped to let the lovers on board have a little private time with each other. Our cart was near the top of the ride, giving us a spectacular view of the park and the city lights. Everything looked fresh and clean from this height, and the lights resembled twinkling, colored stars that had fallen from the sky.

"It's just as beautiful as I remember," Johnny said. "My father, James, used to bring Bella and me here at least once a week to ride the carousel and visit the animals in the zoo." A sad, wistful tone crept into his voice.

I remembered what Joanne James had said about Bella's father dying. "He passed away recently, didn't he? Your father."

Johnny's eyes hardened. "He was murdered. A couple of months ago."

"I'm so sorry." I put a hand on his arm. "I know what it's like to lose someone you love so brutally."

"Is that why you wear an engagement ring, even though there's no fiancé around?"

Surprised, my fingertip sparked. I clenched my fist to keep it from igniting. "How do you know that?"

"I asked around. There's no fiancé or boyfriend in the picture. In fact, no one even knows who you were engaged to, according to Bella."

I dropped my hand from his arm and twisted the ring around on my finger. Nobody had known about my engagement to Travis because we'd thought it would be safer that way. But he'd still died. Travis deserved better than to remain some anonymous, faceless figure from my past.

"I was engaged to a wonderful man. His name was Travis. He was murdered too."

"I'm sorry," Johnny said in a quiet voice. "I didn't mean to pry."

"No, it's good to talk about him. My friends are afraid to ask me about him, to even mention his name. They don't want to stir up bad memories."

Johnny put his arm around me, and I leaned into him. His shoulder felt warm and solid under my cheek. "Tell me about him, Fiona. Tell me about Travis."

So I did. I told him how kind and caring Travis was, how much I loved him, our plans and hopes and dreams. The only thing I left out was our nighttime occupation as Bigtime's resident superheroes and how it had led to his death.

"What happened to the person who killed him?" Johnny asked when I wound down.

The image of Malefica plunging into a vat of radioactive goo flashed through my mind. "Oh, she got what she deserved in the end. What about your father? What was he like?"

"He was a lot like your Travis. Kind, caring, considerate. He was a wonderful father. The only thing we ever argued about was—" Johnny cut off his words.

"Was what?"

He hesitated. "My taking over part of . . . the family business."

"I thought you'd done that already."

"Most of it, yes. But there was one area I wasn't particularly interested in. That's where my father and I disagreed. In fact, I hung up on him the last time we talked about it. It was the last time I ever spoke to him." Sadness and guilt tightened his handsome face.

I squeezed his hand. "Have the police caught the person responsible for his death?"

"The police are useless. They can't do anything about it. But I can. And I will. The people responsible are going to pay. More than they ever dreamed of." The vehemence in his voice startled me. His eyes glittered with anger and a deadly promise.

Johnny turned to me, and some of the anger melted away. "But let's think about happier things. Here we are stuck on top of a Ferris wheel, the whole city at our feet. It would be a shame to let the view go to waste, wouldn't it?"

Johnny pulled me toward him. His eyes glowed like a lion's in the twilight, illuminating the chiseled planes of his face. My heart quickened. My lips parted. I leaned forward. He did the same. And then—

My cell phone rang.

★ 7 ★

We stared at each other, frozen in an almost-kiss. My phone kept ringing out the old song "Light My Fire," by The Doors. The loud, blaring rock tune could mean only one thing. Fiera was needed. My desire to kiss Johnny warred with my duty and responsibilities as a superhero. It was a short, tough battle, but duty won out. Drat. Why did my father have to raise me to always do the right thing?

"Please excuse me." I dug through my purse, grabbed my phone, looked at the caller ID, and snapped it open. "This better be good, Henry."

"Sorry to interrupt, Fiona, but we've got a tip on a possible location for Siren and Intelligal. The chief wants you here ASAP. We're going to go after them and see if we can shut them down."

I was about to respond when Johnny's phone started to ring. I recognized the tune as "I Won't Back Down," by Tom Petty. He gave me a sheepish grin and answered the call. Johnny listened for a moment, then turned away from me and started speaking in a low, hushed voice.

I focused on Henry. "All right, I'll be there as soon as I can. But tell the chief that he's going to pull one of my shifts for interrupting my date." Sometimes, I wondered whether my father used his psychic radar to monitor me a little too closely, especially now that Travis was gone.

"You're out on a date? That's wonderful, Fiona!" I could almost see Henry beaming at me through the phone. "It's about time you started dating again. Are you having a good time? Did he take you somewhere nice? He should try to make a good impression on the first date. Did he bring you flowers? Or chocolates?"

I rolled my eyes. Ever since he'd hooked up with Lulu, Henry thought he knew a thing or two about love. Like most men, the computer geek would be forever clueless.

"He made a terrific impression. See you soon." I hung up.

Johnny finished his call and turned to me.

"That was Henry. He . . . keeps an eye on the store for me at night. There's a problem with one of my suppliers. I'm afraid I'm going to have to cut the evening short and go deal with it."

Johnny shook his head. "This seems to be the night for emergencies. Bella called. One of my business managers is concerned about a potential investor. Seems he wants to back out of a previously negotiated deal. I'm afraid I have to leave as well." Regret tinged his voice, as though he didn't want the evening to end.

I didn't either. To my surprise, I'd been having a wonderful time, memories of Travis and all. There was more to Johnny Bulluci than just a handsome face and hard body. A lot more. I wanted to see him again. Soon. So, I told him.

"I'd like to see you again too, Fiona. Why don't we meet up Monday night?" Johnny asked. "Unfortunately, I have to work this weekend, or I would suggest we get together sooner."

Tonight was Thursday. Monday, Monday. I flipped through my mental calendar. Work in the morning, followed by an afternoon of PR as Fiera, then a benefit that night.

I shook my head. "I can't. I have to attend the annual fundraiser for the Bigtime Observatory. It'll be so boring, all those scientific astronomer types talking about star charts and aliens and whatnot, but I already sent in my RSVP."

In addition to always doing my duty as a superhero, my father had also drilled it into my head how important it was to keep the promises I made, no matter how small or trivial they might seem. But that didn't mean I still couldn't have some fun with Johnny.

"You could meet me there, and we could sneak out afterwards," I suggested.

"It's a date."

He grinned, and my heart fluttered. The man had one hell of a smile. And great eyes. And a terrific body. And . . . The list went on for quite a while.

"So I guess this is good night," Johnny said.

"I guess so."

I stared into Johnny's eyes. Then, I leaned in and pressed my lips to his. He put his arms around me and pulled me closer. This kiss wasn't like the others. Oh, it was still hot and passionate. But there was a gentle sweetness to it, a sense of letting down our cool, guarded, society facades. The rich, charming playboy and the bitchy fashion designer were getting to know each other, faults and all. The Ferris wheel jerked and began to drift downward. We kissed until the ride stopped.

* * *

I had Johnny drop me off outside my store to keep up appearances. I waited until the limo's taillights disappeared, hailed a cab, and went back to my apartment to get my convertible.

Twenty minutes later, I got off the interstate and turned onto a pothole-filled dirt road that seemed to end in the middle of the woods. I kept my foot on the gas, plunging the car into a dark stand of pine trees. My tires fell into a well-worn track, and my headlights bounced off a rock wall up ahead. I flicked them on and off five times in rapid succession. The wall slid aside, and I drove into a lighted tunnel, which stretched out for another mile, before expanding into an underground garage.

The garage, like the rest of the underground Fearless Five compound, was hollowed out of the extensive network of caverns beneath Sublime. Wrenches, screwdrivers, and other tools lined the garage walls, along with cans of oil, wires, and other automotive parts. Five black vans huddled together inside the open space. They were our preferred mode of transportation when we went out into the city at night to fight crime and help with natural disasters. The vans resembled the one from the old *A-Team* television show, only the F5 vehicles had more computer equipment and electronic gizmos stuffed inside them than collagen in Erica Songe's pouty lips. Thanks to Sam's money and Henry's technological genius, the vans were also bullet-, bomb-, and ubervillain-proof.

Henry's small white scooter was also parked inside the garage, along with my father's city-issued sedan. So was Lulu's van. I frowned. What was the computer guru doing down here this late at night? She should be at home trying to hack into the CIA mainframe or hijack the SNN nightly newscast or something equally geeky.

I parked my convertible and strolled over to the metal door set into the far wall. The lights flickered, reminding me that I had only thirty seconds left before the garage would be filled with a potent sleeping gas. I punched in 555, the security code, on the blinking keypad and stepped inside. The door whooshed shut and locked behind me, another layer of security. If someone ever stumbled into the garage from the outside, she wouldn't be able to go any farther into the compound without the code. And once the gas took effect, we could transport her out of the garage without her ever being the wiser. At least, that was the theory. No one had ever breached our defenses before, except Carmen, and now Lulu.

I strode down the halls until I reached the double doors that led into the library. The others were gathered inside, costumes on. My father wore a green and white outfit with a flowing cape that transformed him into Mr. Sage, while Henry's black-and-white uniform and matching goggles morphed him into Hermit. Lulu wore her usual getup of designer jeans and a Bulluci fleece pullover. The cobalt streaks in her hair gleamed under the flickering screen mounted on one wall. Blueprints winked on and off like a pair of bloodshot eyes blinking at me.

"Finally. We've been waiting almost an hour," Hermit said.

I flipped my hair over my shoulder. "I came as fast as I could. I had to get rid of my date first, you know. I couldn't just fire up and come running."

"Was he a little too hot for you to handle, Fiona?" Lulu joked.

I glared at the computer hacker. Another heat-related pun. Ha, ha, ha, ha. One of these days I was going to show her just how hot under the collar I could get. My fingers curled into loose fists. Red-hot sparks landed on the Persian rug under my feet.

My father stomped them out and put a restraining hand

on my arm. "Go get changed and meet us back in the garage. There's no time to waste."

Lulu zoomed out of the room, followed by Henry and my father. I jogged down to the equipment room, punched in the code, and went inside. I grabbed one of my many superhero suits hanging behind a pair of glass doors along one side of the room, and the rest of my gear from another compartment. While I shimmied into the spandex, I glanced at a rack of swords sitting in the middle of the room. I thought about taking them along, but decided against it. Weapons were Sam's—Striker's—thing. Not mine. My flames and fists were enough.

Fiera costume on, I retraced my route to the garage, stopping when I got to the kitchen. I glanced down the hall. Another minute wouldn't hurt. Besides, I needed to keep up my strength in case I got to toast Siren and Intelligal tonight. It was hard to do my sacred superhero duty on an empty stomach. I grabbed three bags of chocolate chip cookies from one of the kitchen counters and continued on to the garage.

Hermit was already in the driver's seat in one of the vans. The side door was open, and the engine idled. I started to get into the van when I realized Lulu was strapped inside. In my seat.

"She's coming?"

"Of course," Hermit said, turning around. "She helped me track down Siren and Intelligal. Since Karma Girl and Striker are on hiatus, I asked her to come along and man the van and comm links, while I help you guys in the field."

"Oh, goody."

I slid into Karma Girl's usual spot in the very back and crossed my arms over my chest. Lulu ignored my hot stare, pulled out her laptop, and started banging away. My father turned around in his seat and gave me a look, clearly wanting me to play nice. That was something else I'd never quite learned to do. At least, not very well. Being an only child, I was used to getting my way. All the time. And I liked it.

I rolled my eyes. But parental guilt could still make me do funny things sometimes, like be polite to a criminal mastermind. "So where are our two ubervillains at?" I asked, attempting to be marginally friendly.

"Right now, they're holed up in an abandoned warehouse on the edge of town, a couple of miles away from the old Snowdom Ice Cream Factory. Or what's left of it."

In other words, the ubervillains were squatting next to a big pile of rubble. The Fearless Five had spent some time at the factory last year during our run-in with the Terrible Triad. The factory had paid the price for being the site of a superhero-ubervillain battle. Not to mention the fact that Carmen had stuffed enough explodium bombs in the building to decimate the whole city.

"How did you find them?" I asked. "I thought they were untraceable or some such nonsense."

Hermit glanced at me in the rearview mirror. "I created a new computer program to track the exhaust fumes from Intelligal's chair. It's powered with a combination of electricity, gas, and some sort of radioactive isotope I haven't identified yet. The point is that it lets off a particular combination of fumes and radiation."

"Clever as always, Hermit," Mr. Sage said.

"I couldn't have done it without Lulu's help," Hermit said.

Lulu smiled at her honey's praise, a goofy grin spreading across her heart-shaped face. She stared at his back, her eyes soft and dreamy. Her obvious affection for him almost made her part of the team. Almost.

"So what do you think they're doing at that factory? Braiding each other's hair?"

I snickered. More than likely, the two ubervillains were trying to pull it out. For partners in crime, they didn't seem to get along too well.

"I have no idea. Their crime wave doesn't make any sense," Hermit said. "One day, they're stealing electronic equipment. The next, they're loading up on computer chips. The day after that, they're taking jewels from Bigtime's finest. I can't figure out what they're up to."

I shrugged. "Does it really matter? They're bad, we're good, and we're going to stop them." Being a superhero had always been rather black-and-white to me. No gray allowed. Nobody looked good in gray, especially superheroes.

Hermit drove through the streets of Bigtime, stopping at a red light. Suddenly, Swifte was there. The speedy, iridescent-clad superhero skidded to a stop in front of the van. He waved at us and dashed away to do whatever it was he did all by himself late at night. Before the light changed, three police cars hauled ass in the same direction. A white van bearing the SNN logo zoomed by a couple of seconds after that.

"What's the problem?" I asked.

"Big traffic accident on the southbound side of the interstate. Looks like fifty cars involved. Injuries, gasoline fires, people trapped in their vehicles, the usual," Lulu explained, staring at her computer screen.

"Should we divert?" Mr. Sage asked.

Lulu pounded a few more keys. "Nah. Swifte's already there, along with the Invisible Ingénues. It looks like they've got things under control."

"How can you tell the Ingénues are on the scene?" I asked.

"Because they're not quite so invisible when they're covered with soot and ash. Look."

Lulu turned the screen around. Sure enough, I spotted two shapely outlines pulling people out of burning, crumpled cars.

"Good for them. Who knows? Maybe they'll finally get the recognition they deserve, and not be so *invisible* anymore." I laughed. Lulu wasn't the only one who could do bad puns.

The others looked at me like I'd just sprouted a third eye. Lulu shook her head and went back to her typing. Mr. Sage stared out the window, while Hermit concentrated on his driving.

I ignored them. It was funny. Johnny would have laughed at my joke. Johnny. My hands crept up to my lips. I could still feel his lips on mine, still smell his rich exotic scent. Maybe I'd call him when I got home. Rich, spoiled playboys kept late hours. It might not be too late for a booty call—

"We're here," Hermit said, stopping the van and killing the headlights.

I peered out the front. We sat at the end of a long, deserted street. Buildings squatted all around us. Even though it was dark, I could see the graffiti on the walls and the broken doors and windows. Trash and debris cluttered the streets and alleyways, spilling out of the tops of metal cans and Dumpsters. A few streetlights flickered on and off, as though in pain.

"Where are we?" I asked.

"About two miles east of Good Intentions Lane," Lulu said.

That explained it. Good Intentions Lane made a mockery of its own name. It was one of the worst streets in Bigtime and the major hangout of drug-running gangs like the Westsiders. Every couple of weeks, we had to come down here and clean out the riffraff. The gangbangers were like cockroaches, though. You could never get them all, and they always scuttled back out from their hiding places when the lights were turned off—or when there were no superheroes or cops around.

"The factory's a block ahead on the right," Hermit said. "I figured you could go through the front, Fiera, while Mr. Sage and I went in through the back."

"Works for me." We always sent the muscle in first. Me.

We piled out of the van. Hermit, Mr. Sage, and I activated the cameras in the *F5* insignias on our costumes and shoved miniature two-way transmitters into our ears.

"Check, check," Lulu said, her voice crackling in my ear. We checked back to her.

Lulu's slender fingers danced over the keyboard, and her laptop whirred and sputtered. "All right. You guys are online. I've got visual and audio on all of you."

"Then let's rock 'n' roll," I said.

"Be careful," Lulu said.

Hermit squeezed her hand. "Always."

We locked Lulu in the van and crept down the block. Discarded candy wrappers and empty soda cans littered the street, crackling under our boots. Enormous rats scurried back and forth in the debris, their eyes red pinpricks of light in the semidarkness. I glared at the odious little monsters. Maybe if I barbecued a couple, the others would get the message and run away. Probably not. Rats were nasty, tenacious creatures. Rather like ubervillains.

The wind shifted, whipping trash into the air and gusting down the street toward us. The smell of rotten garbage, wet fur, and fresh dirt filled the night. I also caught a whiff of something sickeningly sweet, almost like perfume. My nose twitched. For a second, I felt slow and limp and languid, like my body wasn't my own to command. Then, the scent was gone, overpowered by the filth around us. The weak sensation faded. My eyes scanned the street, but I didn't spot anything moving among the piles of trash, except for the foot-long rodents.

We rounded the corner of a building. A cracked parking

lot stretched out in front of us, leading to a low square building set back from the dilapidated street a couple hundred yards.

"This is it. This is where I tracked Intelligal's chair to. It used to be a television factory way back when." Hermit hit a few buttons on his handheld supercomputer. "Here are the entrances and exits. You should go in through the front *here*, Fiera. Mr. Sage and I will come in back *here*, and we'll meet in the middle *there*." He pointed to various squiggles on the screen.

"Front door. Got it."

We huddled together in the shadows. Our eyes went to each other's faces. Despite our powers, we knew that one night all of us might not come back. It had happened before when we'd least expected it. And it could happen again. I put my fist over my heart. Mr. Sage and Hermit followed suit. Courage, all.

Then, one by one, we eased toward the factory and the ubervillains inside.

I waited for Mr. Sage and Hermit to slip into the dark alley that ran along the side of the building before I scurried across the parking lot. I made it to the entrance without incident and glanced over my shoulder. Nothing.

A set of uneven steps led up to the front door, which was boarded over with rotten-looking two-by-fours. I paused. Looking. Listening. Nothing. I started up the steps, which shrieked and groaned like a woman in labor under my weight. I winced. Good grief. I bet they'd heard that in the next time zone. I might have a variety of superpowers and skills, but moving quietly wasn't one of them. So, I did what I do best—I put a little muscle into the situation.

I yanked the boards off the building and tossed them

over my shoulder. The door followed three seconds later. Darkness spilled out from the interior, and I stepped inside. I made my way through a series of abandoned offices that lined the front of the building. Moonlight shimmered in through the broken windows, painting the square, empty rooms with an eerie gray glow. The usual assortment of crushed cigarettes, empty beer bottles, and used condoms covered the floor. How romantic.

I found a set of metal doors that led into the factory and peered through the grimy windows on them. The doors opened up into one enormous room. Assembly lines, pipes, and more snaked through the open space. I couldn't see the back wall for all the metal zigzagging everywhere. I couldn't see very far into the factory at all.

"Anything, guys?" I whispered.

"Nothing so far, Fiera. We're at the back door ready to come inside," Hermit said in my ear.

"Lulu?" I asked.

"Everything's fine, as far as I can tell."

"All right. Here I go."

I tried the metal knob. Locked. Not for long. I gave it a good tug, pulled the knob off, yanked the door open, and stepped through. I paused. Waiting. Watching. Listening. Everything was still and quiet and hushed inside. I moved slowly, staying in the shadows, and trying to keep my chunky boots from clacking too loudly on the hard floor. I went a hundred feet, then two hundred, then three. Pipes, pipes, and more pipes. The place seemed endless.

I stumbled and almost cracked my head on a metal support beam. I muttered a curse and looked down. A power cable curled around my feet. Unlike everything else in the building, it wasn't coated with a layer of gray dust and cobwebs. It looked brand-spanking-new.

At last. A clue.

Keeping one eye on the black cable, I moved farther into the factory. I realized it was getting brighter. There was a light up ahead.

"I think I've got something," I whispered. "Lights in the factory."

"Then go with your hot self," Lulu replied.

I rolled my eyes and kept moving. I rounded the edge of one of the assembly lines and stopped. I'd finally gotten to the belly of the beast, as it were. Halogen bulbs illuminated the scene. Computers, power cables, and more clustered together. Bits and pieces of metal littered the floor and a couple of steel tables. Soldering irons, wire cutters, and other tools crouched on wooden stools and plastic milk crates. Blueprints and schematics and weird diagrams hung on a cork board. It was your usual ubervillain–mad scientist lab. Intelligal was hard at work on something.

Some sort of giant, radio-karaoke-like thing stood in the middle of the makeshift workshop. I spotted a cordless microphone, a bunch of wires, and what looked like a flat-screen plasma monitor. I squinted. Were those diamonds lining the thin screen?

"Are you getting this, Lulu?" I whispered.

"Every last pixel," the computer hacker muttered. "Although I don't have a clue as to what that thing is or does."

I didn't really care what it did. When it doubt, smash. That was my philosophy. I raised my fist and focused, ready to punch through that metal like it was a piece of paper. Suddenly, I realized the hairs on the back of my neck were standing straight out. Not good.

I hit the ground rolling. A blue lightning bolt zigzagged over my head and rattled off into the darkness. Now, I don't have my father's psychic abilities or even Carmen's inner voice, but after some fifteen years as a superhero, I know when an ubervillain's trying to get the drop on me. Siren had been quiet as death, but the electrical charge in the air from her powers had given her away.

I popped up on my feet and turned around, a fireball in my hand. "Hello, Siren. So nice to see you again."

The ubervillain stood behind me, looking as voluptuous as ever in her electric blue suit. For once, the zipper was at a reasonable level, showing just a hint of cleavage. Evidently, Siren knew her charms would be utterly wasted on me. That or she was just cold.

"I wish I could say the same, Fiera. You and yours just keep showing up wherever Intelligal and I go," Siren purred. "Wouldn't you much rather put those nasty fireballs away and have a nice talk with me? I'm sure we have a lot in common, being such strong, powerful women."

Her husky tone wrapped around my body, slowly tightening its grip. I concentrated on the fire inside me, burned away the coils, and ignored the hypnotic pull of her voice. That trick was really wearing thin. I hated women who relied solely on their bodies to get them through life. I wasn't above using my feminine wiles to work things to my advantage every once in a while, but I also used my brains, brawn, and general bitchiness in equal parts as well. Besides lightning bolts, all Siren seemed to have was her body. What would the ubervillain do when her voice went? Or when her bazooka boobs started to sag? She wouldn't be nearly so alluring then.

"Honey," I said. "You're going to have to do a lot better than that. Your two-bit persuasive thing might work on weak-willed, sex-starved men, but not me. Where'd you learn that trick anyway? Hookers High?" When in doubt, taunt the enemy. It always worked on the society circuit.

Siren's eyes glittered with rage. A crackling energy ball popped into her hand. Her white, French-tipped nails curled around it like she was caressing her lover. "I could just electrocute you."

My body burst into flames. "You could try."

A loud roar filled the air, cutting off Siren's clichéd retort. Good grief. It sounded like a couple of tanks were rolling my way. The floor trembled beneath my feet.

"Lulu, what the hell is that?" I shouted.

Lulu squawked something in my ear, but I couldn't hear her over the rumbling. Ten seconds later, I got the answer. A sleek, silver and black motorcycle grumbled to a stop in between Siren and me. A motorcycle? In the middle of a factory?

A figure clad in black leather pants sat astride the huge vehicle. Angel wings shimmered on the back of his tough-guy jacket. Johnny Angel. He was a minor player in the superhero-ubervillain scene in Bigtime, not really on one side or the other. Angel was more intent on riding his motorcycle around the city late at night and raising hell than anything else. The local motorcycle gangs loved him and often tagged along, whooping and hollering and making pests out of themselves.

But Angel wasn't all bad. Sometimes, he helped out people who needed it. Damsels in distress mostly. Women about to be mugged. Women who were carjacked. Women fleeing abusive boyfriends. To them, he was an angel. To the Fearless Five, he was a minor blip on the radar screen.

"Well, if it isn't Johnny Angel. Back from the dead so soon?" Siren cooed. "And here I thought Intelligal had finished you off for good with her heat-seeking missiles."

I frowned. What the hell was Siren talking about? Johnny Angel wasn't dead. He was sitting right there between us—

Angel swung one leg over his bike, and I caught a glimpse of his face. His smooth, unlined face. With a start, I realized that he was around my age. Usually, this wouldn't be of any importance, as most superheroes and ubervillains fell in the twenty-to-forty age range, with a few exceptions like my father, who was creeping up on fifty-five, or the

Tween Terrors, who hadn't hit puberty yet. But the last time I'd seen Johnny Angel, he'd been limping down an alley, struggling to keep up with the thug he'd been chasing. Lines and sweat had painted his strained red face. Gray had glistened in his brownish hair. He'd moved slowly, as though every step hurt.

He'd been an older man, just like my father.

Not this guy. He moved with a loose, easy confidence. Blond hair. Tan face. Light eyes. Black and silver wing-shaped mask. That was all I saw before Angel tossed his jacket aside and turned to face Siren. I frowned. Johnny Angel might not be an ubervillain, but he should know better than to turn his back on me. I was Fiera, for crying out loud. I could melt his ass like a candle, if I wanted to.

"There's a new Angel in town," he snarled in a low throaty voice. "And you're going to pay for what you did to my predecessor."

Siren put her hands on her hips and laughed. The dulcet tones rang like church bells, all sweetness and light. "Now why would you want to hurt little ole me?" Siren lowered the zipper on her suit, exposing more of her buoyant chest. She focused her eyes on Angel like a snake trying to hypnotize a helpless bunny. "I'm just a simple girl who's trying to make a name for herself in the big, bad city."

Yeah right. And I was the freaking Tooth Fairy.

Angel stilled, struggling against the pull of Siren's voice. Since the ubervillain's attention was focused on Angel, her tone didn't bother me as much as usual. I circled to one side, easing to the left of them.

"Are you guys hearing this?" I muttered.

"Every word," Mr. Sage whispered in my ear. "We're almost there to back you up. Let them keep talking."

Siren and Angel stared at each other, ignoring me. I took the chance to study the man. He was taller than his predecessor, his skin darker, his hair longer. My gaze swept lower, tracing over his leather jacket and the pants he'd poured himself into. And he was definitely in much better shape than the previous Angel. The old guy had a bit of a potbelly.

Now, I'd run into my fair share of superheroes and ubervillains over the years. I'd seen more buff bodies, rippling abs, and bulging biceps in skintight spandex than I could remember. But Angel gave buns of steel a whole new meaning. I frowned. But there was something strange about his skin. It almost looked hard—

"Am I interrupting something?" a tight, cold voice cut in.

My head snapped up. Intelligal hovered over us in her chair. Damn. I'd forgotten about her during my perusal of Johnny Angel's new, improved body.

"It's about time you got here," Siren snapped. "Take care of them. Now."

Intelligal hit a button, and two missiles spewed out of the depths of her chair.

Right at Angel and me.

★ 8 ★

I immediately hurled a fireball at my incoming missile. The two met in midair and exploded. Smoke, ash, and sharp bits of flying silver metal filled the factory. I ignored the smoldering debris and turned to help Angel. But it was too late. The missile was bearing down on him. Angel was going to get blown to hell and back in two seconds.

But he didn't run or duck or even try to leap out of the way. Instead, Angel curled his hands into fists, held them down by his legs, and flexed. Please. All the chiseled muscles in the world weren't going to save him from a rocket. The missile hit him in the chest and exploded.

I threw up my hands to ward off the bloody man chunks and brain matter that were coming my way. To my surprise, nothing hit me, except a few bits of metal shrapnel that stung my hands and arms. Dust and soot hung like thick clouds in the air. I waved the smoke away from my face and squinted through the soupy fog.

My mouth gaped open. Johnny Angel stood in the exact

spot where the missile had hit. He was still alive, although his bike was a smoldering piece of melted junk now. Incredible.

"Is that all you've got?" Angel mocked.

The explosion had ripped into his white T-shirt, black leather pants, and boots, but the man himself didn't seem to have a scratch on him. His hair wasn't even mussed. Now *that* was a neat trick.

"Do you care to explain this, Intelligal?" Siren hissed, taking a few steps back.

"He . . . he should be dead!" Intelligal sputtered. "Those are hundred-load explodium missiles! He should be nothing but a stain on the floor!"

Angel kicked aside his melted motorcycle and stepped forward. "Well, I guess it's a good thing I have a superstrong exoskeleton then, isn't it?"

My eyes narrowed. Wait a minute. The old Angel hadn't had any superpowers that I'd known of, just a souped-up motorcycle. It looked like this guy was the new and improved model. My eyes strayed back to the hard body. In more ways than one.

"Don't just hover up there!" Siren screeched. "Gas them, you fool!"

I started forward to body slam Siren into next week when a puff of light blue smoke exploded in my face. I coughed and gagged and tried not to retch. It was the same odd smell that I'd inhaled before outside the factory. The sweet, noxious stench worked its way down my throat and into my lungs. My arms and legs felt like gelatin, all loose and wobbly. Beside me, Angel choked and sputtered. We both slid to the ground, caught in a cloud of blue gas. I tried to focus. Where were Hermit and Mr. Sage?

"Hurry up! Get it loaded!" Intelligal's voice drifted through the fog.

Metal screeched. Something hit the floor. Siren cursed.

Somehow, I rolled over onto my hands and knees. Those bitches didn't know who they were dealing with. I was Fiera. Member of the Fearless Five. Protector of the innocent. Superhero du jour. A little knockout gas wasn't going to keep me from kicking their asses. Slowly, very, *very* slowly, I crawled forward. Metal dug into my hands and scraped my knees, but I ignored the pain and kept going. After about twenty feet, I broke free of the cloud. I drew in a deep breath of soot-filled air. I still felt weak and disjointed, but some of the feeling returned to my arms and legs.

Too late. Siren stuffed something in the side of Intelligal's chair and hopped on the arm. The helicopter rotor popped up out of the back, and the chair whirred and flew right over me. I pointed my finger at them, but I couldn't find the strength to muster up so much as a single spark. I couldn't even roast a marshmallow, the shape I was in right now.

A pair of familiar green boots flashed in front of my face. "Fiera! Are you all right?" Mr. Sage asked, his eyes bright with concern.

I coughed some more. "Johnny Angel . . . still . . . in . . . there," I wheezed. My tongue felt like I'd eaten a whole tube of sugar-flavored toothpaste, sticky and gooey sweet. Yuck.

"I'll get him," Hermit said.

He took a breath, held it, and plunged into the blue gas.

"A little help, please!" Hermit called out. "He's too heavy for me!"

Mr. Sage reached into the cloud and helped drag Angel free of the fumes. I got to my feet, wobbling back and forth like a newborn fawn. The others weren't in much better shape.

Something smacked against the front of the building. The windows that weren't already busted out shattered with a collective roar. The factory quivered and trembled like a feather floating on the breeze.

"Intelligal's firing explodium missiles at the factory! The whole place is going to come down on top of you! Get out! Get out now!" Lulu screamed in my ear.

I took another breath. My head cleared, and most of my strength returned. I put my arm under Johnny Angel's shoulder, and my knees threatened to buckle. Hermit was right. He was heavier than he looked. The other superhero and I half carried, half dragged Angel toward the back of the factory.

"Back there!" Hermit shouted, pointing toward a door a couple of hundred feet away.

Mr. Sage stopped long enough to grab some of Intelligal's weird schematics and drawings, then followed us.

A hundred feet to go. More explosions ripped through the building. Pipes creaked and snapped like dry twigs, while the floor ripped and bucked like water.

Fifty feet. Fire shot through the air above our heads. Smoke seared my lungs.

Twenty, ten, five . . .

We stumbled out the door and down some steps. The night air, still reeking of garbage, revived me the rest of the way, and the fire inside me flared back to life. Behind us, the building moaned and creaked. The front section collapsed with a long low groan, and the resulting shockwave threw us fifteen feet forward. We scrambled up and kept hobbling along, trying to get clear of the dust and debris.

About a quarter mile away, we lunged out into the street and stopped. Angel slumped against the side of a nearby building. Hermit put one knee on the ground, while Mr. Sage rested a hand on his shoulder. I put my hands on my hips, trying to get my breath back. Superstrong exoskeleton indeed. Superheavy was more like it. The four of us stood there, gulping down air.

After a few minutes, Johnny Angel straightened. His eyes swept over us. Then, he turned and started to walk away.

"Hey! Come back here!" I grabbed his arm.

"Let go of me!" he snapped.

He tried to shake me off, but I tightened my grip. It was like trying to squeeze a cement block, but I held on. Super-strength came in handy sometimes.

"Who are you? What happened to the old Johnny Angel?"

"None of your damn business."

I pointed a smoking finger at his chest. His skin felt like solid steel through the thin fabric of his ripped blackened T-shirt. "When you waltz in when I'm trying to apprehend two ubervillains and almost get my friends and me blown to smithereens, then you make it my business. What the hell did you think you were doing in there?"

His face hardened. Angry gold flecks sparked in the depths of his eyes, which glowed a rich green. "None of your damn business."

"We're not going to hurt you, if that's what you're worried about," Mr. Sage said in a calm, soothing voice. "We only want to talk."

Hermit nodded. Smoke smudged his thick goggles.

Johnny Angel stared at the three of us. Outnumbered. He nodded. "All right. We'll talk."

He stared down at my hand on his arm. I dropped it, even though I didn't want to let go.

Angel leaned back against the side of the pockmarked building. From his pants pocket, he fished out a pack of cigarettes and a black lighter that had somehow survived Intelligal's missile. Silver angel wings gleamed on the dark surface. He lit his cigarette, drew in a long drag, and blew smoke out his nostrils, showing us what a badass he was. Please. One snap of my fingers, and that cancer stick would blow up in his face like a grenade. I should light up the cigarette anyway.

Didn't he know those things would kill you? Or perhaps his lungs were as hard as his chest. And his head.

After another couple of puffs of his cigarette, Johnny spoke. "I'm the new Angel. I have been for a few months now, ever since Siren and Intelligal killed my predecessor."

"We hadn't heard. How did it happen?" Mr. Sage asked, his voice soft and kind. My father. Always the diplomat.

Angel stared at the ruined factory, which smoldered behind us. "The two muscled in on some of the High Riders' territory. The motorcycle gang asked the old Angel to get rid of them. He owed the gang a favor, so he took the job. It was going to be his last gig, since he'd been training me to take over as Angel. One night, he tracked down the ubervillains and confronted them. He told them to get out of town or else. They just laughed at him, and Intelligal fired off some of her heat-seeking explodium missiles. He tried to outrun the missiles on his motorcycle, but he never had a chance." Sad, bitter anger colored his low throaty voice.

"Because he didn't have superpowers," Hermit said.

Angel nodded. "All he had was his bike. It wasn't fast enough."

I stood to one side and listened to the question-and-answer session. Generational superheroes and ubervillains were rare, but not unheard of. Fathers and mothers who moonlighted for the greater good or evil often passed down their powers or some variation thereof to their children. When the old folks got tired of fighting or creating crime, the youngsters donned the cape and spandex and took up the family mantle. It didn't even have to be a family member. More than one aging hero and villain had plucked a young orphan off the streets, trained her, and introduced her to Bigtime and the world as the new whomever. Pistol Pete and Hangglider were classic examples. If I remembered correctly,

Johnny Angel had been around in three incarnations now, counting the new guy.

"But you have powers, don't you?" Mr. Sage asked. "I believe you mentioned something about an exoskeleton?"

Angel rolled up the sleeve of his tattered T-shirt and flexed his bicep. At first, I couldn't see the difference between his bicep and anybody else's. Well, it might have been a bit more defined than the average superhero's. But when I looked closer, I realized there was a hard look to his skin, almost like it was stretched over steel. Plus, I could just make out a faint, weblike pattern in it.

"When I concentrate and focus on what I want to do, I'm impervious to pretty much everything. Missiles, guns, grenades, lasers." Angel's eyes flicked to me. "Fire."

"Fascinating," Hermit murmured, tapping a few buttons on his computer and angling the camera embedded in his suit for a closer look.

"We're very sorry for your loss," Mr. Sage said. "Believe me, we know how hard it is to lose a member of your team. But killing Siren and Intelligal won't bring back your friend and mentor. And it won't ease your pain. We need to capture them and turn them over to the police before they hurt someone else. That's what superheroes do. It's our duty. Dishing out your own brand of vigilante justice isn't the way."

"Turn them over to the police? Why? So they can spend a couple of weeks in prison before they break out and come back to Bigtime? The police in this town are useless. They always have been, and they always will be," Angel scoffed.

Ouch. I glanced at Mr. Sage. His face was smooth and unreadable, but his eyes glittered. Being the chief of police, he didn't think his men were useless. Quite the opposite. They provided valuable support to the superheroes in town, as well as taking care of the more ordinary, mundane crimes.

"I'm going after Siren and Intelligal, and there's nothing

you can do to stop me." Angel's green eyes shimmered in his tight face. "Get in my way, and you'll be sorry."

"What are you going to do?" I asked. "Kill us too?"

"If you get in my way—yes. I will kill you, superheroes or not. I won't hesitate. Not for a second. Remember that. Or suffer the consequences."

With those words, Angel turned and stalked into the darkening night.

"Can you believe the nerve of that guy? Telling us, the Fearless Five, to stay out of his way or he'll kill us? He must have a pair of steel balls on him to go along with that exoskeleton," I snapped.

"Fiona," my father chided. "There is no need for such language."

"Well, he must," I muttered.

After Johnny Angel huffed and puffed and stormed away, Lulu had brought the van around, and we'd gone back to Sublime. Now, we were gathered in the underground library, reviewing the mission and planning our next move. The others clustered in front of the film screen, staring at the footage from inside the factory. I sat in the corner, munching on the cookies I hadn't had a chance to eat in the van, along with a couple of cheese burritos, a tray of tortilla chips and hot salsa, Spanish rice, refried beans, and a gallon of raspberry iced tea. The fight with the ubervillains and dragging Mr. Two-Ton Ego around had zapped a lot of my energy, so I'd made Henry stop at Olé, an all-night Mexican joint, before we headed home.

"Right now, I'm more worried about that doomsday-looking contraption the ubervillains were building. Not to mention whatever it was they gassed you with, Fiona," Lulu said.

"Gas, missiles, flying chairs, weird inventions. It comes with the territory." I took another bite of my cheese burrito. Spicy Monterey Jack cheese melted in my mouth. Ah, so good.

"Speaking of the gas, I collected a sample for the chief to analyze," Henry said, holding up a glass tube full of light blue fumes. "I got it while I was trying to drag Angel out of the cloud. It looks like a fascinating chemical compound."

Only Henry would stop in the middle of a battle to take a scientific sample of the enemies' weapon of choice. I rolled my eyes. I loved him like a brother, but he was such a complete geek.

"Judging from the effect the gas had on Fiona, I'd say it contained some sort of superpotent muscle relaxer," Chief Newman said, lacing his long fingers together. "Perhaps even a power inhibitor."

"Smelled like cheap perfume to me," I said. "As befitting Siren."

My nose twitched. I'd taken a steamy shower and washed my hair twice, but I could still smell the gas. It clung to my body like Joanne James on a widowed billionaire's arm. Even the extra onions and hot sauce on my burritos couldn't quite overpower the sweet, jaw-locking taste in my mouth.

"Whatever it is, I need to make some sort of antidote for it," the chief continued. "Especially since it didn't seem to affect Siren and Intelligal in the slightest."

I looked at my father. "Whatever you do, just make sure it doesn't taste like toothpaste."

* * *

I spent the next few days working. During regular business hours, I finished up the businesswear line for fall and took care of a thousand other fashion-related details. Then, at night, it was time to suit up as Fiera, answer my fan mail, and squash the evildoers who crossed my path.

The rest of the Fearless Five worked just as hard as I did at their day jobs, and at night, we all focused on Siren and Intelligal. The chief started cooking up some antidote to neutralize the stuff they'd gassed us with, as well as putting the final touches on some earplugs to block Siren's hypnotic voice. But Henry couldn't figure out what their radiolike device did, and Lulu couldn't find whatever abandoned building they were holed up in.

Still, we searched, prowling the streets in the F5 van. A few times, Johnny Angel zoomed by on a new shiny silver bike. We tried to flag him down, but he always ignored us, the hardheaded egotistical snot. We even gave chase in the van a couple of times, but he was always too quick for us to catch or darted into some narrow space where we couldn't follow. Showoff.

As for the other Johnny, Johnny Bulluci, I didn't see him, since we were both so busy with work. That didn't stop me from thinking about him, though. I replayed our date over and over again in my head. He was a rich, spoiled playboy. Smooth, suave, used to getting his own way. But he'd also been kind, considerate, and caring. How many guys would have sat there listening to a woman gush about her dead fiancé? Not many. We'd clicked, connected that night in the park. I was beginning to think maybe Johnny Bulluci had potential beyond being Rebound Guy.

Johnny hadn't forgotten about me either. The day after our date, he had a black pepper–seasoned steak from Quicke's delivered to my office. I squealed so loud when I opened the package that Piper thought I'd gotten a box full of diamonds or something equally expensive. I returned the favor by sending two tickets to the Ferris wheel and a funnel cake to Bulluci Industries. Two hours later, I'd received a stick of cotton candy and a stuffed purple rabbit. We exchanged gag gifts the rest of the day. A sense of humor was another thing I liked in a man. Life was too short to be taken seriously. Especially when you went around town wearing body-hugging orange red spandex and shooting fire out of your fingertips.

Monday rolled around. I left the final details of the fall collection in Piper's capable, anal-retentive, obsessive-compulsive hands and went home early to get ready for my latest public appearance as Fiera.

Every couple of months, SNN, the *Exposé*, the *Chronicle*, and the other media outlets in the city sponsored *Meet Bigtime's Superheroes* in Paradise Park. The events were a chance for regular folks to mix and mingle with their favorite superheroes and learn about our powers, as well as raise money for some worthy causes. The members of the Fearless Five took turns attending the functions, and I was the lucky superhero today. I didn't mind too much, though. It was fun to show off in front of people. Kids, in particular, always got a kick out of my fireball-juggling skills.

Once I was suited up, I flipped a switch just inside the door. It looked like any other light switch, but it was a special feature Henry had installed for me when I'd moved into the apartment. The switch sent out a signal that scrambled the building's security cameras and locked down all the elevators except for the one I used for five minutes. Since I had the whole floor to myself, I didn't have to worry about nosy neighbors—just about getting out of the building without being seen.

I rode the elevator down to the fifth subbasement, the very bottom of Tip-Top Tower. The doors pinged open, revealing a dark space filled with metal trash chutes and overflowing Dumpsters. Black mold covered the damp walls, and the air smelled of rotten pizza, greasy French fries, and overripe fruit. Tip-Top Tower might be one of the most exclusive buildings in Bigtime, but it still had to have a place to collect tenants' trash, just like every other apartment complex. Nobody, not even the maintenance men, came down here unless they absolutely had to. Lucky for me.

I walked to the very back corner of the subbasement, where a metal door stood. The lock and knob were long gone, and the door had a smushed look to it, like a bag of chocolate that had been out in the sun too long. I pointed my finger at the door, letting out a steady stream of concentrated flame, and traced along its borders. The metal heated up in seconds, casting a red-hot glow onto the rotting trash. I pulled the door open, stepped through, and repeated my welding process, sealing it behind me. The building managers thought the door had been melted shut by a long-ago gas explosion. They didn't know it was my secret way out of the building. Slipping out of my apartment in my costume unseen by the other tenants was a necessary skill that I'd perfected over the years, especially since I couldn't just go up to the roof and fly away like Hangman and Rocket Ron and the other winged types.

I strolled through the dark passageway, using my flaming hand as a torch. The passageway twisted and turned underneath a couple of city blocks. It was part of a network of old tunnels that ran under most of the downtown area and was one of the main reasons I'd chosen to live in Tip-Top Tower.

A pinprick of light flashed up ahead, and I dimmed my hand. The tunnel opened up into an alley close to the Bigtime Public Library. A few weeds and some loose bricks cluttered the entrance, along with the backside of a metal Dumpster. I shimmied through the space between the Dumpster and the alley wall. I peeked around the corner of the metal container, but I was the only person in the alley. With its Dumpsters, bits of smelly garbage, and cracked pavement, the alley wasn't the sort of place most people would willingly walk into, even during the middle of the afternoon.

There were other ways out of my apartment building, but I'd found this to be the quickest and safest. Even if someone moved the Dumpster and stumbled into the passageway, they'd never get through the door at the far end without some sort of superpower. Even then, there was nothing in the tunnel that could be traced back to me. I wasn't dumb enough to leave costumes lying around or stupid enough to write FIERA WAS HERE on the walls.

Once I was satisfied that no one was watching, I slipped out into the main street with the city's other citizens. Most folks didn't give me a second look. There were so many superheroes in Bigtime these days that people didn't get too excited unless we were going fist-to-fist with ubervillains on top of a skyscraper somewhere. Still, a few people stopped and asked me for autographs, which I graciously signed.

I made my way to Paradise Park. An enormous banner across the front entrance proclaimed that it was A SUPER DAY FOR SUPERHEROES! Thousands of people, parents with kids mostly, along with the requisite fanboys, crowded into the park anxious to see their heroes in the flesh and fur. And of course, some folks from Slaves for Superhero Sex had shown up. SSS was a cult group whose members put themselves in danger in order to get close to heroes and villains. You could spot them a mile away. They always thought they had to dress up in cheerleading, French maid, and other costumes to attract the attention of their favorite hero. I thought they were all fruitcakes.

I headed for the check-in station, where a twentysome-thing woman carrying an enormous clipboard barked orders at her teenage underlings. A headset clung to the side of her square sunglasses, while pens, paperclips, a stun gun, and more hung in the mesh khaki vest that covered her chest. Abby Appleby. She stabbed a pen at a boy who didn't look old enough to shave yet.

"You! Go take the Caffeinator a fresh supply of chocolate bars and coffee. Now!"

The poor kid grabbed a box of candy and a bag of beans and scurried off to do her bidding like he had jets attached to his sneakers.

Abby zeroed in on me and plastered a smile on her face. "Fiera. Glad you could make it. If you'll follow me, I'll show you to your booth. Everybody else is here already."

Abby Appleby was one of the premiere event planners in Bigtime. She did everything from weddings to birthday parties to funerals. Abby had a reputation for throwing fantastic events, as well as bringing everything in on time and under budget—no matter how many toes and legs and other things she had to break to get it done. She was also one of Piper's best friends. It was no wonder, given how tightly the two of them were wound.

"Here we are," Abby said, stopping in front of a wooden booth decorated with orange and red cardboard flames and the *F5* insignia.

Next door, a tall, Nordic-looking woman created snow-cones with her bare hands, covered them with sugary blue goo, and dished them out to a line of anxious kids. A giant snowflake flashed like a strobe light on her ice blue costume.

"You're putting me next to Wynter again?"

Wynter looked up from her snowcone making. Her blue eyes frosted over at the sight of me. Fire and ice never mixed, and Wynter and I had never gotten along. She was a bit cold and distant for my liking. I'd never once seen her smile or laugh, not even when she was taking out Hot Stuff, her archenemy.

"Sorry," Abby apologized, pointing to another booth. "The only other spot I have is down at the end with Halitosis Hal, and you know I can't put the two of you together."

I followed her finger and spotted the other superhero. Halitosis Hal was a short guy with a wide, but solid frame. His costume was a putrid green color, but it worked with his dark skin and hair. He was busy handing out gas masks to the folks lined up in front of his booth, which was decorated with cardboard cutouts of garlic, anchovies, and other smelly things.

No, Abby couldn't put me down there. As his name suggested, Halitosis Hal's superpower was his superbad breath. One whiff of it could stop the strongest ubervillain in his tracks. In addition to smelling like something that died two months ago, Hal's breath also contained a mixture of nitrous and other flammable gases. Whenever we got too close to each other, things blew up. And not in a good way.

"I understand," I said, slipping into the booth.

For the next three hours, I juggled fireballs, made my fingers flash like sparklers, bench-pressed parents, and scampered around in my skintight spandex costume, much to the delight of shrieking kids and fawning fanboys. I, of course, was among the more popular superheroes in attendance. Folks lined up three deep around my booth to see me light myself on fire, get autographs, and snap up official Fiera merchandise.

Everything was going fine until Kelly Caleb arrived. She had her game face on today—a smart red suit, perfect makeup, flawless hair. She was like a blond version of Erica Songe, except her suit wasn't slit down to her belly button and up to her hips. Kelly wandered through the rows of booths with her SNN cameraman, chatting and shaking hands with the superheroes like they were her close, personal friends. She even hugged Halitosis Hal and Pistol Pete. Hugging. Please. Superheroes did not *hug* people. At least, not this superhero.

The news reporter stopped in front of my booth and gestured for her cameraman to shoot some video of me juggling fireballs. I thought about using one of them to melt the television camera, but decided against it. I'd promised my father that I wouldn't set anything on fire at the park today. I supposed that included nosy news reporters.

"Fiera."

"Kelly."

"I was wondering if I could have a moment of your time." The news reporter gave me her trademark toothy grin.

"I'm sort of busy right now."

My pointed tone didn't faze her. "It will only take a few minutes. You and the other members of the Fearless Five haven't given me an interview in months, ever since you introduced Karma Girl as your new member. I'm beginning to think you're ignoring me on purpose. And I'd hate for that to be the case. Heroes like Swifte give me all the interviews I want. Since you're so busy, maybe I should go see if he's here. I'm sure he'd love to be the featured lead on the evening news, especially since he's got that new videogame to promote. From what I hear, it's selling extremely well. Even better than your action figures."

Kelly's voice was mild, but her tone was just as sharp as mine had been. The message was clear—play nice or else. If it had just been me, I would have ignored her. But I had a duty to the rest of the F5 team to make us look good—whether I wanted to or not. Unfortunately, duty was about doing a lot of things you didn't want to.

So, I snuffed out the fireballs and plastered something that resembled a smile on my face. "Well, I suppose I can give you a few minutes."

Kelly shoved a microphone at me and peppered me with questions. What I and the other team members had been up to. How Karma Girl was fitting in with the rest of the Fearless Five. If we'd heard anything from Malefica and the other members of the Terrible Triad. She skillfully moved from one topic to the next and crammed in more questions in five minutes than most reporters could get to in half an hour. Even I couldn't deny that Kelly was good at her job. She was still a reporter, though. One that I didn't like, no matter how fabulous she looked in the suit that I'd designed.

After another round of nosy questions, Kelly wrapped up the interview and told her cameraman to stop shooting.

"Now, that wasn't so bad, was it?" Kelly asked.

"No," I muttered. "I suppose not. It could have been worse. Erica Songe could have been here."

I hadn't meant for Kelly to hear me, but she did. The reporter's face tightened at the mention of the other woman.

"Not a fan either?" I asked.

"You know we're all just one big happy family at SNN." Kelly smiled, although it looked more like a grimace. "Erica has her uses."

I couldn't resist twisting the knife a little. "Like covering Black Samba and Granny Cane rescuing those trapped firefighters a couple of days ago? I saw the news and was surprised to see Erica on the scene. I thought superheroes and ubervillains were your exclusive beat at SNN. Or is that one of Erica's uses?"

Ice filled Kelly's eyes, turning them the same cold blue color as Wynter's snowcones. "I know what you're implying, but nobody muscles in on my territory. I'm the number one superhero reporter in this city, and I plan on keeping it that way—whatever it takes. Now, if you'll excuse me, Fiera, I need to get this on the air for the six o'clock news. Thanks for the interview."

Kelly jerked her head at the cameraman, and the two of them left the park. Sometimes, I thought corporate politics were just as dangerous as superhero-ubervillain battles, although without the building-leveling explosions. I shook my head and returned to my fans.

After Kelly left, the event wound down, and the other superheroes started packing up, ready to go out and prowl the streets for the night. I gave my regards to Abby, who was now barking orders at the clean-up crew, and headed for home.

I started to walk back to the alley next to the library. On an impulse, I cut through a row of pine trees that marked the park's borders and headed for Bigtime Cemetery. A wrought-iron gate surrounded the sloping green expanse, and marble tombstones, pinnacles, and angel statues dotted the manicured lawn. The wild carousel music and shrieks of glee from the park faded away to mere whispers.

My steps grew slower, heavier as I headed for my destination, but I pushed on until I reached a white marble tombstone. The words TRAVIS TEMPLETON TEAGUE. BELOVED BY ALL flowed across the marker. A few wilted flowers and cracked, faded, weather-worn action figures surrounded the gravesite. People didn't leave as many flowers and cards as they used to. Superheroes and ubervillains came and went in Bigtime, and most folks were slowly forgetting about Travis aka Tornado.

Not me. I would never forget him. Never. I crouched down, straightening the action figures and arranging the flowers into a tidy pile. I did that for a long time, thinking about him and how much love there had been between us. My heart ached, and hot tears steamed off my flushed cheeks.

Travis had been taken from me before his time. It was

cruel, unfair, and there was nothing I could do about it. But he was in a better place now, watching over me. I knew he was. I twisted my engagement ring around my finger. I would give anything for Travis to be here with me now. But that would never happen.

It was time to move on. To date again. To laugh again. To fall in love again. My father was right. I couldn't live in the past forever, and Travis wouldn't want me to. He would want me to be happy, to be with someone who made me happy, whether it was Johnny Bulluci or someone else further down the line. I quit twisting my ring and stood.

"I love you, Travis. I always will." I pressed a kiss to my hand and put it on top of the tombstone. The sun-warmed marble felt smooth as glass under my fingers.

Then, I turned and walked away.

★ 10 ★

After leaving the cemetery, I slipped back into my apartment, stripped off my superhero suit, and got ready for the observatory benefit.

I took extra care with my *I-might-have-sex-tonight* beauty rituals. Daydreaming about Johnny had fired up my hormones even more than usual. I liked him. He liked me. Why shouldn't we have a little fun after the party tonight?

Then, it was time to pick my dress for the evening. I hadn't seen Johnny in a few days, and I wanted to remind him just how fabulous I was. I walked up and down the rows of clothes in my massive closet, pulling things out, tossing them aside, grabbing even more outfits. After about thirty minutes of contemplation, I decided on a jade green ball gown with a high neck, long sleeves, and a skirt that reached to my ankles.

From a distance the dress looked very prim and proper, but the back was completely exposed, showing off my shoulders and muscles, while the sequined fabric clung to my body, hinting at what lay beneath. I pulled my hair back into a smooth, coiled bun. Strappy silver stilettos and long, dangly emerald earrings completed the sophisticated look. Perfect.

I eyeballed my purse. Something was missing from the mess inside. Lipstick, compact, cell phone, credit cards. I remembered what I'd forgotten. I rummaged around in my nightstand drawer and drew out a couple of dust-covered condoms. I stared at the foil packages, and the old, nagging doubt flared up inside me.

Despite my visit to the cemetery, I couldn't quite shake the feeling that I was betraying Travis by moving on. But Travis would want me to be happy. He would. And Johnny made me happy. For the moment. He might turn out to be a loathsome little toad tomorrow, but tonight, he was Mr. Right.

I damped down the guilt and stuffed the condoms in my purse. If you were going to play around, you should be safe doing it. I was already on the pill, but a girl couldn't be too careful, even if she was a superhero. Better to have the condoms and chicken out, than push ahead without them.

I drove my convertible to the benefit, top up to preserve my hair, handed the keys to a tuxedo-clad valet, and walked up the curving steps to the observatory. Situated on a towering hill on the outskirts of town, the Bigtime Observatory was the highest point in the city, farther up than even the gleaming skyscrapers downtown. A museum to all things star-related sat on top of the hill, along with the round white dome that housed the observatory's powerful telescope and other sensitive scientific equipment. The observatory was also connected to a nature center and park, where people could come and get up close and personal with smaller woodsy animals like owls, otters, and foxes. A man-made river flowed down the steep hill, through the woods

and animal habitats that surrounded the observatory, forming a waterfall and small lake, before continuing its journey
toward the city and out into Bigtime Bay.

Every spring, the scientists who ran the observatory and
nature center put away their pocket protectors, telescopes,
and black glasses, and threw a party to raise enough money to
keep operating for another year. In addition to scientific re-
search, the observatory was a favorite with Bigtime teachers,
who brought thousands of students to the facility every year
to stargaze, visit the animals, and swim in the lake. Science
wasn't my favorite thing, not by a long shot, but my pockets
were deep enough to get me invited to the party every year.

I gave my engraved invitation to the guy working the
door and stepped inside. The observatory featured square
white rooms, sharp angles, and high vaulted ceilings. Scientific instruments with names too long to pronounce, detailed star charts, and planetary images adorned the walls,
along with interactive displays about physics and astronauts
and trips to the moon. The displays had already captivated
some of Bigtime's finest, who were pushing buttons and
staring at the flashing lights like kids high on sugar.

I walked to the museum's main auditorium, where most
of the school programs were held. The semicircle of hard
wooden chairs had been replaced with circular tables, and
big models of planets dangled from the ceiling. A band
played swing tunes on the stage at the far end of the room,
while waiters dispensed food to the hungry crowd. Through
it all, the observatory's scientists tried to blend in with the
suave, sophisticated businessmen and women. But it was
easy to tell who was who. The scientists kept tugging on
their too-tight ties and ill-fitting dresses.

I grabbed a glass of champagne and roamed through the
crowd looking for Johnny Bulluci. All the usual partygoers
were in attendance, with Joanne James and Berkley Brighton

holding court in the middle of the auditorium. The sparkle from Joanne's engagement ring would blind a bat at thirty paces. My father stood near them, schmoozing with a couple of lonely widows. I caught his eye and waved.

To my surprise and displeasure, news reporter Erica Songe was also on the scene. She stood at the far end of the room next to a short, slender woman. The contrast between the two was striking. Erica's voluptuous form was poured into a pink dress that looked like transparent pieces of tissue sewn together. The flimsy garment exposed far more than it covered up, and more than a few men had their eyes firmly fixed on Erica's cleavage. How trashy.

The other woman wore a black, kimono-style garment that covered her from neck to feet. The bulky fabric swallowed her up, hiding any hints about her figure. Her mousy brown hair was pulled back into a tight bun, and a scowl painted her pasty face. Tortoiseshell glasses perched on her nose, which was set rather high in the air. She might as well have had NERDY SCIENTIST tattooed on her chest. A tall, fat cameraman hovered nearby, downing champagne like he was dying of thirst. I didn't blame him. I'd drink too if I had to work with the likes of Erica Songe.

A familiar motorized whir caught my ear, and I zeroed in on Henry and Lulu. Henry had traded in his usual polka-dot bow ties for one of my classy tuxedoes, while Lulu wore a scarlet dress that showed off her pale skin and blue and black hair. The two huddled in a corner by themselves, engaged in an intense conversation. Henry held on to to Lulu's hand and said something, almost pleading with her. Lulu shook her head. Henry dropped her hand, turned on his heel, and stalked away. Lulu stared at his retreating back. What was that about?

Determined to find out, I marched over to the other woman. "Trouble in paradise?"

"You'd like that, wouldn't you, Fiona?" Lulu looked away, but not before I caught the gleam of tears in her dark eyes. "For Henry to dump me."

The hurt tone in Lulu's voice made me hesitate. I didn't like the computer hacker. I'd made no secret of that. We'd come too close to getting killed last year to take any more chances than necessary. Letting Lulu Lo, one of Bigtime's computer geniuses and not-quite-aboveboard citizens, in on our secret identities wasn't the smartest thing we'd ever done.

But Carmen trusted her, and Henry loved her. And Lulu loved Henry, from what I'd seen. I loved Henry too, and I wanted him to be happy. If Lulu made him happy, well, I supposed I could live with her. After all, I'd come to live with Carmen. So, I decided to put my personal feelings aside and do my duty to support Henry—and his hacker honey.

"No, I don't want Henry to dump you."

Lulu snorted. "Oh, come off it, Fiona. You can't stand me."

I ignored her comment. "Why would Henry dump you? Are the two of you fighting? The two of you never fight." In addition to having superstrength, I was also supertenacious, especially when it came to the people I cared about.

"It's nothing. Absolutely nothing," Lulu muttered. She hit a button on her wheelchair and zoomed away.

I started to melt her tires to get her to stop, when a low voice sounded behind me.

"Hello, beautiful."

My heart fluttered. I put my most dazzling smile on my face and turned around. Johnny Bulluci stood behind me, wearing a perfectly fitted tuxedo that showed off his golden hair and bronze skin. My eyes zipped up and down him. The man looked yummy enough to eat. And I was always hungry. For all sorts of things.

Johnny leaned in and planted a kiss on my cheek. His

lips felt warm even against my flushed skin. I closed my eyes, drinking in his spicy aroma.

"Hello yourself, handsome."

Johnny's eyes raked over me in a slow fashion. He let out a low whistle. "Nice dress."

I smoothed down the slinky fabric. "I thought you might like it."

"I do. A lot." He gave me a wolfish grin and took my hand. "Come on, I want you to meet my grandfather."

Johnny led me through the chattering crowd. More than a few eyebrows rose when we passed, and hushed whispers broke out in our wake. Gossiping about everyone and everything was one of the main activities in Bigtime society. Actually, in Bigtime in general. Tomorrow, we'd be the talk among the city's matrons, more than a few of whom'd probably like to foist their daughters off on Johnny. Too bad. The man was mine. At least for tonight. I tightened my grip on his hand. And I was planning on keeping him all to myself.

Johnny strolled over to a table set against the wall, where Bella sat with their grandfather. Tonight, Bella wore a simple peach-colored satin sheath dress that brought out her tan skin. Pearl combs glinted in her amber-colored hair, while her usual silver angel charm hung around her throat. The two of them rose at our approach.

"Fiona."

"Bella."

"Nice dress," we said in unison.

We looked at each other, not sure if we were being catty or not. A slow smile spread across Bella's face. I grinned in return, and we laughed.

Johnny drew me forward. "Grandfather, this is Fiona Fine. Fiona, this is my grandfather, Roberto."

"I've long been a fan of your work, Miss Fine." Roberto Bulluci's voice was just as rich and cultured as Johnny's, except his accent was far more pronounced. He bowed low, pressed a kiss to my hand, and gave me a sly wink that would have been right at home on a much younger man. "And please call me Bobby. All my friends do."

I laughed. "Well, I see where Johnny gets his charm from."

"Johnny has told us quite a bit about you, including your fondness for steak. You must come have dinner with us one evening, Miss Fine," Bobby said. "Perhaps Bella will let me have some red meat and wine if you do."

Bella's lips pursed as though she'd bitten into a lemon. "Grandfather, you know the doctor said you shouldn't eat—"

Bobby Bulluci waved his hand. A silver ring set with diamonds sparkled on his pinkie. "Bah! I'm seventy-two years old, Bella. If I want to eat steak and drink fine wine in my golden years, then I should be able to—no matter what any doctor says. They're all fools anyway."

Bella put her hands on her hips. "Not if you want to live to see seventy-three."

Bobby eyed his no-nonsense granddaughter. "Just like your father, you are. Everything must always be by the book." His tone was light and teasing.

"Well, perhaps if he were here, I'd have an easier time keeping you in line and out of trouble," Bella said.

Her words hit a little too close to home. A cold shadow fell over the three of them at the mention of James Bulluci. Johnny's hand tightened around mine.

"Let's get some champagne," I said, trying to lighten the darkening mood.

It worked. Just like always. A waiter came around, and we grabbed tall flutes filled with bubbling golden liquid. I kept up a steady stream of chatter, and slowly but surely, the darkness faded away and the ice broke. Then again, it usually did when I was around.

Bella and I talked about our fall lines. I was going for a

hip, yet preppy look. Lots of bright, multicolored plaid. Lots of blazers. Lots of chunky jewelry. Bella, meanwhile, had chosen to focus on every Bigtime woman's favorite color—black. How boring. I was sure her clothes would be exquisitely made and very beautiful, but the girl really needed to mix it up a bit. She needed some color in her life—in more ways than one.

After we exhausted the world of fashion, Bella drifted off to speak to one of the society types about her latest dress, leaving me alone with the men. After a couple of false starts, the boys and I found a topic we could talk about—soccer.

"Soccer is the true football," I said. "Americans really don't know what they're missing. Anybody can kick a ball with his foot. Bouncing it off his head is what takes *real* talent."

Bobby's green eyes lit up. "Ah! A woman after my own heart."

We chatted about various European leagues and teams and the latest scandals, and Johnny jumped in with his thoughts. After about half an hour of sports talk, Johnny took my arm again.

"I'm sorry to leave you alone, but we really need to mingle for a while, Grandfather," Johnny said. "I'm sure Fiona has some friends that she'd like to say hello to tonight."

"Of course, of course. Just as I have some lovely ladies that I would like to speak to as well."

Bobby winked and pointed at a group of older women standing by the bar. The spry septuagenarian strode off, his walk tall and strong. He strolled right into the midst of the women, and more than a few of the elderly ladies perked up at his presence.

"Your grandfather is a real character," I said. "Very charming, very lively."

Johnny smiled. "He's always up to something. That's why I love him."

We moved off into the crowd and made a circuit of the auditorium, speaking to people we knew, including Chief Newman. My father's eyes grew dark and curious when I introduced him to Johnny.

"I've heard a lot about you, Mr. Bulluci," my father said, shaking Johnny's hand.

Johnny looked at me. "I hope it's been good."

"So far. So far, my boy."

The two of them started talking about manly things, like cars and sports and fine cigars. Johnny turned out to be quite an expert on the last subject, giving my father tips about what cigars to buy and where to get them from.

"I didn't know you smoked," I said.

Johnny shrugged. "Occasionally. Not so much since I came back to Bigtime. Americans are very uptight about it, far more so than Europeans. It takes the fun out of it. Plus, Bella won't let me smoke in the house. She's a real stickler for things like that."

As the conversation progressed, my father kept lacing his fingers together and peering into Johnny's eyes, as though deep in thought. His own eyes seemed to be glowing ever so faintly. I frowned. Johnny moved off to speak to one of Bella's friends, and I grabbed my father's arm.

"Stop that!" I hissed.

"Stop what?"

"Trying to read his mind."

"Would I do something like that?"

My father smiled and tried to look innocent. Please. I didn't have to be a psychic to know he was faking.

"You've always done it, ever since I started dating boys in high school. Remember the guy who took me to the prom? I thought he was going to have a heart attack when you started asking him about the hotel room he'd booked for the two of us for after the dance."

My father chuckled at the memory. I rolled my eyes.

"So what's the verdict?" I asked.

My father frowned. "I'll get back to you on that."

Johnny returned before I could interrogate Chief New-man further about his cryptic comment. An anorexic widow dripping with jewels wiggled in between us and pulled my father onto the dance floor. Johnny and I made another lap around the room. It was close to midnight, and I was ready to move on to the next part of the evening—whatever it might entail.

"Are you ready to blow this joint?" I asked.

Johnny opened his mouth to reply, when a low sultry voice cut in.

"Mr. Bulluci. Hello. So nice to see you again." Erica Songe batted her long black lashes at Johnny. They were fake, just like her lips and boobs. "Oh, Fiona. I didn't see you there."

"Erica," I said through gritted teeth. Up close, the re-porter's filmy dress was practically transparent, giving every-one a view of all her charms, including Johnny. "That's a nice little dress you're wearing."

"Isn't it just fabulous?"

Erica put her hands on her curvy hips and preened. The woman actually thought I was being serious and giving her a genuine compliment. Please.

"Actually, I prefer a more understated look on a woman." Johnny smiled and put his arm around my waist. "It leaves more to the imagination."

"But sometimes the real thing's so much better than your imagination," she purred.

I rolled my eyes. The woman had no shame and zero class. Slut.

Johnny's cool green eyes flicked over her. "Not in this case, I think."

Erica's mouth opened and closed as though she couldn't

believe there was a man alive who didn't want her. Who could resist her. She pouted, sticking her lower lip out as far as it would go. If she kept that up much longer, her whole face would explode.

But I had to give Erica credit, she recovered quickly. She brushed off Johnny's comment like it was nothing more than a piece of lint sticking to her see-through dress. She gestured to her cameraman, who was still guzzling champagne, and whipped out a microphone. The guy wobbled over and pointed his video camera in our general direction.

"Well, while I have you cornered, what do you think about the benefit? I'm covering this tonight for SNN."

"Really? Why?" I asked. "Shouldn't you be out chasing down superheroes and ubervillains like Kelly Caleb?"

"Kelly is a bit limited in what she can do, poor girl. The network wants to broaden its horizons beyond just superheroes. I'm the go-to-girl for the more high-profile assignments these days," Erica replied in a smooth tone.

In other words, Erica had somehow wrangled the assignment away from the other reporter. I didn't like reporters much, but Kelly Caleb was good at her job. If there was any scoop to be had, she was the one who knew about it. I wondered who Erica had to sleep with to beat out the other woman. That was the only way I could imagine that she'd one-upped Kelly.

"Care to comment about the benefit, Johnny?" Erica shoved the microphone and her chest in Johnny's face.

"Well," he said, keeping his eyes fixed on Erica's face. "I think the observatory is an important asset to the community . . ."

While Johnny expounded on the virtues of the Bigtime Observatory, nature center, and sundry related programs, I wandered away and grabbed a couple of crab cake appetizers from a passing waiter. I would have taken the whole tray away from the guy, but there were too many witnesses.

Instead, I polished off the batter-dipped bites, licked the crumbs off my fingers, and watched Erica interrogate Johnny. A scuffle sounded, and the kimono-clad scientist I'd spotted with the reporter earlier stopped next to me. The woman stared at the curvaceous news reporter. A disapproving frown covered her white, makeup-free face.

"Not enjoying the show?" I asked.

"Oh, preening for the camera and throwing herself at men is what Erica does best." The woman sniffed. "After a while, the spectacle gets old."

"You sound like you know her pretty well."

"Unfortunately," the woman replied, "we share the same gene pool."

I eyed her. With her headache-inducing bun and buttoned-up-to-there dress, the woman didn't look a thing like Erica *I'm-so-slutty* Songe. "Cousins?"

"Sisters. Unfortunately."

"I'm Fiona Fine, and you are . . ."

"Irene Songe."

We shook hands. Irene's grip felt as cold and passionless as an ice cube. It matched her pale face. We stood there drinking champagne and watching Erica do her best to let Johnny Bulluci know she was up for anything, anytime. After about five minutes, Johnny managed to extricate himself from Erica's clutches and head back to me. Erica trailed along behind him, not quite ready to admit defeat. The cameraman grabbed some more champagne. It was a wonder the guy could still stand—or that his liver didn't burst.

Erica stopped short when she spotted her sister talking to me. "Enjoying yourself, Irene?"

"Of course," Irene replied.

The two women looked at each other with barely disguised hostility. Definitely no love lost there. One sister an exhibitionist, the other a repressed, wound-up scientist. I couldn't imagine why they didn't get along.

Erica turned to Johnny and flashed him another smile. She opened her mouth to proposition Johnny yet again, but he beat her to the punch.

"It was so nice talking to you, Erica. But if you'll excuse us, Fiona and I have somewhere we need to be. Now."

Johnny offered me his arm, and we walked away. I looked back over my shoulder and smiled at Erica. Her face reddened, and her hands clenched into fists, as though she wanted to stab me with her microphone. Let her try. I could kick her ass blindfolded. Irene whispered something to her, and Erica turned and snapped at her sister.

"Forget about her," Johnny said. "You're the only woman I have eyes for tonight."

I smiled at him. "Smooth. Very, very smooth."

"Let's get out of here," Johnny said, his eyes burning into mine. "And go somewhere a bit more private."

My stomach quivered. "Let's go," I said.

He pulled me toward the door.

★ 11 ★

We strolled out the back of the auditorium and onto a stone balcony that overlooked the gardens and nature preserve that surrounded the observatory. Acres of flowers, grassy knolls, and low bushes stretched out before us into the dark night before melting into the black woods. A few other couples stood on the balcony, whispering, drinking, and enjoying the scenic view.

"Care to go for a walk in the moonlight?" Johnny asked.

"I'd love to."

We picked our way down the stone steps and onto one of the crushed-shell paths that wound through the tame jungle. Antique streetlamps lit the way, along with the moon and stars above. A steady breeze blew from the north, pushing a few wisps of clouds across the sky, and bringing with it the heady scent of roses, orchids, and more. But all I was aware of was Johnny walking next to me. His spicy cologne tickled my nose, and his body felt warm and solid next to mine.

We strolled in silence, leaving the noise and gaiety and

lights of the benefit behind. Crickets chirped in the dew-covered grass. A bullfrog let out a loud bellow. Doves cooed and fluttered in the trees above. We crossed a stone bridge that arched over the manmade river. Water gurgled below our feet.

"Come on," Johnny said. "Let's take a detour."

He took my hand and led me down a path that curved back under the bridge. After going under the bridge, the river tumbled down a hill, forming a small, fifteen-foot-high waterfall. The water pooled into a shallow lake a little less than two miles across before rushing on down the hillside. Fiberglass picnic tables and stone benches dotted the lake's edge. Brilliant moonlight bounced off the water's surface, making it shimmer like liquid silver. Cattails and other vegetation surrounded the water's edge, and a few waterlilies floated in the pool, bouncing up and down on the rippling waves.

"It's beautiful," I whispered.

"Want to go for a swim?"

"Now? In the middle of the night?"

I loved to swim, loved to lose myself in cool, soothing water and rhythmic strokes. But coming up to the lake for some late-night swimming, skinny-dipping, and a little necking was a popular pastime for local teens and college students. When Johnny had said he wanted to go somewhere more private, I'd been thinking about my apartment, specifically my bed.

Johnny grinned, his teeth flashing in the darkness. "Why not? There's nobody around but the two of us. I won't tell if you won't tell."

He slipped off his jacket and shoes and put them on a nearby bench. His shirt and pants soon followed. All I could do was stare at the man before me. I'd thought there was a body to die for under those clothes, but I had no idea how deadly it was. Sculpted biceps. Rippling abs. Solid muscles. My eyes dipped lower. Everywhere. Yummy. Johnny Bulluci was one fine-looking man. I closed my hands to keep unwanted sparks from shooting out of my fingertips.

I ogled him a minute longer, then laughed. "Cherubs?"

Johnny put his hands on his hips, proud of his boxers. Fat, happy-looking cherubs frolicking on puffy clouds decorated the slick, silk fabric. "Just because I'm no angel doesn't mean I can't wear them. Now, are you coming or not?"

I hesitated, twisting the ring around my finger. The time for being wishy-washy was long gone. I stopped and let out a long, hot breath. "I'm coming."

I stripped off my dress and high heels, folding the fabric into a neat pile. It would have a million wrinkles in it, but I could always make another one just like it. In a moment, I was standing there in a lacy green bra and matching panties. I always wore the good underwear when there was a chance of someone else taking it off.

Johnny's eyes traced over my body. "You know, I think Erica was right. The real thing is so much better than my imagination."

I smiled and lifted my chin up. "Of course it is, when I'm involved."

We strolled down to the water's edge and plunged into the frothy spray. We treaded water a few minutes, letting our bodies adjust to the cool temperature. Even though it was the middle of May, the water hovered around seventy degrees, a bit chilly for most people. Not Johnny, though. He swam and dove like a duck. If anything, the water invigorated him. Or perhaps it was just the sight of me in my wet skivvies. Yeah, that's what I was going with.

"Is the water too cold for you?" Johnny asked.

"No." I was never cold. But the hunger in Johnny's eyes made me shiver.

We swam back and forth in the pool, shrieking and splashing water and pulling each other under like a couple of teenagers. After about half an hour, we headed for shore. We flopped onto the grass and stared at the smattering of stars high above.

"It's so peaceful here," I murmured. "So beautiful."

"Not as beautiful as you," Johnny whispered in a husky voice.

I stared into his eyes. This was it. Decision time. The old guilt flared to life inside me. But Travis was gone, and Johnny was here. Now. With me.

So, I kissed him. His tongue met mine, and I was lost.

My bra and panties disappeared before I knew what had happened. So did Johnny's boxers. Everything else faded away until there was nothing but the soft grass below us, the stars above, and Johnny's hands on me.

We lay there for a long time. Kissing. Stroking. Caressing.

Johnny pulled back. He pushed a wisp of hair off my face and stared into my eyes. His own glistened like jewels in the moonlight.

"I want to do something for you, Fiona," Johnny said. "Do you trust me?"

I went quiet and still. I wasn't good at trusting people. I'd gone through too many battles with too many uber-villains to give my trust lightly to anyone. But there was something about Johnny that made me want to trust him. Made me want to lower my defenses. Made me want to believe in him. "Yes, I do."

"Then roll over onto your stomach."

I did, and to my surprise, he started to massage me. There was nothing overtly sexual about it. Just Johnny's firm hands kneading my body with the detachment of a large Swedish woman. He started at my feet, moving up my calves to my thighs. His fingers worked on my ass, molding, sculpting, before going up to my lower back and shoulders. He even worked on my head, loosening my hair from its wet bun and massaging my scalp.

Heaven. Sheer heaven.

"Now, the other side," Johnny whispered.

I turned over onto my back, eager for more. Much, much more. Johnny repeated the process, this time starting with my neck and working his way down. His fingers pressed gently into me, soothing away my doubts and fears. His sure hands moved to my breasts, massaging each one in turn. My nipples hardened under his touch, but Johnny ignored them and went on with the massage, focusing on my stomach, before sliding lower.

I trembled when he reached my pelvic area. I thought he might slip his fingers inside me, but Johnny moved on as though he wasn't the least bit interested in that part of my anatomy. He worked on my thighs, then calves, then feet. Slowly, the fireball of guilt and tension in my stomach faded away, replaced by a different, though no less dangerous, sort of liquid heat.

"That was wonderful," I sighed when he finished. "Absolutely wonderful."

Johnny grinned. A devilish light sparked in his eyes. "Baby, if you thought that was wonderful, how about this?"

He eased my thighs apart and lowered his mouth to me. I gasped at the sudden, unexpected sensation.

"Do you like that, baby?" he asked.

I buried my fingers in his hair and whimpered.

"I'll take that as a yes."

Johnny delved into me like I was a delectable dessert just waiting to be sampled, and he was a sugar addict. His tongue. His fingers. Stroking. Caressing. Driving me crazy.

Sweet, painful pressure built up in my body, and I thought my hair would catch fire from the sensation. But I'd learned long ago to dampen down the physical manifestation of my power during sex. To let all that fire melt into liquid desire coursing through my veins.

"Johnny . . . I . . . can't . . . wait . . . much . . . longer," I panted, fingers clenching the grass.

"You don't have to, baby," he murmured. "I'm ready for you."

We kissed, then I rolled Johnny onto his back. I reached for my purse and pulled out one of the dusty condoms. Johnny tried to take it from me, but I pushed him back against the ground.

"Let me," I whispered, tearing the packet open with my teeth.

I trailed my fingers up and down his long length before slipping the condom over him. Johnny's eyes widened at the sensation, and he hissed.

Then, I got on my knees and straddled him, taking his stiff shaft deep inside my fiery body. Johnny was so much more than just ready for me. *Hard* didn't do the man justice. Even *steely* couldn't quite describe it.

"Oh, baby, you're so tight," Johnny murmured. "So tight and hot and wet."

I rocked back and forth, thrusting against him. Johnny's hands stroked my breasts as I rode him, squeezing my nipples until they ached and throbbed along with the rest of me. It only made me want him that much more. All that sweet liquid fire bubbled up in my veins like a volcano about to erupt. A moment later, it did. An orgasm tore through my body, and I cried out. So did he, and we rode up into the stars together.

Sometime later, I slumped over Johnny with him still inside me.

"That was fantastic," I said, nuzzling his neck. Sweat covered my body, and my heartbeat slowly returned to normal.

Smoke puffed away from the ends of my fingers, but you could barely see it in the darkness.

"That was fantastic, but we're not done yet," Johnny said.

He eased me off him and got rid of the condom. Then, he pulled me to my feet and led me down into the lake. The water washed away the slick sweat and cooled my feverish body, as much as it could. Johnny kissed the back of my neck while his hands slid around and covered my breasts, rubbing my nipples until they were hard and aching once more.

"Come on," he whispered, withdrawing his hands.

I followed him. Johnny walked up the bank and tugged me over to one of the picnic tables that flanked the lake.

"This looks about right," he said.

"Yes, it does."

Johnny reached for me, but I eluded his grasp, grabbing another condom from my purse. Then, I went down on my knees and took his shaft in my mouth. Johnny gasped in surprise. He staggered, and his back went against the table.

"You're not the only one who likes to be shocking," I said.

I ran my tongue up and down his penis, while my fingers stroked him. Johnny twitched and trembled with every flick of my hot tongue. Now, I was the one in control. Just the way I liked it.

Not for long, though. Johnny reached down and plucked the condom from me, unrolling it in record time. Then, he picked me up and placed me on top of the picnic table. My legs locked around his waist. Johnny leaned over me, bracing his hands on the cool fiberglass. He stared into my eyes for a heartbeat. Then, he thrust into me. His hungry mouth covered mine, hushing my cries and moans of pleasure.

Johnny plunged into me over and over again. My hands were everywhere. His hair. Neck. Chest. Abs. Our tongues dueled back and forth even as we pushed together. I couldn't get enough of him. I urged him on, wanting him to go deeper and deeper.

So, he did.

And I loved it.

Every fantastic, pleasurable, white-hot second.

★12★

Afterward, we lay there on the cool grass for a long time, looking at the stars and lying in each other's arms.

"This is perfect, absolutely perfect," I said.

"Yes, yes it is," Johnny replied in a soft tone.

"So where do we go from here?"

Johnny propped his elbow up and stared into my eyes. "I want to keep seeing you, Fiona, if that's what you're asking. I might be a rich, spoiled playboy, but I have been known to engage in actual relationships, every now and then. Especially with such an incredible woman like you."

It was exactly what I was asking—and exactly the response I wanted.

"Good. I might be a bitchy fashion designer, but I've also been known to indulge in relationships—with certain equally fabulous people."

"And do I fit that bill?" Johnny asked.

"Absolutely. I want to keep seeing you too." I trailed my fingers down his abdomen. "All of you."

Johnny grinned and reached for me again.

Eventually, we put on our clothes and headed back to the observatory. It was closer to morning than midnight now, and the birds and bugs and bullfrogs had quieted down to sleep. Only a few drunken stragglers remained at the benefit, sitting at tables and guzzling down what was left of the champagne, along with the science types who had organized the event. But they were too busy counting money and tallying up checks and contributions to notice Johnny and me and our disheveled appearance.

Johnny walked me outside, and a sleepy-looking valet retrieved my convertible. I threw my purse in the car and turned to face Johnny.

"Dinner tomorrow night?" he asked, cupping my cheek in his hand.

I hesitated. I liked Johnny, I really did, but the sex hadn't been as casual as I thought it would be. Quite the opposite. I'd been looking for a rebound guy, not somebody long-term. But this felt like the beginning of something big, something serious. Despite our earlier promises to keep seeing each other, I didn't know exactly how I felt about the sexy businessman. Other than hot and bothered.

"Come on. You promised Grandfather you'd come. You wouldn't want him to miss out on his steak and wine, would you? He was really looking forward to it," Johnny wheedled.

I laughed. "Far be it for me to let your grandfather down. Dinner tomorrow night. Or rather tonight. Eight o'clock?"

"It's a date." Johnny flashed me another sexy grin, leaned in, and kissed me.

It was another fifteen minutes before I was able to get in my car and drive away.

I entered my apartment at six in the morning. I tossed my purse on a table and sank onto the scarlet upholstered sofa. A smile spread across my face. Tonight had been fabulous. Completely, wonderfully, absolutely, perfectly fabulous. I stretched my arms over my head. The dry spell was over. I was totally satisfied. Johnny Bulluci should have been a sculptor instead of a businessman. The things that man could do with his hands. And tongue. And lips . . .

My thoughts strayed for a little while, replaying the evening over and over again in my mind. But my stomach rumbled, and I realized that I was starving. Sex really was great for burning calories, not that I had any problem in that department anyway. And it was definitely a lot more fun than exercise.

I was halfway through a gallon of strawberry cheesecake ice cream when the phone rang. I frowned. Who could be calling me at this hour? Johnny? My heart quickened.

"Fiona Fine."

"Well, it's about time you got home," Carmen said. "I left you a message hours ago."

I looked at the answering machine. Sure enough, the red light blinked on and off. I'd been so busy thinking about Johnny that I hadn't even noticed it. "Sorry. I was out."

"Don't worry. I didn't want anything important. But tell me, how was your date?"

"What date?" I mumbled through a mouthful of melted ice cream.

"The hot date that ended in you having fantastic sex."

The spoon slipped from my fingers. "How do you know that?"

"I can hear it in your voice. You're practically purring, Fiona. And the chief called and said you disappeared with some hot new guy you've been seeing. That the two of you were looking at each other a certain way. I just put two and two together."

I cursed and picked up my spoon. Carmen's inherent nosiness could be so annoying sometimes, especially when coupled with her new empathic powers. Didn't I have any secrets from anybody anymore?

"I'm happy for you, Fiona. That you found somebody you like. I really am. It's time you got back out there again. Now, if only I could get Lulu to—" Carmen cut off her sentence.

"Get Lulu to what?"

"Nothing. Never mind."

"What's going on with Henry and Lulu?" I asked. "It looked like they were fighting at the benefit tonight."

Carmen was silent. "You'll have to ask Lulu about that."

"I did. She told me to buzz off. She almost ran over my feet with her wheelchair." I scraped the bottom of the ice cream carton.

"Well, I wouldn't worry about it. The two of them will work things out. Eventually."

The last luscious bite of ice cream melted in my mouth. Gone already. Damn. I should have gotten the grocery service to deliver more than just one gallon. "Well, if they do break up, can I finally set Lulu's hair on fire?"

"Fiona! That's not very nice."

"What?" I asked. "She's always telling me how *hot* I am. I'd like to show her how right she is. Just once."

"Henry and Lulu are not going to break up. They're just having a little problem right now."

"But you're not going to tell me what it is."

"No. It's not my place to say anything." Carmen switched

gears. "Now, back to you and the hot guy. How was it? I want all the juicy details."

I sat back against the cushy sofa. Carmen was the closest thing to a girlfriend that I had, and I couldn't exactly talk to my father about this. Plus, I felt like bragging. Just a little bit. All right. A lot. Who wanted to be modest when Johnny Bulluci was in the picture?

"Wonderful. Absolutely wonderful. The man knows how to use his hands very well, if you know what I mean. As well as other parts of his anatomy."

"So, who is the mystery guy?"

"Johnny Bulluci. Bella Bulluci's brother."

"I didn't know Bella had a brother."

"Well, she does. I met him at the wedding. He was the guy who thought he could take out Siren and Intelligal by himself."

"You met him at the wedding? Really?"

I rolled my eyes at the note of triumph in Carmen's voice. "Yes, really."

"Tell me about him," she said.

So I did. I told Carmen how funny and charming and wickedly sweet Johnny was. How he made me laugh. And how he had reduced me to a puddle of oozing mush.

"He sounds terrific," Carmen said.

"He is," I admitted. "I just don't know what to do about it."

"What do you mean?"

"Well," I said. "At first, I was just going to have a fling with him to get my feet wet again, so to speak. But I really like him. A lot more than I thought I would. That's complicated enough by itself. Then, there's the whole secret-identity thing. I've never figured out how you tell a guy, *Oh, by the way, I moonlight as one of the most famous superheroes in the world. I can create fireballs with my hands and bench-press a couple thousand pounds.* It's not exactly pillow talk. Most guys are intimidated by things like that, especially the super-human strength part."

"You're not thinking about telling him that you're Fiera, are you? You've only known the guy a few days!"

I wanted to point out that Carmen hadn't even known Sam's real identity before she'd slept with him, but I was too relaxed and mellow to quibble over that fact. Tonight, anyway.

"Of course I'm not going to tell him that I'm Fiera. How stupid do you think I am? I've been a superhero a long time now. It's not something you just blurt out to people."

It'd be a long, long, *long* time before I told Johnny what I did in my spare time. If ever. I'd had more than one guy dump me as a result of my nighttime escapades. Guys had one of two reactions when they learned about my secret identity—they freaked out and broke up with me, or they got totally kinky and wanted me to dress up in the Fiera costume for them. It was rather embarrassing when you had to get your father to mind-wipe your boyfriend because he couldn't handle the fact that you could break his arm like a peppermint stick or barbecue him with a thought. Or when he wanted you to play dress-up in the bedroom all the time.

"Well, whenever you tell him, if Johnny can't understand your other job, he's not worth having. Just take it one day at a time. That's what Sam and I did in the beginning." Carmen hesitated. "But you need to be careful, Fiona."

"Why's that?" I got off the couch and opened the refrigerator door, still hungry.

"The chief told me about your run-in with Siren and Intelligal the other night. Those two are up to something, I'm sure of it. Something big. Something dangerous."

"Is that what the voices in your head are telling you?" I snickered.

"Yes," Carmen snapped. She tended to get a little touchy

about her powers sometimes, just like newbie heroes always did. "That's what the voices in my head are telling me."

"All right, Mom, I'll be careful." I pulled a frozen pizza out of the refrigerator, tore off the wrapper, and put it on a baking sheet.

"Good."

I wiggled my fingers, spreading flames over the ham, pineapple, and cheese concoction. "So how's the honeymoon going? Where's Sam at?"

"Right here beside me."

My eyes narrowed. "Are you guys still in bed? Isn't it like noon over there by now?"

"Eleven o'clock actually," Carmen said in a cheery voice. "You didn't think you were the only one who got lucky last night, did you?"

After eating my pizza, a bag of chips, three cinnamon buns, and washing it all down with a six-pack of soda, I went to bed. Due to my late night out, I didn't get to work until almost noon. Good thing I owned the place, or I would have been so fired. I strolled into Piper's dust-free office, and the Hispanic woman gave me a sly smile.

"Someone must have had a good time last night," Piper said, her eyes sparkling. "A *very* good time."

"Why do you say that?"

She jerked her head at my office. I opened the door to find more flowers and chocolates crammed into the room than I'd seen in my entire life. There were three times as many as before, and they covered every single surface, even the floor. It looked like the Petal Pusher had set up her evil, flower-filled lair inside. I picked up one of the boxes scrunched next to a towering bouquet of white roses. Godiva chocolate bars filled with raspberry. Johnny Bulluci definitely had good taste.

Piper leaned in the doorway. "Like I said, you must have had a *really* good time last night."

I just grinned.

I spent the rest of the day working. At least I tried to. It took almost an hour to clear out some of the flowers so I could actually get to my desk. More often than not, I ended up mentally replaying last night with Johnny. I'd catch myself staring at the flowers and chocolates and smiling. Well, at the flowers anyway. The chocolates didn't last past twelve-thirty.

Eventually, I buckled down and got busy. I okayed Piper's final pricing suggestions on the fall line and contacted the necessary fabric suppliers. I called a few of Bigtime's rich society types to let them know their orders would be available for pickup next week and signed a variety of forms and initialed them in triplicate. I even answered all my outstanding Fiera e-mails.

Piper came in the office around three, bearing bags full of burgers, soups, salads, and desserts from Quicke's.

"You're a lifesaver," I said, unwrapping a double cheeseburger as fast as I could without burning off the cellophane. I bit into the warm, cheese-covered bun. Mayonnaise, chargrilled meat, tomatoes, onions, and more exploded onto my tastebuds. Ah, heaven.

"I know. You should give me a raise. A big one." Piper snitched a French fry from one of the bags.

I nodded, too caught up in my burger to protest or smack her hand away from the fries. I didn't like people messing with my food, especially eating what was mine. That was how nasty, fire-filled accidents happened.

"And don't forget. Joanne James is coming in at four to talk about her next wedding dress."

I groaned. "Is that today?"

Piper nodded. "Yep. You told me to set it up, remember?"

I groaned again and stared at the white paper bags. "So

that's why you brought me all this food. You were softening me up. Trying to bribe me with burgers so I wouldn't weasel out of the appointment."

"Guilty as charged," Piper said, breezing out. "But it worked, didn't it?"

I just took another bite of my burger.

Joanne James arrived at exactly four. She glided through the front door like she was the queen of Bigtime, even though she wouldn't officially get that title until she married Berkley. She wore a sleek lavender Bulluci suit and matching heels that set off her blacker than black hair. Amethysts bigger than small potatoes ringed her thin throat. They looked like something out of a Cracker Jack box. Except I knew the necklace was real. It had to weigh a ton. I didn't see how Joanne held her neck up with that thing strung on it, much less walked around. When you factored in her golf ball–size engagement ring, the jewelry she wore probably weighed more than her scrawny body. Like most women on the society circuit, Joanne was painfully thin.

"Fiona, darling!" she cried out, removing a pair of over-sized black sunglasses studded with diamonds.

"Joanne, darling!"

We airkissed and told each other how fabulous we both looked. Once the fake pleasantries were out of the way, I led Joanne to one of the many spacious consultation rooms that branched off the storefront. The area featured plush chairs, a low settee, flowers, and sample books of all the garments I'd designed, along with trays of fabric swatches. A round raised dais and three-sided mirror stood in the middle of the area. It was everything I needed to outfit the fabulously wealthy—and unbelievably picky.

A knock sounded on the door, and one of the clerks came by with a tray of vanilla-crème-filled chocolates and champagne. Joanne nibbled on one of the sweet confections, while I gulped down two glasses of the bubbly.

"Leave the bottle, and keep the booze coming," I muttered to the clerk. "Slip me something stronger, if you've got it."

She nodded with sympathy. She'd had a few run-ins with Joanne herself. The clerk left, and Joanne settled herself on the settee, sitting up smartly as to not wrinkle her five-thousand-dollar suit.

"First of all, let's talk price," I said.

It was always better to lock down the money up front. That way, I wouldn't spend my time and energy coming up with something fabulous only to have some penny-pinching rich bitch try to stiff me on the bill. Joanne was particularly notorious for doing that. Sometimes, I thought she should have gone into business instead of trolling for husbands. She was a tough negotiator.

Joanne waved her hand. The sparkles from her ring made my eyes hurt. "Money is no problem. Charge whatever you want for the dress. Berkley is footing the bill for everything. It's his wedding gift to me. I told him that I wanted the wedding of my dreams, and he is more than happy to give it to me. He's very sweet that way."

Sweet wasn't the word I would use. *Besotted fool* would be more appropriate. But if Berkley Brighton wanted to blow his whiskey millions on the wedding and throw some of that money my way, who was I to argue? Still, I couldn't stop myself from asking the painfully obvious question.

"Haven't you already had the wedding of your dreams? You have been married five times now."

"Of course. The first one left a lot to be desired, but the last four were absolutely wonderful. But there's always room for improvement, Fiona." Joanne polished off her chocolate. "Now, on to the color. I was thinking of something in a rich red. Burgundy maybe, or perhaps scarlet."

"Scarlet?" I said. "Are you sure? What about white? Or maybe a nice ivory or pale pink?"

"I look like a ghost in white and utterly washed out in ivory. Pale pink? Disgusting. Besides, it's not like I'm some sweet young thing who's never been with a man. I've been around the block, several times, and we all know it."

Despite her other faults, Joanne didn't mince words or pull punches, not even regarding herself. I admired that small part of her personality.

"All right, red it is," I said, pulling out a thick book.

For the next half hour, Joanne looked at fabric swatches. She settled on a crushed velvet in a deep wine red color that contrasted nicely with her blacker than black hair and pale skin. Next, it was on to the dress itself. I showed her some preliminary sketches I'd done for various lines.

"No, no, no, no." She flipped through the pages. "Too poofy. Too saccharine. Too much tulle. Too many sequins. Wait a minute. This. Now this, I like."

Joanne pointed to a sketch, and I snorted. I should have known she'd pick that one. The dress featured a long, flowing, almost transparent silk skirt and a lace-up leather bustier. The dress was a little too slutty for your traditional brides, looking more hooker than virgin. I'd actually been thinking of adding it to my lingerie line for next year.

"Are you sure?" I asked. "I was going to use that garment for a more intimate line of apparel."

"Absolutely. That will look marvelous on me." Joanne's voice rang with certainty.

Lingerie for a wedding dress? Well, it'd certainly look good in red.

Joanne stripped down to her undies so I could take her

measurements. I couldn't really tell how old Joanne was, given her ageless-looking face and rumored propensity for plastic surgery. But she still had a fabulous body, trim and toned, if a bit on the bony side. Tiny amethysts sparkled on her lilac-colored underwear, matching the jewels around her neck. Talk about flaunting your wealth.

Once that was done, I draped a piece of white muslin over her and started shaping it into the dress she'd picked out so she could see how it would fit and look.

"The wedding's in two months. When will you have the dress done?" Joanne asked.

"We'll do the final fitting in a couple of weeks."

"Good." Joanne's eyes met mine in the mirror. "I want this dress to be especially fabulous, Fiona. The best thing you've ever done for me. This is going to be my last wedding, and I want to look my very best."

I stifled a giggle. "Your last wedding? Are you sure about that, Joanne?"

A dreamy, faraway look crept over Joanne's unnaturally smooth face. "Oh, yes. Berkley is everything I've ever wanted in a man. Kind, caring, sweet, richer than a sultan, fantastic in bed. He's a very generous lover, the best I've ever had."

I almost swallowed a pin. The woman looked as besotted as a teenager with a movie star. Joanne James truly in love? A scary, scary thought.

"He always makes sure that I'm satisfied, and he does the most marvelous thing with his . . ."

Somehow, I managed to focus on the dress and block out most of the details of Joanne's sex life with Berkley. Those were mental images I definitely did not need.

"Then again, you'd know how important the bedroom is in a relationship, wouldn't you, Fiona?"

"What? What did you say?" I mumbled through a mouthful of pins.

"I'm talking about you and Johnny Bulluci." Joanne gave me a sly look in the mirror. "The two of you looked quite cozy at the observatory benefit last night. Until you disappeared, that is. Tell me, are the waterfall and lake still as beautiful as I remember?"

"I wouldn't know," I replied in an even tone, resisting the urge to stick a sharp pin in Joanne's bony ass.

I'd known we'd be the talk of town after slipping out of the benefit, but Joanne's catty tone still irked me. What I did with Johnny was nobody's business but mine. Especially since I wasn't quite sure what I was doing with Johnny yet. Other than having amazing sex.

"Now, now, Fiona. We're all friends here. Like father, like son."

I shook my head. "I really have no idea what you're talking about."

"I'm talking about the fact that James Bulluci and I used to meet at the observatory, go down to the waterfall, and become otherwise engaged for several hours. I hadn't realized Johnny had taken up his father's bad habits until I saw you two slip away from the party last night."

"You knew Johnny's father?"

"Oh yes. James Bulluci and I were quite the item at one time, although he was several years older than me." Joanne preened. "I was in high school, and he was finishing up his second business degree at Bigtime U when we started dating. He was such a sweet boy. He even gave me his college football ring. I wore it until we broke up shortly before he graduated. I hated to give it back, though."

"Why? Was it covered with diamonds?" I couldn't resist the dig.

"Oh no. It was made out of silver and onyx, if you can believe that. Completely worthless. But it had the most beautiful design of wings on it."

I frowned. Wings? On a college class ring? I flashed back to Johnny's cherub boxers and his silver watch and Bella's necklace. The Bullucis seemed to have a strange fascination with winged, angel-like spirits. One that bordered on obsession. Who knew? Maybe they were the ones who supplied Angel with all his embossed gear.

A vague unease filled me at that odd idea. I couldn't quite put my finger on why connecting Angel to the Bullucis upset me. But it did. For a moment, I felt like Carmen listening to the voices in her head. That couldn't be good.

"James was very, very good with his hands, from what I remember. We spent many hours down by that waterfall skinny-dipping and doing other things . . ."

Joanne chattered on about James Bulluci and his magnificent hands, chasing my stray thought away. I finished pinning up the dress, and Joanne twirled around and looked at the rough copy.

"You've outdone yourself again, Fiona. This will be perfect, absolutely perfect."

It'd come with a perfect price tag too. I'd make sure of that. Joanne slipped out of the dress and back into her suit. She fluffed out her hair and put on a fresh coat of lavender lipstick.

Joanne eyed me in the mirror. "Come on, Fiona. Everybody saw you with Johnny at the benefit. Give me something, some little detail, to share with the girls at the spa."

I stared at Joanne. Then, I smiled. "Like father, like son."

★13★

I finished up with Joanne James and sped home. I was due at the Bulluci manor at eight, leaving me less than two hours to get my fabulous self ready. Of course, I always looked fabulous, but I really wanted to knock Johnny's socks off. Along with the rest of his clothes.

I took a shower and dried my hair in a nanosecond. Then, I paced back and forth through my closet, trying to find the perfect dress to wear, while I scarfed down a couple of bags of key-lime cookies. The gown couldn't be too casual—or too revealing. I wouldn't want to give Bobby Bulluci a heart attack by shoving my cleavage at him à la Erica Songe. Although from the way the old man had worked the crowd at the benefit the other night, maybe I was the one who should watch out. Charm seemed to run in the family, except for Bella, who was far too serious and uptight for her own good.

I decided on a short, sleeveless, silver lamé number with lots of cowgirl-like fringe in strategic places. The requisite stilettos and bag polished off the look, along with large diamond studs and a matching tennis bracelet. Joanne James wasn't the only one who could sparkle like an electrified disco ball when she wanted to.

By the time I was dressed, it was creeping up on seven-thirty. I put the gas pedal to the floor and roared across town in my convertible to the Bulluci manor in record time, traveling fifteen miles through heavy traffic in about ten minutes. Swifte couldn't have done much better himself.

Tires squealing, I took an exit off the interstate and threaded my way through more traffic before pulling onto Lucky Way. Old, twisted Cypress trees and Spanish moss hung over Lucky Way, bathing it in long, soft shadows. Lawns as smooth as carpet led up from the street to some of the priciest homes in Bigtime. We were talking castles here, turrets, moats, and all. Joanne James had a mansion in the area. So did Berkley Brighton, Nate Norris, Wesley Weston, and all the other power players.

I double-checked the address Johnny had given me and turned into a driveway that curled up a steep hill. The wrought-iron gates swung open at my approach. The black pavement curved into a circle that went by the front of the house before looping back around on itself and flowing down the hill. I pulled up to the front steps, got out of the car, and paused to stare at the massive building. I'd been to the mansion a couple of times before during some of Bella's fashion shows, but it still wowed me. It wasn't as large as Sublime, but the house had an old-world feel to it that I admired. The red-tile roof, wide stone arches, and numerous balconies and patios reminded me of a villa on the coast of Italy or Greece. Perhaps Bobby Bulluci had built it to remind himself of his homeland. Either way, the manor had a bright, cheery feel. In the light of day, it would be even more impressive.

A tuxedo-clad butler greeted me at the front door,

crooked his finger, and beckoned me to follow him. We moved deeper into the house, and my eyes roamed over the rich furnishings. In a way, it was exactly like Sublime. Tapestries covered the walls, and statues and other pricey knickknacks clustered in curio cabinets.

But as I looked around, I noticed there was a definite, odd pattern to the finery. Almost every single item had some sort of angel-like figure on it. Fat cherubs smiled from frescoes on the walls. Wings adorned the backs of tall chairs. Miniature halos dangled from a pair of crystal wind chimes. Even the light fixtures looked like marshmallow clouds drifting by. I'd have to ask Johnny about his family's strange obsession.

We reached a massive wooden door. The butler knocked once before pulling it open. My gaze went to the knob, which was shaped like an angel's head, halo and all. It was kind of creepy.

"Miss Fiona Fine." The butler bowed and left the room.

I strode inside. Johnny, Bella, and Bobby sat on a long sofa staring at an enormous plasma-screen television. Soccer players shouted and screamed and slammed into each other on the flickering monitor.

"Johnny. Bella. Bobby."

They echoed my greeting, but Johnny and Bobby's eyes remained glued to the television. I snorted. Men. Bella rose and walked over to me. She wore a shimmering dress of the palest pink imaginable. Despite Joanne James's hatred of it, the color looked wonderful on Bella, and the embroidery on the bodice was exquisite and dainty. I peered closer at the pattern. Tiny angels ran along the high-fitting neckline, and the usual silver angel charm ringed Bella's throat. What was it with these people and angels?

"Sorry about them," Bella said, rolling her eyes at her male relatives. "I told them that you'd be here at eight sharp, but they just had to check out the highlights from today's games. Didn't you, Johnny?" Bella leaned over the couch and mussed her brother's tawny locks.

Johnny swatted her hand away. "Fiona likes soccer too. She completely understands. Don't you, Fiona?"

He looked and sounded like such a little boy that I had to laugh. "Believe me, I understand. My friend Sam never leaves the house without seeing what the latest football and hockey scores are."

After several more loud, jovial, clichéd comments, the sportscaster bid his captivated audience good night, and Johnny clicked off the television. "Now it's over."

Bobby came around the couch and bowed to me. "And now we can properly entertain our lovely, lovely guest." The old man pressed a dry kiss to my hand.

"All right, that's enough of that," Johnny growled in a playful tone. He took my hand away from his grandfather.

"Afraid the old man might be too smooth for you, eh, Johnny boy?" Bobby elbowed his grandson in the ribs and shot me a playful look.

"Of course not," Johnny replied in an even tone. "I not only have my father's charm, I have my mother's good looks as well. No woman can resist the combination."

Bella crossed her arms over her chest. "I don't think Fiona will be as easily swayed as that."

"Oh, I don't know. I think I've made considerable progress so far. We had a wonderful time at the observatory benefit, didn't we, Fiona?" Johnny grinned.

The feel of Johnny's hands, his lips, his tongue on me, in me, flashed through my head. For the first time in a very long time, I blushed. "Yes, we did," I murmured, catching his dancing eyes. "Yes, we did."

Bella looked back and forth between me and her brother,

frowning. She really needed to lighten up. Bobby clapped his hands together.

"Come! Let's eat! I want my steak and wine and chocolate." Bobby beamed at me. "And not necessarily in that order."

"Grandfather . . ." Bella warned.

Bobby pulled himself up to his full height. "We have a guest tonight, Bella. I will not insult her by eating that tasteless gruel the doctor calls food in front of her. The chef has prepared an excellent meal, and we will all dine well tonight."

Bella sighed, giving in to the old man. I didn't envy her. Bobby Bulluci was quite a handful, even if he was on the downhill side of seventy. I put my hand on Johnny's arm, and he escorted me to the dining room. It was a long, narrow room with a long, narrow table that looked like it could seat five hundred people and then some. More tapestries lined the walls, including one that featured more fat, happy cherubs shining their gleaming halos on puffy clouds.

The more I stared at the cherubs, the more I wondered why the Bullucis had so many of them. So, I asked.

"You guys seem to have a thing for angels. Everywhere I turn, there they are. Is your family crest a halo or something?"

Bella's mouth dropped open. Bobby's step faltered. Johnny's arm tensed under my fingertips.

"I'm sorry, did I say something wrong?"

My eyes flicked back and forth among the three of them. What was *that* about? You'd think I'd just uncovered a skeleton in the hall closet or their secret identities as superheroes or something.

Secret identities as superheroes . . . I frowned. I'd seen a lot of angels lately, mostly adorning the clothes and sundry gear of Johnny Angel. Could the Bullucis be connected to him? If so, how? Bobby and Bella certainly weren't the motorcycle rider. And it wasn't like Johnny could actually be Angel . . . could he?

No, I decided. Johnny didn't have Angel's attitude problems. Besides, Johnny hadn't even been in the country until recently, and Angel had been around Bigtime for years. At least, his old incarnation had been. I didn't know how long the new guy had been prowling the streets.

Johnny forced himself to relax. "Of course not. Angels aren't our . . . family crest." He looked at his grandfather. "But we all like them. It's sort of a family . . . tradition to collect them."

"Oh."

I didn't quite believe his explanation, although there was no real reason for me not to. But I decided to let the matter drop. I wasn't as nosy and paranoid as Carmen. I didn't think everyone was harboring a secret identity or wearing a spandex suit underneath his tuxedo. In fact, I didn't really care who was who as long as they stayed out of my way.

We sat down at one end of the table. Servants hustled in, bringing with them tempting dishes that smelled like they'd come down from heaven itself. My stomach rumbled, and I forgot about my unease and suspicions. The bag of cookies was long gone.

"Grilled filet mignon, roasted potatoes, fried zucchini, Italian bread, butter, a Caesar salad, and enough olive oil to grease a car." Bella looked at her grandfather. "Going all out, aren't we?"

Bobby smiled. "Well, I had to make sure we had enough food for our guest. Johnny told me that she has quite the healthy appetite."

Bella's eyes flicked to me. For the second time that evening, I found myself blushing. My stomach gurgled again, this time loud enough for everyone to hear. Bella looked shocked by the grumbling sound, while the men seemed amused.

"Guilty as charged," I said, reaching for the nearest dish.

We spent the next hour dining and making small talk. The Bullucis were a delightful bunch, merry and funny with no hints of the self-importance and pretentiousness that plagued so many on the society circuit. They didn't take themselves or anyone else too seriously. Even Bella loosened up a bit and let me see that she had a dry, biting sense of humor under her by-the-book facade. She was the straight woman who kept the men in line. As much as she could anyway.

But I was most impressed by the food. Everything was just as scrumptious as Bobby had promised it would be. The vegetables were fresh, crisp, and perfectly seasoned. The bread was warm and chewy. And the steak was so tender I could have cut it with a toothpick.

I took big portions of everything and wolfed them down in about fifteen minutes. Then, I went back for seconds. I finished those up about the time the others had washed down their first helpings with a superb bottle of wine. I eyed the platters, wondering if I dared to take any more food. I didn't want to come across as a total glutton. Johnny saw me eyeing the potatoes with barely restrained desire.

"Let me guess. You didn't have breakfast or lunch again today," Johnny said, sliding his half-eaten steak over to me.

I looked down at the juicy, medium-well steak. A man who gave up his food for me? I could get used to this. Quite easily. The thought startled me, but not enough to make me turn down the meat. I stabbed my fork at him. "You guessed it."

So, I ate the rest of his steak.

And the bread.

And the potatoes.

And the wine.

In the end, I gobbled down more than the three of them put together. Bella looked back and forth at me and the now-empty platters. Then, she turned her gaze to her brother. Johnny shrugged. Bella probably thought I had an eating disorder, just like Piper did. I'd probably find more pamphlets on my desk in the morning. Ah, well. The steak alone had been worth it.

More servants appeared to clear the dishes away and present us with a monstrous, three-tiered cake. The flavor came as a bit of a surprise to me, although it really shouldn't have.

It was angel food, of course.

The cake, topped with cherries, chocolate sauce, and whipped cream, was just as wonderful as everything else had been. I ate four big pieces and put my fork down in contentment. Steak and potatoes were wonderful, high-calorie, filling, stick-to-your ribs food. I'd be all right until I got my midnight snack.

"Well, I don't know about you young folks, but this old man is ready for bed," Bobby announced, pushing his chair away from the table. "Too much wine and food make me sleepy these days."

Bella also rose to her feet. "I'll help you, Grandfather." She looked at Johnny and me. "I'm sure Johnny and Fiona would like some time to themselves."

Johnny turned to me. "I'll show you around the house." The devilish glint in his eyes told me that the tour would probably end up in his bedroom. I wasn't sure quite how I felt about that. Other than hot and panting.

Bella and Bobby disappeared up a flight of stairs, while Johnny led me down a series of wide hallways. Strolling through the house was a little like walking through a church. More angels decorated everything from paintings to furniture to even the carpet under our feet.

We reached a hall filled with large oil paintings. Smiling, similar-looking people sat in the portraits, their eyes filled with light and joy. I didn't need Johnny to tell me that I was staring at pictures of the Bullucis through the centuries.

Johnny tugged me down the hall, stopping at a portrait of a middle-aged man on a motorcycle. "This is my father, James. I wasn't sure if you remembered him or not. He wasn't much for the society scene, preferring to concentrate on looking after our business interests. He rarely attended events, preferring to leave that to Bella and Grandfather."

I stared at the picture. Blue eyes. Tan skin. A mane of chestnut hair. James Bulluci had been a handsome man. But the more I looked at the picture, the more it bothered me. There was something else very familiar about James Bulluci. Something in the eyes and the set of his jaw reminded me of—

"And this is my mother, Lucia," Johnny continued, pointing to the next portrait.

My tremulous thought fled. Johnny hadn't been bragging earlier when he'd said he'd inherited his mother's good looks. Blond hair. Green eyes. Fabulous figure. Tawny skin. Lucia Bulluci was a goddess in mortal form.

"Funny, I don't remember her either," I said, staring at the picture.

"She died when I was a teenager," Johnny said. Sadness colored his voice, a sadness I recognized.

"My mother died when I was young too," I said, squeezing his hand.

"What about your father? You don't talk about him much."

I hesitated. I couldn't tell Johnny who my father really

was, but I didn't want to deceive him either. "Oh, he's . . . around. His work takes up a lot of his time, and we don't see as much of each other as we'd like."

It wasn't a complete lie. The only times I got to see the chief these days were when we went out as Fiera and Mr. Sage to do battle with Bigtime's ubervillains or braved the society crowd at the latest benefit.

"What does he do for a living?"

"He's in, ah, security." Another half-truth.

"Like a bodyguard?"

"Sort of." Did protecting the citizens of Bigtime from ubervillains qualify you to be a bodyguard? I supposed it did.

"What's his name?"

Finally, an easy one. "Sean."

"Sean? That's very Irish."

I laughed. "We're a very Irish sort of family. My mother's name was Finola."

"Irish, huh? Does that mean if I kiss you, I'll have good luck for the rest of the year?"

I tossed my hair over my shoulder. "I don't know about having good luck in the future, but you just might get lucky tonight."

"Well, then, let's test your theory out right now," he murmured.

Johnny dipped his head forward and kissed me. His lips felt like liquid fire on my own. I opened my mouth, and Johnny darted his tongue inside. He tasted like chocolate and wine, and his spicy scent filled my nostrils. Yummy.

Johnny eased me up against the wall. We kept kissing, our tongues moving back and forth. I raised one leg around his waist. Johnny's sure, confident hands moved up and down my body. Kneading. Caressing. Sculpting. He moved from my breasts to my stomach down to the junction between my thighs. I hissed as he stroked me through my silken panties, and a warm, heavy wetness pooled between my legs.

"Would you care to continue the tour? Say, upstairs?" Johnny nibbled on the side of my neck.

Tingles of pleasure shot through me. My neck was *very* sensitive. I dug my fingers into his hair and pulled him closer. "Is that where your bedroom is?"

"Mmm-hmm." Johnny continued to kiss my neck as one hand cupped my breast. "So what do you say?"

Breathless, I couldn't speak. I raised his head and stared in his shimmering green eyes. I opened my mouth to respond, but Johnny swooped in and cut me off with another hot kiss.

Then, the worst thing in the world happened.

My cell phone rang.

★ 14 ★

"That's becoming a rather annoying habit of yours," Johnny said, his lips still touching mine.

"Sorry," I muttered. "It's one I'm trying to break."

Johnny stepped back and dropped his hands. I bit my lip. All worked up and no relief in sight. The things I gave up for my city. Stupid superhero duty.

I dug through my purse, grabbed my phone, and snapped it open. "What *is* it, Henry? I'm right in the middle of something."

"We've got a lead on Siren and Intelligal," Henry replied, not the least bit put off by my fierce growl. He'd long ago grown used to it. "We're heading out soon to see if we can track them down and stop them. The chief wants you here ten minutes ago."

I stared at Johnny, who leaned forward and pressed another kiss to my neck. I closed my eyes. Mmm. "Do I have to?" Whining just a bit.

"Well, you don't *have* to, of course," Henry replied. "We could go after the ubervillains by ourselves. But since you're the strongest and since we're down two members, it might be a good idea for you to come in. You do have the most fire-power, after all."

I snorted. "Firepower? You've been hanging around Lulu too long."

"I have not," Henry snapped back. "And you should be nicer to her, Fiona. If I get my way, Lulu will be part of the team permanently."

I narrowed my eyes. Permanently? I didn't like the sound of that. What was up with Henry and the computer hacker? "What do you mean by that?"

"None of your business at the moment. Now, are you coming in or not?" he asked.

Johnny's hand slipped under my short skirt and started creeping upward. He stroked my thigh. For a moment, I couldn't speak.

"I'll be there as soon as I can." I snapped the phone shut.

"Let me guess. Henry has more problems at the store." Johnny arched an eyebrow.

"Unfortunately."

"Perhaps you should think about getting another night manager. He always seems to call you at the most inappropriate moments," Johnny said.

"You're telling me. I'm sorry I have to go, Johnny. I was having a fabulous time." Regret tinged my voice. It had been wonderful spending the evening with Johnny and his family. And then being alone afterward with the man himself.

"I know, and I understand. But since you have to leave, we should make the most of this brief time we have together, shouldn't we?"

Johnny flashed me a wicked, wanton grin and sank to his knees in front of me. Johnny stroked my thighs with his fingers. I gasped at the sensation.

"Tell me to stop, and I will," he said in a quiet voice.

I couldn't say a word, and I didn't want to. For a moment, Travis's face flashed through my mind. Then, Johnny moved his hand, and the image disappeared.

"Go ahead." My voice was thick and husky with passion, desire, need.

Before I knew what he was doing, Johnny had pushed my skirt up and my panties down. I stepped out of the filmy lace and kicked them down the hall. Johnny hooked one of my long legs over his shoulder. Then, he leaned forward and put his mouth on me.

Licking. Tasting. Teasing. Driving me insane.

I dug my hands into his shoulders. "Johnny!" Begging him to stop. Wanting him to go on.

Johnny chose to think of my strangled cry as one of encouragement. He quickened his pace, his tongue probing deeper and deeper with every sure stroke, as though he wanted to lick his way to the very core of me. Liquid desire flowed like thick lava through my veins. Pressure built deep in my stomach. My whole body trembled.

And then—

An eruption of epic proportions. But in a good way.

I just stood there, wrapped in the soft blanket of sexual bliss. Afterglow, people called it. I felt as warm and fuzzy as a fleece blanket that had just tumbled out of the dryer.

"Wow!" That was all I could say.

"I aim to please," Johnny said, rising to his feet. "Again . . . and again . . . and again . . ." He planted more kisses on my throat. His tongue flicked over my rapid, throbbing pulse.

"I have to go," I said in a weak tone, even as I drew him closer.

We kissed long and slow and deep. Johnny's hands moved up and down my body. I kneaded his back, his chest, his abdomen with my grasping fingers. I wanted to touch him. All of him. Over and over again until we were both sweaty, satisfied, and utterly spent. And then some. But Johnny had other ideas.

"Oh, I think we have a little more time left," he said, grinning.

Johnny went down on his knees again.

It was close to midnight by the time I reached the underground garage at Sublime and parked my convertible next to one of the Fearless Five vans. It'd been almost half an hour since I'd left Johnny, and I couldn't stop smiling. I'd even been humming on the drive across town. Humming! I never hummed. Superheroes did *not* hum.

I made my way to the equipment room and changed into my orange red Fiera outfit. I felt good tonight, charged, pumped up. Like I could take on Siren and Intelligal with one hand tied behind my back. And it was all thanks to Johnny. Oh, the things that man could do with his tongue . . .

A loud squawk sounded, cutting through my sexual daydreams.

"Fiona, are you almost ready? You've been in there almost twenty minutes." The chief's voice cracked over the underground intercom system.

"Coming."

Since my dinner had been burned away by my time with Johnny, I stopped by the kitchen, made myself ten tomato-and-cheese sandwiches, and grabbed a two-liter soda before heading to the library. The others waited inside.

"Hello, all," I said in a cheery tone. "Ready to go kick some ubervillain ass?"

They just stared at me.

"What?" I asked. "What's wrong? Why are you all looking at me like that?"

The chief cleared his throat. "You're glowing, Fiona."

I looked down. Sure enough, a soft, orangey glow enveloped my entire body. I hadn't even noticed it, and I was pretty good about keeping my flare-ups in check. Even when I let myself go, most of the time I emanated more of an angry red. I glowed orange only when I was extremely relaxed or very, very happy. I was both right now.

"Well, well, someone must have gotten lucky tonight," Lulu drawled. "Did we have a *hot* date, Fiona?"

I narrowed my eyes at the computer hacker. A spark flew from my fingertip. My orange glow took on a reddish tint. One day I was going to get her for those stupid heat-related puns. One day soon . . .

My father cleared his throat again.

But not today. Too many witnesses around. So instead of frying Lulu from the inside out, I tossed my hair back.

"As I matter of fact, I did have a *hot date* tonight. Unlike you two. Let me guess. You've been sitting here all night pounding away on your keyboards trying to track down ubervillains. Is that your idea of a good time, or are the two of you still not over your tiff from the benefit?"

Lulu's lips tightened into a thin line. Henry stopped typing. The two of them looked at me, then each other, then back at their computers. I stared at my father. He shook his head, his way of telling me not to butt in. I glared at him. Lulu had just shoved her way into my business, but I couldn't get a little get-back? *So* not fair.

I learned long ago there was only one thing to do when life wasn't fair. So, I marched over to the table with its *F5* insignia, put my feet up, cracked open my soda, and started eating my melted-cheese-and-tomato sandwiches.

★15★

While I polished off my midnight snack, Henry and Lulu used one of their umpteen computer programs to pinpoint Siren and Intelligal's exact location. Surprise, surprise, the ubervillains were holed up in another dilapidated warehouse. This time, though, they were near the downtown area. So, we loaded up the van, exited the garage, and headed toward Bigtime.

We'd just gotten on the interstate when Lulu frowned.

"Uh-oh," she said.

"What?" I asked. "What's wrong now?"

"SNN just cut into their charity benefit. Halitosis Hal and Pistol Pete were engaging in a mock fight to raise money for the children's hospital. Pete would fire his pistol at Hal, but his breath would stop the bullets in midair. Funny stuff."

"But now . . ." I prompted.

"They're live at the construction site where the city's building the new sports complex. The whole thing's collapsed."

Lulu stared at her laptop. "Kelly Caleb's on the scene. She's saying that Swifte got trapped inside while he was trying to rescue some of the construction crew."

"Why is a construction crew working on a building after midnight?" I asked.

"It's a city contract, and the sports complex is two months behind schedule due to the snow we had this winter. They've been working round-the-clock shifts for the last six weeks to try to get back on track," Mr. Sage said. "Is anyone else on the scene besides Swifte? Anyone providing security or backup for him?"

Lulu shook her head. "Not yet. The police, fire, and rescue squads are there, but no other superheroes." She hesitated. "It looks pretty bad."

She turned the laptop around to us. The skeleton dome of the sports complex had folded in on itself, like a deck of cards knocked over by a gust of wind. Hoarse screams and shouts could be heard over Kelly Caleb's clipped voice. Sirens flashed blue and red in the distance, while dust drifted through the air, obscuring the camera's view. Lulu was right. It looked bad.

I stared at my father. His face was smooth, but his eyes glowed neon green. He was reaching out with his psychic powers, trying to tap into people's vibrations, emotions, fears. "It is bad. The worst accident we've had in some time. Turn around, Hermit. We need to go help."

"What about Siren and Intelligal?" I asked.

"They'll have to wait," Mr. Sage said. "This is more important. Agreed?"

I'd been looking forward to getting another chance to wrap my hands around Siren's scrawny neck and squeeze until her head popped off her overinflated body. But I'd just have to settle for moving rocks around and saving sweaty construction guys instead. It wasn't a bad trade-off. "Agreed."

Hermit whipped a U-turn, and we headed back toward the collapsed building. You could see the smoke and dust miles away, billowing into the night sky like a mushroom cloud.

"Hermit?" Mr. Sage asked.

"I know," he answered. "Step on it."

Hermit's hands tightened around the wheel, and we made it to the construction site in less than seven minutes. He might be unnaturally fond of computers, but Hermit could drive when he put his mind to it. I thought it was one of his most useful skills.

We stopped the van in a dark alley about two blocks from the construction site. Lulu outfitted us with two-way earpieces and turned on the cameras in our suits. Once we were set up, Hermit, Mr. Sage, and I jogged over to the scene, while Lulu stayed in the van to monitor us and the news channels.

People were everywhere, like ants running around a pool of hot honey. They crowded into the streets, climbed onto parked cars, and hung out apartment windows high above to get a better view of the action. They chattered like magpies, their voices building to a cacophony of high-pitched, excited sound.

I plowed into the crush, trying to clear a path. "Excuse me, excuse me, coming through. Now. Move, please. Thank you." I kept up a steady stream of patter as I zinged people with hot flashes to get them out of the way.

Finally, though, someone took notice of us.

"Look! It's Fiera!"

"And Mr. Sage and Hermit!"

"The Fearless Five are here!"

Claps, cheers, and whistles sounded. People got the message and stepped aside to let us by. I smiled and shot a few sparks off my fingertips, my signature move. Folks roared in response. It was always nice to be recognized. That was another perk of being a superhero. People knew you wherever you went, and you never had to wait in line for anything.

A woman darted through an opening in the crowd and clutched at my arm. "Please! Please! You've got to help them! My husband is trapped in there!"

I'm used to such tearful pleas. I've heard thousands of them during my time as a superhero. But the raw panic in her eyes touched my heart. I'd felt the same way about Travis aka Tornado every time he'd gone out on a mission. Panicked and worried and slightly crazed.

"I'll do my best, ma'am." I patted her arm, careful not to burn her, and gently shook off her hand.

The three of us made our way to the police barricade, where the esteemed members of the press waited. My eyes scanned over the crowd, and I spotted reporters from the *Chronicle*, the *Exposé*, and of course, SNN. Word of our arrival had already spread, because Kelly Caleb was ready and waiting for us. She shoved her microphone in my face the second we approached the cops. The white lights of her television camera cranked up like headlights in my face. I squinted against the blinding glare.

"Fiera! Fiera! Have you come to help? What's the status of the trapped workers? Do you think you're too late already?"

"Later, Kelly," I snapped and kept moving. Unlike Swifte, I didn't have time to give interviews *before* I saved people.

Besides, reporters were always so difficult. Why couldn't they just leave us alone to do our jobs? Public's right to know, my ass. All the public needed to know was that I would do my superhero duty—to protect and serve—no matter what.

We went around the police barricade and entered the construction site, which was cordoned off from the street by a metal chain-link fence topped with razor wire. Cranes and bulldozers and backhoes sat behind the fence, along with tin trailers, cement mixers, trucks, and portable toilets.

Police, fire, and other emergency rescue officials hovered around the back of a pickup truck, where a beefy guy with a dirt-covered face sat. His arm was in a makeshift sling, and cuts and bruises dotted his bulging body. He looked like he'd just barely escaped the collapse himself, but he was busy looking at several papers.

The police let us through, just like they always did, and Mr. Sage headed straight for Beefcake.

"What's the situation, sir?" Mr. Sage asked in a calm, but strong voice.

Some of the tension dribbled out of the cluster of people around us. That was my father for you. He could calm down a hurricane if he wanted to. He'd done it many times before.

"I'm Jim, the foreman. I was overseeing the night shift when she came down. Scariest thing I've ever lived through." His eyes flicked to the destroyed building.

"Any idea what caused the collapse?" Hermit asked, punching some buttons on his handheld computer. No doubt he was accessing the building's blueprints, looking for structural weak spots and the like.

"Not a clue." Jim hesitated. "But right before she came down, I heard this . . . sound. Sort of like purring or something. It was the oddest thing."

Some of the policemen chuckled. A few meowed. The foreman shot them angry stares.

"Well, that's what it sounded like to me," he growled.

"Instead of just standing around, why don't you boys in blue get in gear and get my folks out?"

That shut the cops up real quick. I gave Jim an encouraging nod.

"Please. Let us offer our assistance," Mr. Sage cut in.

Jim nodded. "I've been going over the blueprints. We've got some folks in sector two." The foreman pointed to the area in question. "Swifte arrived about two minutes after she went down, but more of the building gave way and sealed off the entrance. He went in there, but he hasn't come back out. Neither has anyone else."

"All right," Mr. Sage said. "The first thing we need to do is shore up that section so it won't cave in on us when we go in. Fiera, you move the big pieces out of the way. I'll use my telekinesis to help and make sure that everything doesn't come falling down on you."

I nodded. Standard operating procedure. This wasn't the first collapsed building we'd seen in Bigtime. We'd run into and dug our way out of more than a few ourselves.

"Let me help too," a cool voice cut through the air.

I snapped my head around. Johnny Angel stood behind us, looking like his usual badass self in his shiny black leather.

"What are you doing here?" I snapped. "I thought you were busy with your vengeance mission. Shouldn't you be plotting ways to run down ubervillains with your bike?"

"I heard about the collapse on television. I just want to help," he said in a quiet, defensive tone.

"Us too," a pair of feminine voices chimed in.

My eyes darted over the crowd. I couldn't see them, but I knew they were there. Finally, I spotted two pairs of footprints in the dirt about ten feet away. I squinted and could just make out the faint outline of two curvy figures. It was like I was looking at something through cloudy water.

"The Invisible Ingénues. It's been a while since we've seen you girls." I'd been hanging around Lulu too long. I just couldn't seem to stop with the bad puns.

"Oh, we've been around . . ."

"Just like always."

The Ingénues were sisters who had a strange habit of finishing each other's sentences. I'd wondered more than once if they were joined at the hip. I couldn't tell, though, since they were invisible.

I looked at Hermit, who shrugged. I turned to Mr. Sage. His eyes glowed for half a second, and he nodded.

"All right, Angel, Ingénues," Mr. Sage said. "We can use all the help we can get. Let's move, people."

Jim told us a few more pertinent details. Some of his folks had called in sick, and he'd been working with a skeleton crew. "There were thirteen of us inside when she went down. Me and five others made it out. That leaves seven, plus Swifte."

Once we got all the information we could from Jim, we stepped through the police barricade and approached the building. The sports center—what was left of it—looked like a doll's house that had been upset by a child's angry tantrum. Steel beams as thick as my body stuck up at weird angles. Bricks, concrete blocks, wires, cables, and more spilled down from the towering heap of metal. Every once in a while, something deep inside the structure would moan and creak and groan.

"Right here," Hermit said. "That's where the entrance was."

Steel beams and pieces of building the size of small cars covered the exit. Nothing I couldn't handle. I cracked my knuckles and did a few stretches to limber up. It was always important to stretch before undertaking big tasks. I might be a superhero, but I could still blow out my knee or tear my biceps.

"Which side do you want, Ingénues?"

Like most superheroes, the girls had some muscle on them, especially when they worked together.

"We'll take . . ."

"The left side."

"Good. I've got the right then."

I looked over my shoulder, making sure no one was behind me so they wouldn't get hit by the boulders I was about to toss back. Then, I went to work.

So did Johnny Angel. In addition to having a superhard exoskeleton, Angel was stronger than average. After twenty minutes, the four of us had cleared a space big enough for a couple of people to walk through. I peered into the darkness. More beams lay inside crisscrossed over each other like the teeth of a zipper. Whoever went in would have to be very, very careful. It would be worse than walking through a maze of razor wire—one that could come down on your head and crush you at any moment.

"It might work better if Fiera and I went inside together. She can hold up the roof and move things as needed, while I drag the people out," Angel suggested. "As long as I keep concentrating on my exoskeleton, the debris won't hurt me."

Mr. Sage peered into the dark hole. "You're right. Hermit and I will stay here with the Ingénues and monitor the building from the outside. I'll use my telekinesis to try to steady some of the structural points. Be careful. Both of you."

I pressed my fist to my heart. Mr. Sage and Hermit did the same. The Ingénues had seen the salute before, but Angel stared at us. Curiosity glimmered in his eyes.

I turned to him. "All right, Angel. Follow me."

I took a deep breath and stepped inside the collapsed building.

The inside was even worse than the outside. The main support beams had crumpled in on each other like cheap tinfoil. Dust hung in the air like a wet blanket, and debris littered the uneven ground. Rocks slid and shifted under our feet with every step we took. It would have been safer to walk through a minefield, but we plunged inside anyway. We had to. People were counting on us. I wrapped myself in flames to light the way, careful not to burn too bright, so I wouldn't ignite whatever gas or chemicals might be in the air.

I didn't have many fears, but being in a small, unstable space was one of them. I could feel the weight of the building hovering over my head. All that metal. All that steel. All that concrete. Just waiting to come crashing down and bury me forever. It reminded me of the unbreakable glass tube I'd been stuck in last year when the others and I had been captured by the Terrible Triad. I'd felt the tube pressing in on me in the exact same manner. I panted for air.

"Just take deep breaths," Angel said, touching my arm. "It'll help."

I stiffened, hating myself for letting my nervousness show. Still, the feel of his hand reminded me that I wasn't alone in this. And that there were eight people somewhere in here that were in much worse shape than me. I had a duty to help them. I couldn't afford to chicken out now.

I drew in a breath and let it out slowly. My nerves steadied.

"Fiera, turn left. According to the heat-sensing camera in your suit, there's a thermal image about a hundred yards ahead of you," Hermit's voice crackled in my ear.

"Copy that." I jerked my head at Angel. "This way."

We eased through the metal maze. Ten yards in, twenty, fifty, a hundred. I upped the dimmer on my body and peered into the darkness, trying to see something, anything that resembled a human form. A flash of shimmering white caught my eye. "Swifte!"

I eased over to the superhero. Now I knew why he hadn't made it back out of the building. Two metal beams had crashed down on him. One lay on his leg, the other on his back. His costume was torn in several places, and blood blackened the dirt under his body. For a moment, I thought he was unconscious or maybe even dead, but Swifte turned his head to stare at my boots.

"Hey, Swifte. What's shaking?" I asked.

The superfast superhero grinned into the dirt. "Not much at the moment." His voice was raspy and strained. The beam must be pressing down on his lungs, making it hard for him to breathe.

"You know, I've never seen you like this before. Usually, you just zip in and zip out of these situations," I said, being my usual bitchy self to lighten the mood.

He shrugged. Or at least, he tried to. He got about halfway there before stopping in pain. "Normally, I do. But it's a little more difficult when there's a thousand beams raining down on you at once."

"Well, hold still. We're going to get you out of here."

Swifte shook his head an inch. "Get the others out first. I'm all right." He grimaced.

"Are you sure?" Angel asked. "Because you look pretty messed up to me, man."

"Get the others out first," Swifte wheezed. "They're only a couple hundred yards up ahead."

"Noble to the end, huh, Swifte?" I asked.

"Just doing my job, Fiera. Just doing my job."

I could respect that. While we talked, I heard the sound of buttons being punched in my ear.

"Swifte's right. I've got more images about two hundred yards farther in," Hermit said.

"All right. We're going to get the others out. But we'll be back for you in a few minutes. Okay, Swifte?"

The superhero chuckled. "Of course. Unfortunately, I'm not going anywhere at the moment."

I nodded to Angel. "Let's go."

Hermit guided us through the remains of the ruined building. It was slowgoing, but ten minutes later, we stumbled onto the rest of the construction crew. They huddled together in a space about the size of a large desk that was amazingly free of debris. Other than cuts and scrapes, a few broken bones, and having a decade or so scared out of them, the men and women were in remarkably good shape. Somebody upstairs had been smiling on them tonight.

Angel surprised me again. One by one, he pulled the men and women to their feet. He spoke to them in soft, soothing tones and guided them back through the metal maze. If I hadn't known better, I would have thought that Johnny Angel was one of Bigtime's finest superheroes. I stayed behind to help calm the others while they waited for their turn. Every other minute, the building creaked and shrieked like a tree caught in a hurricane, but it stayed up, thanks to my father and his mind of steel.

Angel put his arm around the last construction crew member, and the three of us headed back to Swifte. I picked up the beams pinning down the speedy superhero, and Angel pulled Swifte out from under them. The superhero's suit was in tatters, and blood stained the opalescent fabric a dark scarlet. A long, deep gash decorated his right thigh where shrapnel had cut into him. I winced. Blood didn't bother me, but Swifte's wound looked nasty and painful.

"I don't think you'll be running any marathons anytime soon," Angel said, staring at the superhero's leg.

"That's what you think," Swifte said.

He took a step as though to dart away. I caught him before he smacked into the ground.

"Easy, big boy," I said. "There'll be plenty of time to disappear on us later."

Swifte mumbled something under his breath.

"You're welcome," I replied.

I picked up Swifte and carried him outside, while Angel took care of the construction guy. The four of us emerged from the building, and the crowd erupted into wild, happy cheers. Cameras flashed. Sirens sounded. People whistled and clapped and yelled until they were hoarse. The roar was deafening.

I put Swifte down in the back of an ambulance and struck my best, classic superhero pose. Hands on hips, stomach in, breasts out. The crowd cheered even louder. I smiled and shot more sparks off my fingertips. A little good press never hurt anyone. There were so many heroes in Bigtime these days it was hard to stand out from the crowd.

A couple of paramedics came over to treat Swifte. Mr. Sage and Hermit moved to stand beside me.

Mr. Sage put a hand on my shoulder. "Good work, Fiera."

"Thanks, Dad," I said in a soft voice only he could hear.

My gaze went to the people we'd pulled from the rubble. I stared at the worried husbands and wives who hovered over their injured spouses as the paramedics checked them out. I thought of Travis. He would have loved to have been part of such a successful rescue. But he wasn't here. And he would never be again.

But the thought didn't make me feel as empty, as hollow inside, as it usually did. I could remember the good times now, instead of just the aching pain of Travis's loss. I knew Johnny Bulluci had a great deal to do with that.

Speaking of Johnnies, I drifted over to Angel, who was standing next to his motorcycle smoking a cigarette. I didn't really want to say *thank you*, especially to someone who'd threatened to kill us if we got in the way of his pursuit of Siren and Intelligal. But I had to. My silly superhero honor wouldn't let me not do it. "Thanks for helping me out in there. I don't do so well in tiny spaces."

"No problem. I'm glad you let me help." Angel's eyes wandered over to the construction crew members, who were hugging and kissing their weeping spouses and children. "We did a good thing tonight."

"Yes, we did."

We exchanged a smile, in sync for once. Angel turned and got on his motorcycle.

Something clinked, and a spot of silver on the black pavement caught my eye.

"Hey, wait! You dropped your watch." I leaned down, picked up the silver watch, and turned it over so I could see what time it was. It had to be almost three in the morning by now—

I froze.

A pair of silver angel wings decorated the watch's black face. I recognized it immediately. It was the same watch Siren and Intelligal had stolen at Carmen's wedding. The same watch I'd handed back to Johnny Bulluci.

Johnny Bulluci.

Johnny Angel.

My eyes flew to his face. And I knew they were one and the same.

"Thanks," he said, taking the watch from my sparking fingers. "I'd hate to lose this."

Angel snapped the timepiece around his wrist and gave me a mock salute. Then, he fired up his motorcycle and rumbled away into the night.

All I could do was stare at his retreating form.

PART TWO

The Honeymoon's Over

★ 16 ★

After shaking hands with everyone, working the crowd, and reluctantly giving interviews to reporters from SNN and the two newspapers in town, the *Chronicle* and the *Exposé*, we piled into the van and headed back to Sublime.

The others chattered about the rescue and wondered who or what could have brought down the massive sports complex. I sat in the back and stared out the tinted windows. Brooding.

Johnny Bulluci was Johnny Angel. I was still trying to figure out what it meant. How I felt about it. The guy I'd been having a hot fling with was actually a . . . a what? He wasn't a hard-core ubervillain like Malefica, but Angel was no, well, angel. At least, his last incarnation hadn't been.

Johnny's anger over his father's death. Angel's vow of revenge on Siren and Intelligal for killing his predecessor. All those freaking angels in the Bulluci mansion. I hated to admit it, but Carmen was right. We superheroes weren't the brightest bunch when it came to disguising our real identities.

I could have firebombed myself for not seeing Angel's real identity sooner. Say, before I'd gone and slept with him.

"You're awful quiet, Fiona," the chief said in his thick brogue. "Is something wrong?"

"I'm just tired." I was tired. And cranky. And famished. Not to mention the shock I'd just received.

"Well, I don't want to pry, but if you want to talk about it, I'm here for you."

Grateful that he wasn't going to read my mind tonight, I nodded and returned to my brooding.

I crashed in my underground suite at Sublime and didn't get up until almost four the next afternoon. I hadn't slept well. In my dreams, Johnny Bulluci had kept morphing into Johnny Angel and back again until I couldn't tell where one man started and the other ended. Not the most pleasant dream to have about your lover. Especially when you moonlighted as a superhero who was supposed to fight crime, and your honey was out to kill a couple of uber-villains, no matter what. And it was your responsibility to stop bad things like murders from taking place, no matter how much someone might deserve it.

Grumbling, I got out of bed, showered, and went to the kitchen. I wolfed down five pizzas, three hamburgers, a twelve-pack of soda, two chocolate cheesecakes, an apple pie, and three gallons of vanilla ice cream. I always ate more when I was angry or upset. Johnny's secret identity was more than enough to make me both.

After polishing off my late lunch, I went to the library looking for Henry. I wanted him to get me all the information on Johnny Bulluci that he could find. I opened the double doors and stopped short. Instead of Henry, Lulu sat inside the spacious room. The fan in her laptop whirred to life at my arrival.

"Oh, you're here—" I started to say *again*, but I caught myself.

"Nice to see you too, Fiona," Lulu replied.

"Where are the others?"

Lulu typed a few buttons on her computer. "The chief had some big city meeting he had to go to about the collapse of the sports complex. Evidently, the powers that be want to know why it happened and how much it's going to cost to clean it up and get the project back on track."

No big shock there. Assessing the damage was the first thing the Bigtime city government did the morning after accidents like last night's incident. They set aside one morning a week to devote to all the buildings, cars, and streetlights the city's superheroes and ubervillains destroyed. Epic battles might have been bad for the historic structures in the city, but they kept the local construction companies in business. There was always a building boom of one kind or another in Bigtime.

"And Henry?" He was the one I was really interested in at the moment.

"He's down at the Complete Computer Company trying out some new microprocessor for his technology column in the newspaper. He won't be back until late tonight."

Damn. Where was the computer geek when I needed him? There was nothing I could do about it, though, short of calling Henry and demanding that he torpedo his job to help me. I knew from past experience that wouldn't work. For some strange reason, Henry actually liked his crummy day job at the *Exposé*. He would play hooky from work only if one of the Fearless Five was in mortal danger—or his precious computer was about to explode.

I sat down in my usual seat at the F5 table and drummed my fingers on the top. Sparks flew everywhere, adding more scars to the scorched wood. My stomach rumbled. Lunch was gone already.

"Do you need something, Fiona?" Lulu asked.

"Why do you ask?"

"Because you look just like Carmen did when she was hot on the trail of a superhero she was about to expose. All tense and twitchy and bothered."

Being compared to Carmen aka Karma Girl Cole didn't help my sour mood. But I stopped drumming my fingers. Lulu would find out about Johnny when I told Henry and the chief. I might as well tell her what I wanted and get the information now. I didn't want to wait a second longer than necessary to get the goods on Johnny Bulluci. I wasn't good at waiting. Patience was something else I'd never seen the virtue in.

"I need everything you can dig up on Johnny Bulluci."

Lulu arched an eyebrow. "Why is that? Is he your new honey?"

"Yes, he's my new honey," I snarled.

"Mmm-hmm." Lulu shot me a coy look. "So that's who had you all *hot and bothered* last night."

I rolled my eyes at her obvious pun. "Yes, that's who had me all *hot and bothered* last night. But there's more to it than that."

"Sure there is," Lulu smirked.

She was getting on my last nerve, so I did my best to shut her up. "Oh, there's a lot more to it. I'm pretty sure he's really Johnny Angel. You know, the guy who rides around on the motorcycle? The one who threatened to kill us?"

Lulu stopped typing. Her head snapped up. "No way!"

"Way."

I told her everything. About Johnny's anger over his father's death, the family obsession with angels, the watch. All of it.

Lulu let out a low whistle. "So you've been getting hot 'n' heavy with the guy who's vowed to destroy Siren and Intelligal, and the Fearless Five if you get in his way."

I shot my finger at her. "You've got it."

"And I thought I had problems," Lulu muttered.

My eyes narrowed. "What do you mean by that? What's going on with you and Henry?"

Lulu looked at her computer screen and refused to meet my hot, searching gaze.

"Oh come on," I snapped. "I spilled to you, now you spill to me. I won't laugh, if that's what you're worried about." At least, I'd try not to.

"Henry asked me to marry him," Lulu said in a soft tone.

Straight arrow, geek-to-the-max Henry aka Hermit Harris had proposed marriage to one of the most notorious computer hackers in Bigtime. A woman who could expose us with a click of her mouse. Fabulous. Just fabulous.

"When?"

"Three weeks ago."

I thought back. "Wasn't that the weekend you guys went to that big ubergeek conference in Gotham?"

Lulu glared at me. "It was not an ubergeek conference. It was a computer symposium about Internet security."

I snorted. "Like there's a difference."

"Anyway," Lulu continued with her story. "We stayed at this quaint little bed-and-breakfast just outside the city and went to the conference during the day. One night when we came back to the room, everything was covered in rose petals. There were flowers and champagne. Henry had hidden the ring in a chocolate cake. He had it made in the shape of a laptop. It was so romantic." Lulu's eyes went all soft and dreamy.

Rose petals? Champagne? A ring hidden in a computer-shaped chocolate cake? Henry was more of a romantic than I'd given him credit for. In a completely geeky sort of way.

"Well, that's wonderful, isn't it?"

My voice didn't come out too strangled. I, of course, thought Henry was making a terrible mistake, just like I'd thought Sam had been making a terrible mistake when he'd started boinking Carmen when the Terrible Triad was after us. But I forced myself to be polite. For once. For Henry's sake.

Lulu stared at me like I'd just said the dumbest thing in the world. Maybe I had. A superhero and a computer hacker? Not a good combo.

"Look at me, Fiona. I'm in a wheelchair, in case it's escaped your notice. It's not all hearts and flowers, you know."

"So? Lots of people are in wheelchairs. It doesn't seem to bother Henry any, so why should it bother you?"

Lulu sighed and pushed a wisp of black and blue hair out of her face. "You wouldn't understand."

"Is it because of sex?" In relationships, just about everything came back to sex in the end. Sex or money. Or both. "The two of you do have sex, don't you?"

"Of course we have sex," she snapped. "Just because I'm in a wheelchair doesn't mean I don't have needs. That Henry doesn't have needs. In fact, Henry and I have sex quite frequently—"

I held my hand up. "Don't tell me. I don't need the mental image of you two supernerds going at it. It's bad enough Carmen and Sam do the nasty in every corner of the manor imaginable. I don't want to hear about anyone else or I'll never be able to sit on the furniture again. So if sex isn't the problem, what is?"

Lulu stared at her still legs. "I'm not just paralyzed. I can't have kids either," she mumbled.

"What?" I asked, straining to hear her. "What did you say?"

"I can't have kids. I can't marry Henry because I can't have kids. There. I've told you what's wrong. Are you happy now?" Tears shimmered in Lulu's dark eyes.

"So what?"

Her mouth gaped open. "So what?"

I shrugged. "So what? So you can't have kids. Lots of women and men can't have kids. Besides, do the two of you even want kids right now? Aren't you a little young for that? You're not even thirty yet."

"No, we don't want kids *right now*. But someday we would, and I can't give them to Henry." More tears puddled in her eyes, threatening to spill down her ivory cheeks.

"You could always adopt," I pointed out. "There are lots of great kids out there that need a good home."

Lulu shook her head. "It wouldn't be the same."

"Why the hell not?"

Lulu stared at me as if the answer should be obvious. I was getting rather tired of that look. I wasn't a mind reader like my father was. I couldn't discern someone's innermost thoughts with a single, soul-searing gaze. Beat it out of them, yes. Fry them alive? Always. But glean pertinent information with a quick look? No, not so much.

"Because of Henry's power."

"What does Henry's power have to do with you not being able—Ah." The lightbulb switched on inside my head. "If you can't have kids, then Henry couldn't pass his mind-melding power on to the next generation of Lo-Harrises."

"Bingo. If we adopted a kid one day, we'd love her to death, but she wouldn't have Henry's power."

"But you don't even know that Henry's kid would get his power anyway. Or that it would manifest in the same way. Sometimes, these things skip a couple of generations."

My father and I were a prime example. It had been my mother and her fiery temper that had influenced my power, not my father's calm sensibility. Johnny and James Bulluci were another pair that proved my point. Johnny had a power his father had probably never dreamed of. But that's what happened when you battled ubervillains on a regular basis. The villains always seemed to live in the nastiest places, surrounded by acres of radioactive waste. The goo wasn't good for your skin or hair—or for your genes. More than one hero had her powers altered by being exposed to radioactive waste over the years. And if it didn't get you, then it would more than likely get your kids and change them in some way—either good or bad.

"I don't think Henry would care about whether or not his kid had powers. He'd love him or her just the same."

Lulu shook her head. "I've run the numbers. There's a good chance the kid would either have Henry's power or some other manifestation of it. I don't want to take that chance, that opportunity, away from Henry."

Run the numbers? Lulu was making decisions about her love life based on some statistics a computer program had spit out. How romantic.

The other woman eyed me. "Haven't you ever thought about having kids? About passing your powers on? Isn't that what you would want?"

I thought about it. I'd been a fire-starting hellion when I was a kid. Everyone on the street where we'd lived in Ireland had thought that I was an arsonist and hopped up on steroids. Only the fact that my father was a policeman had kept me out of juvenile detention. Even as a kid, I had a tendency to beat up bullies.

Travis and I had talked about having children, about the fact that we might pass our powers on to them. Travis had been thrilled with the idea, but I was more ambivalent about it. Don't get me wrong. I loved having superstrength and the ability to zap a pizza with my eyeballs. But powers weren't the be-all and end-all of the world, as Carmen was so fond of reminding me. Sure, superheroes got plenty of perks, but being one was a lot of hassle too. The long hours and late nights. The constant beatings and narrow escapes. The continual drain on my finances. Having to make nice with the likes of Kelly Caleb, Erica Songe, and other members of the press. My constant need to eat everything in sight. It got old sometimes.

But the most important thing I'd learned over my years of being a superhero was this—having powers couldn't keep you safe from all the big, bad things out there in the world. Travis's death was proof of that.

I answered Lulu. "It'd be nice to pass my power on, but it wouldn't determine if I loved my kid or not. And it sure as hell wouldn't keep me from being with the man I loved."

I opened my mouth to further argue my point, but Lulu snapped her hand up.

"I don't want to talk about it anymore," she said through gritted teeth. "Talking won't fix anything, especially not my shriveled-up ovaries and useless legs. Let's get back to your problem."

She pounded away on her laptop, signaling the end of our conversation. For now.

I started drumming my fingers on the table again while Lulu typed and clicked and muttered under her breath.

"Oh, go hoover down a pizza or something," Lulu snapped about five minutes later. "I can't concentrate with you giving me the laser gaze. All those heat waves make my computer freak out."

"Fine," I sniffed, threw my hair over my shoulder, and flounced out of the library.

I stalked to the underground kitchen, but I didn't *hoover*

down a pizza as Lulu had so indelicately suggested. Instead, I ate three boxes of sugar cookies and drank two gallons of milk. I was just finishing up when Lulu's voice bellowed out of the intercom.

"I've got the information. You can come back to the library now."

"Gee, thanks," I said, draining the last of my milk.

By the time I returned to the library, Lulu had compiled several inches of paper on Johnny Bulluci. A printer whirred and chugged in the background, spitting out more reams.

"How did you get so much information so fast?" I asked.

"Carmen showed me how she does it," Lulu said. "She's still working on Frost and Scorpion's real identities, although they didn't leave a trail for her to follow like Malefica did. Carmen doesn't think any of them died at the ice cream factory, not even Malefica."

"I doubt any of them are dead myself," I replied. "Unfortunately, ubervillains are very resilient. One or all the members of the Terrible Triad will come back to Bigtime someday, and we'll be ready for them, real identities or not."

"Anyway, I set up a couple of computer programs to facilitate the process. I'm just printing the last of it now," Lulu said, tidying up some pages. "This is all pretty normal stuff. School, college, business honors. Lots of friends, female and otherwise. Until three months ago."

"When his father died, and he took over as Johnny Angel."

"You betcha." Lulu grabbed the last of the pages from the printer and shoved them into a thick blue binder. "After that, the life of Johnny Bulluci gets a bit more murky."

"Naturally."

Life was always murky in the world of superheroes and ubervillains. For someone like Johnny, who wasn't on one side or the other, it would be positively gray. And I hated gray.

Lulu tossed me the binder. "Knock yourself out." She

paused. "And try not to set those on fire, okay? I don't want to have to print them out again."

"I won't, Mom," I muttered, settling myself at the round wooden table.

Lulu steered her chair toward the door.

"Hey, Lulu?"

She stopped. "What?"

"Thanks. I really do appreciate it."

I'd said *thank you* twice now in less than twenty-four hours. I really was going to have to quit freaking out and getting people to do me favors.

She nodded. "Back at you."

"What did I do?"

Lulu stared at me. "You listened." Then, she opened the door and zoomed away.

★17★

I waited until the sound of Lulu's wheelchair faded away. Then, I cracked open the binder and started reading.

Lulu had compiled quite a bit of information on James John aka Johnny Bulluci. Age thirty-six. Hair blond. Eyes green. Blah, blah, blah. I knew the boring facts already. I wanted to get to the good stuff.

I skimmed through pages detailing Johnny's progress in high school and college, as well as the business accolades he'd received over the years. To my surprise, there were more than a few of those. I flipped through pages of earnings and stock reports. Since Bobby had retired and Johnny had taken over the majority of Bulluci Industries, the company had almost doubled its profits. Johnny was definitely more than just a sexy guy. He was a shrewd businessman who wasn't afraid to take risks. Sam would approve.

Finally, I found what I was looking for—James Bulluci's obituary. It had appeared in both the *Chronicle* and the *Exposé*.

Lulu had even downloaded the transcripts off the SNN archive service for me.

> *James Michael Bulluci, 58, died in a fiery car accident on Feb. 7. According to Bigtime police, an unknown driver apparently hit the rear of Bulluci's silver Mercedes, causing the gas tank to explode. Bulluci's body was badly burned and partially disintegrated. He was pronounced dead at the scene. The family will receive guests at 6 p.m., Feb. 10, at Bigtime Funeral Home. The burial will take place at 10 a.m., Feb. 11, at Bigtime Cemetery. In lieu of flowers, the family asks that donations be made to the Cure Cancer Research Facility . . .*

I frowned. Died in a fiery car crash? I wondered how the Bullucis had pulled off that lie. They must have paid someone in the coroner's office to look the other way. Or perhaps one of them had some sort of psychic power or mind-control gizmo. It didn't really matter how they had done it. Only that they had.

I kept reading. The obit went on to detail James's life and his work at the helm of his family's company, as well as his many contributions to Bigtime charities. The local media had covered the funeral, of course, since the Bulluci family was so prominent in Bigtime society. I'd been out of town on a business trip and hadn't gone to the funeral, but I remembered Sam talking about attending and what a sad day it had been.

I stared at a picture of Johnny with his arm around Bella, comforting his weeping sister. Johnny's mouth was set in a hard, tight line. Even though the picture was in black-and-white, his eyes practically glowed with fury. The casket stood in the foreground. It was closed. Not surprising. If Intelligal had killed James Bulluci with explodium missiles like Angel claimed, there wouldn't have been enough of him left to put in a spoon, much less a casket. Died in a car crash, my ass.

After the funeral, there were no more mentions of James Bulluci or Johnny Angel. For a while. Then, about a month after the funeral, SNN reported an Angel sighting at the Everything Electronics Store in downtown Bigtime.

Wait a minute. That name sounded familiar. I closed my eyes and thought back. That was one of the places Siren and Intelligal had hit during their crime spree. I remembered because we'd gone tearing after them when they'd robbed the store, but we'd lost them in traffic. All Siren had to do was crook her finger, and twenty cars had slammed into each other. I snorted. Men. And people thought women drivers were hazardous. Please.

I kept reading. According to the television transcripts, Angel had shown up just as the reporter was leaving. That's why we hadn't spotted him that time, but he'd been tracking them even then.

I wondered how he did it. And how he'd known the ubervillains were in the factory a few days ago. Did he sit by the police scanner at night like the newspaper reporters did? Or did he prowl the streets like the roving crews for SNN? Maybe his father's old motorcycle gang friends had given him the heads-up. Perhaps his grandfather helped him. Or even Bella. She had to know the family secret. She might even have some sort of power herself, since Johnny did. She was probably too uptight to use it, though.

As the months went by, more and more sightings of Johnny Angel were reported. He always popped up where Siren and Intelligal had been, sometimes missing them by minutes. Occasionally, he'd save somebody from a burning building or chase off some would-be rapists, but he spent most of his time hunting the two ubervillains. Trying to get his revenge.

Revenge. Johnny wanted revenge on the ubervillains for killing his father. I couldn't blame him for that. When I'd thought Travis had committed suicide because Carmen had exposed him, I'd wanted to tear her into little pieces and feed her to the fish in the marina. My father had to slip me sleeping pills for a week before I'd calmed down enough to even think about letting Carmen live.

When I learned that Malefica had actually murdered the man I loved, I'd gone ballistic. If I could have gotten my hands on the ubervillain, I would have ripped the skin from her body an inch at a time, sewn it back on, and started all over again. And again. And again. So, I didn't begrudge Johnny his revenge. I understood the need for it all too well.

But in the end, revenge wasn't as satisfying as it seemed. There had been plenty of people and ubervillains who had done me wrong over the years. Caveman Stan, the Undertaker, Frost, Carmen, Malefica. Some of them had gotten their comeuppance and then some. Caveman Stan had been buried alive in a cave-in. Frost got attacked by his own monstrous creations. Malefica had disappeared into a vat of radioactive goo.

But it had all been so hollow, so anticlimactic. Oh, the idea of revenge tempted you with its sweet, deadly song, whispered sly promises in your ear. But it didn't bring back the person you loved. It didn't change the past. It didn't heal your hurt. Revenge only made you feel that much more empty inside. At least it had me.

No, Fiona Fine didn't begrudge Johnny Bulluci his revenge. But as Fiera, the superhero, I was honor-bound to stop him. I was in the business of saving lives, not taking them. Not even the lives of ubervillains the world would be better off without. It wasn't for me to decide who lived and who died. That had been one of the first lessons my father had drilled into my head when I'd decided to become a superhero like him. I might be powerful, but I wasn't God. And according to Carmen, karma took care of everybody in the end, good and bad. From what I'd seen so far, she was right. Bad things had a way of happening to bad people. It might take a while, longer than it should, but in the end, you got what you deserved.

But if I stopped Johnny from taking his revenge, things would end between us. I knew his secret, what he did when he thought no one was watching. The knowledge would only fester and rankle between us until the connection we had turned into something sour and rotten.

I didn't want that to happen. But I couldn't ignore my calling, my duty either. And I didn't know if I could risk telling him the truth about me, about what I did when no one was watching.

So what was I going to do?

$\mathcal{I}$ sat in the library staring into space, brooding, and eating candy bars until the others came in around eleven that night.

"Fiona, is something wrong?" the chief asked, his green eyes bright with concern.

I licked a bit of caramel off my finger and shoved the binder over to him. "Oh no. Nothing. Nothing at all. Everything's just dandy. In fact, I've been reading up on a good friend of mine. Johnny Bulluci. Aka Johnny Angel."

My father froze, his fingers hovering over the binder. "Johnny Bulluci is really Angel? Are you sure?"

"You've got to be kidding," Henry said, his glasses gleaming in the dim light.

I shook my head. "Unfortunately, I'm not. It's all there. Read it for yourselves."

Henry and the chief pored over the pages, while I told them about Johnny's watch and all the angels floating around the Bulluci household.

"You found this information yourself?" the chief asked Lulu.

She shrugged. "I've been getting pointers from Carmen. She's right, you know. It really is easy to figure out who you guys are."

"It makes sense," Henry said, pushing his glasses up his nose. He leaned over his computer and started to type. "Each Bulluci generation has had at least one son in it, and we know Johnny Angel is a generational superhero-ubervillain. Not to mention the fact that one of Bulluci Industries' specialties is the production of custom motorcycles. It all fits together. The secret identity, the business, everything."

Something Johnny had said before echoed in my mind. "He told me once that the only thing he and his father ever argued about was his taking over part of the family business. I didn't think anything of it at the time, but he must have been talking about becoming Johnny Angel."

"But now he is Angel," Lulu pointed out. "And we know what he wants."

"To kill Siren and Intelligal for murdering his father," I replied.

Chief Newman put his hand on mine. "Fiona, I know Johnny is your . . . special friend, but we can't let him kill Siren and Intelligal. That's not how we do things around here. We put ubervillains behind bars. We don't execute them. Just because we have superpowers doesn't mean that we're above the law. And neither is Angel."

"I know," I said in a low tone. "We've got to stop him. No matter what."

"No matter how much you might like him," my father said in a kind tone. "No matter how much you think you might come to care for him."

"I do." I rubbed my aching head. "I do care for him. And that makes this whole thing suck even more."

★18★

We sat there in silence, each of us digesting this latest secret-identity exposé.

And a loud bell blared out.

Henry jumped like Siren had just electrified him with a couple of thousand volts. I thought his polka-dot bow tie would pop right off his neck, along with his plaid sweater vest. Henry punched buttons on one of his many computers. His fingers flashed over the keyboard faster than Swifte zipping down the freeway.

"I've got them!" he said. "I've got Siren and Intelligal!"

We clustered around his computer.

"Where? Where are they?" I asked.

Henry punched some more keys. "They're downtown. Right next to Oodles o' Stuff."

Oodles o' Stuff was the shopping center of shopping centers in Bigtime. The mall of malls. The store of stores. The multistoried building had more levels than a wedding cake and featured everything from clothes to jewelry to makeup to consumer electronics. The only thing I didn't like about the store were its subbasements, where last season's Fiona Fine originals could be had for up to 75 percent off. Oodles' extreme sales cut into my profit margins far more than I liked.

"What would they be doing there?" I asked. "They wouldn't be dumb enough to try to rob the place, would they?"

Like Quicke's, Oodles was considered neutral territory for everyone in Bigtime. After all, even villains had to shop for essentials from time to time—namely, boots, masks, stilettos, and neon, sequined spandex. Oodles carried all of the above in large quantities.

But the owners of Oodles weren't stupid. They knew better than to rely on the kindness of ubervillains—or your average shoplifter. The store had one of the best security systems in Bigtime. Guards, dogs, lasers, cameras, steel doors, ink-filled security tags. Not to mention the superheroes who shopped there during regular business hours. Oodles had more security than some of the banks in town.

Then again, Siren could charm just about anybody out of just about anything she wanted to in record time. Oodles' security wouldn't faze her or Intelligal a bit.

"Well, Swifte did stop them from taking everyone's jewels at the wedding, and Oodles has more jewelry than anyone else in town," Lulu pointed out. "Maybe Siren and Intelligal need to stock up on diamonds or something. There were gems all along the border of their radio device."

"I don't know why they're there," Henry said, still typing. "But they've been popping up in and around the area for a couple of days now. Maybe they've set up shop somewhere downtown. Intelligal must have figured out how I found them last time, because she masked the exhaust system on her chair. But I locked in on that strange gas she gave you guys. It contained a small amount of a very rare radioactive isotope that I was able to track through the atmosphere—"

I held up my hand. "Enough of the geek talk. It doesn't matter what they're doing at Oodles, only that we've tracked them down. Let's go." I took a deep breath. "Before Johnny Angel beats us to them."

Ten minutes later, we were suited up and in the van. Hermit zoomed out of the underground garage and raced through the empty streets.

Worries and fears rattled around inside my head like electrified dice. Siren and Intelligal were deadly enough on their own, but now we had Johnny Bulluci aka Johnny Angel to worry about. What would I do if Angel showed up? What would I do if he tried to kill the ubervillains? Or worse yet, tried to hurt one of us for getting in his way? I didn't know the answers to my troubling questions.

My father leaned over and took my hand. "Don't worry, Fiera. It will work out all right in the end. You'll see."

I squeezed his hand, comforted as always by his cheerful, optimistic calm.

"Mr. Sage is right. We might not even see Angel tonight," Hermit called out from the driver's seat. "I was only able to trace the ubervillains by using my radioactive isotope tracker. Angel's not exactly known for his technological devices."

I brightened. "So he probably can't even track them on his own. Excellent."

"Unless he's watching for us," Lulu piped up. "The van's pretty easy to spot. If I were Angel, I wouldn't even try to find Siren and Intelligal on my own. I'd just be looking out for the Fearless Five. Because where you guys are, ubervillains are sure to follow."

My good mood vanished, and I glared at her. "You're not helping."

"Well, forgive me for thinking."

We rode in silence the rest of the way. Since it was so late, downtown was largely deserted, and Hermit was able to park right in front of Oodles. Normally, at this time of night, steel bars and shutters would have covered the store's plate-glass windows, along with the revolving doors that led inside. But the bars were up, and light spilled out from the building. Siren and Intelligal were here all right. Uber-villains were always so brazen when it came to strong-arm robberies.

"Same procedure as before?" I asked. "You boys in the back, me in the front?"

Mr. Sage nodded. "You've got it. And Hermit and I have whipped up something special for tonight, just in case Intelligal decides to spread some more of her gas around." He held up a small white pill.

I took the pill and gulped it down. "So this will keep me from having gas?" I snickered.

Lulu groaned. Hermit rolled his eyes. Mr. Sage just smiled.

"Oh, come on, Lulu," I said. "It's not any worse than the corny puns you come up with."

"That was terrible, Fiera," Lulu said. "Absolutely terrible."

"Yes, this will keep you from being affected by the gas," Hermit said. "It absorbs the gas before it gets into your bloodstream, sort of like an *RID* pill. But it only works for about twenty minutes. Mr. Sage and I haven't come up with a permanent solution yet."

"And it will probably only work half as long for you, Fiera," my father added. "Maybe even less, given your rapid metabolism."

"You know you could make millions from flatulent Americans if you could perfect it."

No one responded. Ah well. Some people just didn't have the vision I did. While Mr. Sage and Hermit ate their pills, Lulu gave us all earpieces and activated the cameras in the F5 insignias on our suits. Then, it was time to get out and about and see if we could catch us a couple of ubervillains hell-bent on destruction, world domination, and the like.

Mr. Sage and Hermit ran around to the back of the building. I marched over to the first door I saw and shoved through it, not even bothering to be quiet or sneaky. I wanted to get this over and done with before Angel showed up. I didn't want to face Johnny just yet. Not until I figured out how I really felt about him. And how big an obstacle our secret identities were going to be to our blossoming relationship. With Travis, it had been so easy. We'd both known who we were when the lights went out, and we'd both been on the same side. But things wouldn't be that simple with Johnny and me. Not by a long shot.

A couple of large, vicious-looking Dobermans lay inside the door. At least, they would have been vicious-looking if they weren't snoring like lumberjacks and piled on top of each other like puppies. Ten feet behind the dogs, four guards slumped against counters full of designer handbags. They too were sleeping, and slightly goofy smiles curved their faces.

I sniffed. The sweet, sickening stench of the ubervillains' gas lingered in the air, although there was a slightly more floral aroma to it this time, almost like jasmine. It didn't take a rocket scientist to figure out that Siren and Intelligal had used the blue gas or some variation of it to knock out the guards and dogs. At least they hadn't killed them.

"Hey, guys, I found the dogs and the guards. At least, the ones on this side of the building." I pointed the camera in my suit at the snoring piles so Lulu could get a look at them. "Everyone seems to be having sweet dreams."

"They'll be all right," Lulu squawked in my ear. "They have good, steady vital signs, and according to our analysis, the gas gets flushed out of people's bodies pretty quickly. They'll probably just sleep for a couple of hours. Keep going, Fiera."

The first floor contained women's clothes and accessories, from lacy lingerie to simple socks to stern business suits to slick panty hose. Even though the store had closed only a few hours ago at midnight, all the clothes hung neatly from the racks, and the sweaters, shirts, and other items were folded and stacked on wooden tables in tidy piles. The staff at Oodles prided itself on making sure everything was meticulously arranged and easy to find.

I was happy to note that some of my goods, including my latest collection of affordable cocktail dresses, were prominently featured in a display near the middle of the first floor. I stopped to straighten a mannequin's wayward spaghetti strap and continued on. I walked up to one of the many maps located throughout the store. My eyes scanned over the diagrams and lists of products and services available on each floor. If I were Siren and Intelligal, where would I go? What would I need to complete my scheme for world domination? I thought back to the device I'd seen in the abandoned warehouse and the spare bits of metal that had been lying around. Parts. That's what I'd need.

"I'm heading up to the third floor, where the consumer electronics are," I said to the others.

"Roger that," Mr. Sage replied in a tinny voice. "Hermit and I will go up to the fifth floor, where the jewelry's located."

I headed for the nearest escalator and walked up a flight of frozen steps. The second floor was devoted to home goods, like kitchen appliances, bedding, and shower curtains. I resisted the urge to see how many of my new linens were left on the shelves and climbed the next flight of stopped stairs.

The staff at Oodles was also known for its marketing savvy, which was why the third floor was split between menswear and consumer electronics, with electronics taking up the majority of the space. Someone had realized long ago that men were far more likely to drop a couple thousand dollars on plasma-screen TVs instead of business suits.

"I'm on three. I'm heading in," I whispered to the others.

"Be careful," Hermit whispered back to me.

I slid behind a row of suits and headed for the electronics side of the floor. I stopped every few feet, looking and listening, but all I could hear was the hum of the air-conditioning system, and the others breathing in my ear. I wandered through the rows of televisions, computers, and digital cameras, searching for the ubervillains and exchanging hushed updates with the rest of the gang. After a few minutes of searching, I found the ubervillains' spur-of-the-moment lair.

It was the same setup as before. Someone had shoved a cash register and displays of chocolate bars off a long counter to make way for the strange, radiolike device. Lots of tools and blueprints and papers were also strewn about the area, and more electronic junk sat in a shopping cart. I picked up something that looked like a subwoofer for a speaker. Maybe the villains were getting into the car stereo installation business. I tossed it aside.

"You getting this, Lulu?" I asked.

"Yep, but focus on the blueprints this time," Lulu chirped in my ear. "I've got plenty of pictures of the actual device from the other night."

I did as she asked, pointing my chest and the camera hidden there at the writings and scribblings and schematics on the counter.

"Interesting. It seems to be some sort of sound device," Lulu murmured.

I snorted. "I could have told you that. The thing looks like a giant radio."

I wandered among the debris, getting pictures of everything for Lulu. Siren and Intelligal were nowhere to be found. They must have been supremely confident to leave their doomsday device sitting here by itself. Or supremely stupid. It was all the same when it came to ubervillains. Besides me, the only thing that was talking was a television set tuned to SNN, where Erica Songe preened for the camera.

When I was done taking images for Lulu, I went back to the radio-looking gizmo and reared back my fist.

"Shall I smash it to bits?" I asked the others.

"Why don't you just stand guard over it?" Hermit suggested. "I'd love to take a look at the device and see some of Intelligal's handiwork. The ubervillains aren't up here on the fifth floor, although there seems to be some jewelry missing. We'll be down in a minute."

I rolled my eyes. Hermit was such a technology nerd. But I did as he asked, leaning against a display filled with the newest laser-jet printers. I opened my mouth to tell him to double-time it when a mechanical whir sounded above Erica Songe's voice. Intelligal floated into view.

The two of us stared at each other.

"You again! Can't you go set yourself on fire or something?" Intelligal muttered.

I didn't bother responding. That was another comment I'd heard about a thousand times. Instead, I grabbed the biggest printer I saw off one of the tables and hurled it at the ubervillain. The action surprised her, and she didn't have time to get her force field up before the printer smacked into the bottom of the chair.

The plastic case shattered, and parts pinged everywhere, along with a good amount of colored ink. Intelligal fumbled for her controls. The chair spun round and round like a child's top before slamming into a thick, metal support beam and sliding to the floor. A bit of smoke spewed out from the back of the trunk, like a car with a coughing fit.

The impact threw Intelligal out of her seat, and she hit a counter hard before sliding off. She sprawled on the floor, and I stood over her. The ubervillain looked small and sad and lost without her massive gadget-filled chair. She stared up at me, her eyes dark and unreadable behind her thick black glasses.

Someone started to clap.

I turned. Johnny Angel stood behind me, looking dangerous in his head-to-toe black leather. My heart sank. Where had he come from?

"Very nicely done," he said.

"What are you doing here?" I snapped. "Are you following us?"

Angel tipped his head. "Guilty as charged, I'm afraid. I saw your van outside and couldn't resist following you. Now, if you'll just step aside, I'll finish the job you so elegantly started. I owe the old Angel that much." His voice twisted with guilt, and I knew that Angel, that Johnny, was thinking of his father.

I looked at Intelligal. The ubervillain blanched and scooted backward on her heels, like a crab scrabbling along a sandy beach. She bumped into a glass counter and stopped, trapped. She didn't have any powers without her ruined chair; otherwise she would have used them on me. Right now, Intelligal was as helpless as any other Bigtime citizen. My heart heavy, I turned back to Angel.

"I'm afraid I can't let you do that," I said. "It's my duty to turn her over to the police."

"And it's my duty to avenge my predecessor, no matter what. Now, get out of my way." Angel took a step forward. His hands curled into fists. "Don't make me hurt you to get to her."

"I can't let you kill her so you can take your revenge. I'm in the business of stopping ubervillains, not murdering them."

"Then it's a good thing I don't have such qualms."

Angel marched straight at me. I knew he wasn't going to stop. Not when I was standing between him and Intelligal. Angel wouldn't stop. Neither would Johnny Bulluci. It was my bad fortune that they were one and the same.

And that I was Fiera, member of the Fearless Five. Protector of the innocent. Defender of democracy. Superhero du jour. I couldn't just let Angel murder Intelligal, no matter how much he wanted to, no matter how much she might deserve it. My duty, my code of honor as a superhero, wouldn't let me.

So, I slow-pitched a fireball at him, making sure to give him enough time to defend himself. Angel stopped and flexed, his skin taking on a hard, chiseled look. The liquid ball of heat hissed through the air and exploded on his chest. Angel's jacket and T-shirt disintegrated into ash. On the bright side, that gave me an eyeful of nicely toned man-flesh. On the dark side, it didn't slow him down a bit.

Smoke boiled in the store, setting off the fire alarms. Sprinklers dropped down from the ceiling and spewed out a puffy, white, heat- and flame-retardant foam. Oodles had contingency plans for just about everything, including a superhero-ubervillain battle in the middle of the store. It had happened before when Gentleman George and the Dapper Duke both wanted the same silk ascot. George had won, but by the time the fire was out, the ascot had been reduced to ash.

Angel laughed and tapped his chest. It sounded like metal ringing. "Superstrong exoskeleton, remember? Your fireballs won't hurt me a bit, but I'll forgive you for that one, Fiera."

I looked back at the ubervillain. Intelligal had flopped

over on her hands and knees and started crawling around the counter. Sweat poured down her face, and a bit of blood darkened the side of her silver suit. She must have injured herself when the chair hit the support beam.

Angel kept coming, his green eyes as hard as jade. My eyes flicked around, trying to figure out a way to stop him without hurting him too much. He was on me in a second.

"Move out of my way, Fiera," Angel growled, his eyes focused on Intelligal. "Or else."

I was out of options and out of time.

So, I punched him.

★19★

I really should have restrained myself. It was like trying to punch through granite or slamming my hand into a wall of concrete. Pain pulsed through my fingers, up my wrist, and into my arm and shoulder.

"Son of a bitch, that hurt!" I cursed, shaking my hand. I'd have bruises tomorrow for sure.

"I told you, Fiera. You . . . can't . . . hurt . . . me," Angel emphasized. "Now stand aside. Or else."

"Or else what?" I taunted, stalling for time.

Time to do what, I hadn't a clue. My options were severely limited. Johnny Angel was strong, and with his heavy exoskeleton, I'd have a hard time wrestling him or pinning him to the ground until the others came to help. I couldn't keep him at bay with my fireballs without destroying the entire floor. The only thing I could do would be to beat on him a little, but my blows wouldn't have any effect as long as he was concentrating on his exoskeleton.

"Or else, I'll move you. And I don't think you'll like it."

My eyes darted back and forth. I didn't want to hurt Angel aka Johnny Bulluci, but I couldn't let him kill Intelligal either. I just couldn't. Not and still call myself a superhero. I spotted a long, thick pipe among the junk in the shopping cart. I came up with a hasty plan. The only kind of plan I did, really.

I sighed. A great big heaving *I'm-such-a-wimpy-girl-I-just-have-to-give-in-before-I-break-a-nail* sigh. "All right, you can have her. Just let me tie my shoes first."

My excuse was totally lame, but it worked. The girly sigh, combined with my Barbie-doll looks and baby blues, gets 'em every time. Angel's eyes dropped to my shoes, and the hard, chiseled look left his skin.

"Tie your shoes? But you're wearing boots—"

I reached over, grabbed the pipe, and smacked Angel with it. That got his attention. He staggered back and fell to one knee.

"Kinky. I like it," he mumbled. Blood welled up out of the cut I'd sliced across his left cheek.

He got back up and charged at me, but he forgot to concentrate on forming his exoskeleton—exactly what I'd been counting on. I sidestepped him and whacked him across the back with the pipe. But Angel limped to his feet again. And again. And again.

Every time Angel got back up, I hit him. Every time, the pipe got a bit heavier in my hands. Every cut, every bruise made me feel sick inside. Every blow I gave him was like a knife in my own heart. Despite his faults and desperate need for vengeance, I really liked Angel aka Johnny Bulluci. I hated to hurt him. I hated to hurt all innocents. But he'd left me with no choice. Sometimes, being a superhero really sucked. Damn duty.

Angel's skeleton might have been superstrong, but so was I. With the pipe, I was able to put a few dents in him.

Drops of blood slid down his chest like a trail of rubies. The sight made me want to retch. But he kept coming at me. Stupid, stubborn fool.

Didn't the man realize that he was beaten? Evidently not, because Angel stumbled to his feet after a long moment of kissing the floor. He seesawed back and forth like a kid's teeter-totter. Then, he took a step forward. He wasn't going to stop until I killed him. Well, I wasn't going to do that. Not to Angel. Not to Johnny. I'd had enough of this. I marched over to him.

"You really should have stayed down that last time," I snarled.

I reared back and gave him the ole Fist-o-Might. I put everything I had into the punch. All my strength, all my anger, all my guilt, all my shame. My fist cracked against his jaw, and Angel crumpled to the ground like a paper doll. I let him. Maybe the fall would knock some sense into that hard head of his, although I doubted it.

This time, Angel didn't get up. He lay there on the floor. I drew in a deep breath and threw the pipe away. I didn't want to look at it. Or the blood trickling out of the many wounds I'd inflicted on Angel. On Johnny. I closed my eyes. What had I done?

A gloved hand settled on my shoulder. I shrieked, reached back for the hand, and flipped the person it belonged to over my shoulder. A blur of green slammed into the floor in front of me.

Mr. Sage's masked face stared up at me. His mouth opened and closed in pain, and his eyes rolled around in his head like marbles. I cringed. First my lover, now my father. I was batting a thousand today. Who was next? Some orphan out on the street? How about a senior citizen on his way home from the bingo parlor? Maybe I could knock Lulu around a little. That would make my day complete.

"Oh, sorry about that. You startled me."

I reached down and helped Mr. Sage to his feet. His green eyes were dark and dazed. I kept a hand on his arm to keep him from plummeting back to the floor.

Hermit moved over to the unconscious Angel. "Fiera, what, uh, happened here?"

"I had Intelligal cornered, and Angel showed up. He wanted me to step aside so he could finish her off—Intelligal!" During my sickening fight with Angel, I'd forgotten about the supersmart ubervillain.

I whipped around. She was gone, along with all the blueprints, the shopping cart full of stuff, and the curious machine she'd been working on. Her chair sat where it had fallen, slowly getting covered with sticky, white foam, just like everything else in the store.

Damn. I put my fist through a computer monitor, not even caring about the mess I made. I couldn't believe I'd been so stupid as to let her get away. She'd been injured, for crying out loud. What kind of superhero was I? I beat up on people who helped me and let ubervillains escape. Maybe it was time to hang up the skintight spandex and mask. I punched through another monitor.

"Easy, Fiera. Easy," Mr. Sage said, stepping back to avoid the flying debris. "It's not your fault she got away, so please don't destroy any more of Oodles' stock than necessary."

"Was there any sign of Siren?" I asked.

Hermit shook his head. "Not a trace of her, although there was a smashed jewelry case on the fifth floor. It looks like Intelligal broke in alone." He spotted the ruined Intellichair and brightened. "But at least she left her chair behind. I've been itching to get my hands on it and see the technology she's got hardwired inside it."

Hermit pulled out his computer and started to walk toward the chair.

Mr. Sage's eyes glowed. "No, Hermit!"

A tall skinny cylinder popped up on top of the chair, and a red light flashed on and off. Red lights were never, ever good. I didn't have to be psychic to know what was going to happen next. I grabbed Hermit by the back of his black-and-white suit and sprinted toward the escalator, dragging him along behind me.

"Get Johnny!" I screamed at my father.

Mr. Sage used his telekinesis to pick up Johnny's unconscious form, which zipped ahead of him. Johnny sailed down the frozen escalator with Mr. Sage right behind. Hermit pounded down after them.

"Go, go, go!" I shouted.

Being the strongest and fire-resistant, I stayed in the back this time, so I could shield the others from the force of the explosion—

Intelligal's chair self-destructed with a roar. I don't know what sort of explosive she had in that thing, but it packed one hell of a punch. Even better than my trusty Fist-o-Might. The others had just reached the bottom of the escalator and I was halfway down when the shockwave from the explosion knocked me into them. I felt like I was a human bowling ball, and they were a set of pins. We went down in a tangle of limbs, boots, and spandex. The building shook, and fire raced down the escalator, threatening to roast the others. I scrambled on top, trying to shield them from the searing heat. But it wasn't going to be enough.

Another set of sprinklers dropped down from the ceiling and spit out a pale, blue foam, adding to the mounds of white. The color scheme reminded me of some sort of winter wonderland. But the blue foam did its job, and the fire snuffed out just as it hit the bottom of the escalator—inches away from our feet. A second later, fans rumbled to life, pulling the smoke and soot from the explosion up out of the building. Bless Oodles and its efficient safety system.

The foam covered everything. By the time we got to our feet, we were ankle-deep in the stuff. Everybody was a little shaken up, but nobody had any serious injuries. Nobody except Johnny. Hermit managed to prop him up against a table full of blenders. Blood dripped from the cuts on his face and chest, a bright scarlet contrast to the white and blue around us.

"Let's go," Mr. Sage said. "The ubervillains are gone, and the fire department will be on their way to assess the damage. There's nothing more we can do here tonight. We need to get Angel back to Sublime and treat his injuries."

I sighed. I knew I'd done the right thing by stopping him, but seeing him there on the floor beaten, bloody, and bruised made something twist deep inside me. I knelt down beside him and brushed his hair back from his face.

"I'm so sorry, Johnny. So sorry," I whispered. "But you wouldn't stop. You wouldn't listen to me. And I couldn't let you do it. I just couldn't."

He didn't respond. So, I picked up Angel, heaved him over my shoulder, and followed the others out of the building.

Two hours later, I stood outside one of the underground sick bays in Sublime. I stared through the tinted glass window at the unconscious Johnny Angel. After waking up the unconscious guards and filling them in on what had happened, we'd ridden back to the manor in silence.

I'd put Johnny in one of the sick bays we used when we had unexpected guests. The chief and Henry had treated Angel's cuts and bruises with their magic mojo pills, salves, and ointments. I hadn't beaten him as badly as I feared, and the chief promised me that he would make a full recovery. It didn't ease my guilt any, though. Now, the four of us waited outside the room trying to decide what we were going to do when Angel woke up.

"Beating up the guy you're sleeping with. That's twisted, Fiona, even for a superhero," Lulu said, attempting a joke.

"He didn't exactly give me a choice," I growled. "I couldn't let him just kill Intelligal, especially when she was completely out of it. They call that *murder*, you know."

My father placed a comforting hand on my shoulder. "You did what had to be done. We know you'd never intentionally harm someone, Fiona. Don't we, Lulu?"

The computer hacker didn't quite meet his gaze. Or mine. "Sure, we know that, Chief Newman."

"What you think I might do or not do doesn't matter. The fact is that I beat Angel to a bloody pulp."

If it had been Scorpion or Frost or some other ubervillain in that bed, I would have been beaming like a comet, proud of whipping an evildoer. Now, I just felt sick and cold and tired.

My eyes traced over Johnny's face. We'd left his mask on, of course, but bruises had already started to form on his golden skin. A white T-shirt stretched over his chest, while a cotton sheet covered the rest of his body. An IV dripped antibiotics into his arm, while more machines monitored his heart and blood pressure. Johnny looked so sad, so battered, so broken lying in that hospital bed. And it was all because of me.

Even worse, it could happen again if Johnny kept on with his mission of vengeance. I couldn't bear to stop him. Not Johnny. Not again. My heart couldn't take it.

In that instant, I made a decision. Probably a bad decision, probably the wrong move to make, but it was the only plan I could come up with. I looked at the others.

"I have to tell him that I know who he is, and I have to tell him who I am too."

Everyone stilled. Then, Lulu whistled. Henry pushed his glasses up his nose. The chief laced his fingers together.

Finally, Chief Newman spoke. "Do you think that's a good idea, Fiona?"

I shrugged. "I haven't got a clue. But it's the only way I can think of to get him to stop this vendetta. We got lucky tonight. If Intelligal hadn't been injured, she could have killed us both. She could have gassed us and shot us and not thought twice about it. Next time, we might not be so lucky. Maybe if Johnny knows who I really am and knows I'll see that justice is served, he'll think twice about killing the ubervillains."

"You think he cares for you?" the chief asked. His eyes glowed a second, like the quick flare of a cigarette.

I thought back to the time I'd spent with Johnny. Our dinner at Quicke's. Riding the Ferris wheel. Sneaking out of the observatory. Swimming in the lake. Dinner at his house. The way he kissed me. The way he held me. The way he made my heart quicken when I thought about him.

"I don't know exactly how he feels about me," I replied. "But I care about him. I have to try to stop him before he hurts himself—or somebody else."

From inside the sick bay, Angel let out a low moan. The sound tugged at my heart. He was beginning to come around. I put my mask back, opened the door, and stepped inside the room. The door hissed open, and his head turned in my direction at the sound.

"Well, if it isn't my favorite sadist," Angel said. His voice was thick and slurred like he'd been drinking instead of unconscious.

I settled myself in a chair next to the bed. My eyes

flicked to the many monitors that surrounded Angel. Heart, lungs, brain. Everything was fine, despite the smackdown I'd given him. Relief filled my body, along with guilt and shame.

"I'm sorry about that," I said in a low voice, not quite looking into his bleary eyes. "But you didn't give me a choice."

"No, I suppose I didn't." He rubbed his bruised jaw. "You've got quite the right hook going there. Especially when you're swinging something heavy to go along with it."

I didn't respond. There was nothing I could say to change the fact that I'd just kicked his ass. He was taking it better than I had expected, though. Most men would have been curled up in a fetal position and whimpering by now if they'd been knocked out by a woman, even one with super-strength. No matter whether they were ubervillains or not, getting beaten up by a girl was enough to make the strongest man just fall to pieces.

"Where am I?" Angel asked, looking around at the gleaming medical equipment.

"At Fearless Five headquarters. In one of our sick bays. It's where we bring team members to rest and recuperate when we get injured—or other people who need medical attention."

Angel struggled to sit up. I put my hand under his shoulder to help him, but he flinched and jerked away. I dropped my hand and stepped back, my heart heavy and aching. I twisted my engagement ring around my finger. His eyes went to the ring, and my hand stilled.

Angel managed to raise himself up. He fell back against the bed, panting a bit from the effort. When he got his breath back, his eyes went around the room again, more focused now. Taking in every little detail. Then, he peeked under the covers. In addition to being the chief of police, my father was also a first-rate doctor. He'd cut Angel's skin-tight pants off so he could examine his whole body. I'd been torn between watching and leering and staying away. In the end, I'd stayed away, not wanting to see any more of the damage I'd done than necessary.

"Nice jammies," Angel said. "Do they come with the room?"

How he could crack a joke at a time like this, I didn't know. But some of the anguish dripped out of my heart. "You might say that."

Angel examined the rest of his body, flexing his arms and legs and making sure everything was in working order, more or less. His hands went up to his face and the mask that was still there. His head snapped around to me.

"Did you . . ."

I shook my head. "No, I didn't peek and see who you really are under there. Neither did the others."

Tension ebbed out of his body.

"I didn't need to look under your mask," I continued. "Because I knew who you were already."

"Really?" he said in a fake, cheery, carefree voice. "And who do you think I am?"

"Johnny Bulluci."

Angel looked at me. His shoulders sagged. Then, he did the last thing I expected him to do. He reached up and yanked his mask off. Johnny Bulluci stared back at me. Green eyes. Tawny hair. Golden skin. My gaze traced over his features. He was still as handsome as handsome could be, even with the blue and purple bruises that colored his face.

"How did you figure it out?" he asked in a low voice.

"You gave yourself away with all those angels," I replied in a soft tone. "All angels, all the time."

Johnny's green eyes narrowed, and he looked at me.

Wondering. Thinking. Remembering. And he knew. Just as I had known. The knowledge blazed in his eyes.

There was only one thing left to do. I reached up and took off my own mask.

"Hello, Johnny," I said.

★ 20 ★

The act shocked him as much as his unmasking had startled me.

Johnny's eyes widened. "Fiona? You're really . . . Fiera?"

"In the flaming flesh," I said, tossing my mask on the foot of the bed.

We stared at each other. Then, Johnny threw his head back and laughed.

He laughed . . .

And laughed . . .

And laughed . . .

"What's so funny?" I growled.

"This! Us!" he said, wiping away tears of mirth from his battered face. "Look at us. You're a superhero, and I'm . . . well, I'm not exactly as pure as vanilla. We just got into a knock-down, drag-out brawl over the life of an ubervillain who doesn't deserve to live. You beat the snot out of me, and now I find out the superhero who kicked my ass is, in fact, the woman I've been seeing. It's absurd. It's ridiculous. It's just . . . funny!"

Johnny started laughing again. Then, he winced and grabbed his taped ribs. His laughter died on his lips. My heart sank down into my rumbling stomach. There was nothing funny about what I'd done to Johnny Bulluci, nothing humorous or amusing about the beating I'd given him. All to save Intelligal's worthless ass.

"It's not funny," I said in a cold tone. "It's—" I bit my words off, shocked and more than a little disturbed by what I'd been about to say.

"It's what?" Johnny asked. "What were you going to say?"

I rolled my eyes. "It's karma."

"Karma? Where are you getting that from?"

I sighed. "I have this *friend*, for lack of a better word. She thinks that everything we do affects everybody else in the world and that our actions determine events in our lives. That there are no coincidences, basically. That everything is destiny. Fate. Kismet. Karma."

I was glad Carmen wasn't here to hear me use her catchphrase and superhero name. I'd scoffed at her view of the world more than once. If she knew I was bandying around words like *karma*, I'd never hear the end of it. Ever. Lulu would probably tell her all about it, though.

Johnny's green eyes narrowed. "Karma? As in Karma Girl? Wait a minute. Isn't that the name of one of the Fearless Five now? The new member who took over Tornado's slot after Malefica killed him—" Johnny stopped, guessing the rest of my secret.

"The man you were engaged to, the guy you're so in love with, it was Tornado, wasn't it? The superhero?"

I closed my eyes and nodded. "Yes, he was the man I was engaged to. And yes, Karma Girl is the name of the woman who took his place on the Fearless Five team."

Johnny sat still, digesting everything. Me being Fiera. Me being engaged to a superhero who'd been murdered. Him being beaten down by the woman he was sleeping with. I couldn't quite read the emotions swirling in his beautiful eyes, but I had to try to explain things to him. Johnny Bulluci had become very important to me these last few days. I wanted him to understand me, accept me. I needed him to.

"Johnny, I—"

A whoosh sounded at the far end of the room, and the doors opened. To my surprise, the others trooped in. Costumes on. Masks off.

"What . . . what are you doing?!" I squealed.

The chief and Henry exchanged unapologetic shrugs.

"He knows who you are, he'd figure out the rest of us eventually. We thought we'd just speed along the process," Henry said.

I sat back in my chair, dazed. Good grief, if we kept this up, everybody in the greater Bigtime metropolitan area would know our secret identities. We really needed to stop telling people what we did in our spare time.

Johnny's mouth dropped open. "Chief Newman? The chief of police in Bigtime?" He stared at the chief, who was still wearing his green and white costume. "You're Mr. Sage, the psychic superhero?"

"Guilty as charged," the chief said, looking at me. "I'm also Fiona's father."

Johnny's head snapped back to me. "Hold on. You said your father was a bodyguard. That his name was Sean and that you didn't get to see him as often as you'd like because of his work."

I winced and shrugged. "The chief's first name is Sean. And he is a bodyguard, sort of. I mean, he *is* a superhero. That's like being a bodyguard, except of the whole city instead of just one person. And we don't *really* spend a lot of time together—"

"Except when you're out chasing ubervillains," Johnny finished.

I winced again.

His eyes moved over to Henry and his black-and-white outfit. "And who are you?"

Henry stepped forward and offered Johnny his hand to shake. "I'm Henry Harris, aka Hermit."

"Hermit, the technical whiz, right?" Johnny gave Henry's hand a hard squeeze.

The black superhero stepped back, wincing and cradling his hand. "Guilty as charged."

"You're the Henry who calls Fiona at odd hours with those weird emergencies?"

"That's me," Henry said. "Sorry if I've been interrupting your dates lately, but we've had some situations going on these past couple of days, as you're well aware."

Johnny's eyes moved over to Lulu. They lingered on the blue streaks in her black hair. "And who are you? Karma Girl? You're not dressed in silver. In fact, you don't really look like her. And not to be rude, but she's not in a wheelchair. Unless that's part of your disguise or something."

Lulu laughed. "Oh no. I'm not Karma Girl. Not even close. I'm Lulu Lo."

Johnny frowned. "I've never heard of a superhero named Lulu."

"Oh, I'm not a superhero. I just help the Five out from time to time. I'm sort of a sidekick. A groupie, if you will."

I glared at Lulu. Superheroes did not have *groupies*. At least, not the real pros like us. Debonair might have legions of them, but not the Fearless Five. Lulu made us sound like we were some sort of strange rock band. Or encouraged those weird people who belonged to Slaves for Superhero Sex.

Henry put his arm around Lulu. "She's also my fiancée."

Lulu scowled. "Actually, that has yet to be decided," she said, shrugging off his touch.

Henry pushed his glasses up his nose. "Well, when exactly are you going to get around to deciding that?"

He sounded more than a little annoyed. I stared at the mild-mannered computer guru. Henry never got really cross, not even when I melted his computer wires. But now, he sounded rather like me when I hadn't eaten for a couple of hours—ready to explode.

"I told you that I needed more time to think about your proposal, and I told you why," Lulu snapped.

"It's been almost a month already," Henry snapped back. "Either you love me and want to marry me, or you don't."

"Of course I love you," Lulu replied. "With all my heart. Even if I want to throttle you right now."

Henry's eyes narrowed. Lulu crossed her arms over her chest and glared at him. Johnny looked back and forth between the couple, apparently amused by the squabbling supernerds.

My father stepped in between the feuding lovers and cleared his throat. "Why don't we take this discussion to the library and leave Fiona and Johnny alone? I'm sure they have plenty of things to discuss."

He squeezed my hand once, then walked out of the room, followed by Henry.

Lulu's dark eyes flicked back and forth between the two of us. "Yes, lots of things to . . . discuss." She snickered, then motored away.

The door whooshed shut behind them, and I let out a long breath.

"Sorry about that," I said. "Usually, we're not so boisterous. At least not Lulu and Henry. They're the quiet ones of the gang. They hardly ever fight and never in front of other people."

"It's okay," Johnny said. "It took my mind off my ribs for a few minutes."

I grabbed his hand and stared into his eyes. "Johnny, I want you to know how sorry I am. I truly, truly am. But I couldn't let you kill Intelligal. I just couldn't."

He dropped his eyes. "You know she's evil. She and Siren have tried to kill you before. And when you figured out who I was, you knew the two of them killed my father. Why couldn't you have just let me deal with her the way I wanted to?"

"Because I'm a superhero. I have a code of honor that I follow. I don't kill ubervillains, no matter how heinous their crimes are. I only hurt others to protect myself or innocent people. If I went around killing ubervillains or punishing everyone who broke the law in whatever manner I saw fit, I wouldn't be a superhero anymore. I'd just be a vigilante, dispensing what I saw as justice."

"A vigilante? Is that what you think I am?" Johnny asked, his eyes bright and hard in his bruised face.

"No." I shook my head. "I don't think you're a vigilante. I think you're a son who misses his father very, very much."

"Then, why didn't you let me have her? Why?"

"Because killing her and even Siren too won't take away your pain. It won't bring your father back, Johnny. Nothing will do that. Believe me, I know."

His eyes burned into mine. "What do you know about pain? You still have your father by your side. Fighting with you. Just like always. Mine is dead, Fiona. Dead. And he's never coming back."

Travis's face flashed through my mind. His kind eyes. His sweet, happy smile. I turned my ring around my finger.

"I know your pain, your need for vengeance, a lot better than you think. Malefica murdered Tornado, the man I loved. The man I was going to marry. Don't you think I wanted to kill her for that? Don't you think I wanted to rip her black heart out of her chest and squeeze it until it burst like a piñata?"

"You said that the person who killed your fiancé got what she deserved. What happened to her? What happened to Malefica?"

I flashed back to that fateful night in the Snowdom Ice Cream Factory. I was trapped in a glass tube. And cold. So cold. And angry. And fearful. "Carmen Cole, Karma Girl, dropped her into a vat of radioactive something-or-other."

"So, she's dead."

I shook my head. "We don't know that. No one's seen her since. Ubervillains are sort of like movie monsters. They always come back, even if they've been beaten, stabbed, shot, burned alive, and beheaded. I won't believe Malefica or the other members of the Terrible Triad are dead until I see their bodies."

"But Malefica is probably dead. Or at least horribly mutated." Johnny's voice was flat, cold, icy.

"Yes."

"You got your revenge, Fiona. Malefica paid for what she did to you and yours. So why are you denying me my vengeance?"

I let out a long breath. "Inadvertently, yes, I did get my revenge. But it didn't bring Travis back. It didn't change the pain I felt when he was murdered. Can't you see? If you pursue your vendetta against Siren and Intelligal, it won't help you in the end. You could even die in the process, and where would that leave Bobby and Bella? Grieving for you *and* your father. Would you cause them more pain just to kill a couple of worthless ubervillains?"

Johnny didn't respond. He looked at me, then turned over and rolled onto his side toward the wall. Away from me.

Suddenly tired, I let out a long sigh. Our conversation was clearly over. For now.

So I did the only thing I could. I opened the door and left the room.

I left Johnny to his brooding, stalked to my suite, and crashed onto the king-size bed. It was approaching dawn, and I was worn out. For once, I was even too tired to eat.

I fell into a dark dreamless sleep and woke up around noon. To my surprise, I felt a little better. I knew Johnny's secret, and now he knew mine. I didn't really like keeping secrets, especially from a man I was sleeping with. One that I had come to care about. It was so much easier just to say what you wanted to, when you wanted to. Consequences be damned.

I took a hot shower and pondered my wardrobe for the day. I planned to give Johnny the grand tour of the Fearless Five headquarters, and I wanted to look damn good when he saw me. I needed to look good. I had a feeling I'd have to amp up the old Fiona Fine charm in order to get Johnny to forget about our boxing match and his kissing the ground multiple times last night. If he ever really could.

I riffled through the small, dark area. Unfortunately, I didn't have quite the selection or closet space as I did in my apartment back in Bigtime. There were no lights in the closet, no stacks of shoes, no rows of purses, no chests filled with jewelry. Just a couple of pitiful metal racks that weren't nearly long enough. In fact, Sam had limited me to one measly, ordinary-sized closet. He said the underground space was too valuable to use housing my enormous clothing collection. The man was so misguided sometimes. Just because the love of his life preferred ratty T-shirts and ripped jeans to real clothes didn't mean the rest of us should have to suffer.

I settled on an available-but-casual outfit so I wouldn't seem too eager. I'd done that already the other night, when Johnny had me moaning and begging for more against the wall. I put on a pair of tight, low-cut jeans that hugged my curves and a sleeveless black top that laced up the front. It looked like something a working girl might have worn in an Old West saloon. Combined with the jeans, a pair of stilettos, and a black velvet choker, I had the whole *hooker-with-a-heart-of-gold* look going on. I turned, admiring myself in the mirror over the dresser. I liked it. I hoped Johnny would too.

I closed my eyes, strategizing. I'd go check on Johnny and, if he felt like it, give him the grand tour of the place. Then, maybe we could have lunch. My stomach rumbled. Well, maybe Johnny could have lunch, and I could have whatever he didn't eat. And everything else in the refrigerators. All the refrigerators. Upstairs and downstairs.

I put on my makeup, brushed my golden hair until it gleamed, and headed for the sick bay. I peeked in through the window, not wanting to disturb Johnny if he was still asleep. But he was gone. The covers on the bed were thrown back, and the machines stood still and silent. My eyes flicked up and down the corridor. No broken glass, no busted doors. Johnny hadn't bashed his way out of the sick bay like Carmen had once. So where was he?

I spent the next twenty minutes stalking up and down the carpeted corridors of our underground lair. I checked the kitchen, the game room, the gym, the entertainment room, the garage. I reached the library. If he wasn't in here, I'd send out a red alert. I cracked the door open and stuck my head in. Johnny was inside. Relief flooded my body, followed by a far more potent feeling.

I stared at him. Green eyes. Tawny skin. Golden hair. A hard body sent down from heaven itself. It was no wonder the Bullucis were obsessed with angels. With their golden good looks, they could have passed for the winged guardians themselves.

Johnny prowled around the room with a predator's deadly grace. The bruises on his face and arms had faded to a soft purple, and most of the cuts had already sewn themselves shut. Johnny—Angel—must be a quick healer too. Most superheroes and ubervillains were. You sort of had to be in this business.

"Hey there, handsome," I drawled in a light tone and stepped inside. I wanted things to go better today than they had last night. I needed them to. "What are you doing in here?"

"I'm looking for a phone," Johnny said, eyeing Henry's many computers, wires, and other gadgets. "That's just about the only thing you people don't seem to have around here."

"Why do you want a phone?" My heart sank. I didn't want him to leave just yet. Not until things were right between us, and I'd convinced him to let the Fearless Five handle Siren and Intelligal.

"When I'm out riding around as Johnny Angel, I check in with Bella and grandfather a couple of times a night. It's been over twelve hours since I last contacted them."

I slapped my hand against my head. "I'm so sorry! I should have thought of that last night. They're probably worried sick." I would have been. I'd always been worried when Travis had gone out on missions by himself. "Come on. You can use the phone in my room."

I led Johnny down the twisting corridors to the one that housed our underground suites. His eyes flicked over the signs on the doors that designated whose room was where. They lingered on the one that read TORNADO.

I opened the door to my suite, and we stepped inside. Johnny strode ahead, taking in the furniture and knickknacks.

Johnny's gaze focused on Travis's picture before settling on the enormous bed. A wave of hot, fiery anticipation shot through my body.

"So this is where you stay when you're fighting crime. I like it. It looks like you."

I glanced around. Red sofa, black chairs, tile floors, white walls, fireproof paintings. The room was almost an exact copy of my apartment, except without the extra much-needed closet space. "Thanks. The phone's over there by the bed."

Johnny's lips twitched up into a seductive smile. "Really? How interesting." He gave me a long, steady stare that made my hormones flare to life. "Perhaps we'll explore that area of the suite later. Unfortunately, right now I really do need to make my phone call."

A few sparks shot off the tips of my fingers and landed on the slick tile floor.

"Dial five to get out of the manor," I said in a helpful, slightly flustered tone. Like Joanne James, I was no innocent, quaking virgin, but something about Johnny Bulluci made me quiver deep down inside.

Johnny punched in a series of numbers on the black phone. "Hey, it's me."

"Where the hell have you *been?*"

I winced. I could hear Bella's high-pitched screech across the room.

"Grandfather and I have been up all night!"

"I'm sorry," Johnny said. "I was unavoidably detained, but I'm fine now. In fact, I'm with Fiona."

"Fiona?" Bella squawked. "Did the two of you have a sleepover? Is that why you didn't call and check in last night? You should have told me where you were going, Johnny. If I'd known that you and your new girlfriend were having fun, then I would have done something nice for myself. Like gone to bed at a decent hour instead of sitting up, waiting and worrying about you."

"We did something like that," he replied. "I'm sorry I didn't call sooner."

Bella spent the next five minutes tearing into her brother for his lack of manners and total disregard for her feelings. "The next time you stay out all night with your girlfriend, you'd better call me, Johnny Bulluci. Or else it will be the last time you're ever with a woman. And I do mean *ever*."

"I'm sorry, Bella. I really am. It won't happen again." Johnny glanced at me. "Although I suppose I should tell you that I probably won't be home tonight either. Fiona and I are right in the middle of something important. So, don't wait up for me."

"You—you—you!"

Bella sputtered incoherently, then slammed down the phone. The crack sounded like a concrete block being splintered. Johnny winced and rubbed his ear.

"She sounded really angry. I'm sorry I got you into trouble."

Johnny shrugged and put the phone back in its cradle. "This isn't the first time I've forgotten to check in. Bella will get over it. Eventually."

"I hope so. For your sake. I always thought Bella was so cool, so calm, so collected, but she didn't sound like someone I'd want to cross. Not even as Fiera."

"You have no idea. Bella can get a little worked up at times. And when she does, well, strange things happen." Johnny ran his fingers through his thick hair. "But I'm yours for another day, at least. So, how do you want to spend it?"

I knew exactly how I'd like to spend the day. In bed. With Johnny. I stared at him, wondering exactly how injured he still was—

"But before we do anything, do you think I could get some real clothes to wear?"

My eyes traced over his body, and I realized that Johnny was only wearing the white T-shirt and pajama bottoms we kept in the sick bay. The clothes were so thin, they were practically transparent. More sparks fluttered from my fingertips, and I curled my hands into fists to keep them from igniting. Now was not the time to ogle Johnny. Not after I'd beaten him senseless only a few hours ago.

"Come on," I said. "We'll find you some clothes, then I'll show you around."

"Are you sure about this, Fiona?" Johnny asked half an hour later. "I know this might be upsetting for you."

I closed my eyes. "It's fine. Really, it is."

After half an hour of riffling through the suites and pitifully small closets, we'd come up with nada. Nothing came close to fitting Johnny. My father's and Sam's shirts and pants were too small across the chest and too long. Henry's clothes were too short and too mismatched. Besides, I wasn't about to make Johnny wear polka-dot bow ties with plaid sweater vests. That was just cruel. Which meant the only one other place to look for men's clothes in the manor was in Travis's room.

I opened the door to Travis's suite, and we stepped inside. My heart twisted, the way it always did when I came in here. A fine layer of dust covered the coffee table and entertainment center. The bed was bare, stripped of its sheets, and the magazines and knickknacks had been removed from the bookshelves. A couple of months ago, I'd packed up Travis's things and stacked them in some cardboard boxes in a corner of the room. I hadn't had the heart to get rid of them or donate them to charity. Not yet. I turned the ring around on my finger. The diamond glowed under my hot hands.

Johnny put a hand on my shoulder. "Are you sure this is okay? I really don't mind wearing the pajamas."

My eyes slid over his perfect biceps. I didn't mind him wearing the pajamas either. Or even nothing at all. That was the problem. "No, this is fine. Someone should get some use out of Travis's clothes. I've been meaning to donate them to charity. I just haven't gotten around to it yet."

I stepped away from Johnny and tore into one of the boxes marked CLOTHES. I handed him a pair of jeans and a T-shirt that bore the logo for the Weather Channel. "Here. Try these. They look like they're about your size."

Johnny nodded and stepped into the bathroom. He came back out wearing the clothes I'd given him. "They fit well enough," he said, turning around. "How do I look?"

He looked perfect, of course, just like always. But my eyes misted over just a bit. That had been one of Travis's favorite T-shirts. I'd given it to him as a gag gift for his birthday last year.

"Fine," I said, dropping my eyes. "Let's get out of here."

We closed the door, and I took a deep breath. Remembering Travis was always a little difficult for me. So was going into his old room and realizing that he'd never come striding into it again. Still, it wasn't quite as hard as it had been in the past. Johnny had made it a little easier for me. I only hoped I could do the same for him and his pain over his father's death.

I took a step forward. My head spun around, and I braced myself against the wall.

"Hey, are you all right?" Johnny asked, his eyes bright with concern. "If me wearing Travis's clothes bothers you that much—"

"It's not that. Sorry. I'm just a little light-headed. I get that way when I don't eat enough."

Johnny stared at me. "Really?"

My stomach chose that moment to let out what amounted to a plaintive wail. *Feed me . . . feed me . . . feed me now*, it whined.

Johnny's eyes widened. "I didn't know a person's stomach could make that particular sound. Especially for that long."

"Fiery metabolism," I explained. "I have to eat quite a bit every couple hours or I get light-headed and weak. As you can tell from my complaining stomach."

"Don't worry about it. I could use a little something to eat myself. Food first. Then, we'll explore. Deal?"

My stomach rumbled again. "Deal."

I led Johnny to the underground kitchen and cracked open the refrigerators. I pulled out almost everything that was in there. Johnny started making some turkey-and-Swiss sandwiches. I couldn't wait any longer, so I grabbed a frozen pizza and tore off the cellophane covering. I wiggled my fingers, and flames covered the pie. Thirty seconds later, the pizza was done. I put it on a plate, folded the pizza over, and prepared to sink my teeth into the cheesy, greasy concoction.

"Can I have some of that?" Johnny stared at me, a knife in one hand and a fork in the other.

"Sorry," I said, putting down the pizza. "Everybody around here's pretty used to my, ah, habits. Sometimes, when I'm hungry, I forget my manners around other people, including how to share my food. Here. Have some. Please."

Johnny cut himself off a large slice, while I inhaled the rest of it. We sat there in silence, munching on pizza and sandwiches. After about twenty minutes, Johnny pushed his plate away. I kept eating.

My eyes zeroed in on the half-eaten sandwich on his plate. "So, are you going to eat that?"

Johnny shook his head and laughed. He slid his plate over to me. "I seem to be doing this a lot around you."

"Oh? What's that?"

"Missing meals."

I rolled my eyes at his bad joke. Johnny chuckled, and the tension between us lightened. Soon, we were laughing and talking and joking just like we had before we'd discovered each other's secret identities—and our confrontation at Oodles o' Stuff. We were having such a good time I almost forgot that less than twenty-four hours earlier, we'd been at each other's throats. Almost.

"I know this must have come as a shock to you," I said, polishing off a bag of chocolate chip cookies. "Our secret lair. Me having superpowers. Especially the superstrength. That freaks a lot of people out, especially guys."

"Actually, I think I always sort of knew," Johnny said.

"Really? How?"

"I'm not quite sure. When I was Angel and I ran into you guys, I thought you looked very familiar. That you reminded me of somebody I knew. I just couldn't quite put my finger on who it was."

I narrowed my eyes. "You don't happen to have an inner voice that whispers to you, do you?"

Johnny shook his head. "Sorry. Psychic powers aren't my forte."

Good. We had enough mind readers around here. It was getting to where a person couldn't even *think* anything in private. Especially anything naughty.

"And there was the food, of course. You ate so much and were so thin I thought maybe you were bulimic or something."

"You're not the only one."

Johnny continued with his story. "Plus, that night we had dinner with Bella and Grandfather, when we were looking at the portraits, your body was . . . warm, hot even. Unnaturally so." A rueful grin crossed Johnny's face. "I thought it was me at first, but I guess I can't take credit for that now, can I?"

"Oh, it was mostly you," I said, blushing just a bit as I remembered my outrageous behavior. I'd begged Johnny for more . . . and more . . . and more.

"Really? Well, then, I'll have to remember that."

And there he was, standing in front of me. "And exactly how I went about doing it."

Johnny lowered his lips to mine. I closed my eyes, reveling in the sensation. His tongue licked the corner of my mouth, and I opened it. Johnny plunged his tongue inside even as he pulled me toward him. His hands ran up and down my back. I tangled my fingers in his hair. I breathed in, letting his spicy scent make my head swim.

But I couldn't fully enjoy the kiss. I kept seeing myself hitting Angel with that metal pipe, his blood zipping through the air. With a sigh, I broke off the kiss and stepped back.

"Johnny, about last night—"

He put his finger to my lips. Another fiery flare shot through me. "Let's not talk about business today." He smiled that crooked grin I knew and loved so well. "Didn't you say something about a tour?"

"This is incredible. Absolutely incredible." Wonderment filled Johnny's green eyes. Which were pretty wondrous in and of themselves.

During the last hour, we'd done a complete sweep of the underground lair. The library, kitchen, suites, game room, equipment room, everything. Now, we stood in the training room watching a computer simulation of our previous battle with Siren and Intelligal at the factory near Good Intentions Lane.

"The equipment, the computers, the holograms. Where do you guys get the money for all this stuff?" Johnny asked, his eyes moving from the lifelike holograms to the rows of computers and blinking lights. I could almost see him trying to calculate the cost of everything.

I shrugged. "Being a superhero isn't cheap, so it helps that Sam's a billionaire."

"Who's Sam?" Johnny asked.

"Sam Sloane, the businessman," I replied. "He's Striker, another member of the Fearless Five, and one of the wealthiest guys in the city. He has plenty of money to burn on our superhero gear. And I don't do so badly myself either. Fiona Fine Fashions has a very healthy profit margin."

Johnny's eyes slid over my shirt and jeans. "I'm sure it does, with such a beautiful woman running it."

I smiled, pleased at the compliment. A lot of things about Johnny Bulluci pleased me.

He turned back to the holograms that flickered in the training room below us. "Do you have more of these? I'd love to watch them."

"Of course. But they're so boring. Why would you want to look at—" I knew why Johnny would want to watch our training simulations. He wanted to know more about Siren and Intelligal. Every strength. Every weakness. Every habit. He had to, if he was going to kill them.

"Oh, Johnny."

"He was my father, and he was blown away. Can't you understand that?" His voice was hard with emotion. Anger. Rage. Grief.

"Of course I can understand it." I put a hand on his shoulder. "No matter what else has happened, you have to know that I'm sorry for your loss. Losing a loved one is never easy, no matter what the circumstances are. Losing your father the way you did is especially painful. I know you think that I'm against you, that the Fearless Five are against you, but we're on your side. We want Siren and Intelligal brought to justice just as much as you do. They're planning something—something that could hurt a lot of innocent people. We've got to stop them before they get a chance to do it."

He didn't respond, but his eyes went to my hand on his shoulder. They lingered on my diamond ring.

"Is there anything I can say to get you to change your mind? To work with us?" I said in a soft voice.

Johnny stared at me. "You have your duty, your code. And I have mine. I'm sorry, Fiona."

Then, he turned and walked away.

★ 21 ★

Johnny returned to the sick bay and spent the rest of the afternoon in bed recovering his strength. I paced around the library and brooded for an hour, before heading to the kitchen and polishing off everything I could get my hands on. Cookies, chips, pies, pizzas, cold cuts, cheese, bread. If it wasn't nailed down, I ate it. If I'd had enough salt left, I would have gnawed on a couple of table legs. But I'd used it all on my French fries. Damn.

The chief came in late that afternoon after his shift and checked Johnny's vitals. I stood in a corner and watched.

"Well, it looks like you're healing up nicely, Johnny," the chief said, listening to Johnny's heart through a stethoscope. "In addition to your exoskeleton, I also believe you have a bit of regeneration. Then again, most superheroes do."

"I'm not a superhero," Johnny said.

He didn't speak to me. He didn't even look in my direction.

"Well, everything appears to be in order. I think you can

return home tomorrow, if you wish. Try not to do anything too strenuous for a couple of days, though. Okay?" the chief asked.

Johnny nodded his head. "Okay. I'll get out of your hair first thing in the morning."

"I'll drive you back to Bigtime," I volunteered.

He stared at the tiled ceiling and shook his head. "That's all right. I'll just call a cab to take me back into town."

"You can't exactly do that," I pointed out. "We're a couple hundred feet underground here, you know. Plus, there's our whole secret-identity thing. Calling a cab would officially blow our cover."

"Then, I'll go upstairs and call a cab from there. I'll be fine. I always am."

Our gazes locked. Johnny pulled the covers up to his chin and rolled over on his side.

Shutting me out again.

Tired, grouchy, and frustrated, I went to bed early. And I dreamed . . .

I stood between Johnny and Siren. We were all in costume, standing in the middle of an open field. Spring green grass stretched for miles in every direction, contrasting with the gaudy colors of our suits. And the gunmetal gray of the pistol in Johnny's hand. It was a large weapon, more like a cannon than an actual gun.

Siren stared at me with her hypnotic blue eyes. "Are you just going to stand there and let him kill me? Or are you going to be a real superhero and save me?"

Her voice sounded harsh and demanding. I could feel her will wrapping around me, squeezing my thoughts, my actions into her wishes and desires. My feet moved of their own accord until I stood in front of Johnny.

"Please, Johnny," I begged. "Please don't do this. Don't make me choose between the two of you. She's not worth it. She's nothing compared to you. Please, please don't do this."

Johnny raised his gun and pointed it right at me. I opened my mouth to beg, to plead with him one more time. But he didn't listen. He pulled the trigger. The bullet punched through the air, slamming into my heart. Breaking it—

I woke up with a gasp and bolted upright. My heart pounded. My hair cracked and sizzled and hissed with fire. My fingertips glowed. Sparks flew everywhere, smoldering on my silk sheets. My eyes zipped around the room.

My room. I was in my room. Slowly, I relaxed. It was a dream. Just a dream. Just a nightmare. I flopped back against the bed and rubbed my blazing eyes.

For now.

I stripped the sheets off the bed so they wouldn't catch fire, then lay back down. I tried to go back to sleep, but for once, it eluded me. Hot and sweaty, I got out of bed and grabbed a couple of thick towels and an itty-bitty bikini from my stash of swimsuits.

It was time for a midnight swim, something I'd started doing after Travis had died. I hadn't slept well for months after his murder, and swimming was the only thing that calmed me down. The gentle splash of the water, the weightless feel of it against my skin, the rhythmic, repeated kick of my arms and legs soothed something primal deep inside me. For a little while, I could forget about my troubles, my pain, my anger. I could lose myself in the water. Plus, I didn't have to worry about getting emotional and setting the pool on fire. I'd melted more than one treadmill that way.

I walked through the deserted halls of the underground lair. We were taking the night off, given the disastrous events of the previous evening. My father had gone back into the city to finish up some paperwork regarding the mess at Oodles. Henry and Lulu were around somewhere, probably huddled in the library *type-type-typing* away on their computers, but no one was officially on call.

I made my way to the exercise room. Unlike my pitiful closet space, Sam had spared no expense in outfitting the gym with the best treadmills, elliptical trainers, and strength-training devices money could buy. Row after row of gleaming machines sat in the long room, along with shelves full of exercise DVDs. Free weights, exercise balls, and yoga mats hung in racks in a corner of the room, which smelled like sweat, rubber, and old gym socks.

We couldn't afford to let ourselves go or ubervillains would wipe the floor with us. And then there was the PR side of things. Nobody—not the public and certainly not SNN—wanted to see out-of-shape superheroes. Even the older heroes like Granny Cane kept themselves in tip-top condition. They needed to in order to sell their toys and video games. Given my fiery metabolism, I didn't have a problem keeping the weight off, but the others had to work at it.

I strolled past the machines, opened a door, and stepped into the pool room. Sam had spared no expense here either. Cushioned lounge chairs and umbrella-topped tables crouched on either side of the Olympic-sized pool, along with metal lockers full of scuba, snorkeling, and other diving equipment. In addition to saving people on the mean streets of Bigtime, we'd also done more than a few underwater rescues. At least once a month, some civilian ran his car off the Skyline Bridge and into the marina. Or a cruise ship tipped over and had to be righted before it sank to the bottom of Bigtime Bay.

But perhaps the most unusual feature of the pool room was the ceiling. Instead of the usual tiled ceiling that hovered above so many of the hallways in the underground lair, this one featured embedded 3-D holograms similar to those in the training room. A knob on one wall let you set the ceiling to whatever scene you wanted to look at, from rolling clouds, to lightning, to several of the better-known constellations. I chose the *night sky* setting, remembering my time with Johnny at the observatory. The ceiling dimmed to a dusky gray, and a smattering of stars twinkled to life, along with a full moon. I hit another knob, and the soft sounds of crickets and other forest creatures filtered into the room. Ah, perfect.

The faintest hint of a spring breeze brushed my face, and I felt some of the tension ease out of my body. I spread my towels out next to the shallow end of the pool and did a few stretches to loosen up my tight muscles. Then, I climbed up the twenty-foot diving board, bounced once, and plunged into the deep blue water.

The wetness closed over me, blocking out everything else. Johnny's stubbornness, his vendetta, my fruitless attempts to stop him, these new feelings I was developing for him. I swam and swam, going from one end of the pool and back again in a thoughtless rhythm.

I popped up for air and found myself staring at a pair of bare feet. Slightly hairy, very male feet. My eyes snapped up.

Johnny towered above me, clad only in his pajama bottoms. "Hey there."

"Hey," I said, not quite sure what he was doing here. I swam over and sprawled across the steps that led down into the water.

Johnny followed me. He sat down on the edge a few feet away and dangled his legs in the warm water. I tried not to notice how the fabric clung to his toned calves. Or how see-through it became when wet.

"I wanted to talk to you about earlier today," Johnny said. "I acted like a complete ass. I'm sorry."

"There's no need to apologize."

"Yes, there is. You were trying to help me, and I shut you down." He drew in a deep breath. "It's just, I don't know, I can't think straight where Siren and Intelligal are concerned. It just hurts too much. All I can focus on is my father and what they did to him. But I took my pain, my frustration, out on you today. I'm sorry for that."

"Forget about it. I understand. Really, I do."

Johnny nodded. "That's what makes it so hard sometimes."

He stared out at the shimmering water, then back at me. "Care for some company?"

"I'd love some. Doing laps gets pretty boring after a while," I joked, trying to lighten the mood.

I swam back out into the middle of the pool, so Johnny would have room to ease himself down into the water. To my surprise, he followed my progress alongside the edge of the pool, grinning.

"Cannonball!" Johnny shouted, throwing himself into the water.

An enormous wave washed over me. Water stung my face, and I laughed. Johnny came up for air, and we treaded water. We swam back and forth in the pool for a while.

After about half an hour, we raced back to the shallow end and got out. We flopped onto the thick beach towels and stared at the fake stars high above. If I hadn't known better, I would have sworn I was lying on a deserted beach somewhere instead of underneath one of the finest homes in Bigtime.

"It all looks so real," Johnny said. "Like you could almost reach up and pluck the stars out of the sky."

"Sam, Henry, and the chief do a good job with the holograms."

We lay there, still and silent and staring at the stars. I

thought about asking Johnny one more time to forget his vendetta, to leave Siren and Intelligal to us. But I didn't want to ruin the moment, so I kept quiet—for a change.

My stomach, though, had other ideas. It let out a long, gurgling roar that would have put Yeti Girl to shame.

Johnny turned over on his side and looked at me. A grin spread across his face. "Let me guess. No lunch or dinner, right?"

My stomach rumbled like thunder. "Oh no, I ate enough lunch and dinner for thirteen people. But unfortunately, my metabolism never, ever stops. Not even when I'm asleep."

"Well, we better get you fed before you waste away to nothing. We can't have you fighting crime on an empty stomach, now can we?"

I laughed, and Johnny pulled me to my feet. I grabbed my towels, and we headed for the underground kitchen.

I plopped down on one of the metal swivel stools, while Johnny yanked open the door on one of the refrigerators. He stared inside, then glanced over his shoulder at me.

"I know." I cringed just a bit. "It's probably a little empty in there."

"I'm sure I can find something for us to snack on."

Johnny turned back to the refrigerator, and I used the opportunity to study him. His pants were still slightly damp, accentuating every muscle in his perfect body. Exoskeleton or not, the man looked like a marble statue come to life. One that was perfectly proportioned. My eyes dipped lower. Everywhere.

"So, what do you want?" Johnny asked, rummaging around in the frosty depths. "I think there's still enough roast beef left for a couple of sandwiches."

I was hungry, but not for food for a change. I hungered for Johnny. And I was going to do something about it. Right now.

"Here, let me see what I can find."

I strolled over to the refrigerator and scanned the contents. Johnny was right. There wasn't much left, except a couple of boxes of baking soda and a few condiments. Even I couldn't eat ketchup, mustard, or mayonnaise straight out of the bottle, no matter how famished I was. My eyes roamed over the metal racks. But it wasn't a complete loss. I plucked out a skinny can.

"Whipped cream?" Johnny asked. "You're going to eat chocolate whipped cream and nothing else?"

I grinned. "Absolutely."

I shook the can. Then, I leaned over and squirted a little on the corner of Johnny's mouth. I flicked my tongue over the chocolate frost and licked it off, lightning quick. I repeated the process on the other corner of his mouth. Then, on the side of his neck. Then, in the hollow of his throat. Whipped cream had never tasted so good.

"Fiona . . ." Johnny said in a husky tone.

"What's the matter? Don't you like whipped cream?" I asked in a coy voice.

Johnny put his hands on my hips and rested his forehead on mine. His light touch made me burn that much more. "Are you sure you want to do this with everything that's happened? With everything that's between us? Because Siren and Intelligal are still out there, and I'm still—"

I put a bit of whipped cream on my finger and pressed it to his lips. "Enough about them. We're here now, and that's all that matters. Besides, I'm still hungry." I licked the chocolate confection away. "Aren't you?"

Johnny stared at me. Then, a slow wicked grin spread across his face. "Baby, I'm always hungry."

He took the can from me and squirted some of the cream into his mouth. I reached up and pulled his lips down to mine. The frothy chocolate melted as our tongues stroked back and forth. Even as the whipped cream disappeared, the liquid heat inside me grew and grew until it was a bonfire raging out of control, burning me alive. And there was only one thing that would douse the flames, only one thing that would cool my desire. Johnny. Now.

Right now.

I sank to my knees and pulled Johnny down with me. He lowered me the rest of the way to the floor. The tile was cool and slick beneath us, but I didn't feel it. All I could feel, see, taste, hear, smell was Johnny.

Our kisses grew longer, harder, deeper, until we were both frantic and dizzy with need. We clawed at each other's clothes, ripping aside the thin barriers. My bikini was shredded away. So were his pajama pants.

Johnny squeezed my breasts. I raked my nails down his back. He kissed my neck. I nibbled on his ear. Our legs tangled together, and fire throbbed and pulsed through my body, rocking me to my molten core. With one thought, we moved into each other. The white-hot feel of Johnny sinking into me made me cry out with pleasure.

It was quick and hard and good. We climaxed and lay there panting on the tile.

Johnny drew me into his arms and nuzzled my neck. I closed my eyes and stroked his damp hair, careful not to singe it with my sparking fingertips. A soft, warm glow wrapped around my body.

"Don't you go to sleep on me just yet," Johnny said.

I looked at him through slitted eyes. "Why not? Good sex always makes me sleepy. I think I held up my end of the bargain just now."

Johnny reached over my head and grabbed the stray can of chocolate whipped cream. "Because, baby, we still have half a can of whipped cream left."

Johnny shook the metal can. He leaned over and spread

the cream on my nipples, my stomach, then farther down to more interesting places. The creamy frost felt like dew drops on my flushed skin.

"Johnny, what are you up to?"

He grinned and lowered his mouth to me.

★ 22 ★

I woke up a couple of hours later in Johnny's arms. We were still in the kitchen, stretched out in front of the refrigerator. A couple of beach towels covered our bodies. I stretched my arms above my head. Every part of me felt warm and languid and relaxed. A sigh of contentment escaped my lips. I felt so satisfied, so peaceful, so loved.

A hand stroked my cheek. I turned, and Johnny was there. He rose up on one elbow and stared into my eyes.

"Hey there."

"Hey there yourself." I pressed my lips to his for a quick kiss. "That was pretty incredible."

"Yes, it was. Although I'd use a better adjective than merely *incredible*. Lots of things are *incredible*. Give me something stronger."

I arched an eyebrow. "Fantastic?"

Johnny shook his head. "Something stronger."

"Unbelievable?"

"Nope."

"Tip-top?"

Johnny shuddered.

"Super-duper?"

Johnny snapped his fingers. "Super-duper! That's it! Fiona Fine, we have just made *super-duper* love together. Wouldn't you agree?"

"And then some."

We kissed again, and Johnny flopped onto his back. He stared up at the ceiling, and his smile faded away. I knew he was thinking of his father. And how he would never experience such pleasure again.

"Tell me about your father," I asked, snuggling into the crook of his arm to distract him. "I told you about Travis. Tell me about your father, James."

"Are you sure you want to hear about him now?" Johnny asked. "That's sort of an odd conversation for pillow talk."

I gestured at the tile floor beneath us. "Well, we're not on pillows, we're on the kitchen floor. And I'd like to know more about your father, more about Johnny Angel."

"All right."

Johnny told me everything about his father. How he'd been heartbroken when his wife Lucia had died. How he'd struggled to raise Johnny and Bella alone. How he'd given them everything he had. His love, his time, his business. Johnny's love for his father radiated from him, along with some emotion I couldn't quite identify.

"When was the last time you spoke to him?"

Johnny's eyes darkened. "The night before he died. I was still in Greece then, and he called me to talk about a business deal I was working on. Then, we started talking about the other family business—Johnny Angel. He wanted me to come home to Bigtime and take over as Angel. He said he was getting too old, that he'd almost let a mugger get away from him a couple of weeks ago. I refused. I told him that life wasn't for me. The fighting, the patrolling, the gang wars. It wasn't what I wanted."

"And then he died," I prodded in a gentle tone.

Johnny sucked in a deep breath. "And then he died. Two days later, Bella called me, frantic. She hadn't heard from Dad. I flew home at once. We went out to where he'd last been seen. We found some of the pieces of his motorcycle. They were charred and burned almost beyond recognition. And we found his watch. The glass case was busted, but it was still in one piece. That watch was my grandfather's, the original Johnny Angel. My dad never went anywhere without it. We knew then that he was dead."

My heart ached for Johnny. I touched his face with my fingertips, and Johnny pressed a kiss to my hand.

"I turned over our Greek operations to one of the other business managers and moved back home. I vowed to find the people responsible and make them pay."

"Siren and Intelligal."

Johnny nodded. "A contact in one of the local biker gangs overheard the two of them talking about how they'd killed Angel. They were bragging about it at Quicke's one night. When I found out it was them, I swore a blood oath to my grandfather and Bella to kill them and avenge my father. And I will honor my vow."

I opened my mouth to protest. To tell him once again that the Fearless Five would bring the ubervillains to justice. Johnny wasn't having any of it, though. His fingers slid down my breasts, past my stomach. They penetrated me, exploring. I closed my eyes. Heat waves of pleasure sizzled through my body. I was so hot you could have fried bacon on my forehead.

"That's . . . not . . . fair," I rasped, digging my hands into his smooth, broad shoulders. "I . . . can't think . . . straight . . . much less . . . argue . . . when you . . . do that."

Johnny grinned. "Baby, nothing's fair in love and war. Isn't that how the old saying goes?"

He didn't have to reach for me. I threw myself into his waiting arms.

We made love four more times. On the floor. On the countertop. Against the refrigerator. Sitting on top of a stool. The last one was particularly interesting. I'd never look at a chair the same way again.

When we were done, Johnny went back to the sick bay, and I slipped back into my suite. We both would have been much more comfortable in my bed, but I didn't want the others to know everything we'd done just yet. I wasn't worried about their disapproval. Despite Johnny's desperate need for revenge, the others knew he was a good person deep down inside. Besides, I'd never needed other people's approval anyway.

No, I didn't want the others to know everything just yet because if they knew, then I'd have to admit to myself that Johnny and I were having more than a casual fling. That we were officially a couple. An item. Together. And that I was slowly but surely starting to forget about Travis.

I sat down on my bed. With a start, I realized that I hadn't thought about Travis in hours now. Days really. Oh, he crossed my mind every now and then, but he didn't fill my thoughts anymore. My heart no longer ached like a rotten tooth, pulsing and throbbing with each strained beat. My eyes flickered to the beaming picture on my nightstand. Travis's blond hair and brown eyes looked strange to me, almost as if I were seeing him for the first time. The pain of his loss wasn't the only thing fading from my mind. My memories were getting fuzzed over as well. And that's what really scared me. I didn't want to forget him. Didn't want to forget anything about him.

But I was.

My fingers traced over his wide smile. The diamond on my finger sparkled like a small sun on my hand. "Well, I suppose you know about me and Johnny by now. You'd like him, I think. He's a lot like you. Fun, energetic, full of life," I whispered. "He'll never take your place, but I like him. And he likes me. He makes me laugh, just the way that you used to. I've missed that. Laughing."

Talking to a picture of a dead man was rather silly, of course. He wasn't going to talk back to me or suddenly appear beside my bed as a shimmering ghost. Whispering to Travis was something Carmen would do while listening to those pesky voices in her head. But it made me feel a little better, even if Travis didn't respond. Even though he never would again.

I snapped out the lights and went to sleep.

The next morning, I stood in the sick bay with Johnny and the chief, who was giving him one more exam before discharging him. Johnny grinned at me while Chief Newman checked his temperature, pulse, and blood pressure. The last of his cuts and bruises had healed up, and Johnny looked no worse for wear, despite the fact I'd gone to town on him with a lead pipe. I didn't feel quite so guilty about it as I had before. I figured last night had made up for it a little bit. Pleasure. Pain. There was a thin line between the two.

The chief tapped his knees with a metal hammer, making a hollow, ringing sound. Johnny slipped his hand in mine, while the chief continued his ministrations. I liked the solid feel of Johnny's skin next to mine. All of his bare, naked, smooth, supple skin next to mine. His hard, muscled body on top of me. Under me. Beside me. In me—

"Fiona? Are you listening?" Chief Newman rumbled.

I snapped back to reality. "Of course. What did you say?"

"I said that Johnny's fine, except he seems a little tired this morning. You wouldn't know anything about that, would you?" The chief turned his blue eyes to mine.

I flashed back to our time together in the kitchen. I could still taste the chocolate whipped cream on my lips. "Of course not."

"I did tell him to avoid strenuous activities," the chief continued. "But I don't think he heeded my warning."

Strenuous wouldn't be the word I would use to describe last night. Perhaps *vigorous* or *long-lasting* or the previously agreed upon *super-duper*.

My father kept staring at me. His eyes glowed, like a match burning. Johnny looked back and forth between the two of us, still grinning.

"Johnny doesn't seem to be one to heed warnings," I said.

"That sounds like someone else I know," the chief replied.

I tossed my hair over my shoulder, but I couldn't help the blush that crept up my cheeks. I'd just been busted for having a little nookie-time fun by my own father. Way to go, Fiona.

The chief finished up his examination, pronouncing Johnny fit to take on the world once more. Johnny put on some more of Travis's old clothes, and we headed back to the city in my convertible. It was a beautiful May day, with plenty of sunshine and a steady breeze. I put the top down, tilted my face up, and drank in the vibrant rays. Johnny leaned his head against the back of his seat and did the same.

We didn't speak on the way back to Bigtime. I didn't know what to say to Johnny, other than to ask him once again to abandon his vendetta against Siren and Intelligal. I wasn't sure how he would react to that.

We pulled into the long, curving driveway of the Bulluci manor about ten that morning. I stopped the car outside the front door and killed the engine.

Johnny turned to me. "Come in. Stay with me for a while."

I stared up at the house. A white lace curtain in one of the upstairs windows twitched and fell back into place. "I'm not sure that's such a good idea. Unless I miss my guess, Bella's waiting somewhere inside ready to pounce on you and demand an explanation. Given how your last conversation went, I imagine there'll be some yelling involved too."

"That's precisely why I need you to come with me. To protect me from my big, bad, nasty sister." Johnny grinned.

I found myself grinning back. "I do so admire manly men, especially those who quake at the thought of facing their little sister."

Johnny shuddered. "You don't know Bella. She might seem mild-mannered and sweet, but once she gets going, she's hard to stop."

"Well, if you insist . . ."

The truth was that I wanted to spend more time with Johnny. Every waking minute if I could. Anything to keep him close to me, to keep him safe. Anything to keep him from trying to fulfill his vendetta.

"I do insist with you, Fiona. Always."

Johnny pulled me inside, and we wandered through the angel-filled rooms, searching for the rest of the Bullicis.

"Bella? Grandfather? I'm home," Johnny announced. His voice boomed through the sprawling mansion.

No response.

"Come on," Johnny said. "I know where they are."

He led me to the den. Bella sat on the long sofa, watching some art restoration program on the enormous television.

A sketch pad lay on her lap, but she snapped off the screen at the sight of us.

"Well, it's about time you got home," Bella said in a tight, cold voice. Her hazel eyes shimmered like liquid gold with anger. "I hope the two of you enjoyed yourselves these last few days. Some of us were working."

"I didn't mean to be gone so long, but I ran into a bit of trouble. Fiona helped me out of it." Johnny strolled to Bella's side and planted a kiss on her cheek like nothing was wrong.

Bella narrowed her eyes. "What sort of trouble? Did the two of you run out of condoms or something?"

I arched an eyebrow. I wouldn't have thought quiet, shy Bella would have the gumption to say the word *condoms* out loud, much less in front of other people. Perhaps still waters really did run deep.

"Not exactly," Johnny said. "Fiona beat the stuffing out of me."

Confusion and worry spread across Bella's face. "How would she be able to do that? Your exo—" She cut off her words and looked at me.

I rolled my eyes and tossed my hair over my shoulder. All these innuendos and shortened sentences and half-truths were really starting to annoy me. So I did what I did best. I snapped my fingers, and a fireball popped into my hand. With my other hand, I picked up the sofa—with Bella still sitting on it. She let out a squeak of alarm and clung to the side of the furniture.

"This is how," I replied.

Bella's eyes zipped back and forth from me to the fireball to the sofa to Johnny and back to me. Comprehension filled her face. "You're Fiera?" she screeched. "The superhero? A member of the Fearless Five?"

I winced. Bella could almost match Siren when it came to her piercing voice. "That's right."

Bella's golden gaze flicked to her brother. "Why are you telling us your secret identity?" She tried to be cool and casual, but panic sparked in her eyes.

"You don't have to pretend, Bella. Fiona knows that I'm Johnny Angel. She knows everything. About me, about Father, all of it."

Bella's mouth dropped open. She almost tumbled off the sofa. "Johnny! You didn't!"

"He didn't really have a choice," I said. "I did beat the stuffing out of him. But I knew who he was before then."

Bella turned on her brother. "Johnny, how could you be so reckless? Letting someone guess your secret identity. The family's secret identity."

I gestured at all the cherubs and angel wings and halos in the room. "It wasn't that hard to figure out. In fact, it's pretty obvious. You know, you guys might want to think about redecorating just a little bit. The angels are a dead giveaway."

"That's what their grandmother always thought, but I never listened to her."

We turned at the sound of Bobby Bulluci's voice. The old man stood in the doorway, staring at the three of us. His eyes went to the fireball in my hand and the sofa I had hoisted in midair. Busted again. If I kept this up, I might as well just take an ad out in the *Chronicle* or the *Exposé* announcing my secret identity to the entire world. Hell, maybe I'd just rip my mask off at the next superhero gathering at Paradise Park in front of Kelly Caleb. The SNN reporter would get the news out in no time flat. On the up side, I'd save a fortune in masks.

Bella rubbed her temples. "Let me get this straight. You

knew that my brother, the man you've been dating, was Johnny Angel, yet you still beat up on him?"

"That's right."

"Johnny, do you care to explain this?" Bella crossed her arms over her chest, looking more like an uptight school-teacher than a cutting-edge fashion designer.

"It's a long story," Johnny said. "Let's sit down."

I put the furniture and Bella back on the floor and snuffed the fireball out. We sat down on the lowered sofa, and Johnny spent the next ten minutes filling Bella and his grandfather in on everything that had happened since we'd had our knock-down, drag-out brawl at Oodles o' Stuff.

"Incredible," Bobby said. "All these years I've wondered about the Fearless Five, who they really were, and here you are, Fiera, sitting in my living room. Incredible."

I shrugged in a modest sort of way. It was always nice to be thought of as incredible. My eyes went to Johnny. Or super-duper. I cleared my throat. Since all of our cards were on the table, I might as well appeal to Bella and Bobby to help me with my mission. My very personal mission.

"My friends and I have spent the last two days trying to convince Johnny to leave Siren and Intelligal to us. The two of them are planning something, and we need to figure out what it is and stop them before they hurt anyone else."

"It is not simply a matter of stopping them," Bobby said. Tears gathered in his eyes, and he suddenly seemed old and small and frail. "I believe in the old ways. Eye for an eye, blood for blood. Those two killed my James, my son. They should be killed in turn to set things right."

"I understand your pain, sir, truly I do," I said. "But killing them won't bring your son back. It won't take away your sadness."

Bella nodded. "That's what I've been trying to tell them for months now. We've already lost Father. We don't need to lose you too, Johnny."

"He has a duty to his family, to carry on the legacy—" Bobby started.

"Oh, screw the stupid family legacy," Bella snapped. "I'd rather have Johnny home safe and sound any day than lose him to your silly legacy."

The two of them glared at each other. Yikes. And I thought I could get hot under the collar when I was angry. I had nothing on Bella Bulluci.

Disgusted with the men in her family, Bella grabbed her sketchpad off the sofa and threw it onto the glass-topped coffee table.

Crack!

The pad hit the table with a loud smack, and the glass split down the middle. The two pieces fell on top of each other, along with an assortment of coasters, magazines, and a mug that hit the floor and shattered.

When the noise faded and the glass and dust settled, I looked at Bella. Wondering.

"It's nothing," Bella muttered, avoiding my eyes. "Just another part of the stupid family legacy."

One that was getting more interesting and unusual by the minute.

"Maybe you should go and let us talk about this, Fiona," Johnny said in a soft voice. He squeezed my hand. "Please?"

I looked at the three of them. This was a family matter, and I wasn't part of the family. The thought made me sadder than I would have imagined.

"All right. I'll go. For now. But think about what I said. Let the Fearless Five handle the ubervillains. It's what we do."

"It's what Johnny Angel does too," Bobby replied. "It's

what we've done for three generations now. We take care of our own. We always have, and we always will. That's our family's real legacy."

I didn't have a response. Johnny's eyes begged me to go before things got any more heated. So, I left.

★ 23 ★

I drove to my office. Paperwork cluttered my desk, along with the remains of the wilted flowers Johnny had sent me. I stared at the dried-up brown petals and hoped they weren't an omen. That my relationship with Johnny wouldn't soon be as dead and decayed as they were.

I rolled my eyes. Sheesh. I was getting as bad as Carmen and my father looking for doom-and-gloom portents of the future. I shoved the flowers into the trash can and stared at the piles of messages on my desk, the notes from suppliers, all the thousand small details that needed seeing to. I really needed to get to work.

But I couldn't concentrate on any of it, not even my Fiera fan mail. All I could think about was Johnny and his family. I paced around my office. Bella had agreed with me, that the Fearless Five should be the ones to take care of Siren and Intelligal. But Johnny and his grandfather hadn't. And I knew they wouldn't. Their honor, their code, their legacy was just as important to them as my superhero duty was to me. Why did men have to be such fools sometimes?

"If you don't cut that out, Fiona, you're going to poke holes in the floor with your stilettos," Piper called out from the doorway. "You don't want a repeat of last time, do you?"

I grimaced. The last time Piper was referring to was when I'd put my foot through the floor after a particularly grueling fitting session with Joanne James. It was either that or put my foot through her bony ass. Joanne had gotten off lucky that day.

"Why don't you use the balls I got you?" Piper suggested.

In addition to leaving eating disorder and other self-help pamphlets on my desk, Piper was also fond of giving me gifts like those rubber balls you squeeze in your hands. She thought I needed to relax.

Piper kept staring at me, so I yanked open my desk drawer and rummaged through the mess inside until I came up with one of the rubber gizmos, which was a little smaller than a tennis ball. I rhythmically flexed my fist around the puny ball.

Piper smiled, happy that she'd gotten me to do her bidding, and disappeared back into her office.

I waited to make sure she wasn't coming back. Then, I squeezed the ball with all my might. It only took me a second to turn the rubber into a handful of goo. I tossed it in the trash and watched it smolder.

Piper was right. It did make me feel better. I always enjoyed melting things.

I worked the rest of the day, stopping only to eat a quick but massive lunch at Quicke's. Every so often, I'd look at the phone, hoping Johnny would call. Hoping he'd

tell me he'd changed his mind about going after Siren and
Intelligal. That he was giving up his quest, his mission, his
vendetta. But he never did. Men never called when you
wanted them to.

I left work around six and headed back out to Sublime.
Tonight was my night to be on duty in the library. I rolled
my neck around, trying to ease some of the tension that had
built up there. I'd zapped all of the rubber balls I could find
in my desk, but they hadn't helped much. Maybe I'd be
able to do a few laps in the pool after my shift ended. Maybe
not, the way things were going. It hadn't exactly been a
banner week so far. Except for my time with Johnny in the
kitchen.

I stopped by the kitchen and made myself a couple of
ham-and-cheese sandwiches, grabbed two bags of chips, and
put a bottle of soda under my arm before heading to the library. One of the doors was cracked open, and loud, angry
voices bounced down the hall. I frowned and quickened my
pace. What the hell was going on?

"I don't see why you have to be so stubborn," Henry's
voice floated through the door. "I love you, and I want to
marry you. What could be simpler than that?"

I peeked inside. Ah, the two lovenerds were squared off
above their flickering computer monitors, each one glaring
at the other.

"There's nothing simple about it, and you know it," Lulu
snapped back. "Your power is a precious gift. You deserve to
have kids who will follow in your footsteps—who'll have
your mind-melding power and help others with it."

"You're acting like there's no hope," Henry said. "But
there are things we could try. Medical advances like in vitro
fertilization or a surrogate mother. And researchers are developing new methods all the time."

Lulu shook her head. "But you should be able to have

both—a woman who loves you and who can give you kids. It shouldn't be this hard. Your power is too important to waste—"

"Oh, stuff my power." Henry shoved his glasses up his nose. "I wouldn't care if my power went away tomorrow, as long as I had you."

Lulu's face softened. Even I melted a little. Wow. Giving up your power to be with the person you loved? That was the ultimate sacrifice for superheroes and ubervillains alike.

Lulu drew in a deep breath. "We both know I can't have kids. And unless they come up with some sort of super-science in the next couple of years, I won't ever be able to have children. I don't want you to give that up for me, Henry."

"But we can adopt," Henry persisted. "It wouldn't matter to me. You know that."

Lulu shook her head. "But they wouldn't have your powers. You're far too strong and your power is far too important to let it end with you."

Henry opened his mouth to protest again.

I cleared my throat, not wanting to hide outside any longer. "I hate to interrupt, but it's my turn to be on call."

The computer gurus stared at me, shocked that I'd overheard their conversation. I strolled inside, sat down at the table, put my feet up, and started eating sandwiches like I hadn't heard a single word of their heated argument.

Henry and Lulu glared at me, then each other. Both of them looked at their monitors and began to pound away on their computers. I supposed that's what geeks in love did after they had a fight. Scary.

After I finished my sandwiches and assorted munchies, I flipped through the stack of fashion magazines Sam kept in the library for me. But my heart wasn't really into dissecting the latest looks from Paris and Milan. All I could think about was Johnny. I wondered where he was right now. What he was doing.

Was he getting ready to suit up and prowl the streets as Angel? Or had he taken my advice to heart and was staying home where he'd be safe? I didn't know.

After about an hour of silence, Lulu let out a loud yell. "I've got them!" she cried. "I've got them! I've got them!"

"Who? What? Where?" Henry asked just like a good journalist would.

The two of us darted over to Lulu and peered into her computer monitor. The hacker's thin fingers pounded the keyboard so hard I thought she was going to punch through the plastic keys.

"They're holed up in one of the buildings down by the marina," she said, pointing to a city map on her wide screen. "Right there next to the fish-packing plant."

I put my hands on my hips. "The marina? What would they be doing at the marina? There's nothing down there but boats and water and rotten fish. And, of course, the occasional dead body."

Lulu stared at me. "How am I supposed to know what goes through the minds of ubervillains? But that's where they're at, according to my calculations."

"I'll call the chief," Henry said. "If we're lucky, we can trap them in the building and take them down. There's nowhere for them to go but out into the water. It shouldn't be so easy for them to slip through our fingers this time."

He moved to his computer, pressed a few buttons, and spoke into a microphone. My father's voice boomed into the room, and Henry told him the situation.

While they talked, I thought about calling Johnny. Perhaps if I asked him to fight with us instead of against us, it might satisfy him. Then, I remembered the pain in his eyes when he'd told me about his father's death. The cold hard rage in his voice. No, Johnny Bulluci aka Johnny Angel wouldn't be satisfied until Siren and Intelligal were dead. But perhaps I could save him from himself. And my heart in the process.

Henry cut the connection to the chief. "He's in the area checking on a burglary. He'll be here in fifteen minutes."

"Good. Then let's go end this thing. Once and for all," I said.

★ 24 ★

The chief arrived, everyone suited up, and we piled into the van. Thirty minutes later, we skidded to a stop in front of the entrance to the Bigtime Marina.

Bigtime was situated on the eastern edge of New York, right on the Atlantic. The ocean cut into the middle of the city, almost like a jagged shark bite. It and the manmade river that flowed down the hill from the observatory formed Bigtime Bay. The bay's waters were calm and shallow for the most part, making it the perfect place to come for a swim or day of sailing. Some of the society folks like Berkley Brighton and Devlin Dash even had their own private islands out in the middle of the bay, offering them impressive views of the city skyline.

Hermit eased the van over a couple of speed bumps. During the day, the cobblestone marina was a pedestrian area closed to vehicles, so the boating types had to wait until after sunset to put their ships into the water. In addition to fleets of sailboats, the marina featured a maritime museum where kids could pet stingrays and the like, and stores that carried all things nautical, from clothes to scuba gear to bait. A wooden pier stretched out like a finger into the bay. It was popular with people from all walks of life, many who came to fish and feed the flocks of gulls.

We left the sailboats behind and headed for the less glamorous side of the bay, where the loading docks, shipping yards, and industrial plants crouched against the water's edge like barnacles.

"Before we go in, everyone be sure to take their gas pill." Hermit passed out the medication to each of us. "Remember, it only lasts about twenty minutes, so we need to get in and take down Siren and Intelligal as quickly as possible."

"And we're sticking together this time," Mr. Sage said. "I don't want anybody being ambushed by the ubervillains or Angel, if he decides to make an appearance. We all go in together. We all come out together. Agreed?"

Hermit and I nodded.

"Then, let's go."

Lulu outfitted us with the usual cameras and transmitters, and the three of us left the van.

"Be safe," she called after us, looking at Hermit.

"Always," I replied, pressing my fist to my heart.

We tiptoed through the dark shadows, the bay a pool of black ink on our right. A few lights bobbed up and down on the water, and a foghorn sounded in the distance. A steady breeze blew the smell of salt to us. It made me want some pretzels.

"According to Lulu's calculations, Siren and Intelligal are holed up in that building over there." Hermit pointed to one of the frozen-fish-stick-processing plants.

I wrinkled my nose. Fish sticks. I hated fish sticks. They were just about the only food I wouldn't eat. The stench alone was enough to make me gag. Why did ubervillains always have to pick the dingiest, dirtiest, most disgusting places imaginable for their supersecret, diabolically evil lairs? You'd think that, every once in a while, they'd spring for a nice room at the Bigtime Plaza or something. Most of them stole enough jewelry and other pricey baubles to stay anywhere they wanted to, anytime they wanted to. But no. Ubervillains skulked about in the shadows, and we always ended up saving the world in some abandoned, out-of-the-way dive.

A loud rumble cut through the air, and my heart sank like a cement block tossed in the bay. I knew that sound. A pair of halogen headlights popped into view down the street, and Johnny Bulluci aka Johnny Angel slid his motorcycle to a halt in front of us. His eyes warmed at the sight of me, and he shot me a crooked grin. My heart sped up, and I found myself smiling back. Then, I remember why Angel was here—to kill the ubervillains who had murdered his father. My smile faded.

Still, I had to give him a chance, no matter how far-fetched it might be. "What are you doing here, Angel?"

"Just looking after things, including my girl. Is that a crime?" he asked, his green eyes bright.

"Not as long as that's all you're doing. Is it?"

Angel shrugged. He drew his lighter out of his pocket and fired up a cigarette. "I spoke with Grandfather and Bella. The three of us decided that I should work with you, instead of against you. For now."

Meaning he'd play nice until we had Siren and Intelligal right where he wanted them. I opened my mouth to protest, but my father cut me off.

"All right, Angel," Mr. Sage said. "We're a couple of hands short, so you can join us if you wish. But you follow our lead."

Angel nodded his head. "Of course."

I stared at my father. What was he thinking? He was

psychic, he had to know that Johnny Angel had no intention of letting us turn Siren and Intelligal over to the Bigtime police. Hell, I wasn't a psychic, and I could see it.

Johnny parked his bike, and the four of us headed for the fish-stick plant. It was a short, squat building that jutted up against the side of the bay. We faced the back part of the building, where the docks were that the fisherman used to drop off their daily hauls of tuna, flounder, and shrimp. The front of the building faced one of the downtown streets a couple of blocks over.

"Don't you guys think this is sort of odd?" Lulu said in my ear.

"What's that?" my father asked.

"Well, in my somewhat limited experience, ubervillains usually choose abandoned buildings to set up their headquarters. According to my information, Fred's Fried Flounder Fish Sticks is the main supplier of fish sticks in Bigtime."

"Who cares?" Angel asked. "All that matters is that they're in there, and we're going to get them. One way or another. I'm tired of waiting. Let's go."

Angel headed for the plant. I looked at my father, then Hermit. They shrugged. I shook my head and followed Angel.

I not-so-gently wrenched open one of the loading-dock doors, and we stepped inside. The four of us formed a line and searched the area. Lulu was right. Fred's Fried Flounder Fish Sticks was very much a working operation. Everything was neat and orderly and clean, from the rows of forklifts to the stacks of cardboard boxes to the few workstations and desks that we passed.

We did a complete sweep of the facility. Other than a couple dozen industrial-size freezers full of frozen fish sticks and your usual assembly-line setup, there was nothing inside. No power cords. No radiolike device. No wires. No tools. No blueprints. No ubervillains. Nothing.

We backtracked to the center of the factory, hoping to find something we'd overlooked. Still nothing. Angel cursed and lit another cigarette. Hermit typed on his hand-held computer and murmured to Lulu. My father laced his fingers together, deep in thought. I put my hands on my hips.

A chill swept over me that had nothing to do with the freezers. My nose twitched. I smelled something rotten, and it wasn't fish sticks.

"This doesn't feel right," my father murmured.

"Oh, I wouldn't say that. I think it's about time you got here," a sultry voice drawled out.

The four of us turned. Siren stood behind us, holding a curious-looking microphone in her manicured hands. Diamonds gleamed on the black metal surface. Intelligal floated high above. She flipped a couple of switches on a device that looked like an oversized boom box. It too was studded with diamonds.

Angel's hands clenched into tight fists. He started forward, but I caught his arm. He took half of a step forward. I tightened my grip, stopping him.

"Not yet," I whispered out of the corner of my mouth.

For a second, I thought Johnny would shake me off and launch himself at Siren. But he paused. I nodded my head at him. Maybe I had finally gotten through to him.

Because no matter what happened, Johnny wasn't going to kill the ubervillains. I wasn't going to let him. It wasn't the Fearless Five way. It wasn't my way, and I didn't want it to be his way either.

And I hated to admit it, but Lulu was right. This was a little too pat, a little too rehearsed for my liking. The ubervillains were up to something. Well, more so than usual.

"You're probably wondering why we're here tonight," Siren said.

Her soft breathy voice curled around me like a rope. I reached for my inner fire and burned the coils away.

"Intelligal told me about Angel and Fiera's tussle the other night, and I had an idea. Instead of trying to fight you off, I should bend you to my will, make you all my little puppets. Intelligal and I are going to need some help to fully implement our scheme."

"And what scheme would that be?" I said.

"Oh, the usual," Siren said. "Take over Bigtime, then the world."

That was our cue to move. I loosened my grip on Johnny's arm and tensed my muscles, ready to strike. He did the same. My father's fingers fluttered, and Hermit fixed his computer on Intelligal's chair. But before we could move, Siren held the strange microphone up to her lips.

"Now, now, I don't want to fight. Why do the four of you?" she purred.

The microphone amplified the sultry hypnotic pull of Siren's voice a hundred times. A thousand times. I stopped cold. Maybe even a hundred thousand times. My brain screamed at my muscles to move, to attack, to lash out at Siren, but I couldn't quite make myself do it. The others stood frozen beside me.

"I don't want to fight, do you? Why don't you clasp your hands behind your backs and stand there like good superheroes?" Siren lowered the zipper on her neon blue costume, exposing cleavage that would have put the Great Wall of China to shame.

Since Siren's voice had more effect on men than women, the others did as she asked without question. Even my father, the great psychic, couldn't resist Siren's command with her new toy firmly in hand. The men had their hands behind their backs before she'd even finished speaking.

Not me.

Maybe I was just too much of a hothead to be easily controlled. Maybe my will was just a tad stronger than the others'. Or maybe I just hated the ubervillains more for what they'd done to the Bullucis, to James, to Johnny.

So I didn't succumb to Siren's sultry song. Instead, I reached for my inner fire, concentrating on the searing, pulsing flames deep within me. I grabbed them and held on tight, focusing my energy on *my* fire, *my* anger, *my* will. The sweet, gauzy haze of Siren's voice melted away like snow in a firestorm. My arms twitched.

The microphone. I had to destroy that damned microphone. Then the others would be free, and they could help me.

"What's going on?" Lulu squawked in my ear. "Hermit, Mr. Sage, what are you doing? Why are you listening to her? Hermit, can you hear me?"

I blocked the computer hacker's voice out of my mind. I couldn't answer her and fight off Siren at the same time.

Siren noticed that I hadn't done as she'd asked. She frowned and raised the microphone to her pouty lips again. "Siren says, *Put your hands behind your back, Fiera.*"

I took a step forward. Sparks flew from my fingertips. Then another step. My hair hissed with fire. Another step. My body started to glow like a liquefied ruby. One more step.

Every step got a little easier, a little faster. The bitch wasn't going to control my mind. I didn't care what kind of souped-up karaoke machine she had. No way, no how. I was Fiera, for crying out loud. Protector of the innocent. Superhero du jour.

"Go to hell, Siren," I muttered through gritted teeth.

"Gas her! Now!" Siren roared.

Intelligal hit a button on her chair, and that sickly sweet blue gas floated over me. I must have burned away Hermit's antigas pill, because the feeling immediately went out of my arms and legs. The fire inside me snuffed out. I fell to the cold, slick floor, my arms and legs flopping around like a fish trying to breathe in the bottom of a boat.

"Now, Siren says, *Lie still.*"

I growled at the silky, hypnotic purr. I couldn't move my arms or legs, and I didn't have my fire to sustain me. So I did the only other thing I could think of. I bit down on my tongue. Hard. Blood filled my mouth. The coppery taste washed away some of the sugary sweet gas and grounded me.

"Never."

Siren stared up at her sister. "What's wrong with her? Why isn't she a puppet like the others? You told me this thing was foolproof." She tapped her long nail against the top of the microphone.

Intelligal shrugged. "I never said it was foolproof. Only that ninety-seven percent of the population could be put under your control by using it. As for Fiera, she seems to have a stronger will than the others. And she's female. You know you've never been able to get along with other women, even when you use your power to its fullest extent."

"You're right, of course. Oh well. Three superheroes will be more than enough to help me carry out our plan."

The ubervillain leaned over me, giving me a close-up view of her overinflated breasts. They matched her ego perfectly.

"Sorry, Fiera, but Intelligal's right. I'm just not into chicks. Since you won't play nicely, you won't play at all." Siren laughed. "Siren says, *Throw her in one of the freezers, Angel. Now.*"

"What? Don't be a fool, Siren. Let me blast her with my explodium missiles," Intelligal said, flipping switches on her chair. "Let's kill her. Immediately."

Lulu let out a loud shriek of dismay in my ear. I winced.

"Hold on, Fiera. I'm leaving the van! I'm getting out right now!" the computer hacker screamed.

Through my earpiece, I heard the hydraulic lift hiss to life on the van. But it was too little, too late. Lulu wouldn't get here in time to save me. There wasn't anything she could do against two ubervillains anyway. And there wasn't any radioactive goo around that could turn her into Super Lulu.

"Come on, Siren," Intelligal said. "Enough of this nonsense. One missile and Fiera will be history. Forever."

"Calm down," Siren snapped. "Look at her. She's as helpless as a baby. She's no threat to us now."

Siren dug her pointed boot into my ribs. I couldn't even feel it.

"Besides, you just finished calibrating the machine. I don't want the shockwaves from the explosion throwing it off. Otherwise, we'll have three pissed-off superheroes to deal with. I don't think they'd take too kindly to the brutal demise of their comrade. That just might be enough to snap them out of their trances. And your missiles make such a mess of everything." Siren fluffed out her black curls. "You know how I hate to have bad hair."

Intelligal scowled, but her hands dropped from the switches. I let out a quiet sigh. Thank heavens for ubervillains and their vanity.

But my relief was short-lived. Angel jerked forward like a robot. He put his hands under my arms and hauled me to my feet. I dangled against him like a wet noodle. Limp and completely lifeless.

"Please, Angel. Please don't do this. Fight her. I know you can." My tongue felt thick and heavy in my bloody mouth.

Angel's eyes remained blank and expressionless as a piece of paper.

"Mr. Sage? Hermit? Snap out of it, guys! She's an ubervillain! Fight it! Fight her commands!"

My two fellow superheroes didn't respond. They didn't even seem to hear me. Instead, they stared at their new mistress, eager for another task.

Siren laughed. "Tearful pleas won't do you any good, Fiera. Your friends are now under my control. If you haven't figured it out by now, this device that Intelligal rigged up amplifies my power incredibly. With it, I'm going to enslave the people of Bigtime, then the rest of the world . . ."

I tuned out her long-winded self-congratulatory explanation. Ubervillains always thought they had to explain every single, tiny, minute detail of their schemes. When you've heard one plan to take over the world, you've heard them all. It doesn't really matter what the brilliant plan is—as long as you figure out a way to stop it.

But one thing Siren said did catch my attention.

"And if city officials don't believe I'm serious, well, I'll just have to remind them about our demonstration at the sports complex a few days ago."

"What? You used your karaoke thingy to bring down the sports complex?" I asked. "That's why it collapsed?"

"Of course," Intelligal answered. "That was our dry run, so to speak, to test the maximum power of the device, as well as its effect on solid matter. It was very effective, exceeding all of my calculations."

Siren preened. "All it took was a couple of throaty whispers set to the right frequency to make the whole thing come tumbling down."

I opened my mouth to ask another question, but the ubervillains were ready to wrap up their gloating. Siren snapped her fingers. Angel, Mr. Sage, and Hermit stiffened to attention at the sound.

"Siren says, *Take her to the freezer, Angel. Now.*"

Angel dragged me back toward one of the many freezers that lay inside the plant and threw me down. Siren, being ever-so-helpful, opened the door. Cold air blasted out. If my arms and legs hadn't felt like soggy tissue paper, the frigid chill would have made even me wince. I focused my eyes on Angel.

"Come on, Angel. Fight her. Fight Siren. Do it. For me. Remember that night by the lake? When we made love? Our time together in the kitchen?" I pleaded, trying to spark some sort of memory. A super-duper memory.

"You two are an item? Well, isn't that sweet? Super-heroes in love. Or at least lust." Siren slithered up to Angel, and her eyes roamed over his hard body. She leaned in and slid her manicured nails down Angel's chest to his crotch.

"If you can inspire such devotion from Fiera, I just might have to give you a ride once this is over with." She cupped him, and her face lit up. "Oh my, what a nice package."

I wanted to rip the bitch limb from limb for touching my man like that. My hands jerked and spasmed. If only the gas would wear off, I would fireball her trashy ass. Hell, I'd boil the whole bay with her in it.

Siren snapped her fingers again, and Angel dragged me inside the freezer. It was one of those large, walk-in freezers favored by restaurants and, evidently, fish-stick factories. Boxes and boxes of fish sticks lined the walls. Blowers set into the ceiling churned out a steady stream of air, and a thick layer of ice covered everything. Frost gathered in Angel's tawny hair, making it gleam like pure silver.

As a superhero, I'd been in plenty of tight spots before. I'd been thrown through walls, slammed through floors, dropped off high-rise buildings. So I wasn't ready to panic just yet.

"Angel, please. I know you care about me. Don't you

know how much I care about you? Don't you know how much I love you?"

I hadn't planned on saying the words. Hadn't really thought about them before. But as soon as they came out, I knew they were true. I did love Johnny Angel aka Johnny Bulluci. Somewhere, in the middle of this craziness, I'd fallen for the rich biker playboy. I loved him for his crooked grin, his devotion to his family, the way he could always make me laugh.

So I said it again. "I love you, Angel."

Nothing.

Angel didn't smile. Didn't look at me. Didn't even blink.

I poured my heart out to him, and he didn't even care.

He didn't respond to my desperate, heartfelt plea, and that hurt me worse than anything Siren had in mind.

I'd appealed to Johnny's feelings for me. Evidently, he didn't have any because it hadn't worked. It always worked in the movies. I'd seen it work for Carmen and Sam. What was wrong with Johnny and me?

I shoved that painful thought aside and focused. I knew Johnny pretty well. What else did he care about? What else was important to him? What would snap him out of his trance? Finally, the answer hit me.

"Johnny Angel," I said in a hard, sharp voice. "Your family needs you. I *need* you. You're not responsible for your father's death. Your father made his choice a long time ago. He knew the dangers. He knew the risks. It's not your job to avenge him and uphold the family honor. But if you don't fight Siren, if you don't *try*, we're all going to die. Your friends. Your family. Me. All of us are . . . going . . . to . . . die."

For a moment, Angel's face cleared. His hand slowly went to his jacket, and he fumbled with something in his pocket. Angel leaned over me. Concentrating. Trying. Something slipped from his fingers onto my stomach. I stretched my numb hand out and managed to cover up the lump of cold metal.

"Siren says, *Leave her there*," the ubervillain cooed.

Angel's eyes widened. Sweat beaded and froze on his forehead, but he didn't move away from me.

"Stop stalling!" Siren roared into her microphone. "Get out of there now!"

With a jerk, Angel straightened. He turned and walked out of the freezer. The last thing I saw before he shut the door were his eyes. They were ice green.

Frozen.

Just like his heart.

PART THREE

Breakup
Blues

⋆ 25 ⋆

The door slammed shut, and the metal bar on the other side clanged into place. Trapped. I was trapped in an industrial-strength freezer. With fish sticks. Things were definitely not going as planned. Then again, they rarely did in my line of work.

But what hurt more than my present situation was my heart, which felt as if the Ringer had used it as a punching bag. Johnny had succumbed to Siren's song. He hadn't cared enough about me to fight her off. Neither had Hermit or Mr. Sage. I wasn't thrilled with my team members right now, but Johnny's betrayal was the one that wounded me the most.

Oh sure, he was under the influence of a hypnotic ubervillain with more cleavage than a lingerie model. Oh sure, she had a fancy device that could enslave 97 percent of the population. Pitiful excuses, at best. I'd told Johnny that I loved him, and he'd still abandoned me.

My fingers twitched. But maybe not entirely. Hands

shaking, I uncurled my palm. Johnny's, Angel's, lighter lay inside. A spark of hope flared to life inside me. In the end, Johnny had tried to help me. To give me a way out. Maybe I could forgive him, if I got out of this alive.

My body felt limp and tingly from Intelligal's power-diluting gas, but I didn't have time for such weakness. If I didn't get out of here soon, I'd freeze to death. Even with my fiery superpowers, it would only be a matter of minutes before I was one big icicle. I hated to be cold, and I hated fish. But here I was, trapped with both. Ah, the glamorous life of a superhero.

"Lulu?" I asked, my voice weak and small. "Lulu, can you hear me?"

The computer hacker didn't answer. Not even static cracked in my ear. The thick door must be blocking the signal, meaning I was on my own. Fabulous.

Somehow, I managed to roll over onto my knees. I could still taste the sickeningly sweet gas in my mouth, mixing and mingling with my blood. With my free hand, I scraped up a mound of frost off the floor and shoved it into my mouth. The ice crystals melted, washing away some of the gas. My head cleared, and I felt a little stronger.

I kept repeating the process until I had cleansed my mouth. My arms and legs twitched and jerked and spasmed, recovering from the effects of Intelligal's gas. I crawled to the middle of the freezer and slung my numb limbs around until I faced the door. It was a thick metal door, designed to keep the cold in. Well, not for long.

My fingers trembled. I grasped the lighter and slowly clicked it. Once, twice, three times. Four, five. Nothing happened. I couldn't quite grip the cold, slick metal with my weak, tingling fingers. *Focus, Fiera, focus!* I'd been in tighter spots than this, most notably when Prince Horrid had captured me with plans to add me to his harem as one of his pliant dancing girls. I'd gotten out of that mess. I'd get out of this one too. I was Fiera, for crying out loud. Member of the Fearless Five. Protector of the innocent. Superhero du jour. It was what I did.

Just when I thought I couldn't hold it another second, the lighter sparked on. I cupped the tiny weak flame like it was the most precious thing in the world. To me, it was. Slowly, my hands warmed. The lighter's small flame fed my own inner power. My fingertips started to glow as the fire inside me rekindled. I concentrated on burning the rest of the limp, languid feeling from my body. High metabolism, help me now.

My emotions had always fueled my powers, and I grabbed hold of them. I remembered how Siren had tricked us, how she'd turned my friends against me, how the bitch had put her hands all over Johnny. I focused my anger, let it rage through me with the heat of a thousand suns. The fire inside me grew and grew and grew.

I formed a fireball with my hands. I took careful aim and threw it at the door. It exploded onto the cold metal, making it shriek and groan. Steam filled the freezer. I formed another fireball.

Then another one . . .

Then another one . . .

Then another one . . .

Ten minutes later, the last remains of the door melted away. I got to my feet, still a little shaky, and stumbled through the melted edges of the white-hot metal.

"Fiera! Fiera! Where are you?" Lulu's voice squawked in my ear.

"Over by one of the freezers," I said, sliding to the ground.

A motor whirred, and Lulu stopped in front of me, tires smoking.

"Where the hell have you been?" I muttered, trying to rub the rest of the feeling back into my arms and legs.

"I got here as quick as I could. I'm not Swifte, you know," Lulu said in a defensive tone. Her eyes dropped to her wheelchair and legs. "Not by a long shot."

I bit back my angry retort. It wasn't Lulu's fault. She'd done the best she could. And I had other things to think about right now. Like how to rescue the others and stop Siren's evil plan to take over the city. "Did you hear Siren? Did you see where they went?"

"I heard everything, but by the time I got out of the van, it was too late." Lulu shook her head. "Siren and Intelligal shepherded the others into a car on the far side of the building. They sped away before I could fix a tracker to it."

I cursed. This was no time to be sitting around. I grabbed on to the remains of the melted door and pulled myself up. At least, I tried to. My arms buckled, and I wobbled back and forth, before falling and smacking my ass against the cold concrete floor. I cursed again, loud and long, hating my sudden weakness.

"Whoa there, tiger!" Lulu put a hand on my shoulder. "You're not in any position to be walking around right now. It's a miracle you got out of that freezer alive."

"Well, I can't sit still. And it's not like you can carry me out of here. Do you have another suggestion?"

Lulu patted her lap. "Hop on board the Lulu Lo Express. I can drive us both out of here."

"You can't be serious."

"Oh, I am. Henry likes to ride around on my lap all the time."

I groaned and put my head in my hands. "Too much information, Lulu. Too much information."

*   *   *

In the end, I didn't have a choice. After a good five minutes of cursing and snarling and trying to heft myself into an upright position, I crawled up onto Lulu's lap, and she motored us back to the van.

"Damn, this thing can scoot," I said, trying to distract myself from the fact I was hanging on to Lulu's neck like we were lovers.

I was extremely glad it was after midnight and pitch-black, and that there was no one around to witness my humiliation. I'd never live down the shame. Fiera, member of the Fearless Five, protector of the innocent, reduced to clinging to a wheelchair to get around. Some superhero I was. I couldn't even stand upright at the moment.

Lulu beamed and patted the side of the chair. "Of course it can. I've got almost two hundred horses in the motor. It tops out at about fifty miles an hour."

We zoomed to a stop in front of the black van. I slid off Lulu's lap and into the carpeted interior. The computer hacker strapped herself in the motorized lift and joined me.

Lulu rustled through one of the first-aid boxes we kept inside and handed me a small foil packet. "Here. Take one of these. It should flush the rest of the radioactive gas out of your system."

I took the packet, which contained a *Radioactive Isotope Diminisher*, or *RID* for short. The pills were the invention of some mad scientist who found himself constantly bombarded by radioactivity while he was researching something or other. They were like vitamins to superheroes, and the Fearless Five used them to keep from getting more mutated than we already were. They'd saved our asses on more than one occasion, especially Carmen's last year when she'd gone up against the Terrible Triad by herself.

I swallowed the pill and felt the effects almost immediately. My limbs grew heavy and substantial once again, my superstrength returned, and my inner fire flared up to its usual slow, steady burn. I sat up. "All right. That did the trick."

"Are you sure you're okay?" Lulu asked. "We can sit here and rest a few more minutes, if you need to."

"I'm fine. And we don't have any time to rest. We need to get our boys back."

"How are we supposed to do that?" Lulu asked. "Carmen and Sam are halfway around the world, and Henry and the chief are under Siren's spell, along with Johnny. We're a little short of superheroes right now."

"Oh, don't worry about it. I know a couple of people who should be more than willing to help us," I said. "Let's go."

"Are you sure this is a good idea, Fiona?" Lulu asked.

I put my hands on my hips. "Of course I'm sure it's a good idea. All my ideas are good ones."

I tossed my hair over my shoulder, trying to look more confident than I felt. The truth was I wasn't sure it was a good idea, but it was the only one I'd been able to come up with. Lulu and I needed help, and this was the only place we were likely to get it.

We stood outside the closed iron gates that led up to the Bulluci manor. Lulu pressed the button on the call box again. No response. We'd been standing out here for ten minutes, trying to get somebody to wake up and answer us.

"Oh, screw this." I took hold of the iron gates and looked over my shoulder. "You might want to move back."

Lulu eyed my glowing hands, which were clenched around the metal. "I think I'll do that very thing." She hit a button on her chair and zoomed out of the way.

I ripped open the gate. The iron wasn't nearly as sturdy as it looked, and the gates cracked off their hinges. I didn't

even have to put any real muscle into it. Part of the surrounding wall crumbled in on itself.

Since Lulu's chair could move a lot faster than I could
walk, I hopped back on Lulu's lap, and we scooted up the
long driveway. I was getting almost used to sitting on top of
the computer hacker. Almost.

The chair stopped. I climbed off and pounded on the
front door, which was embossed with a giant B and another
freaking angel wing. "Bella! Bobby! Open up! Now!"

A light flared to life in one of the upstairs windows. A
curtain on the front door twitched, and Bella cracked it
open. She wore a pair of short pajamas with white clouds on
them. Naturally.

Her mouth dropped open at the sight of me. "Fiera? I
mean Fiona? I mean . . . oh, you. What's wrong?" Her eyes
flicked to Lulu. "And who is this person with you?"

I took a deep breath. "Johnny's in trouble. We need your
help."

★ 26 ★

Lulu and I explained the situation to Bella. She woke up Bobby, they threw on some clothes, and we piled in the van and headed back to Sublime. Normally, I would have knocked them out or blindfolded them to keep them from seeing exactly where we were going, but I didn't have time. Besides, sneakiness wasn't my strong suit. That was more Sam and my father's thing.

We led Bella and Bobby through the underground garage to the library. It was a good thing I hadn't used blindfolds, because it was painfully slowgoing with the two Bullucis stopping every three feet to stare at something else.

"Come on, come on," I snapped. "You guys can *ooh* and *aah* over the super-duper, supersecret superhero lair later."

The two of them picked up their pace, and we reached the library. Lulu wheeled around and plugged her laptop into Henry's network of computers. The Bullucis stood at the doorway, mouths hanging open.

"Oh, come in. It's not that sacred." I marched over, pulled them inside, and closed the double doors.

Bella and Bobby cautiously crept farther into the massive library.

"Please forgive my surprise. It's just that I never thought I'd be invited in *here*," Bobby said, running his hands over the *F5* insignia carved into the table.

"Me either," Bella whispered. "This is incredible. Look at all the books you have!" Her eyes flicked over to Lulu and her computers. "And the equipment. It's so amazing!"

After a few more minutes of staring and sputtering, Bella and Bobby sat down with Lulu and me at the big round table.

"Explain it to me again," Bella said, rubbing her head. "I'm still a little confused. Johnny joined up with you guys to take out the ubervillains, but Siren hypnotized the men."

"Right." I nodded.

"How was she able to do that?" Bobby asked. "Surely Mr. Sage would have been able to resist her. He's a powerful psychic in his own right."

"It's that damn microphone she had. It upped her power tremendously." I drummed my fingers on the table. Sparks flew everywhere. "Nobody could resist it but me, and that's only because I was a woman. And totally pissed off."

"It's not just the microphone, Fiona. Weren't you paying attention to Siren? Didn't you listen to what she said?" Lulu asked. "She told you exactly what she and Intelligal are up to."

I shrugged. "Not really. I was more concerned with not being able to move at the time. And in the end, all ubervillains want the same thing—to rule the world. The only difference is the crackpot scheme they come up with to try to help them do it."

"Well, let me tell you, Siren's plan is a doozy." Lulu typed on her computer. Images began to pop up on the film screen hanging on the wall.

"Hey, it's that radio thingy the two of them were protecting so fiercely," I said, staring at the box with its odd wires and diamond-studded frame.

"It's not just a radio thingy," Lulu corrected. "It's a voice amplifier and projector. Or VAMP for short."

I snorted. "How fitting."

"Indeed. Anyway, the VAMP machine is designed to take a sound, like Siren's voice, and distribute it over a wide area."

"Like, say, the whole city?"

Lulu shot her finger at me. "Precisely. Siren mentioned something about a broadcast while she was rambling. They must be ready to use it."

"What happens if they do that?" Bella asked.

"Siren's voice will spread out over Bigtime. Not only does the VAMP machine boost the range of her voice, it also ups the power, which is how the others were brainwashed into doing her bidding. It's really quite an impressive machine. Luckily, I thought to put a filter on everyone's comm links to screen Siren's voice, or I probably would have been under her spell too. But if we don't stop them, Siren will enslave everyone."

"Why would she want to do that?" Bobby asked.

"Who knows why ubervillains do what they do? I quit trying to figure out their motivations a long time ago," I said. "She'll probably do something totally lame and cliché and hackneyed like get people to bring her all their money."

"But wouldn't she have to keep talking into the machine the whole time to keep people under her control?" Bella asked.

We looked at Lulu.

"Not necessarily," Lulu said. "She could record her voice and just loop the recording so that it plays back over and over. The only problem with the VAMP machine is that it's not quite powerful enough to broadcast Siren's voice over the entire city. So she's going to need another power source or a way to piggyback the signal onto one of the radio or television stations."

"Then that's what we need to figure out," I said. "Where the ubervillains are going to go to unleash their doomsday device."

"I'm on it," Lulu said, hands flashing across her keyboard.

We sat there in silence while the computer hacker went to work. Bella and Bobby kept shooting furtive looks around at the maps and globes and books. I got up and paced back and forth behind Lulu.

Lulu glared over her shoulder at me. "You know I can't concentrate when you flounce around like that."

"Well, what do you want me to do?" I snarled. "I can't sit still, and I can't crack any skulls until we get a positive location for Siren and Intelligal."

"Oh, go eat what's left in the refrigerator or something. That's what you usually do."

Lulu turned her back to me and started typing again. I resisted the urge to light her hair on fire.

"Come on, Fiona. I'll go with you," Bella said. "Do you want anything, Grandfather?"

Bobby shook his head. "No. I think I'm just going to sit here and look at everything. If that's all right with you, Fiona."

I waved my hand. "Fine. Just as long as you don't disturb her computer highness over there."

Lulu shot me another dirty look. I just tossed my hair over my shoulder.

*   *   *

Bella and I walked down the deserted halls until we reached the underground kitchen. I opened the doors on the restocked refrigerators, desperately in need of ten thousand calories or so. It'd been a busy night so far, and tomorrow, rather, today would only be worse. I needed to keep my strength up.

"How about some cheesecake?" I asked, pulling a large pie out of one of the refrigerators. "It's triple chocolate, one of Quicke's specialties." The restaurant delivered a couple dozen of the delectable desserts to Sublime every week.

"Well, I really shouldn't. I'm on a no-sugar diet . . ." Bella's voice trailed off as she stared at the luscious cheesecake.

No-sugar diet? No wonder the poor thing was so up-tight. No sugar, no fun, in my book.

"Well, you're going to have a piece tonight," I said, cutting her a slice. "I think we've all earned it. I certainly have."

Bella took the cheesecake from me and poured herself a glass of milk. I thought she'd just pick at the yummy cake, but Bella downed it and came back for seconds. She was a quick eater, just like me. Maybe we'd get along better than I thought.

"I still can't quite believe you're a member of the Fearless Five. And that I'm sitting here with you in the supersecret Fearless Five headquarters." Bella took another big bite of her cheesecake. "It's all a bit surreal."

"Tell me about it. I can't believe you come from a family of generational superheroes. I also can't believe your brother is actually Johnny Angel, and that I've been dating him." I eyed Bella. "Do you moonlight as somebody too?"

"Of course not. Johnny Angel is the only one in our family." She sounded offended, as though being a superhero was some vile occupation.

"Do you have an exoskeleton like Johnny does? Or some other sort of power?"

She hesitated. "I don't know if you'd call it a power, exactly. It's a little strange."

"Oh really? Strange how? Strange like you can manipulate the weather with your bare hands? Strange like you can create unbreakable force fields around yourself? Strange like you can create earthquakes just by thinking about them?"

I stared at the fashion designer. Perhaps if Bella had some hidden superpower, she could suit up and go out into the field with me. I could use all the help I could get when I went after Siren and Intelligal. My eyes flicked over her body. She was about Carmen's size, although quite a bit curvier. Surely, I could find her some sort of costume to wear—

Bella laughed. "Not that strange. I'm just lucky."

So much for that thought. "Lucky? That's not really a power, is it?"

Bella shrugged. "Not really. Not like your power."

"So how does it even work?"

"I just think about things, and stuff . . . happens. Especially when I'm stressed out."

I thought back. "Is that why the coffee table cracked the day I was at your house?"

Bella nodded. "That's one of the problems with it. You can have good luck . . ."

"Or bad luck," I finished. "Show me. Show me how it works. Or doesn't work."

"I can't control it all the time, but I'll try."

Bella stared at me. I looked back at her. Her eyes didn't glow. Her hair didn't snap and crackle. Sparks didn't fly from her fingertips. She didn't seem to be doing anything at all, other than eyeing me. Some power.

But I kept that thought to myself and raised my fork to

take another bite of cheesecake. To my surprise, my hand wobbled, and the cheesecake fell onto the table. What a waste. It was a good thing I still had plenty left. I stabbed another bite. Again, the cheesecake slid off my fork and splattered onto the table. I frowned at the chocolate stains. I wasn't that clumsy, especially when it came to food.

I eyed Bella with suspicion. "Did you make me do that?"

She smiled and cut another piece of cheesecake off with her fork. "What do you think?"

Bella raised the fork to her lips. She was just getting ready to pop it into her mouth when the dessert slipped off the silver tines and joined the rest of mine on the table.

She stared at the chocolatey mess and let out a long sigh. "Unfortunately, it always seems to boomerang around back to me—in a bad way."

Maybe there was something to this luck thing. Too bad Bella didn't know how to control her power. Or at least make Siren and Intelligal have a string of bad, debilitating luck.

We sat there in silence. After I finished off the cheese-cake, I made myself a dozen cucumber-and-tomato sand-wiches, which I ate with three bags of chips, five liters of soda, a box of oatmeal-raisin cookies, another box of crack-ers, a pound of grapes, and a wheel of Gouda cheese.

Bella fixed her amber eyes on me. "So what are your in-tentions regarding my brother?"

I almost choked on my sandwich. "Excuse me?"

"What are your intentions regarding Johnny? Do you care about him? Or is he just a fling to you? Some random guy you can have great sex with?"

I wiped the mayonnaise off my mouth, stalling for time. I'd fallen in love with Johnny Bulluci, but I wasn't sure quite how I felt about it. Much less what I should say to his sister about him.

"I ask because Johnny really likes you. I even think he's starting to fall in love with you," Bella said in a soft voice.

My mouth fell open. I couldn't speak.

"Do you care about him, Fiona? Because if you don't, you should walk away from him when this is over. I know Johnny appears like he's cheerful and carefree and that nothing can hurt him, literally, but you could. He told us about your fiancé. How he was murdered. How much you loved him. How you still wear his engagement ring. If you're not over your fiancé yet, you need to tell Johnny now, before he gets any more involved with you." Bella's eyes bored into mine. "I won't let my brother get hurt, especially not by a superhero. Do you understand me?"

For once, I chose my words carefully. "I care about your brother a great deal. I'm not leading him on. That would never be my intention. As for Travis, I'll always love him. I'll always miss him. But he wouldn't want me to live my life in the past. He wasn't that sort of man. As for me and Johnny, I'm just trying to take it one day at a time. Things are a little . . . complicated between us right now, in case you haven't noticed."

Some of the bright, angry glow drained out of Bella's golden eyes. My words seemed to satisfy her. At least she hadn't cracked the table this time. I'd hate to lose the rest of my food.

"I noticed," Bella said. "Things are always complicated when it comes to my family."

The odd tone in her voice struck me. "What do you mean?"

Bella sighed again. "It's a long story."

"I've got nothing but time until we find the uber-villains."

Bella stared at the refrigerator, but the vacant look in her eyes told me that she wasn't really seeing it. "I don't know much about your childhood being the daughter of a superhero, but I grew up in a home where it was all Angel, all the time. If we weren't talking about Angel or motorcycles or ubervillains, my mother and brother and I were patching up my father and grandfather when they'd come home late at night. Can you imagine being a kid and going through that?"

I flashed back to my high school years, when I'd go out and prowl the streets with my father, fighting crime. They were some of my fondest memories. "Oh, I can imagine."

"When I was a kid, I thought it was so fascinating that my family were the ones behind Johnny Angel. I used to ride on the motorcycle with my father and dream of the day when I'd get to be Johnny Angel." Bella's mouth twisted into a wry grin. "Of course, I didn't realize then that Angel was more of a man's name. And a man's tradition."

"And when you grew up?" I asked, sensing this story wasn't going to have a happy ending.

"I realized how silly it was. Dressing up in a costume, riding around town on a motorcycle, raising hell with other bikers. And I remembered the strain on my mother. How she'd sit up late at night worrying whether my father was going to come home or not. It's the same thing I did with my father before he died. And it's the same thing I do now with Johnny every night when he's gone." Bella rubbed her head. "I don't want to have anything to do with superheroes and ubervillains and weekly battles anymore. I'm so tired of it all. Johnny Angel, the worrying, the constant fear. Johnny was too, until our father died."

I squeezed her hand. "It's not disrespectful, and it's not wrong of you to want to have a superfree life. Some people can't handle the lifestyle. Like you, I grew up around it. But to me, my powers have always been a part of who I am. I couldn't imagine not being a superhero, not trying to help people, but I can understand how you feel."

I took a deep breath. "When Travis was alive, he'd go out

on missions by himself. I'd do the same thing you did—sit up and worry. I wore out more carpets pacing back and forth than you can imagine."

Bella smiled. "You do seem like a bit of a pacer."

"You have no idea."

"What are you going to do if Johnny wants to quit being Angel? Or if he doesn't?"

"I don't know," I admitted. "Let's worry about rescuing him first and dealing with Siren and Intelligal. Then, we'll talk about the complicated relationship stuff."

An hour and another cheesecake later, Bella and I went back to the library to check on Lulu and Bobby. The elderly Bulluci sat in front of one of the computer monitors, flipping through various television channels. He looked extremely bored, until he stumbled across a soccer game. That perked him up a bit.

Lulu sat nearby, *type-type-typing* away on her computer like usual. Sometimes, I wondered if she and Henry did anything but stare at their monitors when they went out on dates. The two of them were never far from an electronic device of some kind or another.

"Anything yet?" I asked.

Lulu shook her head. "I'm still trying to narrow down the list of places Siren and Intelligal might go to turn on their boom box. It has to be somewhere fairly high up so they can hook into a radio or television signal. I've been focusing on SNN and the other local television stations downtown, but I don't know how the ubervillains would get past their security. Most of it is state-of-the-art."

I snorted. "Get past security? Please. Intelligal can just use those cursed missiles of hers to blast their way in."

Lulu shook her head. "I don't think so. Remember in the

fish-stick factory, Siren said the radio is very finely calibrated. That's the reason they didn't explode you right then and there. Siren didn't want to risk the shockwave disrupting the VAMP machine."

"So they'll have to do it real quiet-like. Sneak in and set everything up before Siren goes live."

"Bingo," Lulu said.

"Well, let's get cracking," I said.

The four of us started naming the tallest buildings in Bigtime. Bobby not-so-humbly pointed out that Bulluci Industries was housed in one of the highest skyscrapers in the city.

"What about the observatory?" Bella asked. "Isn't it officially the highest point in the city?"

I flashed back to the benefit and the scientific models I'd seen. More than a few of them remarked on the observatory's height. "It sure is. Wouldn't that be the logical spot for the ubervillains to turn the volume up on their radio? Wouldn't they get the strongest, clearest signal from there?"

"They would. Let me check on something." Lulu pounded away. After a couple of minutes, she stopped. "That's funny."

"What's funny?" I asked.

"I hacked into the observatory's database so I could see what programs were scheduled and how many people might be on the scene in case Siren and Intelligal tried to sneak in with the regular folks. Guess who's doing a live morning show there for SNN in a couple of hours?"

"Who?" Bobby asked.

"Erica Songe," Lulu replied. "And the weird thing is, she's going when there are no school groups scheduled. No tours, no benefits, no press conferences, nothing."

"Erica Songe? What would that little twit be doing at the observatory—"

An odd thought struck me. Erica Songe. I thought back

to my run-ins with the news reporter. Her hissy fit at the shop a couple of months ago. Her relentless flirtation with Johnny. Her pushiness at the observatory benefit. All the pieces slowly formed a picture. For a moment, I felt just like Carmen.

"You know, Erica Songe is a trashy little thing, just like Siren is." I snapped my fingers together, remembering something else. "And she has a sister. Irene something. A total geek, just like you."

Lulu stared at me. "You don't think . . ."

I nodded. "I do think. And so do you."

"Let me pull up some pictures of them off the Internet." Lulu's fingers smacked against her keyboard.

Bella looked back and forth between the two of us. "What are the two of you talking about?"

"We're talking about Siren actually being Erica Songe, a news reporter for SNN," I replied.

Bella, Bobby, and I hunched over Lulu's shoulder as she pulled up photos of the two women. I studied the pictures. Same black hair. Same blue eyes. Same collagen-injected lips. Same supersized boobs. There was no mistake about it. Erica Songe was Siren.

"Hold on a minute, let's see if I can get the sister too." Lulu hit more buttons on her computer.

A photo of Irene popped up on the monitor. Lulu compared it to one of Intelligal. Same black glasses. Same sour expression. Same disdain for Siren and everyone else. I wanted to laugh. Carmen was right. Spandex costumes and bright masks really were very thin disguises. We all might as well go around with our real names tattooed on our foreheads.

"That's her! She's the one who killed my son!" Bobby pounded his fist into his hand and let out a long string of curses. His face turned red then purple with rage and fury.

Bella put her arm around her grandfather's shoulder, trying to comfort and calm him down before he had a heart attack. I turned to Lulu.

"It's them. We agree that it is. Now, let's figure out how we're going to stop them," I said.

"The first thing we have to do is figure out how to resist Siren's voice, especially now that she's going to be plugged into that TRAMP machine," I said. "I can't very well smash it to bits and throttle her if I'm under her spell."

"It's actually called a VAMP machine," Lulu corrected.

I waved my hand. "TRAMP, VAMP, whatever. They both describe her."

"I might be able to help with that," Lulu said. "Henry and the chief were working on some earplugs to block Siren's voice. They're not perfected yet, but they might work well enough for us, since we'll be in the van."

"In the van? I don't want to stay in the van," Bobby protested. "I want to go inside and save my grandson with you."

"You'll need all the help you can get, Fiona," Bella added. "Why don't you let us come with you?"

"Because it's too dangerous. I can't take a chance on one of you getting hurt. I can handle Siren and Intelligal by myself."

Probably.

"But you can't handle Angel, Hermit, and Mr. Sage too," Bella pointed out. "You're going to need some backup."

I paced back and forth. "I need Carmen and Sam, or rather Karma Girl and Striker. Where are they now, Lulu?"

"Carmen called me yesterday before all of this went down. They'd just flown into Rome on Sam's private jet. There's no way they can get back here in time." Lulu looked at the Bullucis. "I think they're right, Fiona. You're going to have to take us with you, whether you like it or not."

I stared at the three of them, eyes shining, faces tight with hope. They were all so ready, willing, and eager to wade into battle and probably get themselves electrocuted or worse. Sending them up against Siren and Intelligal would be like throwing tender steaks to wolves—or to me. The ubervillains would gobble them down without a second thought. I saved innocents. That was my calling, my duty. I didn't put them in danger.

But I didn't have a choice. Not if I had any hope of rescuing the others. Bella was right. I couldn't fight Siren and Intelligal and save the others at the same time. Even Swifte would have been hard-pressed to do it, no matter how speedy he was.

So, I thought about my three new teammates and how to minimize the danger to them. There wouldn't be any radioactive goo around, so they wouldn't become horribly mutated by going with me. At least, I didn't think they would. You could never tell what sort of effect something like that stupid VAMP machine might have on regular folks. Carmen was proof of that.

Besides, Bella had a power that might come in handy. If luck was really a power, instead of just some weird, wild mojo, and if she could get it to work in our favor.

No radioactive goo and a little luck. Maybe things wouldn't go too badly. I snorted. Yeah right.

"Fine, you can come with me, but you have to stay out of the way. Agreed?"

The three of them nodded their heads.

"I mean it," I snapped. "I'm not bringing you along so you can do something stupid, like die a noble, bloody death in order to save the others and the city. That's *my* job. You'll do what I say, when I say it. Or else I'll lock you in the van and take the ubervillains on by myself. Got it?"

They nodded again, a bit more reluctantly this time. Bobby, in particular, shot me a sour look.

I resumed my pacing. "Even with you guys tagging along, I'm still going to need some extra help. Siren, I can handle no problem. It's Intelligal's chair and her stupid missiles that always have me ducking for cover. I need to get her out of that chair, or at least neutralize it, if we have any hope of freeing the others and destroying that VAMP thing."

"You know who you should talk to if you want more fire-power," Lulu said.

"Who?"

"Why, Jasper, of course."

Jasper was one of Lulu's more notorious friends and Big-time's underground bomb expert. If you needed something that went *boom* in a big way, you went to Jasper. What he did wasn't exactly legal, of course. The chief had thought about busting him many times, but since Jasper had helped Carmen rescue us last year, he'd given the demolitions expert a free walk. For now.

"Jasper?" Bobby asked. "The Jasper who lives downtown in that big brownstone?"

Lulu nodded. "The one and only."

"You know him?" I asked.

Bobby shrugged. "I've had use for a few of his items over the years."

"Oh really? Like what?"

Bobby winked. "Oh, this and that."

I opened my mouth to question him further, when Lulu interrupted.

"We should get going," she said. "It's after four now. Erica, I mean Siren, is set to go on the air at seven-ten sharp."

"Then, off to Jasper's we go," I said.

Lulu and I went to the equipment room. I changed into a fresh superhero suit, one that didn't smell like frozen fish sticks, while she gathered up a couple of things we might need, including the earplugs my father and Henry had been working on and some more of the gas-blocking and *RID* pills. Then, we went back to the library, grabbed Bella and Bobby, and loaded up the van.

Just after five in the morning, Lulu and I found ourselves in one of the nicer neighborhoods in Bigtime. A massive brownstone that even finicky Joanne James wouldn't have minded owning towered above us. Bella waited in the van, keeping the engine warm. Bobby sat in the passenger seat and peered out the window. The streets were still and quiet, and the air was cool and smelled of impending rain. The streetlights flickered on and off, confused by the grayish dawn.

Wide, shallow steps led up to the brownstone. Lulu hit a button on her wheelchair, and four jacklike devices sprang out from the sides. The devices hissed as they planted themselves on the sidewalk. They lifted the wheelchair several inches off the ground—high enough so Lulu could roll herself up onto the first step. She started to repeat the process, but I was too impatient to wait. I picked up Lulu, chair and all, and carried her to the front door.

"I can make it up and down stairs by myself," Lulu protested. "I've been doing it for years."

"We don't have time for you to be stubborn and independent," I said. "Now wake up Jasper."

Lulu punched a box on the wall, and a security camera swiveled over to see who was calling at this early hour. I could almost see the lens in the camera widen at the sight of me. I wore my costume, and my hair cracked and sparked with fire. I didn't think Jasper got many visits from the members of the Fearless Five. Well, except from Carmen and Lulu.

The box clicked on.

"What's the word?" a male voice asked over the static.

"The word is *silent night*," Lulu replied.

The camera lingered on us. Jasper wasn't going to let us in. I clenched my hand into a fist. Sparks and smoke hissed out from between my fingers. We'd get in one way or another. I'd make sure of that.

The door buzzed open.

"I thought the word was *boom-boom*," I whispered.

"He changed it right before Christmas." Lulu shrugged. "Jasper has a strange sense of humor sometimes."

No kidding. We entered the brownstone. A tall, thin man appeared at the far end of the hallway. A bathrobe hung on his bony figure, and his hair stuck out at those weird angles that were only made possible by a good night's sleep. We made our way toward him. I moved slowly, keeping my hands in sight and the fire to a minimum. I'd been in the vicinity of one of Jasper's bomb blasts before, and I'd been sore for a week as a result. So, I didn't think it would be a good idea to startle the bomb guru. He might do something stupid, like try to blow us up.

"Lulu, how it's going?" Jasper asked in a cautious voice, his eyes flicking over me.

Lulu extended her hand, and she and Jasper engaged in a series of slaps, high-fives, and other strange finger signals. "Fine, Jasper. Just fine. I know what you're thinking, but don't worry about ole Fiera here. We didn't come here to bust you. In fact, quite the opposite. We need some supplies."

Jasper looked at me. "You need supplies?" he asked in a rather disbelieving voice.

I shrugged. "I'm going up against a couple of uber-villains bent on taking over Bigtime, and I'm four team members down. I can use all the help I can get. Or rather, all the bombs you can give me. And anything else you think might come in handy."

Jasper stared at me. Suddenly, a smile creased his face. "Well, then, who am I to turn away a potential customer? Plus, any friend of Lulu's is a friend of mine. Come in, come in."

He turned and led us farther into the dark brownstone.

"You know I've long been a fan of your work, Fiera," Jasper said in a conversational voice. "Your fireballs are most impressive. The intensity of the heat, the explosion on impact, the massive damage they cause. I'd trade my explodium bombs for them in a second."

The odd praise pleased me, even if it was coming from a somewhat mad bomber. "Thanks. Lulu's told me a lot about your work too."

Jasper gave the computer hacker a pointed look that would have cut glass. "Not too much, I hope."

Lulu patted him on the arm. "Don't worry, Jasper. Your trade secrets are safe with me."

"Good to know," he said. "Good to know."

Jasper punched in a security code and went down a flight

of stairs. I picked up Lulu and her chair and followed him. It looked like Intelligal's lair, except it was much tidier. Wires and bits of metal were stacked in neat piles on top of several worktables. Soldering irons, pliers, and other tools hung from slots in a tall rack attached to one of the thick walls.

"You've done some redecorating, Jasper," Lulu said. "The last time I came here, this place was a mess."

Jasper shrugged. "I decided to get a little more organized. It was either that or blow myself up tripping over things."

Lulu and I froze. We stared at each other, then Jasper. The bomb guru paid no attention to our sudden nervousness.

Jasper pulled out a legal pad and a pencil from a desk in the corner. "So tell me what you need."

Lulu outlined Siren and Intelligal's scheme to take over Bigtime and, subsequently, the world. "So as you can see, Fiera here needs some help."

"What I need, specifically, is a way to disable Intelligal's chair. Of course, I've tried many times myself. Fireballs, superstrength, collisions. Nothing seems to put much of a dent in it, except whatever Intelligal used to make it self-destruct."

"It's probably made out of solidium," Jasper said. "It's very rare and very expensive, but it's the strongest, toughest metal known to man. Explodium won't even scratch it. At least, not by itself. You have to mix some other explosives with it."

"I don't want to scratch it," I snapped. "I want to completely destroy it. Think big fireball. Think catastrophic damage. Think crumpled lump of charred, twisted metal. That's what I'm aiming for. First the chair, then the VAMP device. Maybe even the ubervillains if they get in my way."

Jasper looked at me as though I was the love of his life. His eyes went all soft and warm. "Ah, a woman after my own heart." He took my hand and pressed a kiss to it. "For you, my lady, only the best."

I stared at Lulu. Her lips twitched, and I could tell she was trying to keep from laughing. I rolled my eyes.

Jasper spent the next few minutes puttering around, grabbing strange-looking objects out of various safes and lead boxes hidden throughout the room. Finally, he pulled out a small square box. He bowed to me and cracked open the lid. Nestled inside were ten round, brown-colored objects. They reminded me of chocolate-covered bonbons, although I doubted they tasted as good. My stomach rumbled. I'd have to eat some more food before I went toe-to-toe with Siren and Intelligal.

"For you, Fiera, only the best. This is something new I've been working on. Explodium has become rather passé this last year. Everybody's working with it these days, and you can practically buy it on the street corner," Jasper said. "But this, this is something special. I call it obliteron."

"Obliteron?" I asked.

"Obliteron, because it not only destroys matter, it pretty much obliterates it."

I nodded as if I knew exactly what he was talking about. As a superhero, I'm used to the creative, colorful, and sometimes ridiculous names my fellow heroes and ubervillains call themselves. Halitosis Hal was a prime example. But *obliteron?* For a bomb? Oh my.

Jasper picked up one of the bonbons and rolled it around in his hand. "Obliteron is a special form of explodium, a mixture of it and a few other key radioactive isotopes. I've managed to put my own stamp on it with these little beauties. Inside each of these thick, plastic shells is a liquid ball of obliteron."

I eyed the bonbon. "If it's as dangerous as you say, do you think you should be tossing it around like that? I don't want to get blown up before I get to the ubervillains." That wouldn't help anybody, especially not Johnny, my father, and Henry.

Jasper waved his hand. "Oh, in this form, it's perfectly harmless. You see, I've encased it in a special highly protective plastic shell. You could even play baseball with it, and it wouldn't detonate."

"So how do I arm it?" I asked, reaching for the small ball.

Jasper held it out of my reach. "All it needs is a little heat to fire it up. The plastic disintegrates, and the obliteron becomes active. There's a twenty-second fuse, but I don't think you'll have to worry about that. A flare-up from you will more than do the trick. Along with a stabilizing agent, the outer shell also contains a form of heat-activated superstrong glue. Once the shell starts to melts, it will stick to any surface you throw it at. So once it's hot, let it fly. When it blows, well, let's just say that you don't want to be anywhere near it."

I thought about the observatory. Some of the rooms were cramped, and I had no idea where Siren and Intelligal would set up their VAMP device. I didn't want the others to get caught in the crossfire. "What's the blast radius?"

"Like explodium, obliteron produces a limited blast range, about thirty feet or so. But it packs a hell of a punch and it burns superhot. A couple of these balls would be more than enough to bring down any building, any structure in the greater Bigtime area."

I eyed him. "Like, say, the new paper mill they were going to build out next to the ice cream factory? The one that was going to infringe on part of the observatory's wildlife sanctuary? There was some sort of explosion out there a couple of weeks ago late at night when nobody was around. The damage was so severe that construction was halted. Permanently, I believe."

"I didn't have anything to do with that," Jasper said in a hurt, offended tone.

I kept staring at him.

"I might not be as heroic as you are, Fiera, but I'm not a bad person. I might blow things up, but I never sell my goods to anyone who's going to use them to hurt other people."

"So who do you sell your wares to then?"

He shrugged. "People who want to collect on insurance, mostly. I also get a lot of business from the construction crews in town. A few of the more radical environmental groups. Sometimes, the bomb squad even calls me in to consult on cases. Now, do you want the obliteron or not?"

"I do." I didn't really have a choice. Not if I wanted to save the others and the rest of Bigtime. Besides, I could always come back and bust Jasper later.

Jasper nodded. "Good. Let me package them for you. Don't fire them up until you're absolutely sure you want to blow something up. Unlike some of my other work, these can't be diffused."

He rustled around the underground laboratory, fishing a heavy lead briefcase out of one of the safes. Jasper carefully put ten of the obliteron bonbons in the dark, foam-lined depths. Then, he turned and handed it to me.

"Let me carry them. Better not to take any more chances than necessary. I'm not as hot under the collar as other folks around here." Lulu shot me an amused look out of the corner of her eye.

I gritted my teeth at the bad pun and tried to remain calm. Now was not the time to set Lulu's hair on fire. I would do that later. After I'd rescued everyone and reduced Siren and Intelligal to weeping, wailing heaps on the floor.

Lulu took the case from Jasper and set it on her lap. I eyed a clock on the wall. Just before six. Time to go.

"Ah, before you leave, there is the matter of my fee," Jasper reminded us in a soft voice.

Lulu and I looked at each other.

"How much?" she asked.

Jasper tapped his finger on his lips. "For ten of my obliteron delights? I'd say an even two million would cover it."

I winced. There went my fat fee for designing Joanne James's latest wedding dress. Unless . . . The bomber wore a tattered bathrobe that had definitely seen better days. The slippers on his feet had holes on them, and his socks were threadbare. Plus, everything was the same drab gray color. Rather like Jasper's pale skin. I really, really hated gray.

"How would you like some clothes instead?" I asked. "I happen to know a designer who does incredible work. She makes men's suits that are to die for. Very bold. Very colorful. Just the thing for you to entertain prospective clients in. Or to wear for a night out on the town with your lady. I'm sure my friend'd be happy to outfit you with a whole new wardrobe."

Jasper just blinked.

Ten minutes later, Lulu and I left Jasper's brownstone.

"I can't believe Jasper agreed to waive his two million dollars for a closet full of *clothes*," Lulu said, maneuvering her wheelchair down the sidewalk. "I think Jasper's taken one too many blows to the head recently. Or all the radio-activity is making him go soft."

"It's much simpler than that, Lulu. The truth is that everybody wants to look good," I said in a smug tone. "Even mad bombers. And they're not just *clothes*. I plan on outfitting Jasper with the finest menswear Fiona Fine Fashions has to offer."

Bobby saw us coming. He hopped out of the front seat and opened the side door of the van. Too impatient to bother with the chair lift, I picked up Lulu and deposited her in the van, along with the precious case of Jasper's bombs.

"Did you get everything you needed?" Bella asked from the driver's seat.

"And then some," I said, slamming the door shut. "Now, let's go take those bitches out."

★ 28 ★

We drove through the streets of Bigtime in silence. It was early, and most folks hadn't yet started their commute into the city from the outlying suburbs. Most of them probably hadn't even had their first cup of coffee yet. The sun was just creeping above the tops of the skyscrapers that housed the *Exposé* and the *Chronicle*.

I took the opportunity to eat the emergency bucket of food I had stashed in the van. It was mostly junk food, stuff like candy bars and peanut butter crackers that would keep forever. But all that sweet, sweet sugar was more than enough to give me a boost of energy for the big battle ahead. I wasn't psychic like my father or Carmen, but I had a feeling I'd need it.

We pulled into the long drive that led up to the observatory a little after six-thirty. We didn't see anyone. No cars climbing up the hill. No buses pulling in with sleepy, cranky students. Even the guardhouse at the bottom of the steep hill was empty, although the door looked like it had been ripped off its hinges, along with the gate that blocked the road up to the observatory. I wondered if that's what Siren had needed the others for—a little extra muscle.

But other than the mangled gate, everything else seemed normal, and the place was deserted. Except for two maniacal ubervillains lurking around somewhere. Plus, my hood-winked teammates and the man I loved.

Bella drove the van to one of the garages attached to the side of the observatory. She parked on the lowest level, out of sight from anyone who might be watching from inside. The only other vehicle in the garage was a small SUV bearing the colorful SNN logo. I rattled the door. Locked. I put a little muscle into it, yanked the whole thing off, and set the crumpled metal aside. I rustled through the interior of the vehicle, but there was nothing inside besides your usual assortment of bad CDs, gum wrappers, and empty fast-food cartons.

"Anything?" Lulu asked, smacking her computer, which sat on top of Jasper's case of bombs on her lap.

"Nothing. But at least we know they're here," I replied. "Something wrong over there?"

"Stupid case," Lulu muttered. "I'm trying to pull up the blueprints that I downloaded of the observatory, but the radioactivity from Jasper's bombs is interfering with my laptop. The case he gave us isn't quite as secure as it looks."

"Why don't you let me hold on to those?" Bella asked, sliding the case out from under Lulu's computer. "It might be better for us all."

"A little luck certainly couldn't hurt," I quipped. "As long as it's good."

Bobby laughed. Bella glared at her grandfather.

"All right, folks, gather round," I said.

My three troops clustered near me.

"Okay, here's the game plan. I go in first. Every single

time. If we run into Siren and Intelligal, you guys stay back out of sight. Let me take care of the ubervillains. If the situation gets really desperate, Bella can toss me a couple of the bombs so I can even things out. I said it before, and I'll say it again—I don't want any of you trying to play hero. That's my job. Under no circumstances are you to engage Siren or Intelligal by yourselves. Agreed?"

I looked at each one of them in turn, giving them my *I'm-a-powerful-superhero-so-don't-even-think-about-messing-with-me* look. It seemed to work, because they nodded.

"Okay then. Let's go get our boys back," I said.

We took a few minutes to get our gear together. Lulu passed out the earplugs Henry and my father had been working on and hooked them into her laptop. Like our other equipment, the earplugs were equipped with microphones so we could all talk to each other. Then, Lulu piggybacked her computer onto one of the electrical boxes that lined the empty parking structure. She started to disable the alarm, but someone had already done it.

"Hermit," I said. "That's what Siren needed him for. She probably got Mr. Sage and Johnny to move the gate, then let him do the rest."

Since Hermit had done the hard part already, I opened one of the metal doors that led from the garage to the observatory, and we scuttled inside.

"Where do we go from here?" I asked Lulu in a hushed voice.

Normally, I would have gone in fireballs a'blazing, but I couldn't risk alerting the ubervillains to our presence. Not with the others following behind me like ducklings waddling after their mother.

"According to my calculations, they're probably in the

main auditorium," Lulu whispered. "That would be the most logical place to set up the VAMP device. And if I remember correctly, that's where SNN usually does their live feeds from."

"Then that's where we go."

The four of us made our way through the silent, empty halls. A few of the interactive displays flickered to life as we passed, spewing out facts about the observatory and other scientific babble about stars and planets and black holes. A couple of heated jerks from me, and the machines died a painful, fiery death. We stopped at the edge of one of the observatory's main crosswalks to catch our breath and get a little more direction.

"Time?" I asked.

Bella checked her watch, which looked like a smaller, female version of Johnny's, complete with wings. "Ten minutes until seven."

"We need to keep moving," I said, pushing away from the slick marble wall.

After some more slowgoing, we reached the auditorium. I moved the others back down the hall. Then I dropped down on my stomach, slid forward, and stuck my head around the doorjamb.

We'd guessed right. They were all inside. Siren, Intelligal, Johnny Angel, Mr. Sage, Hermit, and the same weary cameraman I'd seen the night of the observatory benefit. My eyes flicked over my fellow superheroes. They looked no worse for wear, even though their eyes and faces were as blank and smooth as sheets of glass.

My gaze lingered on Johnny, and my heart squeezed in on itself. He looked fine, physically. I just wondered what the toll would be when Johnny realized that Siren had roped him into doing her bidding. That he'd tried to kill me and take over the city on orders from one of the women he hated most in the world.

As for the ubervillains, they stood in the middle of the auditorium in all their foul glory. They must have felt supremely confident in their dastardly plan, because they didn't even have their masks on. I looked at Erica Songe and her geeky scientist sister, Irene. I'd been right on that count too. Stupid, stupid, stupid. Didn't they know something always went wrong with the best-laid plans of ubervillains? And here they were without their masks on running around for the whole world to see.

I shook my head. Ubervillains just weren't as classy—or as smart—as they used to be. Frost certainly would never have tried to take over the world without wearing his mask. Neither would Scorpion or Mad Maria or any of the other colorful certifiable characters I'd battled over the years. If things went wrong, as they so often did, then they wouldn't have their real identities to protect and hide them. Erica's, Siren's, ego was definitely as big as her overinflated chest.

Intelligal fiddled with switches on the VAMP device, which sat on the auditorium stage. Her face was set in its usual dour expression. You'd think she would have been a little happier about her Frankenstein machine finally coming to life. Every once in a while, a loud squawk would fill the air. A series of wires snaked across the floor from the radiolike object and plugged into the SNN camera standing in the middle of the empty auditorium, along with some lights. I eyed the machines and wires. I'd definitely have to do something about those.

As for Siren, she used the fancy VAMP microphone to berate and bark orders at her hypnotized cameraman about the hot lighting ruining her makeup. At least, that's what she did when she wasn't cuddling up to Johnny and rubbing herself against him like a cat in heat. She purred something into his ear. The tramp. Johnny stared blankly ahead, as if he couldn't even feel Siren's slutty hands roaming all over him.

I hoped he couldn't. More than that, I hoped he wasn't enjoying it, dazed though he was. My own hands clenched into fists. A couple of sparks shot up in the air. I was so going to enjoy reducing Siren to a crimson stain on the floor and throwing her ass in jail.

I watched them for a few more seconds before sliding back out of the auditorium into the corridor.

"Well?" Bobby asked in a low voice, his eyes bright. "Are they in there? Is Johnny with them? How does he look?"

"Easy, easy. They're all in there. Siren and Intelligal are fiddling with the VAMP machine. Johnny and the others are fine, if a little spaced out."

"So what's our next move?" Bella asked, clutching the case full of bombs.

I thought. Planning and strategy weren't my strengths, but improvising was. "We'll do what we usually do. Or rather, what the Fearless Five usually do. I'll go in through the front door, and you guys circle around the back. Is there another way to get in there?"

"There's another entrance on the far side," Lulu said, pounding keys. "The one that leads out to the gardens."

Of course. I flashed back to that wonderful night I'd spent with Johnny out next to the waterfall. I allowed myself to remember. All the hot kisses, the soft caresses, the whispered endearments. Then, I pushed those thoughts, those feelings aside. It was time to put on my game face. My angry, *I'm-going-to-kick-your-evil-ubervillain-ass* game face.

"Here's what we're going to do. I'll go in through the front door and toss a couple of fireballs at them. While I've got Siren and Intelligal occupied, you guys go in the back and get the others out. Don't forget the cameraman. Stuff the extra earplugs in their ears. Maybe that will bring them around. If the ubervillains try to stop you, somebody throw the bombs at them and retreat with the others. Any questions?"

Everyone shook their heads no.

I took a deep breath. "Then, let's go."

Lulu, Bella, and Bobby snuck off to skirt around the building and come in through the back of the auditorium. I gave them three minutes to get into position, then eased into the room, crouching behind a row of chairs. Intelligal was still fiddling with the VAMP machine. Siren stood nearby, checking her pale, flawless reflection in a small, compact mirror. I narrowed my eyes. Too bad the Pimpler wasn't here right now. He'd turn Siren's smooth face as red and ragged as the top of a pizza in a matter of seconds.

"How much longer?" Siren asked.

Intelligal checked a watch on her wrist. "Five minutes until the SNN studio cuts to you."

"Excellent." Siren snapped her compact shut and fluffed out her black hair. "Just think, in a few minutes, we'll own this city and everyone and everything in it. No more doing stupid live shots of superheroes flaunting their latest triumph. No more skulking around abandoned factories. No more taking insults from Bigtime's high and mighty. We'll be the ones in control. Permanently."

"Don't get ahead of yourself," Intelligal cautioned. "Things could still go wrong."

Siren waved her hand. "You worry too much. Things won't go wrong. Karma Girl and Striker are nowhere to be found. We've taken care of Fiera, and Mr. Sage, Hermit, and Johnny Angel are under our control."

"Not completely," Intelligal snapped. "They all balked when you wanted them to take off their masks."

Siren's thick lips turned down in a poor imitation of a

pout. Her lips had so much collagen in them that it didn't quite work. "Yes, well, keeping your real identity secret is the very first thing you learn to do as a superhero or uber-villain. It's ingrained so deep in their subconscious even I couldn't break through that particular barrier with my hypnosis. At least, not yet. Don't worry, sister dear. We'll uncover their identities soon enough. And have the rest of the city's superheroes and ubervillains eating out of our hands. Let's talk about something more interesting. What's the first thing you're going to do when we take over the city?"

Intelligal spliced two wires together. "Quit my miserable job here at the observatory. Perhaps use some of the other scientists as test subjects. I'm curious as to what the effect of explodium is on a normal human body. Angel's remains didn't give me much to work with."

My eyes went to Johnny. I thought I saw a bit of anger spark to life in his green eyes, but it was quickly swallowed up by the emptiness.

"And you, sister?" Intelligal asked.

Siren tapped a finger on her lips. "I'm not sure. Perhaps I'll have a little fun with Mr. Johnny Angel here. He certainly has the equipment for it. And I plan on taking certain individuals down a few pegs from their lofty heights. Speaking of Johnnies, perhaps I'll start with Mr. Johnny Bulluci and his trashy cohort, Fiona Fine. What the world sees in that woman's fashion designs is beyond me. Yes, I think those two will be the first ones to feel the new city order under Siren."

I smiled. That was my cue. Siren wanted a dose of Fiona Fine? Well, she was sure as hell going to get it. And then some. I straightened up and stepped into view.

"Oh, why wait another five minutes?" I called out. "Let's get the fun started now."

★29★

Siren and Intelligal's mouths dropped open so far that their teeth almost hit the floor.

"You . . . you . . . you're supposed to be dead!" Siren shrieked. "Frozen solid like the rest of those fish sticks!"

I winced at the high-pitched sound, grateful the earplugs muffled the worst of it. "If I had a dollar for every time I'd heard that, I'd be even richer than I am right now. But enough chit-chat." I took aim and lobbed a fireball at Siren. "I've got some ubervillains to get rid of."

Siren ducked down, and Intelligal soared up into the air. The fireball sailed right between the two ubervillains.

"You missed!" Siren crowed in a loud voice.

The red-hot ball of fire streaked through the air like a meteor and slammed into the television camera in the middle of the auditorium. The wires and camera exploded like firecrackers. Metal and glass zipped everywhere. When the smoke cleared, all that was left of the camera and the large majority of wires attached to the VAMP machine was a puddle of melted black metal.

"No, I didn't." It was my turn to crow. "Oops. Did I break your television camera? So sorry. I think your feed's been interrupted. Permanently."

"You're going to pay for that," Siren hissed.

"Bring it on, bitch."

An energy ball popped into Siren's hand, and she threw it at me. I ducked down, and the ball smacked against the back wall of the auditorium. Sparks flew everywhere, and static electricity gathered in my hair and on my fingertips.

Unnoticed by the ubervillains, the door that led to the gardens behind them opened. Lulu motored into the room, followed by Bella and Bobby. Lulu clutched the open case full of bombs on her lap. The Bullucis ran over to the three frozen superheroes and the cameraman and stuffed the Siren-proof plugs into their ears.

I threw another fireball, this time at Intelligal. She zipped out of the way, and the ball burst into flames on the ceiling. A display of planets hanging there went up like kindling. Somewhere in the distance, a fire alarm blared to life.

"Turn on the machine!" Siren screamed. "Now!"

Intelligal started to whirl her chair around, but I sent another fireball her way. She turned back to me. I kept lobbing my fireballs at the two ubervillains, trying to give the Bullucis enough time to get the others out the back door. Bella stuffed the earplugs in her brother's ears and shot me a thumbs-up. She half pushed, half dragged Johnny toward the door, where the others were waiting.

Intelligal saw the sudden movement out of the corner of her eye. Her mouth dropped open for the second time in as many minutes. "Get them, Siren! Don't let them get away!"

Siren spun, formed an energy ball in her hands, and hurled it through the air with a furious shriek. It seemed to grow in size as it sped through the room, as though all the ambient energy were attracted to it. The ball zoomed through the air toward the others. Right at Johnny's retreating back.

My heart froze in my chest. Even as I started running, I knew I wouldn't get there in time to save him. I wasn't going to be able to save Johnny. The man I loved was going to die.

Again.

Suddenly, Lulu did the one thing I'd asked her not to—she played the part of the self-sacrificing hero and zoomed in front of Bella and Johnny. Siren's energy ball hit her in the chest. Lulu's dark eyes lit up with an inner fire, and her arms and legs twitched wildly. Then, the computer hacker slumped over in her wheelchair. The metal case slipped from her lifeless fingers, and the bombs rolled over the floor like shiny chocolate marbles.

"Lulu!" Hermit screamed. He ran back inside the auditorium.

The sight of Lulu getting electrocuted also snapped the others out of their Siren-induced reverie. Mr. Sage and Angel stormed back into the room. I raced forward. Siren and Intelligal swiveled back and forth between us. They didn't like being in the middle of a superhero sandwich.

"Get the machine and let's get out of here!" Siren screamed.

"I don't think so, bitch," I muttered.

I put on an extra burst of speed and reached the VAMP machine at the same time Intelligal did. A mechanical arm shot out of her chair and grabbed the device, ready to lift it into the trunk on the back of the chair. I grabbed the other side of the machine, latching on to the frame. The VAMP machine seesawed back and forth between us. In the background, I heard Siren battling the others. Energy balls zipped through the air. People screamed and shouted and cursed. Ash fluttered around like confetti.

"Oh, to hell with this," I said.

With a mighty roar, I yanked the VAMP machine toward me and drove my free hand through the metal casing at the same time. Glass tubes and bits of metal snapped deep inside the device, which let out something that sounded like the screech of a wounded animal.

"No, no, no!" Intelligal screamed. "Not my beautiful machine!"

"Hell yeah, your beautiful machine." I grabbed some of the wires inside and yanked them out, along with my hand. Then, I reared back and punched another hole in the side of it. Intelligal's eyes bulged so far out of her head I thought they'd bust through her thick goggles.

"No!" she wailed, sounding just like the broken machine.

I let go the device. Intelligal's chair floated down, and she hovered over the ruined machine. I knew from experience that she'd be out of commission for a few minutes. All the geeky science types hated it when you destroyed their pet projects.

I turned to the others. Bobby and Bella were pushing the unconscious Lulu out the door, while Hermit and Mr. Sage guarded their backs.

But Johnny wasn't retreating with the others. Instead, he stalked toward Siren, who shot energy ball after energy ball at him. Angel flexed and laughed as the bolts bounced harmlessly off his chest.

"Don't you know, you can't electrocute a rock?" he snarled.

"Johnny!" I shouted. "Don't do it!"

He didn't even looked at me. "Stay out of this!"

I raced toward him, desperate to get to him before he got to Siren. My foot slipped on something, and I almost fell. Johnny shot ahead of me, reaching for Siren. I looked down.

One of Jasper's bombs rolled past my feet. It kept going and going across the floor. The bonbon stopped—in front of the still-smoldering camera.

Flames licked at it, and the plastic shell began to melt before my horrified eyes.

"Get out! Get out now! The whole place is going to blow!" I screamed.

With a burst of speed, I grabbed Johnny's leather jacket and yanked him away from Siren. He struggled against me, but I was stronger. Thank heavens for superstrength. I picked him up, panting from the effort, spun around, and tossed him toward the door.

Mr. Sage did the rest. His eyes glowed, and he used his telekinesis to float a still-struggling Johnny outside. I looked over my shoulder. Siren and Intelligal hovered over the machine, trying to salvage it, oblivious to everything else. Including the bonbon bombs rolling around on the floor.

"Get out now!" I yelled. "There are bombs everywhere!"

"Go to hell, bitch!" For once Siren and Intelligal were in agreement. They screamed the epithet at me.

Well, I'd tried. It was all I could do. My conscience was clear. I started running for the back door.

But I wasn't quite quick enough this time. A loud roar sounded behind me, followed by a rush of heat and fire. The shockwave from the bombs threw me forward. I slammed into the back wall of the auditorium and out into the gardens below. Darkness overcame me just before I hit the ground.

★ 30 ★

My eyes fluttered open, and my dazed mind wondered what had happened. Where I was. Why the sun was searing my eyeballs. Then, I remembered. Ubervillains. Battle. Explosion. The usual.

I was lying on the garden overlook on the back of the destroyed auditorium. The stone platform felt rough beneath my cheek. The rest of the fog faded from my mind. I wiggled my toes. Then, my fingers. Everything seemed to be in working order. Good to know. I focused on my arms and legs, moving them just a bit. Pain rippled through my body, but it wasn't anything I couldn't handle, being a superstrong superhero and all.

I pushed myself up on my hands and knees. Debris fell off my back, and glass tinkled out of my hair and crunched under my fingers. I winced at the stinging sensation in my palms. Somehow, I made myself stand up and dug the plugs out of my ears. I groaned and staggered back as more pain ripped through my body. I'd be sore for a week because of this escapade. But that was the price of saving the city and the world yet again.

I turned to look at the auditorium. Or what was left of it. The whole back of the building had been blown out, and nothing remained except the stone platform I was standing on and some smoldering bits of debris and rubble. Soot blackened the air, making it hard to breathe. Jasper had been right. His new bombs made Intelligal's explodium missiles look like toy sparklers. I'd have to come up with some extra-special designs for the bomb guru.

My eyes flicked around the empty ruined shell of a room. Not a trace of the VAMP machine remained. There was a large, charred lump I thought might be Intelligal's almost indestructible chair. I didn't see any blood or body parts, though. I crept inside, careful of the rubble. Something glinted, and I walked over to it. A silver zipper, halfway undone, lay in one of the smoldering piles. I kicked it with my boot, and it disintegrated.

"Fiona! Fiera! Fiona!"

I winced at the loud voices. They didn't mesh so well with the harsh buzzing in my ears. I stepped outside to find the Bullucis scrambling up the broken stone steps.

"Fiona! Are you all right?" Bella asked, putting her hand on my shoulder.

"Fine, I'm fine. Just a little shaken up."

I looked down the steps, expecting to see Hermit, Mr. Sage, and Lulu at the bottom. But they weren't there, and they didn't appear.

"Lulu?" I asked, feeling more concerned than I'd thought possible. The computer hacker wasn't so bad if she'd only stop peppering me with her cheesy, heat-related puns.

Bobby shook his head. "She's in pretty bad shape. Mr. Sage

sent us to come get you so he and Hermit could work on her. She needs to be taken back to the manor as soon as possible."

"I'm just glad you're all right, Fiona," Johnny said, pulling me into a rough, tight hug.

I closed my eyes, savoring the feel of his warm body against mine. I pulled back and just looked at him. Johnny. He was alive, and the ubervillains were gone. Everything was going to be all right. I grabbed Johnny's face and pulled it down to mine. Then, I gave him the hottest kiss I could manage. I lost myself in the feel of him, the smell, the taste.

"Ahem."

I ignored Bella.

"Ahem!"

If she did that any louder, she was going to bring the rest of the observatory down around us. Reluctantly, I broke off the kiss. Johnny brushed my hair back from my face. I touched his lips with my fingers. His green eyes softened. Suddenly, he grinned.

"Now that's how I like to be greeted," Johnny said, reaching for me again.

I stiff-armed him and stepped back. "Hold it, buster. It's going to take a lot more than one kiss to get back in my good graces." I tossed my hair over my shoulder. Dust flapped off the limp dirty locks.

Johnny stuck out his lip in a mock pout. Bella and Bobby just laughed.

My happiness at saving Johnny and the day was muted by the seriousness of Lulu's condition. Siren's energy ball had done quite a number on her. In addition to the burns on her body, the electricity had also interrupted her heartbeat and brain activities. The chief had to shock her twice with the defibrillator in the back of the van when she flat-lined. We raced back to Sublime in silence, and Henry and the chief put her in one of the sick bays moments after we parked in the underground garage.

The Bullucis and I stood vigil outside the room, watching the chief work on Lulu. An hour later, he came out. The chief looked exhausted, and worry lines tightened his long face.

"She's stabilized, but it's still touch and go. If she makes it through the night, then I think she'll be all right. Henry's in there with her. I suggest you all go home and get some rest. There's nothing you can do at the moment."

One by one, we drifted away. Johnny took his sister and grandfather home to change clothes and freshen up. The Bullucis promised to return as soon as they could. I made my way to my suite, stripped off my tattered, ruined costume, and took a long shower to wash away the grime of the fight and explosion. I changed into jeans, stilettos, and a fitted white shirt.

I lay down on my bed, but I couldn't sleep. Even though I'd been up more than twenty-four hours, I was still too wired from everything that had happened. So, I got up and went to the kitchen, where I made a dozen roast-beef-and-cheddar-cheese sandwiches. I put four aside for Henry and the chief and downed the rest of them, along with a gallon of milk and a deep-dish apple pie topped with vanilla bean ice cream. My father found me inside just as I was scraping the last bite of melted ice cream out of the bowl.

"Sorry," I said, pushing him the plate full of sandwiches. "If you wanted pie, you should have gotten here three minutes ago."

"Don't worry about it," he said, taking one of the sandwiches. "I'm used to it."

After the chief finished his first sandwich, he spoke again.

"You've been incredibly strong these last few hours.

Escaping the freezer, figuring out the ubervillains' scheme.
You saved us, Fiona. You saved all of us today. I don't think
I've ever been prouder of you," the chief said, his eyes bright.

I nodded. "I only wish Lulu hadn't gotten hurt in the
process. Is there any change?"

The chief shook his head. "We'll just have to wait and
see. It's out of my hands now."

Hot tears gathered in my eyes. My father opened his
arms, and we hugged for a long time.

The chief left to go to his own suite and shower before
he checked on Lulu again. I went down to the sick bay to give
Henry a break. The doors swooshed open, and I stepped inside. The harsh chemical smell of disinfectant and ointment
filled the room. I walked over to the bed where Lulu lay.

The computer hacker's face was paler than usual, and her
hair stood out like black and blue ink against the white of
her pillow. Thick gauze bandages covered her chest, and she
seemed about an inch away from death. Henry sat by her
side, still in costume, holding her hand and whispering
words of encouragement.

I tapped him on the shoulder. Henry yelped and almost
jumped out of his chair.

"Oh, it's you, Fiona. You scared me."

I pulled up a chair and sat next to him. "How is she?"

Henry sighed. His eyes were dark and sad, and his skin
was almost as pale as Lulu's, despite its ebony color. "The
same. No worse, no better."

"Why don't you go get some rest? I'll sit with her until
you get back," I said in a gentle tone.

"No, I'm not going anywhere. Not until she wakes up."

"You're dirty and exhausted. You're not any good to Lulu
right now."

Henry looked down at his ripped, torn costume. He shifted in his chair, and bits of ash flaked off the spandex. "So what?"

"So, you look almost as bad as she does. You certainly smell worse. Now go." I grabbed the back of his suit and pushed him toward the door. "I'll watch her while you get cleaned up. I promise."

"Come get me if anything, anything at all, changes," Henry said, clutching the door frame.

I pulled his fingers off, but he grabbed on to the other side. "I will. Now go."

After a few more false starts and forceful shoves, I convinced Henry to leave Lulu to me for a little while. I plopped down in the chair beside her bed. After about a minute, I drummed my fingers on my knee. Shifted back and forth in my seat. Fiddled with my hair. If I'd had some gum, I would have blown big bubbles. I'd never been good at sitting still, and I absolutely hated waiting.

But I'd promised Henry. Plus, it was my fault that Lulu was hurt. I was the one who'd let her come along. I should have locked her and the Bullucis in the van where they would have been safe. Instead, Lulu had gone all noble on me and kept Siren from zapping Johnny. I should have been able to take out Siren before she got that shot off. I should have been quicker, smarter, stronger. Now, the computer hacker was paying the price for my mistakes—and her own bravery.

Coulda, woulda, shoulda. Unfortunately, after-the-fact clarity was another thing that went along with being a superhero.

"You know, you need to snap out of this coma thing you've got going on," I said in a conversational tone. "It's not doing you any good, and you've got everybody else worried sick about you. Especially Henry. If you go and die on him, well, I'll have to kill you all over again."

I rolled my eyes. I sounded dumb even to myself. Perhaps dying wasn't the best thing to talk to Lulu about. A good bedside manner was not my specialty. That was Chief Newman's department.

So, I sat there and talked to Lulu about all sorts of things. The battle, how Siren and Intelligal had been toasted by the bombs, how brave but stupid I thought she'd been saving Johnny, how I hoped that Johnny and I could get past today.

"I really, really like him," I said. "And not just because the sex is incredible and he's one of the most gorgeous men I've ever had the privilege to sleep with. I like his sense of humor, his quick wit, his silly grins." I leaned forward and dropped my voice to a whisper. "The truth is that I love him. But let's just keep that between you and me for right now."

After going on for a good while about my feelings for Johnny, I lapsed into silence. I didn't have any more words left in me. So, I clutched Lulu's hand and tried to feel soothing and calm.

I sat beside her, my head bowed, for almost an hour. A small rustle sounded. My head snapped up. Lulu's eyes fluttered open. My breath caught in my throat. This was a good sign, right? I mean, she wasn't going to die on us if she was awake, was she?

"Henry?" Lulu croaked, her voice weak and raspy.

"Hey," I said, leaning over so she could see me. "Henry's not here right now. It's me, Fiona. You're back at the manor in one of the sick bays."

"Henry?"

"Henry's fine, and so is everybody else. The ubervillains are dead."

After a moment of thinking and staring at me, Lulu's eyes cleared. "Fiona. Of course. That's why it's so hot in here."

I rolled my eyes. "You must be getting better if you can crack bad jokes like that."

Lulu chuckled. At least she tried to. She gave up, gasping for air.

"Easy, easy. Don't overdo it."

Lulu nodded. "I'll try. What happened? The last thing I remember is this big blue ball of energy slamming into me."

I filled her in again on the battle at the observatory.

"I'm glad those bitches are dead," Lulu said. "My chest feels like it's on fire."

"Do you want me to get the chief? I'm sure he can give you some more painkillers."

Lulu shook her head. "No, I'm fine. Really sleepy, actually. Where's Henry?"

"Get some sleep. He'll be back in a few minutes."

Lulu relaxed. "You were right about one thing, Fiona."

"Really? What was that?"

"Me being in a wheelchair and having kids or not having kids isn't that important. All that matters is Henry and me and how we feel about each other."

"So, does this mean there'll be another wedding around here in the near future?" I asked. "Because I know this designer who does really fabulous gowns."

"You can count on it," Lulu said, drifting off. "Tell Henry I said *yes . . . yes . . . yes . . .* "

I smiled. "I'll be sure to relay the message."

Lulu's eyes slid shut before I finished speaking.

Later that afternoon, the chief announced that Lulu had stabilized and that she should make a slow, but full, recovery. The computer hacker drifted in and out of consciousness the rest of the day. She came awake long enough to tell Henry that she wanted to marry him, then promptly fell asleep when he leaned over to kiss her. Ah, love among nerds. It was a beautiful thing.

The Bullucis returned that night bearing pasta, wine, and more. After a brief, somewhat subdued celebration in Lulu's room, which the guest of honor slept through, we moved the party to the library. Henry went to check on Lulu every few minutes, while my father entertained the Bullucis with superhero stories.

But I had a different sort of party in mind. One that involved only two people—Johnny and me. I walked over and drew him away from the others.

"Let's get out of here," I said in a low voice. "We need to talk."

Johnny nodded. He put down his champagne, and we slipped out of the library.

"Where are we going?" he asked.

"You'll see."

I dragged Johnny down the halls until we reached my suite. I threw open the door, pulled him inside, and shut it behind us. Then, I wrapped my arms around his neck and lifted my lips to his.

I loved him. I really, really loved him. I'd admitted it to myself and Lulu, and now I was going to tell Johnny. Somehow, some way in the last few days, I'd fallen in love with him. Travis would always be a part of me, always have a piece of my heart. But I was ready to get on with my life. And I wanted to do it with Johnny Bulluci. Mr. Right Now had turned into Mr. Forever.

The kiss went on for a long time. I tried to take a few steps to the side, where the bed was oh-so-conveniently waiting for us to make wild, crazy love in it. But Johnny wasn't cooperating. The kiss ended, and he pulled back.

"Is something wrong?" I asked, eyeing the bed. If I could just maneuver him a few more feet to the right—

"I've been thinking a lot today. About you, me, my father,

Angel, everything. I . . . we . . . we can't be together, Fiona," he said in a low voice.

All thoughts of the bed and what we could do in it fled. "What? Why?" My voice came out as more of a shriek than a wail.

Johnny ran his hand through his tawny hair. "Because of Siren and Intelligal. Because . . . of everything."

"But it's over now," I protested. "We stopped them. The ubervillains are dead. They'll never bother us again. Justice has been served."

"Thanks to you. You saved us all, Fiona. Your father, Henry, me, Lulu, my family. All I did was almost get myself and you killed." Johnny's eyes were dark and troubled. His gaze wandered around the room, settling on something over my shoulder.

"But—"

"No buts. You were right. This whole time, you were right. I let my need for vengeance blind me. I acted like a reckless, selfish fool, and I almost killed you in the process. I let an ubervillain take over my mind and make me her puppet. I put you in a fish freezer and left you to die."

"But you helped me escape," I pointed out. "You gave me your lighter."

Johnny's mouth twisted. "Too little, almost too late. How can I expect you to forgive me for that? I can't even forgive myself for hurting you. How can we be together after everything that's happened? I'm sorry, Fiona. I don't deserve you. I never have, and I never will."

Johnny stared at me, as if memorizing the curves of my face. Then, he opened the door and left the room.

Leaving me alone.

To say that I spent the next few days in a bad mood would be the understatement of the year. The century even. After Johnny left me, I stayed in a perpetual pissy state. I alternated between crying, swimming, and growling at everyone who crossed my path.

And eating. I ate everything I could sink my teeth into. I always ate more when I was heartbroken.

Three weeks after the battle at the observatory, Carmen and Sam returned from their honeymoon. They looked rested, tanned, and more in love than ever. Their happiness and Lulu and Henry's engagement only made me more painfully aware of what I could have had with Johnny if he hadn't been such a hard-headed stubborn ass.

I tried to get through to him, of course. I called him and sent gag gifts and even showed up at the Bulluci mansion with dinner from Quicke's. But Johnny didn't take my calls. Didn't return my gifts. Didn't even acknowledge my visit.

It was a problem I couldn't fix by using my fists or fire-balls or general fabulousness. I didn't know what to do.

Carmen, being the unbearable, cheerful newlywed, made light of my disastrous love life.

"He'll come around eventually, Fiona," she murmured, her eyes vacant the way they always were when she was listening to the voices in her head. "I just know he will."

Stupid voices in Carmen's head. They gave me a shred of hope. But as the days passed and Johnny didn't respond to my reconciliation attempts, my depression only grew. Four weeks after the incident in my suite, I paced around my office. Brooding as usual.

A knock sounded, and Piper entered the room. She set a bag of doughnuts down on my desk. I tore into them like a dog snapping at a bone. Sugar was always good for a broken heart.

"Do you want to tell me what's bothering you?" Piper asked.

"It's nothing a couple dozen of these babies won't fix," I said, shoving a chocolate-glazed pastry into my mouth.

"If you say so." Piper leaned against the doorway. "Well, now that the fall line has finally been shipped out to our suppliers, I had a chance to look over your sketches for spring."

I stared at her, another sticky doughnut halfway to my lips. "What sketches?"

Piper held out a stack of papers. "These sketches. Don't you remember?"

I took the papers from her and flipped through them. My heart sank. They were the drawings I'd done the first time Johnny had sent me flowers. Now, they just reminded me of what I had lost and would never have again. I tossed them aside and ate another doughnut, a cream-cheese-filled one this time.

Piper flipped through the pages of discarded drawings. "I love it, Fiona. The color, the patterns, everything. I think it will be one of your best lines ever."

I snorted. "It's crap, Piper. Garbage. Those designs don't have any edge, any real style. I'm going to totally redo the spring line for next year. I'll do something bold, something daring, something . . . in black, I think."

"Black? You only use black when you're depressed about something." Piper's eyes narrowed. "Or when you have man troubles. What's his name and what's he done to you, Fiona? It's Johnny Bulluci, isn't it?"

Just hearing his name was painful. "What makes you think that?"

Piper sighed. "Because you've eaten a half dozen doughnuts in the space of about two minutes."

"So?" I asked, popping another one of the sugary treats into my mouth. "What does that prove?"

"It doesn't *prove* anything. But it's a bit of a record, even for you. You can talk to me, Fiona. I'm more than your business partner. I'm your friend too."

Piper had such a sweet, earnest look on her face that it made me sigh.

"I know," I said, licking a bit of glaze off my finger. "And I appreciate you wanting to help me through this. But honestly, the only thing that eases the pain is food."

I reached into the bag for another doughnut. My hand clutched at air. I peered into the bag. Empty already.

Damn.

That night, I headed out to the manor, since it was my turn to be on call. Superhero duties went on, broken heart or no broken heart.

I wandered into the library to find Lulu sitting inside.

The computer hacker had recovered from Siren's energy blast, except for the burns on her chest and arms. Even those would heal with time, which meant Lulu was back to compiling information and weaving her web of wickedness on the Internet.

"Where are the others?" I asked.

"Carmen and Sam had some society benefit to go to, and Henry and the chief had to work late." Lulu didn't even glance up from her monitor.

"Oh," I said, feeling deflated. I'd hoped somebody would be around. I'd wanted to go a few rounds in the training room with Sam to burn off some of my pent-up anger and frustration.

Lulu heard the sadness in my tone. "Any word from Johnny?"

I shook my head and started pacing. "Of course not."

Bored, I grabbed a Rubik's Cube off Carmen's desk in the corner and tossed it back and forth in my hands. I put it down when the plastic started to melt. Carmen got a little touchy about people messing with her stuff. But the cube was already too far gone. It slid off the desk and hit Lulu's knee before falling to the floor and soaking into the Persian rug.

"Watch it!" Lulu said, rubbing her knee. "Some of us aren't made out of steel, you know."

I looked at the melted plastic, then at Lulu's knees. What the hell? My eyes widened.

I leaned over Lulu and hit her leg. I didn't give her the ole Fist-o-Might, but I smacked her hard enough so that it would hurt.

"Ouch! What did you do that for?" Lulu glared at me.

I hit her again.

"Fiona! What the hell are you doing?"

"I'm hitting your leg. Can you feel it?"

"Hell yeah, I feel it, and it bloody well hurts—"

Lulu's eyes got as big and round as balloons. "I can *feel* it. I can feel you hitting *my leg*. Do it again, Fiona! Do it again!"

I was happy to oblige her.

"I can feel it! I can feel it! I can feel it!" Lulu screamed.

We started laughing. I kept hitting Lulu, and we both kept laughing and screaming and crying until the chief and Henry walked in an hour later.

They thought we were insane. At first.

Once I explained why I was playing pin the fist on Lulu, the chief whisked her away to do some tests. A few hours later, we gathered in the sick bay to get the results.

The chief pointed to some X-rays he'd taken of Lulu's back and said a bunch of scientific mumbo jumbo about neurons and electricity that I mostly tuned out. I loved my father, but he could be such a bore sometimes, especially when he was in doctor mode.

"Oh, get to the point, Dad," I snapped.

"Please, Chief," Lulu begged. "What does it all mean?"

"Well, I can't be sure without running an extensive battery of tests, but it seems that Siren's energy ball has kickstarted the dead nerves in your spine."

"And what does that mean?" Lulu asked, clutching Henry's hand so hard I thought it would pop off.

"It means, my dear, that one day, I think you'll be able to walk again," Chief Newman said.

There was complete silence.

Then, we all started screaming.

As it turned out, the chief was right. Siren's energy bolt had done a number on Lulu. The huge amount of electricity she'd been hit with had fired up the synapses and nerves and other things that make up a person's spine. In short, Siren had jumpstarted Lulu's body into healing the damage done when she'd broken her back a few years ago. With massive amounts of physical therapy, she should be able to walk again.

The next night, the members of the Fearless Five gathered in the library to celebrate the good news with champagne and chocolate. I stood a little apart from the others, watching them laugh and talk and celebrate. I was happy for Lulu, truly I was, but I still felt sorry for myself. I wanted Johnny here to celebrate with us. I wanted . . . I just wanted him. Always. Forever.

Carmen detached herself from Sam and strolled in my direction. I stifled a groan and downed the rest of my champagne. I didn't have to be a mind reader to know that another unwanted probe of my psyche was coming up. Carmen stood beside me, sipping from her own glass of champagne.

"It's wonderful, isn't it?" she murmured.

"It's just ducky."

She sighed. "I'm sorry you're hurting, Fiona. I really, really am. But you don't have to take it, you know. You can always do something about your situation."

"What do you want me to do? Beg Johnny to love me?" I snapped. "Johnny has made it perfectly clear he never wants to see me ever again."

"You're a fighter. You're Fiera, for crying out loud. Protector of the innocent and all that. So do what you do best. Fight for your man, Fiona. Fight for Johnny."

Carmen moved back to Sam. He wrapped his arm around her waist, and she leaned her head on his shoulder.

Suddenly tired, I gave my goodnights to everybody and went to my suite. I flopped down on my bed, grabbed the picture of Travis, and stared into his dark, smiling eyes.

"It was always so easy with you and me," I said. "Why can't it be that way with Johnny?"

I stroked his face with my fingers, but Travis didn't have any answers for me.

My fingers stilled. Or maybe he did.

The truth was things hadn't always been easy for Travis and me. Sure, we'd loved each other, but we'd also had our share of fights and arguments and problems just like everybody else did. But we'd worked through them all. Together.

I thought about Carmen's words, about how I should fight for what I wanted. I thought about Johnny and how he made me feel. The way he listened to me, laughed with me, loved me.

"She's right," I whispered to Travis. "I hate to admit it, but she's absolutely right."

It was time to fight. Time for a new beginning.

Starting right now.

I went over to the dresser, shoved aside some of my fashion magazines, and gently put Travis's picture down in the clear spot. He looked a little strange, a little out of place sitting there, but I knew I would get used to it.

I'd gotten used to the pain of his loss, and I'd found new love in the process. Johnny would never take Travis's place, but he had an equal share of my heart. He was here now, and we could have a life together. A fabulous life.

All we had to do was fight for it.

I'd never been very good at waiting, and I'd never been a quitter. I wasn't going to give up on Johnny now. Not now, not ever. Miracles really did happen. Lulu was proof of that.

Now, it was time to make a miracle of my own.

★32★

I placed a few strategic phone calls to recruit some spies and put my plan into action the very next night at Paradise Park.

After a leisurely dinner at Quicke's, Bella, Bobby, and Johnny Bulluci strolled into the park at exactly eight o'clock. While Bobby yammered into Johnny's ear about something, Bella flashed me a discrete thumbs-up as they walked by. Everything was in place and right on schedule.

I swallowed the rest of my raspberry-flavored cotton candy and followed the Bullucis as the three of them wandered around the park, keeping a good distance between us. I was also wearing a floppy hat, oversized sunglasses, and a tight-fitting black trench coat so Johnny wouldn't spot me. Bella and Bobby chatted and laughed and even played a few of the carnival contests. Bella won every game she played, even the rigged ones. Bobby bought a large funnel cake from one of the vendors and ate all of it, despite his granddaughter's dire warnings and hot glares.

Johnny just looked pained the whole time. I wondered if he was remembering our first date here. I hoped so. It was why I'd chosen the spot.

Bella pulled Johnny over to the enormous Ferris wheel. The ride stopped, and people filed off. At first, Johnny balked, not wanting to ride, but she whined and pleaded and begged until she got him to the front of the line. I elbowed people aside until I was right behind them. Meanwhile, Bobby went over and talked to the operator, whispering in his ear and slipping him some money.

Johnny sat down in one of the swinging carts, scooting over to the far side. Bella started to get in next to him, but stopped.

"You know what? I just remembered there's somewhere else I need to be," Bella said.

She stepped aside. I tossed my hat and sunglasses to Bobby and took her place.

"Hi, Johnny. What's up?" I slid in next to him and yanked the bar down over us.

"Sorry, folks. This is a private ride," the operator said to the other people in line.

A groan went up through the crowd. The ride started, and we sailed into the air before Johnny could protest, much less get off. Bella and Bobby waved to us once and then disappeared to check out the rest of the park. Johnny didn't say anything, but his eyes looked frantic and confused. I smiled. It was always good to keep a man guessing.

We went round one time as the calliope music played. Then, just as we crested the top the second time, the wheel jerked to a halt. We dangled in the air, high above the shrieking carnival goers.

"Why are we stopped?" Johnny asked. "Did you have something to do with this?"

"Of course I did. So did Bella and Bobby. It was really a team effort."

Johnny sighed. "So how long are we stuck up here?"

"Oh, we're not coming down until you tell me why you dumped me," I said in a cheerful tone.

Johnny stared at the city lights around us. "We've been through this before, Fiona."

"Johnny, I don't care about the past. I only care about the future and you."

He seemed surprised. "You don't care that I attacked you? You don't care that I was a complete ass to you and the rest of the Fearless Five? You don't care that I tried to kill you? You don't care that I let my need for vengeance blind me to everything else? You don't care—"

I put a finger on his lips. "Of course I care. But it's nothing that we can't work through. Together. I'm willing to try. Why aren't you?"

"Because I'm not a superhero. I never have been, and I don't know that I can ever be one. You're Fiera, a member of the Fearless Five. You do good things, important things. I'm just Johnny Angel. A guy who rides around the city on a motorcycle and looks cool because it's what his father used to do, and his grandfather before him."

"I don't care whether or not you're a superhero. As for being Johnny Angel, it's part of your family legacy, and that's part of who you are. I understand that, and I don't want to change it."

"What about Travis?" he asked in a soft voice.

"What about him?"

"You're still in love with your dead fiancé, Fiona." Johnny looked away. "You still have his things. You still have his picture by your bed. You still wear his ring."

I thought back to my conversation with Bella in the

kitchen when she'd accused me of the same thing. The constant looks Johnny shot at my ring and Travis's picture. It all became clear to me. Johnny thought I didn't love him. That's what he was really afraid of. He'd told Bella that, which is why she'd warned me to be careful with him, with his feelings.

I'd made my peace with Travis and his death. Now, it was time for Johnny to do the same.

So, I did something I'd never done before—I took the engagement ring off my finger. A white band marked its place on my hand.

"I love Travis. I always will. But there's plenty of room in my heart, and it's time to move on. That's what I want to do. With *you*. The man I love."

Johnny's head snapped up. "The man you love?"

I nodded and stuffed the ring in my pocket. "The man I love. That would be you, stubborn rock-headed ass that you are. I love you, Johnny Bulluci. Do you believe me? Or am I going to have to beat it into you?"

Johnny's eyes lit up. "No, you don't have to beat it into me. At least, not anymore. I love you too, Fiona."

We kissed, and everything was fabulous. Just the way it should be.

Just the way I was going to make sure it would always be.

"Have you ever made love on a Ferris wheel?" Johnny murmured, pressing a kiss to the hollow of my throat.

I cupped his head in my hands and stared into his magnificent eyes. Passion, love, and more than a little wickedness glinted in the green depths.

I laughed. "A Ferris wheel? Aren't you the adventurous one."

Johnny grinned that sly crooked grin I loved so well. "Always, baby."

He leaned over and looked down at the people below.

"Exactly how long did you tell the operator to leave us dangling up here?"

I smiled. "Thirty minutes."

"Well then, we've got plenty of time, haven't we?" Johnny said and reached for me again.

We didn't come down for a very, very long time.

★ Epilogue ★

Three months later

Johnny and I lay sprawled on the floor in the underground kitchen at Sublime. I put my arm over the beach towel covering our bodies and snuggled closer to him.

"Super-duper once again, Mr. Bulluci," I purred, nibbling on his ear.

"I agree. Super-duper once again, Mrs. Bulluci."

I flashed the square diamond on my hand at him. It was almost as big as Joanne James's was and more precious to me than anything—except Johnny himself. "Not Mrs. Bulluci just yet. We only got engaged last week. And I'm keeping my name. Or at least hyphenating it."

Johnny grinned. "Fiona Fine-Bulluci. I like the sound of that. Especially the last part."

Johnny put his arm around me and pulled me closer. I rested my head on his shoulder, happy, content, and suitably satiated. After taking a dip in the pool, we'd come to the kitchen for a midnight snack. But, of course, things had gotten a little heated between the two of us, especially since I'd made a point to keep a couple of cans of chocolate whipped cream in the refrigerator at all times now.

The door to the kitchen creaked open, and a walker appeared, followed by Lulu. She shoved the metal device forward and dragged her feet toward it. Lulu couldn't walk on her own yet, but she was getting a little stronger every day. Her hands clenched around the frame, and her face was set and determined. Henry followed along behind her.

"Why don't you just use your wheelchair? Just for tonight?" Henry asked.

"No," Lulu snapped. "Using the walker is part of my physical therapy. You know that. Besides, I made a promise to myself that I was going to walk down the aisle at our wedding, and I intend to keep it. No matter how much it might hurt right now."

"But Lulu—"

The words died on Henry's lips as he caught sight of Johnny and me lying on the floor. Lulu spotted us a second later.

Lulu put a hand over her eyes. "Don't mind us. We just came in to get some coffee. We don't see a thing." She peeked between her fingers. "Well, not much. Nice abs, Johnny."

"Thanks, Lulu."

I not-so-gently punched him in his perfect abs. Johnny just grinned. Henry stared at us, while Lulu rustled around in one of the refrigerators.

Henry straightened his ever-present polka-dot bow tie. Then, he turned to Lulu and picked her up.

"Henry!" she squealed. "What are you doing?"

He pressed a quick kiss to her lips. "I don't think I'm in the mood for coffee anymore. Are you?"

Lulu looked at Henry, then down at us.

"Ohhh," Lulu drawled. She wrapped her arms around his neck. "Well, when you put it like that, I think I've had enough coffee tonight too."

Henry headed for the door. Lulu waved at us.

"Hey, Fiona," she called out just before the door swung shut behind them. "Try not to melt the floor tiles again, okay?"

I sat up, fingers sparking, ready to light Lulu's hair up like a firecracker. But before I could focus my power, Johnny pulled me back down on top of him. His hands moved down my body, and I started thinking about a different sort of fire.

"Let them have their fun, baby," he whispered, stroking me. "So we can have ours."

I threw my head back and enjoyed the liquid fire coursing through me. Then, I reached for the almost-empty can of whipped cream we'd dropped in our haste.

"Well, let the good times roll," I said.